Silver
MOON

Silver
MOON

MARTI MELVILLE

First published 2013

This edition published in 2016 by
Doce Blant Publishing
Dana Point, CA 92629
www.doceblant.com

Cover Design by Fiona Jayde Media
Interior Design by the Deliberate Page
Editing by K. H. Koehler Design

Hardbound ISBN: 978-0-9978913-6-2
Paperback: ISBN: 978-0-9994937-0-0
eBook ISBN: 978-0-9994937-1-7

Library of Congress Control Number: 2016917079
Printed in the United States of America

www.doceblant.com

This is a fictional work. Names, characters, places and inci-
dents are the product of the author's imagination and used
fictitiously. Any resemblance to actual persons, living or
dead, including events and locations, is entirely coincidental.

For my sisters: Shari, Mindy, Shelly, and Molly…

(and Wendy, Sue, Lissa, Jennifer, Cindy, and Lois).

By Marti Melville

The DÉJÀ VU CHRONICLES

Special thanks goes to Karen Zabriskie and Lois Cozens for your constant support throughout. As always, I appreciate the patience and dedication of my editor, K. H. Koehler, and cover artist, Fiona Jayde Media—thank you once again for capturing the mystery of the *Déjà vu Chronicles* artistically.

Mark Angeloni, thank you for all the rest.

"The moon is chief over the night darkness, rest, death, and the waters."

(Jan Baptista van Helmont, 1579-1644)

"Fair warnin' be given to all who sail the seas of El Caribe — beware the Midnight Omen and its cursed sister — the Silver Moon."

(Mariel of Wales, circa 1722)

Prologue

DARKNESS BLANKETED THE NIGHT SKY and cast shadows into its deepest recesses. Overhead, a slivered moon bared its toothless grimace where droplets of crimson were drizzled along its surface. A pale mist encircled the orb to reach treacherous tendrils toward the earth. All was still.

The Silver Moon Omen had chosen its victim.

PART ONE

Intention

One

"She's not breathing."

John's muscular hand crushed the blue Ambu bag, and he watched her chest rise with the air pressure. The power of the compression forced pure oxygen into her lungs. He glanced at the clear plastic tubing trailing from the football-shaped apparatus in his hand. He followed the tube to where it was attached to the wall. There was little else he could do—everything possible had been done to protocol. He squeezed the blue bag again and delivered another breath to her lungs. Her chest rose, then dropped almost instantly.

Only inches above his head, the siren screamed. Matching flashes of red and white sliced through the darkness from atop the paramedic ambulance. It travelled a little more than 75 miles per hour. *Not fast enough if she's going to make it*, he thought. Both paramedics riding within the wailing ambulance hesitated to start the Code, given the early hour and slowing traffic. If they could keep her alive just long enough, the waiting team would be more than willing to take over. The Code Blue would be initiated there, inside the ER.

"Did you call it in yet?"

"Just did. They've got a room ready for us. At least we're moving." Martin's voice crackled through the headphones, sounding distant and tinny. "Could be worse, I guess."

Surprisingly, traffic was still cooperative, despite the onslaught of rush hour. Lines of dual lights peppered the freeways with a rainbow array of vehicles. All but one stubborn SUV had pulled off to the shoulder, allowing the ambulance to pass. Martin was a skilled driver in this kind of traffic, but today would test even him. He turned the steering wheel and easily maneuvered the rig around the silver Explorer without slowing below 70. Fortunately, their route swerved onto the next exit only a few yards ahead. He made another turn and followed the long curve of beach before veering off toward St. Luke's Memorial Hospital. The ER was only seven miles ahead.

John manipulated the Ambu bag. Her lungs were failing fast. At the same time, he glanced up at the square monitor that jostled with each bump of the road. The woman's oxygen saturation had dropped again. In spite of the oxygen mask, she was in trouble, and would soon stop breathing altogether.

We're losing her. Apparently, his thought had been expressed aloud, because John heard his own voice ringing metallically through the shared headset.

"How much farther?"

"ETA five minutes. Approaching the exit now. Keep her breathing just a few more minutes, yeah?" Martin's response sounded artificial.

John assessed the woman's pupils. Fading, doll-like, brown eyes were unable to match his gaze. "Not good," came his response, and he felt the ambulance speed up immediately.

Unexpectedly, her pupils shifted as a fleeting moment of consciousness washed over her.

She moved a sluggish glance up to her rescuer. John's emerald green eyes danced, and she watched the left side of his mouth curl into a crooked smile.

"Hello there," he said. His deep baritone purred through the row of perfect teeth that peeked through the partial grin. "You're in the back of an ambulance on your way to the hospital."

She lifted her hand. It drifted up from the paper liner underneath her body, too weak to reach the mask over her face. She tried in vain to move her head, instead. John placed his palm against her cheek for a moment. It worked, and the woman instantly relaxed at his touch.

"It's an oxygen mask. We're helping you to breathe." John's voice always soothed the patients—perhaps due to the lilt of his accent as he spoke. "Try to relax. We're almost there."

She allowed herself to succumb to his warm tones. The woman's consciousness danced on the cadence of

John's unusual brogue. Unexpectedly, her eyes rolled to whites, her eyelashes fluttered, and she fell into unconsciousness.

John compressed the Ambu bag again and looked up through the narrow opening to the cabin. Martin concentrated on the road. A brightly illuminated sign overhead bid them welcome as they passed underneath. White lettering emblazoned on a red background announced the Emergency Department through the dim morning sky. John knew they had arrived. Soon, their patient would be admitted into the chaos of the waiting ER. He sighed in relief.

Martin's voice echoed, thin and tinny through the bulky headphones that covered John's ears. "Dispatch, this is unit Valley Fire 18 on arrival at St. Luke's, oh-five-thirty-four."

John squeezed the bag again and gave his patient another dose of rich oxygen as the ambulance backed up. An accompanying *beep-beep* rang out as the rig moved into position in the hospital ambulance bay. He turned his focus to the rig's rear double doors, pulled off his headphones, and shook his head. Dark wavy hair fell loose along the nape of his neck. He waited for the doors to swing open.

"How's she doing?" Martin asked as he pulled open the rear door and grabbed hold of the gurney's back rail. Together, they pulled it into the dark morning air. The metal frame sprang open, dropping the wheels to the asphalt, while both medics clutched the opposing ends of the stretcher. With one hand, John grabbed a red bag and hoisted it over one shoulder. The other hand remained clamped down over the woman's oxygen mask. Loaded with supplies, the bag pulled a little more than usual, dragging the collar of his navy-blue T-shirt over his left shoulder. Three prongs of an ancient triton inked onto his bronzed skin peeked out—the remains of an old tattoo inscribed into his flesh.

The medics pushed the gurney in unison to the glass doors. As they rolled up the ramp, the glass doors yawned open and hissed the announcement of their arrival.

"She doesn't look good," Martin said.

"Ehhh, she woke up for a minute, but I'm still baggin' her about every other breath." Fresh-faced nurses and young, vibrant techs skimmed by as the medics quickly passed rumpled beds lined up along the long hallway. It was evident from the clutter on the counters that the night had been busy—a relentless clamor of patients until only maybe minutes ago.

Indeed, we didn't get much of a break, either. John shook the thought away. The night had been inter-rupted more frequently than usual by radios crackling and calling for paramedics and other first responders of Valley Fire Department.

"Room 15, guys." The voice was too cheery from the other side of the nurses' station. The nurse's bobbed hair bounced as she turned to face them with a pixie grin spread across her entire face.

Martin nodded thanks and pulled the base of the gurney to the right, while John pushed from the other end. He squeezed the bag and delivered another breath of oxygen. Both medics stayed focused. Martin's job was to find Room 15, while John kept their patient breathing just a few moments longer. They crossed a seemingly eternal length of hallway with long, swift steps. Out of the corner of his eye, John noticed a few inquisitive glances. These seemed to come mostly from nurses pausing in their tasks just long enough to gawk as the paramedics passed by.

It was always the same. Nurses, and sometimes even the female patients, would feign interest in the newly arriving victim, but it was always an excuse to check out the medics. John couldn't help but smile as they turned their attention on him.

"The new guy." He heard the whisper from across the hall. Two young aides in slate blue scrubs stood with backs against the wall. Both looked as if they had just stepped out of high school.

As the medics turned the corner, the number 15 in bold black letters above a doorframe came into view. Pushing through the curtain, they entered Room 15, chased by a handful of emergency department personnel eager to assume care of the woman on the stretcher. Controlled chaos erupted as several hands reached across the bed and grasped hold of the sheet underneath the patient.

"On three. One…two…three…" A tenor voice gave the command, and the woman's body slid across the stretcher to a thin, hard mattress.

Within moments, the shift of care from medics to ER staff was initiated. A tall, bearded man in his mid-thirties strolled in and waited at the foot of the bed. He said nothing, but instead, watched his team at work, keeping one hand submerged in the pocket of his starched white lab coat, while the other pawed at the hair sprouting from his bony chin.

"So, what have we here?" The physician's hand moved down the length of his bony jaw.

"Difficulty breathing. Found by family about an hour ago." Martin glanced from John to the patient and back to the doctor. "John has the report."

Martin flipped the empty Stryker around, moved it out of the now very crowded room, and disappeared down the hallway. All eyes moved to John handing over control of the Ambu bag. A white-haired respiratory therapist pushed his way to the head of the bed and assumed the duty of squeezing the blue bag. John gave a brief report to the physician. Occasionally, he peered at the nurse who had assumed command over the activities in the room, just to be sure she was listening.

"I've been bagging her about every two or three breaths, but she's not holding her sats, and her effort is very weak." John looked at the doctor in the white coat. He was busy stroking his chin. As he spoke, his gaze drifted through the gaping curtain, where he caught

sight of another nurse. Her pale blue eyes danced…
and stopped him midsentence. He watched her move
to one side of the nurse's station.

"Uh, yeah…about twenty minutes down, apparently." His heart pounded as he watched her lean over
the counter to stare at a computer monitor. She moved
again, and her image disappeared—blocked by the physician at the foot of the bed.

He glanced up at the MD, whose only response
was to mutter "Uh-huh," and run his fingers through
his goatee again. John struggled to keep his focus on
the ER doctor's questions.

Hurry up and ask your questions, mate! He forced the
involuntary thought from his mind, but it was immediately replaced by another: *Could it possibly be her?*

A warm sensation spread through his body, and
his heart pounded at the likelihood that it might actually be her.

Two

JOHN P. BUCHANAN, PARAMEDIC FOR Valley Fire, knew her.

"Okay, thanks," he heard the nurse to his left murmur as she looked up from her notes and tossed a flickering smile in his direction.

"No worries," John replied. He clapped the physician on the arm in an effort to appear undistracted. "Doc."

All eyes reverted to the patient, so John ducked through the curtain and walked with long strides toward the exit. Not far down the narrow hallway, he saw Martin pushing through the glass doors with the Stryker. One of the LifeAir pilots had joined him, and they were in a deep discussion about diving with sharks off Hawaii's North Shore.

Apparently, Brett had flown in his patient to the hospital moments ago. John recognized the well-respected pilot. Rumor had it that he looked forward to retirement in just eighteen months, which made sense, given the topic Brett and Martin were so focused upon. The two had worked together for more than two decades, and their "brotherhood" was evident as they exited together through the parting glass doors.

John moved quickly down the hallway. He scanned the nurses' station only five feet ahead. She stood at the counter where he had seen her last, and she was in full conversation with another nurse, someone he had recently met, he was certain. They had been introduced about a week ago, and he thought her name was Maya. She was a lively nurse, and very good with her patients, but Maya did not have the cool elegance and natural beauty of the co-worker standing beside her. The stunning brunette turned slightly toward him as he moved another step closer. He caught the graceful curves of her face and deep blue eyes–pools of sapphire set in ivory skin.

John's breath caught in his chest, and his heart clenched.

Kathryn.

His soul recognized the woman he had loved so dearly once in another time. This day, she stood in simple scrubs at a nurses' station, but every inch was as breathtaking as he'd remembered from before. He knew he had to approach her, to speak to her, to tell her who he was.

He had to tell her that he had returned…again.

She glanced at him, lively and fierce, but without recognition. Disappointment slammed into him and yanked his head down. He could not match her gaze, and his will weakened.

She doesn't know me. The thought burned through his heart, and he felt himself tense as he moved past her. The scent of her hair filled his nostrils with touches of lavender and rhodanthe. *It's her!* Grasping the strap of his medic bag a bit tighter, he fought the overpowering desire to turn back to her and scream, "Kathryn, it is I. Do ye not remember me, lass?" But he held his tongue. His knuckles turned white as he gripped the strap, fighting against the desire to make himself known. He lowered his eyes and strode to the ambulance bay just feet ahead of him.

Martin stood on the other side of the glass doors, still talking to Brett as he wiped down the Stryker next to their rig. John paused, his last hope that she would remember. He could feel her eyes on him, but she said nothing. Lifting the medic bag with his left hand, he slung it over his shoulder in one swift move and sighed bitterly. The heavy bag pulled against his T-shirt once again as it dragged at his left shoulder.

Behind him, a loud gasp shattered his thoughts. He recognized the whispered breath of his beloved Kathryn. Hope forced him to stop, turn, and look in her direction. His emerald eyes flashed.

Yes…yes! Do you see me now?

She stood frozen in place, awestruck, eyes locked on him. Both of her hands were clasped together, covering her mouth as if to stifle the gasp that had just escaped from it. She never blinked, and she matched his stare with eyes that widened as they slowly recognized him.

She knows! The thought rushed over him, and his mouth curled again into a partial smile, revealing his perfect white teeth.

"John, you ready, partner?" Martin called through the glass. A flash of lightning lit up the morning sky. John turned back toward the glass and moved forward as the door yawned open. For the moment, he was at peace, knowing the striking nurse he'd left behind in the ER hallway would again be his.

Three

DENSE CLOUDS CONCEALED A BRONZED coastal sun, rising against murky skies. The haze transformed the atmosphere into a foreboding slate grey. Interspersed among the clouds, blinding flashes of electricity snaked sideways, splitting the morning's solitude. The air grew heavy, and, though time showed the emergence of a new day, all light remained hidden. Morning took on the appearance of a starless night.

John looked out through the open window and gazed up. Another flash of lightning cracked not far above them. His face was instantly bathed in rainwater. It ran in unchecked rivulets down his neck. The road ahead stayed dark, except for the bright beams from the oversized headlights that hit the pavement. Martin navigated the rig carefully over the highway, winding precariously close to the ragged coastline. John inhaled deeply. Whiffs of balmy rain and salty seawater lingered in his nostrils. He glanced to the road ahead and noticed the asphalt had quickly bled into glossy black.

"I guess we need this rain," he muttered half-heartedly to Martin. He wiped his forehead and cheek with the back of his hand as he pulled himself out of the rain and back into the cab.

"Yeah, it's about time, but it's going to make for a busy day, I'm afraid," Martin responded, never shifting his eyes from the road.

John glanced at his partner's hands, gripped at a perfect ten and two o'clock on the steering wheel. Martin's knuckles had turned white, so John decided to change the subject.

"Hey, who's that nurse back there?" He casually attempted to mask his curiosity, but the effort only sounded weak.

"Which one?" Martin's posture stiffened to match his grip.

"The dark-haired one with the pretty blue eyes hidden behind glasses." John glanced out the window. His nonchalant approach to get information was not working. Martin could see right through it.

"Katherine McSomething…" Martin grinned and leaned forward in his seat.

"Katherine." John repeated the name and allowed each syllable to roll over his tongue. His Celtic brogue always made him sound more like a Highlander than he intended. His mind raced, allowing only a muted "Hmm," to escape as an afterthought.

Martin tossed a sarcastic sneer across the seat. "Why? She's probably too innocent for a guy like you."

John shot his partner a look and said nothing. Martin chuckled. "Seriously? You want to meet her? She's definitely cute, but keeps to herself pretty much, I think."

John avoided his partner's gaze and fidgeted with the paperwork lying in his lap. "I think I know her from…" It was just an intuition he had. "I dunno… from somewhere. Not sure. She just looks familiar."

Martin snickered and returned his attention to the road. He'd give John a break and not pursue the topic further. The rain had picked up, casting sheets of solid water across the road. Martin repositioned himself in the seat, leaning forward a little as he slowed the rig to around 50 miles per hour. John could tell from Martin's sudden shift that his partner was concerned. Water poured down from black skies as lightning cracked without pause. Conditions had become hazardous, even for an experienced driver like Martin.

The occasional blurred lights from other vehicles on the road made it difficult to tell where one lane ended and the other began. Martin slowed the rig to 40 as he made the turn onto Highway 18. He could tell the drivers didn't get the dangers of flying across wet asphalt.

"Job security," he uttered under his breath.

John shot a look at his partner but said nothing. Martin blinked as if that alone would clear the sheets of water blurring his view through the windshield. Another deafening crack illuminated the sky in brilliant shades of crimson.

"Red lightning?" John's jaw dropped. He'd seen it before, and tinted lightning was never a good thing.

Silence passed between the men. Neither wanted to answer. Both medics looked at the clouds and took note of the unusual color filling the sky. The muffled pounding of rain beat across the windshield in a rhythmic pulse as the large wipers did their best to clear the constant downpour streaming over the glass. A string of vehicles had pulled off to wait out the storm. Each set of taillights acted as a red beacon, matching the crack of electricity dancing overhead.

"Any available unit respond…"

The radio crackled through their headphones. Dispatch radioed for first responders to a motor vehicle accident on West Seashore Drive.

"Valley Fire Unit 20 responding…" Their voices sounded faint and muffled under a clap of thunder.

"That's lucky for the victims," Martin said under his breath. "Twenty must have been near there. Otherwise the response time would be delayed with this weather."

John stayed silent, focused on the road ahead. Another crack rattled around them, shaking the rig slightly as the sky filled with blue light this time.

"Man, this is a bad one. We must be right in the center of some nasty squall. Did you see how close that one was?" Martin's voice sounded edgy, and he shifted in his seat again.

"Yeah." John's eyes never left the road. "This is a weird storm. Did you see the color of the lightning over there? I haven't seen that since..."

His voice trailed away as his mind travelled to a distant memory. Suddenly, the sky lit up, interrupting his thoughts with another lightning bolt. It snaked its way across the sky with rosy arteries that rose up to thick clouds ablaze with electricity. The upper atmosphere had come alive, clawing at something below, desperately seeking out its prey.

Martin slowed the rig down as they neared the cross street that indicated the highway had ended. An instant later, the sky filled with light again. It was white and steady. John braced for the imminent crack of lightning. But it never came.

Without warning, light flooded the cab from the passengers' side. Almost immediately, they heard the high-pitched squeal of tires suddenly locking, followed by the sound of rubber hydroplaning across asphalt. Martin looked to its source, directly at John's side. His knuckles blanched as he gripped the wheel tighter. Eyes wide, he braced for impact. John faced his partner with terror. He felt a wave of impending doom.

"Hold on...*hold on*! *Holy*..."

Metal crumpled as the front grill of a black pickup met the passenger door of the ambulance. Shards of glass splayed through the air. A deafening screech of steel scraping against buckling steel rang out. Thunder rolled violently through the air, and lightning flashed an ominous crimson. Only a momentary glimpse of the impacted ambulance locked onto the black truck shone in its light. The entire mangled mass slid as one across the wet pavement. Several horns blared, and tires squealed in protest as oncoming traffic maneuvered to avoid the twisted vehicles. Shouts from unknown sources sounded almost in reflex, waiting for the metallic grind to stop.

Time felt like it had become suspended, twisting in on itself, until, moments later, it seemed to stop entirely. John tried to open his eyes, but couldn't make his eyelids obey. He could hear Martin moaning somewhere behind him. A sensation of pure light poured through his body, and he heard the familiar sound of a siren in the distance. The noise echoed hollowly, as if contained within a faraway tunnel. *Surely, this isn't real.* Suddenly, he began to feel weightless, tingling, without restraint. He'd been freed from the molecular mass they call a *body* and felt himself rise.

His limbs became liquid, and he opened his eyes—this time, without effort. Below lay the crumpled remains of the ambulance, impaled by the cab of a black truck. It projected out from where he knew his body lay.

John felt no emotion as he peered down upon the wreckage with only a strong desire to observe. The sirens sounded louder. Simultaneously, he watched the police and fire trucks as they made their way up Highway 18.

First Responders, he thought without sentiment. *That's what I am, too.* But, this time, it wasn't his call. His soul had been freed, and he looked up at a steel grey sky filled with brilliant colors. Vibrant hues twisted and shuddered in time to the electricity there. John smiled as he released his will to the darkness and the dancing energy just above him.

PART TWO

Awakening

Four

ST. ELMO'S FIRE. HIS MIND recalled the term used by seamen to describe the odd electrical lights that sometimes hovered across mast tops on great ships. The memory of a great ship rolling over warm water currents brought him peace for the moment, and he allowed himself to sink deeper into the thought.

Suddenly, a sharp burn seared his chest, radiating through the tissue that surrounded his heart and lungs. He felt the abrupt pounding of his pulse, which forced a breath. He gasped, realizing he hadn't taken air into his lungs for a few moments. His lungs protested, and he heard his own voice cry out with the forced inhalation.

"Kathryn!"

Pain racked his entire body once again, and he felt his back arc reflexively, hyper-extending his spine grotesquely before crashing forcefully onto a solid, cold, wet surface.

"Capt'n? Capt'n?" a raspy voice called out somewhere in the distance.

Water splattered his face, cold and relentless. Each drop landed with force on the surface of his skin. He cried out again.

"Lass…oh, Kathryn!"

His body was heavy, and the sensation of floating dissipated. Aromas of saltwater and linseed oil saturating oak filled his nostrils. Crackling currents in sapphire and crimson flashed overhead, followed by the sound of the ocean pounding against itself not far off from where he lay. Slowly, he opened his eyes and blinked against the rain splashing mercilessly onto his face.

A gentle whisper breathed low and soft next to his left ear.

"He lives…"

He turned his head toward the sound, and instantly, searing pain shot up along his neck and into the back of his skull. Instead of moving, he allowed his gaze to drift toward the gentle voice. Long chestnut hair lay wavy against wet wood beneath them both. Brilliant, blue eyes were fixed on him. He saw her left hand tied securely to a charred grappling hook attached to the mainmast. The entire rod expended pale ribbons of smoke that curled in sinister waves skyward. Its tip pointed dangerously toward black clouds, ready for the next lightning strike.

He recognized her.

"Kathryn?" His voice was barely a whisper.

She blinked in slow motion. Moments lasted an eternity as life shocked his sinews with each breath drawn. Slowly, his strength sluggishly returned to his limbs. He attempted once more to say her name aloud. Each pounding beat of his heart brought renewed vigor, and his voice finally returned. He parted his lips once more and spoke.

"Kathryn."

But she did not respond.

"No!" he called out again. "No, no, no! Don't leave me!" His fingertips traced her skin as her eyes glazed over, glassy and grey. The captain felt helpless and pulled her closer against his body, watching in agony as the woman he loved faded. Her long eyelashes dropped bit by bit, curtaining the vibrancy that had captured his heart until it disappeared completely. At the same instant, her delicate hand fell limp across his chest to rest over the scar—a reminder of the wound she had tenderly cared for not so long ago. He grasped her hand and placed it again over his heart, as it had been only a moment earlier. Her hand remained soft, languid, and cold in his calloused hand. A different pain crushed his chest as he felt his soul shatter with the realization that she had given her life in exchange for his.

"No, don't ye be leavin' me. Not now, not yet," he cried out as he pulled her into his arms and rocked her body, comforting no one. "I'll find ye, me love. I'll find ye again, me Kathryn."

He buried his face in her hair and whispered softly. Cradling her body in his arms, tears streamed down his cheeks as he prayed, then silently cursed God. A small circle of untidy men stood in silence, all eyes on their captain. They said nothing, but stared at the lifeless body of the woman who had sacrificed herself at the mast.

Without lifting his head, Captain John Phillips gave orders.

"Unleash her."

Kneeling next to the woman, Seth's broad shoulders quivered in time with his sobs.

"Aye, Capt'n," he whispered, and wiped his nose on the length of his sleeve. Seth turned swiftly to face the mast. Slicing the ropes with an etched dagger, he freed the woman from the grappling hook. Kathryn's arm dropped to the deck. In a flash, he caught her wrist before it hit the wood surface. Reverently, Seth laid her arm across her body and nodded to the captain before backing away.

"Ay." The captain's Welsh accent was thick. Captain Phillips took in the men facing him. "This is a dark day, indeed. I canna say she'll be the last to leave us."

Crimson flashed as electricity snaked its way across the midnight sky. Lightning wove its way in and out of ominous clouds, threatening to strike the raging ocean without provocation. Glancing skyward, the captain stared blankly. Derelict sails billowed in shreds, lashing wildly against the wind from the mainsail. The boom had been secured, but it still bucked against the ropes. As if in angry protest, the entire ship rebounded as the wind tore across the deck. Captain Phillips stared at the large boom and recalled the crippling pain that had wracked his body when the massive beam had broken free. It had smashed into his chest, trying to overwhelm and destroy him. He could not recall anything after the impact.

"Unlikely an accident."

"Capt'n?"

He hadn't been aware of his own voice. "Nothing… nothing."

"Not making sense. Stunned even now, most likely." The pirate spoke in low tones to one side. Muttered agreement followed.

"Aye, Capt'n. What now? What about…her?"

Captain Phillips scowled, still lost in thought. *Could it be that I'd traversed from this life?* His spine grew cold at the thought, and the realization that Death's icy grip had been loosened by her sacrifice only deepened the pain.

Rain continued its downpour as the sky wept for the loss of the young sorceress on board the great ship. Someone sniffed, and several of the men wiped their faces. Although whether it was from the rainfall or tears remained a secret.

"Give the Capt'n a minute…that's all he needs."

"Aye."

Captain Phillips looked skyward and his tone grew sharp. "Move the lass below to her quarters."

"Aye, Capt'n."

Several men stepped forward and silently bent down to lift the young woman's body. John Paul Archer, the ship's quartermaster, was among them.

"Archer." The captain's voice dropped, along with his glare. "Ye be on the helm."

The warning had not gone unnoticed, nor had the tone of the captain's voice. Archer froze in place, one arm extended, ready to take hold of the girl. He hesitated, ready to question the order, but the captain's warning made him pause, and Archer knew he'd best not cross authority. He held his tongue.

"Aye, aye, sir."

Archer stiffened and moved toward the helm, but not before delivering a searing glance in John Phillips' direction.

"Not now, Archer. Govern your thoughts. I've a devil's soul and cannot tolerate your enmity at present." The captain's distrust was evident. It had been only a few weeks since John Phillips had intercepted the lethal blow from Archer's cutlass saving Kathryn. There'd also been the rumor that he'd tried to strangle her. Phillips knew Archer wanted nothing more than to see the young girl murdered, and the evidence destroyed as fish bait. That would not happen while the captain had breath in his body.

Phillips unwillingly released the young woman's body to the remaining crewmen, who gently carried her away. Mustering all of his strength, he stood upright. Pain shot through his chest and into his back, buckling his knees. He forced himself to stand and face his men.

John Phillips Buchanon.

He had discarded his given surname. The crew, as a means of keeping his identity hidden, used his title exclusively. Captain John Phillips had become his moniker, and the only name to which he would answer.

The captain stood tall, statuesque, and powerful. He faced his crew as the captain of the pirate ship, *Revenge*. Studying the familiar faces of the cutthroats he commanded, Captain Phillips gave new orders.

"Secure the rigging and make fast the sheets."

"Aye, aye, Capt'n," broke over the downpour, as the men scattered in different directions. Each skillfully darted to designated parts of the ship, surefooted despite the slick deck.

"And one of you dogs, tie down that boom er'e it breaks loose and sends ye to your Maker.

There be no healer this time to bring ye back, mind me words!" Captain Phillips shouted.

Again, the cry of "Aye" sounded across the deck as two large men, wearing nothing but naval breeches and skullcaps, held fast to the boom, while a third tied a thick line to the end of the weighty boom. Once secured against the storm, the three turned back to their duties. A single gold hoop earring flashed from the left earlobe of one of the pirates.

"Seth, lad, take me to me quarters." The captain's voice sounded fatigued before he finished speaking. Quickly, the muscular Seth placed steady hands under the captain's broad shoulders. He allowed the officer to sag against him with his full weight.

Once again, pain seared through the muscles of both lower extremities and caused the captain's knees to buckle. Instantly, the ship's gunner appeared at his side, and John Phillips stood upright, supported by the loyal arms of his crew.

"Mister Gow." The captain nodded in appreciation.

Both crewmen ambled with the captain supported between them. The captain urged his companions to follow to the chirurgeon's cabin. Midway, the bosun hesitated.

"Ye best git to yer own quarters, Capt'n," Gow said guardedly.

"Nay, Mister Gow. The lass is me first concern as we have no surgeon, and now, no healer on board. This storm's liable to put us all asunder, lest we break free of it. And there'll likely be injuries before we've reached fair weather. Savvy?"

Gow nodded, wearied from fighting the elements. Obediently, he changed course and followed the dead woman's body below deck. Seth said nothing. Instead, his eyes darted about the ship as if searching for something, while his shuffled steps matched Gow's. With slow strides, the three men made their way to the arched door of the smaller cabin, still filled with the handful of men who had carried Kathryn inside. Something about the room set them on edge. They carried the dead woman deeper into the dark interior of her quarters. The cutthroats' superstition had frozen each man where he stood. The combined crew could do little more than place her body on the small cot tucked against the wall. When they had deposited her, each backed away uneasily into the dim light spilling through the doorway.

When John Phillips entered, he caught sight of his crew's uneasiness. "Nervous pack of pups! Take me to her."

The men exchanged looks with Seth and Gow on either side. Each crewman's eyes widened to the size of grapeshot in the dim light, rarely blinking, as they scanned the chamber for evil spirits. A few crossed themselves, spat upon the oak floor, then hopped in circles on one foot for a time. No one dared look at the body lying on the cot. Few had darted outside before the captain's arrival.

"Aye," came a voice from somewhere in the darkness, but no one moved to help the captain.

"What's the meaning of this?" he barked. He took an unsteady step forward as he pulled free from the cabin boy and bosun.

"Thar be hexes and black magic in here, Capt'n," a beefy crewman muttered. The faded claret neckerchief tied snugly over his grey, stubbled head shook as his chin quivered.

Captain Phillips scowled as the man crossed himself and spat once more for luck.

"Aye," echoed the other men, who began hopping from one foot to the other.

Bundles of dried herbs had been tied together and hung upside down in neat rows from the low ceiling.

The small writing desk and shelf, propped against the farthest wall, were likewise occupied. Vibrantly colored stones, and small white satchels, had been carefully placed in groupings of three. Set in the center of the room, a modest dining table braced a well-burnt candle. The pillar, burned nearly two-thirds of its original length, was adorned with wax that had dried in bubbling rivulets down the sides. Bits of tallow had spilled onto the warped wood and solidified in tiny solid drops. Surrounding all of it, ash and crushed dried leaves lay scattered and windblown—a dusting of what was once a numinous symbol, now left unrecognizable.

"The entire room is naught but the devil's parlor, Capt'n!"

The captain scanned the room. He shivered, and chills ran down his spine as he studied the clusters of herbs, stones, and what looked like tiny animal appendages tied randomly in bundles. He shook his head and purposely dismissed the charms that filled the small cabin.

"You're afraid o' ash an' weeds? What kind o' men are ye?"

"Tools o' the devil, says I." Slade touched the scars that pocked his face—the place she'd cast her first spell against a pirate.

"Aye, Slade speaks the truth." Moody shifted his weight. "She's a witch, Capt'n!"

Turning his attention to the body, Captain Phillips stared at Kathryn lying motionless on top of the well-worn cot. Painstakingly, he moved across the room to where Kathryn lay. There was peacefulness about her expression. She appeared almost joyful as he gazed at her features. Waves of chestnut hair cascaded across the dingy grey linen propped under her delicate head. Hot tears welled and blurred his view of the woman. Irritated and unable to see her clearly, he wiped his face with the back of a torn sleeve.

"She's dead."

"Capt'n…"

"I failed her."

The great Captain Phillips had not been able to protect Kathryn from that final enemy shrouded in death's dark robes. No refuge from such a final state had been found within the confines of the *Revenge*. Evil had discovered Kathryn, and it had taken her from him. *They will pay…they will all pay!* John Phillips' thoughts were as black as the light taken from her eyes. His heart was seared once again with an overwhelming feeling of anguish. Resolution set his features in stone as he turned to face his crew. He would bring her back. Somehow, he would do it.

"Seth!"

He jumped to attention. "Aye, Capt'n?"

"What have ye seen her employ with the dispensin' of her…" Captain Phillips paused, not knowing the exact word to use without setting his crew to hysterics. "Er…healin'?" he finally said.

Seth's stare widened in response, unsure of the various talismans' purposes. "I don't know, Capt'n. She didn't talk much about what she used this stuff for." He waved a hand at the herbs dangling from the ceiling's beam and shrugged his shoulders, then darted across the room.

Captain Phillips pointed to the rack overhead. "Gather somethin', lad."

"Aye." Seth hung his head but quickly set about gathering herbs, stones, and various other bundled amulets. Randomly selecting each item, he held them outward, away from his body, so as not to be hexed by any of it. When he could hold no more, he moved toward the cot. The men made a path and Seth nodded in thanks. "Lilly-livered cowards, all of you," he breathed as he passed by. Abruptly, he stopped near where the captain knelt and dropped the collection onto the edge of the cot.

"Captain." Seth's voice quavered. "It's true I don't know what…what she did with…" He paused, unsure how to answer the captain's question without betraying Kathryn's confidences. She was his friend, after all. Pointing to the piled objects, he continued, shifting his weight from one foot to the other. "These be sommat she does her conjurin' with. Blimey, Capt'n, there's no way to know what these are used for. Kathryn keeps most of the important ones hidden in her coffer." He'd said too much. Slapping both hands over his mouth, Seth shook his head as if doing so would recapture his words.

"What coffer?" the captain responded.

Seth only shook his head more ardently. Captain Phillips studied him a long, hard moment and soon realized Seth had spoken the truth. The crew stood just behind and nervously shuffled their feet. It was apparent the men were awaiting a dismissal that would never come. If one should have to suffer the apprehension of a witch's hovel, they all would suffer. That did nothing to calm the men's rattled nerves. Even in the best circumstances, the surgeon's quarters brought nothing but discomfort to everyone there…everyone, except for Captain Phillips.

"H-how much longer, Capt'n?" Scribbs inched his way toward the door. John Phillips gave no response. He also gave no dismissal. Scribbs remained where he stood.

"There. Fetch that. It'll keep ye busy and less inclined to leave before you're released, Mister Scribbs," Captain Phillips said, nodding to a dark corner.

Set neatly against the farthest wall was a leather pouch filled with surgical tools. It had once belonged to the original inhabitant of the paltry cabin. Unfortunately, the surgeon had been killed almost two years earlier during a fierce battle with Sallee Rover pirates. Since then, the position had never been filled—at least, not until Kathryn had been kidnapped by the crew and taken aboard the *Revenge*. Suddenly, her destiny had changed course, and she had been given the position of the ship's healer by default.

Outside, far above the ship, lightning clapped with a prickliness that startled the crew into a new pattern of hops and crosses. Each jolt lit up the interior of the cramped cabin with steel blue light. Unearthly shadows crawled across uneven crevices hidden in the slats of wood that lined the walls.

"Capt'n," a feeble voice spoke, faltering with each word. "If ye not be needin' me, I best be gettin' 'bout me duties…sir."

Captain Phillips surveyed each of the men in turn. Most of them cowered in the shadows of the now-darkened room. A few dared to lock hopeful eyes with the captain for a moment before returning their gaze to the floor.

"Light the candle, Seth."

"But, Capt'n…we don't know what sort of mischief it might bring in here." Seth backed away from the cot as he spoke. He had proven to be daring, and most certainly a risk-taker, but when it came to superstitions and magic, Seth was a pirate just like the rest of them.

"Well then, we're about to find out, aren't we?" Captain Phillips glanced to where the leather pouch lay untouched. "Mister Scribbs…that satchel, if you please."

"But, Capt'n…"

"Cease and desist your feeble-minded superstitions and bring me that surgeons' pack! And you, Seth, best get that candle lit before I light up your backside!"

Legends spewed from the sea had made most pirates gullible. Swallowing tall tales of creatures and mystic practices were usually met with the sign of the cross, spittle on the deck, and time spent hopping in circles. Simple acts such as lighting a candle bore terrifying significance under the right circumstances. This happened to be one of those times, and try as he might not to, Seth froze in place, as a result.

"But, I don't see it as respectful to her…"

"Light the candle, sir! You'd best not be havin' me ask ye again, savvy?" the captain growled through clenched teeth.

Seth's response rattled through his trembling lips as a dry, whispered, "Aye, aye, sir." He backed out through the door, only too glad to be free of the surgeon's cabin. Quickly, so as not to bring down the captain's wrath upon himself, he took hold of a short, wooden spike he found tied to the starboard side of the causeway. The tip had been wrapped in oakum, and covered with pitch. It smoldered lazily, evidence of its recent use somewhere on deck. As he darted back to the healer's quarters, a thin line of smoke trailed a long grey line behind him as he ran.

Seth cautiously entered the cabin. The handful of crewmates stood clustered together, now a little tighter than when he had left them. Seth's wary glance was returned by blank, fearful stares. Just ahead, resting solemnly on the center of a stout table, lay an obelisk. Its waxy rivers, once dripping over the upper edge, were now still, solid, and cold. It had the unsettling appearance of an altar.

Seth touched the smoldering tip of the oakum to the single wick in the middle of the tallow. Instantly, a tiny flame leapt from the wick, illuminating the room with a pale golden glow.

"Now, boy, bring me that bunker." The captain nodded his head in the direction of the leather coffer.

Seth obeyed and quickly returned with a chest the size of a small crate held precariously between both hands. Cautiously, he set it at the foot of the cot and lifted the lid. The captain peered inside, and though curious, Seth's nerves got the best of him. He leapt to one side of the box just as Scribbs set down the pouch. Both men backed away before any dark incantation could get them.

Abruptly, the air around the box began to vibrate. A deep, almost imperceptible buzz, resonated from an indistinct location. Out of the corner of his eye, Seth caught glimpse of a tiny bird. Its wings fluttered at such a rapid pace, they were merely a blur. The buzzing crescendoed as the creature darted from the box to the captain and hovered for just a moment, suspended in mid-air. The hummingbird literally floated over Captain Phillips' head, pausing as if to inspect the captain. Then the buzzing intensified briefly before the creature soared away from the pirate and over to the cot, where it stopped. The creature descended, alighting to rest precisely on one side of Kathryn's crown.

"A fairy wit' wings, it be." The whisper came from the back of the room.

"Aye," another gasped.

In that instant, a low hum came from another part of the room. This was subtle and soothing as it filled the cabin. Indigo and pink darted between blurred, blue-grey wings as the tiny bird flew. It hovered for just a moment over the captain's head before darting to where the first hummingbird perched.

Captain Phillips said nothing but followed the diminutive creature. It appeared to study him with coal-black, pearly eyes set behind a miniscule beak.

This appears to be more than offerings from a box. Indeed, methinks we're surrounded by magic! His thoughts betrayed him, and he cast a warning glance at Seth. *Hold lad…do not move, as yet.*

The youth froze in place. The admonition was not required—Seth knew this was more than happenstance or coincidence. He leaned away as the second hummingbird took its place near its mate. The sudden lilt of a mourning dove resonated, hauntingly permeating the dense air. The bird cooed a hollow sound as if it were perched in another time, its song a distant memory.

Coo…coo…ooo…ooo.

The assembly grew deathly still. Barely breathing, no one dared even so much as to cross himself. Huddled together, the men prayed silently, and the birds responded.

Coo…coo…ooo…ooo.

John Phillips' demeanor took on an air of acute vigilance. Every muscle tensed as he searched the room for the surreal. Shadows danced in the candlelight as he glanced from one corner to another. His crew remained fixed in place, so filled with terror they were. There was nothing here but darkness, shadows, and the unseen presence of invisible spirits.

Shadows grew deeper under the flickering candle, and Captain Phillips was about to call for a lantern.

And then, he saw it.

Five

BALANCED ON THE SILL OF the circular porthole, a pale grey dove sat. Its wings, tipped on the underside with white, were folded peacefully. A hazy beryl glow radiated from its chest, surrounding the bird in an ethereal light that did not illuminate the darkened room. The almost human eyes blazed cobalt blue as they stared at the young woman lying in death's embrace upon the cot. The dove blinked and cocked its head, and within moments, a second dove alighted alongside it. With the new dove's arrival, an aura surrounded both creatures, growing in intensity and brightness. The light kindled an eerie appearance, almost a mortal look, from the bird that focused hazel, compassionate eyes on Kathryn.

John Phillips shivered as he watched the doves. "This be no accident," he breathed.

Coo…coo…ooo…ooo.

Without warning, a flash of polished steel sliced the air, aimed at the porthole. The birds stayed fixed as the blade passed through them and lodged itself in the grainy wood of the porthole. Rippled currents of rainbow energy shimmered from the unharmed doves that stayed perched at the edge of the porthole. Their eyes darted from the blade to the dead sorceress.

Sounds came from the onlookers as they shuffled in place, combined with audible gasps. Meanwhile, Reed, still wielding the cutlass, stumbled, and the hilt in his hand rebounded.

"Why are they here, Capt'n?"

"Hush!" John Phillips cast another look at the birds, and a deep-set fear bristled at the thought of offending the white-winged visitors. Sensing it would only be a matter of time before one of the crew went off the deep end, should the men continue marinating in their terror, he decided it best to dismiss the lot.

"The doves have a higher purpose and haven't arrived by chance alone. This I know."

"Well, I want no part o' it!" Cade announced.

"Away with ye, then…the lot of ye!"

The men bolted, tripping over one another as they clamored to escape the unholy cabin. Reed, sword still dangling in his hand, shot one last, terrified glance at the perched doves before darting up the short stairwell leading to the deck. Shoved to one side, Seth made for the stairs as last man out.

"Hold there, Seth!" The command sent a chill down his spine. "I'll be needin' yer help with this here, lad. You were her friend, and I'm quite certain the bloody creatures mean ye no harm."

The captain nodded toward the doves perched in the porthole and staring in his direction. As if comprehending human language, both doves nodded their heads simultaneously and a whispered chirrup floated across the room.

"Aye…" The reply barely escaped Seth's lips. He fixed his stare on the pair of birds and stopped mid-step. Without acknowledging him further, Captain Phillips leaned forward and peered into the coffer. Inside laid scattered bits of cloth and what appeared to be the withered petals of some dead flower. Tucked along one side, two large white stones rested beneath a silver cord coated in something that looked like common candle wax. Suddenly, Captain Phillips remembered the stone. He quickly turned back to Kathryn and ran both hands around her delicate throat, exploring her cool, soft skin. He probed further down her back and underneath her silken hair.

Nothing.

"Where is it?"

"I…I don't know what you're lookin' for, Capt'n, but it seems to me that pushin' around a dead body like that might be a bad idea." Seth shifted his weight.

"Nonsense!" Captain Phillips knitted his brows. "I'm obviously looking for…" Cold panic surfaced from somewhere deep inside of him.

His hands trembled as he moved both across her bare shoulders toward her motionless breasts. Still nothing. Afraid of what he had not found, yet afraid of what he might still find should he continue, he pulled both hands away and leapt to his feet, his face almost ashen.

"The Seren is missing!"

Seth stared blankly. "That's a blessing in disguise, Capt'n."

"We've got to find it. It's the key..." Captain Phillips rummaged through the coffer once again. "Make haste and find that stone—the one that glows scarlet when trouble seeks the lass."

"I know which one. Capt'n, if I might say..."

"No, you may not."

Seth ignored him and continued, "...best be grateful it's gone and be done with it."

Captain Phillips met Seth's eyes, which were the size of doubloons. He stared not at the captain, but rather, at the porthole that now cradled three more doves. Seth began to tremble.

"Yer wits have got the best of ye, Mister Seth. I suggest ye get hold of yourself and find that stone... the one she calls the 'Seren.'"

"The Scarlet Seren?" Seth cried, recalling the warning Kathryn had given him to never touch it. "But... but, sir...the stone's cursed!"

"Ay Seth, that be true," the captain said. "But there's no choice in the matter, and this moment cannot be for the faint of heart, says I. Brave men be compelled by good deeds. Now prove yourself and find the bloody thing!"

"I want no part of it. She warned me to stay away from that…that thing!"

"You'll help me find the stone. *That* is an order!" The captain grunted and leaned over the chest.

"Aye, Capt'n." Seth dropped his eyes and began to shuffle around the cabin, searching half-heartedly for a stone he knew would likely kill him, should he find it.

Reaching into the wooden coffer once more, Captain Phillips grasped hold of a bit of cloth and offered it to Seth. "This be dangerous business, lad, fit for the stout-hearted, says I!"

The intended rally did not go unnoticed by Seth. Despite the captain's encouraging words, it wasn't enough to make Seth look harder. He dropped his hands to his lap.

"Start your search topside." Captain Phillips paused, then added, "Smartly there, me bucko!"

The warning rang out, and Seth jumped—not so much in alarm as from relief. He could finally escape the cabin and perhaps get lost for a while. Maybe then, Captain Phillips would forget the task he'd assigned and the cursed stone could be entirely forgotten by sundown.

"Aye, aye, Capt'n!" Snatching the cloth from the captain's outstretched hand, he spun around and dashed out of the cabin.

John Phillips turned his attention back to the healer's coffer. The indigo glow radiating from the doves nearly filled the room. Avoiding the porthole, he gazed into the interior of the wooden chest again. This time, another object caught his eye. Gently, he reached inside and lifted the waxen cord from the box.

Coo…coo…ooo…ooo.

The song, lilting softly at first, grew distinct as the captain carried the silvery object back to its owner on the cot. Placing it in Kathryn's flaccid palm, he turned and faced the porthole. By this time, seven or eight additional doves had joined the others. They perched on the lip of an oak beam stretched across the planked ceiling. The velvet light pulsed throughout the cabin as the cooing intensified. Captain Phillips stared at the doves.

"I don't know what ye want. Nay, it be sommat I want no part of. I've done me best, and it's within your powers to bring the lass back from death's hold. I'll say it only once…" The captain paused and swallowed hard while blinking back tears. He dropped to his knees. "I love her. I would rather it be my life taken so that she yet might live."

Each dove cooed in acceptance of the words spoken by the man. They seemed to understand the pain his heart suffered.

"Save her…please."

One by one, the doves lifted their wings and glided to where Kathryn lay. As they lit upon her, each bird lifted one of the talismans from the edge of the cot and perched with its object clutched in tiny talons, then faced Kathryn. Captain Phillips remained on his knees, his back to them, fearful of what he might witness. The pirate captain sobbed, bent and broken without the woman he loved—helpless to save her from death.

Coo...coo...ooo...ooo.

He caught sight of Seth standing not far off. In his trembling right hand, he clutched the bit of cloth from which dangled the Seren.

"Place the wretched thing alongside her, me boy." The captain choked out the words.

Seth's teeth chattered as he crept silently to where Kathryn lay. He circled her cot, where more than a dozen doves had settled. Distancing himself to just arm's length, Seth reached out a shaky hand and dropped the stone on the edge of the cot next to her. Instantly, two more doves entered through the open porthole, their cobalt light melding with the others, intensifying the radiance already filling the dark spaces. The two birds glided gracefully to the cot, carefully lifted the Seren, and placed it over Kathryn's chest.

"They mean to strangle her," Seth whispered and stepped toward the cot.

A hand reached forward to catch him. "Nay, lad. This is magic, this is. Sommat I know nothing of, but it seems the birds intend to use the stone." The captain held him and nodded for Seth to be still.

Magically, silver strands extending from the top of the stone lifted, then entwined behind the lifeless woman's neck. The ancient symbols etched on the surface of the stone began to glow with the same cobalt blue light that was being emitted from the doves. As if by invisible artistry, the humming began again as the tiny creatures perched near her head lifted in flight. The cooing intensified, and velvet light grew brighter, filling the cabin with gossamer energy. John Phillips watched while Seth stared, wide-eyed, as the birds began their magic, a cry of alarm catching in his throat. An urgency to move closer to the dead woman propelled Captain Phillips forward, closer to the cot where she lay. His actions were sluggish, although immediacy prompted him to obey the largest bird's silent, intense command. Suddenly, a low hum began to vibrate from the Seren, matching the intensity of the birds' coos. There was no way to distinguish from whence the cooing began and the deep pulsing hum had arisen.

One sound, one pulse, one light, one life.

As John drew closer to the lifeless Kathryn, two doves lifted their wings and alighted on his right arm, lifting it and carrying his hand to hover over her. Slowly, the humming increased, separating into colorful tones that vibrated the cobalt light into shades of azure, sea, and sky. His head filled with the pulsating tones and words began to shape themselves.

"A covenant made herewith…the debt yet be paid."

John Phillips listened intently to the lyrical words, drinking in the meaning as his muscles and sinews tensed with each pulsing syllable. Something tore at the flesh of his outstretched hand, yet he did not feel pain as the tissue of his palm separated itself. Sticky warmth spread over his hand, trickling down to where Kathryn lay. He opened his eyes and watched as, drop by drop, his life spilled onto the alabaster stone resting over the pale, still breast of the woman he loved so deeply. As his blood filled the symbolic crevices etched there, his thoughts shifted to images of her—alive, breathing, and vibrant.

He watched the lazy, crimson rivulets running over the edge of the stone and onto her delicate skin. The humming tones intensified, and John Phillips felt the storm suddenly abate as the sea grew eerily calm under his ship.

Seth was unable to move, barely breathing as he watched the magic of the doves at work on the woman and his captain. Almost immutably, a soft whisper of voices began chanting in colorful tones. Ancient Celtic witchcraft swelled as the chanting grew louder and louder with each pulse of tone and light.

"Anadl einioes, Cusan adfer,
(O breath of life, a kiss from the living,)

Grym bywydol Enaid Gwaed."
(Bless the gift of life through a lover's blood.)

Light emanated from the coven of white-winged doves. Hazy mists rose from each dove, revealing the faces of beautiful women hovering above. Ghostly lips moved as the ancient Celtic spell, recited rhythmically, filled the tiny cabin. Captain Phillips' blood continued to spill, an offering of life to the dead Kathryn.

Pulsing, throbbing, pounding, the words grew into a musical orgy until…

Silence…except for one solitary heartbeat.

Lub dub. Lub dub.

Six

SALTWATER, SWEAT AND SANDALWOOD FILLED her senses, surrounding her with an intoxicating power that was sensual and spiritual—a blended synchronicity. She inhaled deeply. The aroma's aesthetic felt safe and familiar. Eyes the color of rare Caribbean gems drifted into her consciousness. *John*, her mind whispered. She wanted to reach out, grasp hold of it and bask in the sensation, but her limbs were heavy, flaccid. And so, she remained still.

Myocardial muscles called out for her to awaken with each heartbeat, weak at first, but that increased in strength with each passing moment. Senses responded as the scent washed through the oxygen she drew in. Her heart recognized it. Each chamber in her heart filled with blood, new, but somehow not her own.

He was near.

She could feel him above her, around her, coursing through her veins with every beat of her heart. She tried to open her eyes, but they wouldn't obey. Instead, perhaps her voice would heed her desire to cry out to him. Silence. How could she make him understand she was here with him again? Awake and alive in a cadaverous body, but somehow anchored to the feeble cot beneath her.

Breathe.

The thought came to her almost effortlessly, and she willed her chest to rise in time with the ascent of the ship as it lifted with the ocean current.

Now fall.

Once again, she willed her lungs to expel the air just inhaled. Her chest's movement matched that of the ship as she felt the *Revenge* drop in time with her exhalation.

"Mmmmm."

A soft moan escaped through the bow in her scarcely parted lips. Just then, she felt deep green eyes fix their warm focus on her pallid face. He had heard her. She listened as he held his breath, waiting for another affirmation that she was, indeed, alive. His heart pounded, beating steady and strong in the silence.

"Capt'n, the men be wantin' a word wit' ye…" A quivering voice abruptly broke the silence. Cade stared through the arched doorway.

"*Hold!*" the captain's response ricocheted back, his eyes never leaving her face.

"But, Capt'n…"

"*Avast*, I say!" His arm shot up as he shouted out the warning.

Cade withdrew. "Aye, aye, Capt'n."

Despite the disturbance, his eyes stayed locked on the young sorceress, and he waited for another sign that life had found its way back to her.

"Ahhh."

The captain caught his breath and stood still while the doves fluttered back to the porthole. They perched there, observing him with their human eyes while he crouched over Kathryn. Soothing sounds gurgled from the birds, intermixed with the warmth of tiny humming as their heads nodded almost imperceptibly. One by one, the white wings spread, and the doves, accompanied by two tiny hummingbirds, departed the ship, flying into the night air. Within moments, they had disappeared into the midnight sky. Only one remained perched in the portal. He felt the human-like stare upon him and lifted his own gaze to meet that of the dove's. The bird held his gaze. It was as if the wizened dove knew him.

Captain Phillips nodded his head. "I'll take care of her…I promise."

"Aahhh." The faint whisper rose again from the cot. She could feel his attention refocusing upon her. Soothing warmth pressed against her temple as his hand cradled, then gently traced her wavy dark hair.

"Kathryn." The baritone voice soothed her, enveloping her, comforting and warm.

"Kathryn. Oh, Kathryn, me bonny lass."

Musk and sea air drifted to her from where he spoke. A familiar sensation rushed through her as she felt her own heart beating vigorously now. Awareness flooded her mind.

Kathryn smiled.

Even though her eyelids remained heavy and closed, her dark lashes spilled pools of warm salty tears that washed slowly down her cheeks.

"Joh-hn."

Her voice felt abrasive in her throat. Again, soft warmth pressed over her skin as she felt the pirate's lips brush across her face, settling over her brow. His kiss was gentle, and she became kindled at his touch. Warming her cheek, she could feel his breath as his lips kissed her again before moving to her jaw.

"I'm here," he whispered in her ear.

She could feel her face was wet with tears, and she knew they were not hers alone. The strong pirate holding her wept as she spoke his name.

"I thought ye were lost to me, lass," he whispered, and his chest heaved.

Kathryn lifted one hand and weakly placed it on the nape of the pirate's neck. "John," she said again, but this time her voice was more than a whisper.

Strong arms pulled her into his chest, where he cradled her body, rocking her as he wept—a caress blending with the roll of the ship that soothed them both. Time passed as the moon rose full, casting pools of light through the cabin that blanketed them both in silver. Kathryn could feel the moonbeams bathing her face, and the sound of a mourning dove resonated from a distance. She lay still, basking in the moment, while her skin, soothed by the pale silver light of the mystical moon, was washed with the tears of the man she loved. He pulled her closer and held tighter, his muscles tensing as if he sensed her thoughts.

Neither the captain nor the witch noticed the white-winged dove with pale blue eyes fluttering up toward the moonlight and out the tiny cabin window. Its silver breast blended with the light of the deep night, mysterious and spectral. It lifted upward with wings outstretched and peered toward the heavens. The tiny creature ascended, cooed, then faded into the light as it disappeared into the feathery mist of the midnight sky.

Seven

"Capt'n! Caaap-tain!" The baritone sounded shrill, edgy, anxious. "Capt'n, ye best set yer eyes upon this, sir!"

John Phillips looked up for only a moment before returning his attention to Kathryn. She forced her eyelids to part as he pulled away. Her vision fanned out vertically, the way curtains part to allow glimpses of what lies behind to come into view. Painfully, she shifted her focus and found his. The captain smiled.

"John," she whispered.

"Kathryn. I thought I'd lost ye, lass."

Again, the anxious call from outside the cabin door beckoned. John Phillips' mouth pulled slightly to one side as he spoke.

"My crew…"

"Aye, go then." The words tore through her blistered throat.

He stood and immediately pitched to one side. She noticed a grimace crossing his face just as he turned away from her. Muscles in his back quivered beneath opaque fabric made sheer with rain and salt water. His face tensed, and he gasped, clutching his ribcage where the boom had caught him. None of his suffering was lost on Kathryn.

"It's not bad, lass."

She said nothing. Haunting visions of a rogue boom tearing free from the sheets and rocketing across the deck ripped across her memory. Flashes of darkness surfaced—the heavy plank that bashed the captain's chest and crushed his heart beneath an imploding sternum. She grimaced as she recalled the images.

His heart had stopped beating. She remembered the spasm in his pulse. Voluntarily, she'd bound her arm to the grappling hook and used her body for a witching stick. The skies had lit up, pulling lightning from the angry sky, through her veins, and into his lifeless heart.

She flinched as the memory of electricity surged along one arm. The cells in her body awakened with her memory, and her heart leapt, knowing this man had survived.

"Stay here, lass. I'll send Seth directly to mind o'er you."

"It isn't necessary."

"Indeed, Madame." Without facing her, he exhaled heavily—whether due to his pain at leaving her, or the injury wracking his body, was unclear. But, whatever his anguish, he willed himself to move. He walked out with long, deliberate strides that masked his trauma.

Kathryn closed her eyes and mouthed the words of an ancient Celtic prayer of gratitude.

The ship lifted and descended, gently succumbing to the deep-water currents, nodding to an unknown Deity's acceptance of the witch's supplication.

"Kathryn?" The voice sounded familiar, deep, and tremulous. "Ahem. Kat?"

"Seth? Is that you?"

Kathryn craned her neck to the left to see who'd entered. She was met with only shadows.

"Aye." He cleared his throat.

"Seth." She paused to swallow back the electric pain still wracking her body. "Step forward. I cannot see you clearly."

"But you're dead…or are you a ghost?"

"Don't be ridiculous, Seth. I do you no harm. Come forward and let me lay me eyes on you, mate."

A hulky silhouette stepped out of the shadows and made its way into Kathryn's peripheral vision. With the broad shoulders of a virile sailor, Seth was not the youth she'd thought he was.

"Ah, Seth." A genuine grin crossed her lips. "Truly a sight for me eyes, ye be." She lifted a weak hand and waved him forward. "Come, tell me…has the captain got you on the lookout for me now?"

Seth nodded and grinned. "Of course. Why else would I be here?" Curls the color of Caribbean sand were tossed to either side of his forehead. He drove his gaze to the floor. It was obvious Seth was rattled.

"Because you're concerned about me?"

"Hardly." His grin widened, then suddenly dropped. "Someone's got to watch over you, Kat. I told you as much not too long ago."

"I suppose you are right, and there's no one I'd rather have by my side right now than you."

He's coolly standoffish, and why wouldn't he be? The thought unsettled her as she watched him. *The poor lad just witnessed his captain bashed about and killed by his own ship's mast. Then he stood by and watched as I was offered up, a sacrifice to the mercy of St. Elmo's Fire, which killed me right in front of him and the crew.* Her brows knitted, and she grimaced. She remembered Seth tying her to the mast, then stumbling backward as the lightning bolt shot down the grappling hook and through her body. *Perhaps it's guilt.*

"You saved him, you know." He did not reply. Kathryn glanced down at the open palm of her right hand and cringed at the sight of burned flesh. She had placed it across John Phillips' chest. She turned sympathetic eyes on Seth.

"Say something."

He lowered his eyes and stayed silent.

Surely, the lad has good cause to be suspicious, and now, with my soul returned to this body, Seth must certainly think me bewitched!

"Seth! Think about how brave you were back there on deck…and quick thinking, too. It was by your design that the captain was saved—a brilliant plan! Although, it must have been difficult watchin' your captain kilt by the angry forces of God's fury! Then, to stand by and watch my soul return to my body…aye, what a loyal friend you are to us both."

"It doesn't make sense." Seth looked at Kathryn, waiting for an explanation. Likely, there would be none, and his body tensed.

"There's magic in this business, 'tis true, Seth. You know it without me sayin' it. There are powers given to some for the blessing of others. You know I have this magic…don't you,

Seth?" She paused for a response, but was met with only uneasy silence. "My mother and grandmother, and many more before them, for generations longer than most can recall, were given the *Gift* of magic healin'. I have that *Gift* for healin', Seth."

Seth cocked his head and met her gaze, which was affectionate and kindly toward him. He could not hold her stare for long and quickly dropped his focus to the floor. Shifting his weight, he nodded that he understood. Clasped between his fingers, he toyed nervously with a roughly knitted wool cap.

"The *Gift* which is given to me is purely for healin'. It's meant to deliver all that is good to the sick and afflicted. There's nothin' evil about it, I'm tellin' you true, Seth. Although, it's not so for Morrigan and her foul sisters. Theirs is the black magic of the Obeah witches."

"I don't know much about the Obeah, and I don't care to, either." Seth crossed himself with one hand as she spoke of the Creole mystics from the dark bayous.

"You know I'm speakin' truth, Seth." She raised a finger to the young man's chest. "You know it in here."

Seth took one step back. His glanced a warning to take heed. Kathryn's hand fell from his chest. It was futile to try to convince him that she meant no harm. Either he was traumatized by the events topside, or his reckless spirit simply wanted to be with the men. Likely, it was both. Seth felt safest when he risked his own life. Somehow, the thought of risking another's life sat unfavorably with him. Kathryn silently accepted defeat and accepted his reservations with a sigh.

"All right then, Seth. What's your business here, really? Did the captain send you after me?"

"Aye."

"Well then, I have a task for you if you won't speak to me." Her words were meant to sting, but Seth stayed impassive, distant. "Help me up, then. I mean to go on deck."

"No! Kathryn, can'be doin' that. The capt'n wouldn't hear of it, and I don't fancy a floggin' at the mast."

"Ridiculous! Capt'n Phillips would do no such thing. I know for myself that he ordered you to watch o're me and tend to my needs."

"Aye, that's exactly what he said." Seth glanced out the window at the sea, obviously wishing he were anywhere else. His fingers pawed at the cap in his hands.

"Well, I'm in need of some fresh air, and this cabin reeks for want of sea breezes. Now take me topside before I take it up with the capt'n himself!"

Kathryn's Celtic temper flared quickly. The staccato of a pirate's lilt suddenly surfaced, suggesting she'd already spent too much time aboard the *Revenge*. Seth glared at her, which she returned with matched belligerence. The two friends dueled in silence, a stalemate that neither would back down from.

"I won't do it," he stated.

"You'll answer to more than just me."

"Your threats don't scare me anymore, Kathryn."

In that moment, she realized their friendship had changed. Now that Kathryn had been summoned back to life, suspicion would surely become her constant companion. She would never be viewed the same, not by Seth, nor by any of the other cutthroats aboard the ship.

She fixed a cool gaze upon Seth as she painstakingly pushed herself up to sit. Unexpectedly, she caught a slight movement as his gaze narrowed in a dark stare. *Is he challenging me?* The effect was not lost on Kathryn.

"Seth, you best mind what you're intendin', mate. I'm not your adversary. Look instead to the black soul who seeks to destroy this ship and all who sail aboard her." She paused, waiting for a reaction from him.

Seth defiantly lifted his chin and continued to glare.

Kathryn shook her head. "That devil is Morrigan, lad. She's evil indeed, and seeks to collect the dead, on land or sea. Her sign is the raven. How many ravens have you seen lately, hmm?"

"A few."

"She's the one ye ought to reserve your anger for… not me." Kathryn's voice had dropped to a whisper—a low, lethal warning.

"Aye, Miss Kathryn," he breathed as he faced the witch. "If that's what the chirurgeon orders, then that's what this sailor will do. But, I warn ye—there's more afoot than what ye think, and ye'd best mind yourself. I'll not be party to your mischief again. You're on your own, Kathryn."

A piercing shriek broke the silence as they stared each other down. The deathly scream cried out again, then suddenly fell silent.

Kathryn turned her head sharply in the direction of the sound. Foamy ashen mist glinted in iridescent colors as it bubbled over the cabin's threshold. Spiderlike, it crept into the cabin with agile, cunning movements. The mist had a life-force propelling it toward them both.

"Silver Moon," Kathryn breathed in barely a whisper.

Her attention snapped back to Seth, who was frozen in place. Terror spread across his face.

"Seth, haste…get me to the window. I must see the moon!"

Seth lurched from his stupor and sprinted to where Kathryn sat on her cot. Without effort, his muscular arms scooped her to her feet. He half-carried her to the tiny porthole window, hoisting her body from the waist just high enough for Kathryn to peer out into the night sky. Caught off guard by the youth's strength, Kathryn blushed. *Impressive.* Seth did not see the look she cast at him.

Suddenly, Seth's focus locked on the door's threshold. His sandy locks waved suddenly as he turned his head, contorting his upper torso, while his hands stayed firmly on the witch's waist.

Kathryn kept her attention skyward, staring in silence into the night. The sea barely moved, a black watery corpse in appearance, lifeless against the night sky. Levitating from the surface like tombstones rising from the earth, an iridescent vapor rose and floated across the water toward the ship. Kathryn held her breath.

"No!"

She tore her gaze from the ghostly apparitions and scanned the black sky for the omen she had hoped would not be there.

"God help us!"

Eight

"SILVER MOON."

Seth turned a terrified look upon her, then shifted his focus through the porthole. His stare followed Kathryn's to the ghoulish orb hovering above them.

"What are ye sayin'? What is a Silver Moon…?" He was too terrified to speak more than the few words that escaped his lips.

"Silver Moon. It's the death omen of the night. Some choose to call it, 'Hell's Grim Tyrant,' due to the death pall cast from the moon overhead. The omen comes from the moon, and its silver tendrils grasp at those it means to take as prey. See there, Seth…it snakes toward us in the darkness, even now."

"Whaa…What do you mean by 'death omen?'"

Kathryn began to tremble. Unsettled by the woman's tremor, his grip loosened about her waist, and he instinctively lowered one hand to the top of his cutlass.

"The moon foretells of events to come. Surely you know of that, Seth."

He nodded. His fingers curled tightly around the hilt and his knuckles whitened as his grip tightened.

"Mariel warned of the moon and its powers when I was but a child. There was a moon omen the very day this crew darkened our village."

"I never saw it. When? When was there an omen? I would have seen it, Kathryn, and I never did."

"It was the day these bloody pirates kidnapped us…the day they took us both away. That omen was the Midnight Omen."

"I swear I never saw it." Seth's voice trailed away as he studied the vapor dripping from the moon.

Kathryn paused, remembering the twilight when her cousin, Winne, had brought her attention to the eerie ring of light surrounding the moon—the same one that now paled Kathryn's face. Mariel had pointed it out, insisting the ghostly aura had prophesied of imminent danger to Kathryn. True to its forecast, that night, a few of the roughest crew from the *Revenge* had arrived at the cottage doorstep, carrying her nearly dead father. They feasted their greedy eyes on the Seren hanging about Kathryn's neck. Out of sheer lust for the treasure she wore, they kidnapped her, bringing her aboard the ship as their prize. Seth had been captured that night, as well. It seemed so long ago, but, in truth, it had been only a year since that fateful night.

Her eyes narrowed. Kathryn wished her grand-mother were with her to interpret it. Mariel's powerful Celtic *Gift* gave her uncanny insight—a white witch's acumen. Kathryn had learned much from her in her short seventeen years in the cottage. But she had not learned all there was to know about the *Gift*. The moon's ominous sign reminded her of that.

"This be pure evil, Seth. There's no warning given but this: Only death and dyin' come from the Silver Moon Omen."

Another piercing scream above them from somewhere on deck jolted them both into staring again at the doorway. Kathryn's body began to tremble. Lapping just beyond the small table that rested off center, the spectral mist crept steadily forward, intent on consuming them. Seth pulled his sword resolutely from the scabbard. The steady scrape of metal on leather sounded above the cries on deck.

"Get me to the captain, Seth!"

"Aye, aye." Seth's eyes darted to the moon outside. "Be mindful of where you step, Kathryn." He waved his cutlass toward the froth now lapping at their feet. "There's somethin' about this...this...this breath of the devil!"

Suddenly, Kathryn stopped. Her eyes widened. "Morrigan! Seth, you must take me topside at once!"

Kathryn's tone left no mistake as to the urgency. Now alarmed beyond terror, Seth reacted instinctively and swept her up in his strong arm, dragging her with him as he made for the doorway. Picking his way carefully along creaking planks of flooring, he placed one tentative step after the other. Cautiously submerging his foot in the vapor, where it disappeared before meeting solid wood beneath, he paused and waited for the worst. Seth looked at Kathryn and nodded.

"So far so good," he said.

She agreed and followed alongside him, examining the vapor as they crept forward. Both kept their eyes glued to the cabin floor, searching the perpetual creeping mist for deadly entities. Each relied on the other's keen eyesight, not knowing what they were looking for.

Seth took another step and a low hiss sounded as they moved deeper into the vapor.

"Avast!" Seth ordered at nothing. He lifted his cutlass high, but somewhat tremulously, above his head.

"Hush, Seth! This is naught but the devil's work and Morrigan its messenger. Keep still, lest ye awaken what e'er foul thing lies beneath!" She stared at the mist now rising above their ankles.

"Aye."

Seth's whisper was barely audible above the vapor's hiss pulsating in a serpent's breath. It was impossible to tell where or if the entity breathed. The ghostly sound was almost an echo that bounced off the walls.

Suddenly, Kathryn's foot struck something unseen. It burned with a searing prick at the tip of her bare toes. She cried out as the pain shot back into her heel and up along her calf.

"What...what is it?" Seth could barely speak.

"I don't know. My foot..."

"Let me see it."

Looking down for the source, she saw both legs cut off just below her knees where the mist lapped hungrily at her skin. Slowly, she lifted her right leg and watched as her calf, ankle, and then, heel appeared intact through the haze. Her limbs remained intact! Still, something beneath the mist had caused the pain to her foot. Lowering her foot into the vapor once again, she felt it—hard against the bottom of her heel. It did not move, and felt strangely familiar. The corner of her mouth twitched slightly as she realized they were standing at the edge of the single stair leading to the causeway.

"Oh!"

"Mind the step, Kat." The words sounded sarcastic, although that was not his intent.

"Right." She sneered and tugged on Seth's supporting arm. "We should keep moving."

Glancing down, Seth nudged his own foot forward until he was likewise tapping the toe of his boot against the wooden stair. The vapor grew thicker as they advanced. Near the top, a radiant glint from off from the mist covered the entire deck of the ship. Kathryn looked to the black sky and studied the luminous body once again.

"Silver Moon…the omen of death," she whispered aloud to herself in disbelief.

Perched just overhead, the moon hovered menacingly, a macabre reminder of the deadly powers of the Caribbean Sea. A faint silver glow encased the orb sprayed with droplets of blood-red shadows. The moon was bleeding. Midnight air stood black and still, though it cast an eerie light, illuminating the surface of the water. The same silver light bathed the entire ship. No longer did the waters churn or the skies lash out with the storm's fury. All was hushed, waiting, prey to the demonic moon. It was as if the *Revenge* and her crew had stopped breathing, too, along with the sea. A demon possessed the night skies and all anyone could do was wait.

Deep within the mist, a faceless shriek pierced the dank silence, and then, just as suddenly, was cut off. Once again, the *Revenge* was quiet, and all aboard her froze. The stillness was suddenly interrupted by the hollow sounds of something bumping along the wooden planks beneath the misty vapor.

Thud…thud…thud, cavernous and dull.

Out of the corner of his eye, Seth spotted a spherical object the size of a small melon rolling to where he and Kathryn stood. Surfacing through the topmost layer and dipping in and out of the mist, the large rolling object appeared, then disappeared, gathering speed as it moved closer and closer. Seth stared hard at the object, blinking his eyes once or twice to bring clarity to them as it neared. He realized at once the startling object was, in fact, something else—something too terrifying to comprehend, yet he could not stop staring at it.

The object rolled closer. Two sets of unblinking eyes peered skyward momentarily before rolling underneath the mist and back down toward the deck. Seth gasped, his voice held silently in his throat as he stared at the ghastly entity making its way toward him. Over and over again, the eyes appeared, then disappeared, in and out of the mist, doll's eyes, never closing, rolling in his direction. The object spun directly toward him until it smacked solid against his left foot with a sickening thud. Unfocussed eyes stared vacantly at Seth from a decapitated head. Seth mouthed a cry but made no sound, unable to scream.

Kathryn felt the youth's horror explode around them both and turned her attention to the head. Lying there was the face of a rigger-mate named Payne. His mouth was frozen open in a voiceless scream, a death mask, which had been silenced by something unseen. Coal black eyes glistened lifelessly under the ominous silver moonlight. Kathryn shrieked and Seth kicked the ghoulish object reflexively. He shuddered at the realization of what he had booted.

The head rolled away and disappeared back into the mist with a fading, hollow thud.

Just ahead, on the right, something rustled, and Kathryn turned to find it. She could see nothing in the dense mist. The whooshing sounded again, and the whiff of acrid, rotting crustacean filled her nostrils. She choked involuntarily on the stench, coughing out the putrid stench that lingered in the back of her throat. At the same time, her skin bristled and a slimy appendage whisked past her feet, making her jump.

Then all was instantly silent once again.

Indeed, we are being overtaken by evil itself. She knew they were doomed, and an unwelcomed validation of her suspicions shot icy shivers up her spine.

Low and guttural, the wet moan of a man in agony rattled the stillness. This time, the cry sounded from somewhere just ahead, toward the starboard bow. A new wave of fear gripped her in anticipation of what she might find peeking through the mist. Frantically, she forced her eyelids tightly closed, hoping to shut it out. Seth reached out a quivering hand and took hold of her. Kathryn did not know whether it was out of fear for her safety, or simply to steady himself, but his grip felt like a vice. She heard the clatter of his cutlass as it hit the deck and figured he must have dropped it. Kathryn could only assume Seth's violent trembling had gotten the best of him. He would no longer be able to protect her.

Just as suddenly, the guttural moan stopped. Kathryn waited for the aftermath. She scanned the mist, afraid of what she would find, but more terrified of what she could not see with her eyes closed. Nothing but mist. Another whooshing sound came from a different direction. She strained to see the cause of it and was met by something hurling through the air above her head and toward the other side of the ship. The object looked like the wooden posts mounted along the forecastle. Typically, these were used for securing cast-off line, but this was not typical, and she knew it was not a post. The object had fingers and a hand. She turned her head away from it, revulsion making her nauseous at the dull thud that soon followed when the arm landed somewhere to port.

The crew of the *Revenge* was dying, one by one, hunted by an evil entity they could not see. Doing nothing would only make them easy prey for this hunter, but she could not force her mind to clear.

"I don't know what to do, Seth," she whispered. The grip on her sleeve tightened, and she felt him shake vigorously. Not wanting to look at him, she glanced down at her feet. The vapor waxed and waned slightly where she stood. It was as if the mist breathed.

Whispered rumbling crawled out of the silence. Something laughed, coarse and deep. The entity was laughing at them.

Kathryn watched the vapor inhale and exhale over her bare feet and felt the ship heave just slightly. Saltwater washed across the deck's surface and lapped at her exposed feet—seawater now stained crimson from the blood of the helpless crew being slaughtered one by one. The skin along her spine prickled, and she suddenly thought of the captain. She tore her gaze from the gruesome scene at her feet and scanned the deck once again for any signs of him.

Terror swept over her at the thought that this could be *his* blood bathing her feet. She shook her head at the thought, praying he might be somewhere near the helm. Still, she had not yet seen him, and the possibility of his death at the hand of this predator haunted her.

Turbulence ripped through the ship again, this time originating from somewhere to her left. Another high-pitched cry rang out, agony-laced and bloodcurdling, before falling silent. An eerie hush once again blanketed the ship, along with the enveloping mist. Kathryn looked toward the cry and could see Seth, fearful and searching. She could just make out a few of the other crewmen silhouetted in the moonlight as the mist heaved back and forth. Their shadowy forms gave them the statuesque appearances of floating where mist met legs or trunks, even heads. She sensed these men were alive and felt a brief sense of relief when a shadowy head suddenly jerked to scan the mist fervently, looking for an unseen predator. Terror filled each one of the faces she surveyed. Death waited to take them one-by-one.

Then she remembered.

Nine

"THE SEREN!"

As Kathryn huddled within the deadly mist, she groped for the object but found nothing but bare skin where the Seren should have been. Powerful, and known for protection, the Sigel of Defense had been gifted to Kathryn on the day of her kidnapping. Nicknamed the Scarlet Seren, the talisman was never to be apart from her. Desperate to find it, she patted her chest and shoulders with both hands in search of the stone. It was not there.

"The Seren! Seth…where's the Seren?" Her voice betrayed the fear that accompanied its absence.

She spun, peering through the mist for any sign of the valuable stone. Nothing was visible below the vapor. Desperate, she cried out to anyone within earshot.

"The Seren…I must find the Seren!"

No one responded. No one moved. There was little chance the men would help her. Frozen in terror, they looked like statues. Mostly, they took measures to avoid the magical pendant that had strangled one of their crewmates. The stone took life at a whim, or so it seemed.

The men were paralyzed, and it was obvious she would not get help from any of them. No one dared assist her, and Kathryn's search grew more frantic. She twisted and pushed her way across the deck, probing through the dense veil that encircled her. She could no longer see Seth, nor did she care. Her only thought was to retrieve the precious Seren.

A low cackle sounded from a distance. It continued, barely audible, and then, grew to a whisper. Kathryn froze. Laughter echoed again. Fear gripped her as she realized what it was that hissed—Morrigan's laugh. Kathryn closed her eyes and waited to be struck down by the evil that laughed at her. While she waited, her lips moved, and she whispered the ancient Celtic prayer for protection. Another voice sounded low and distant from another place as if she could hear it sounding inside her head. Its tone was old and wise.

> *Dun a'n gwaredo eich merch,*
> (God protect this lass)

Without thought, Kathryn repeated the words aloud.

> *Angel pen ffordd, a diawl pen tan,*
> (An angel abroad, a devil at sea)

Kathryn's voice matched the intensity of the terrified men scattered about the foggy deck. Occasionally, the cry of another dispatched pirate would reverberate through the haze—a cry for mercy just before it suddenly fell silent. All who remained alive on board feared most the hush of death's stillness.

Kathryn felt her skin crawl with an uncanny sense that evil crept closer to her. She continued to recite the ancient words that sounded in her head.

> *Gwarcheidwad Amgylchedd y dwr,*
> (Guardian of the water)

> *Yr alwad hon i amddiffyn*
> (This call to protection)

The Welsh witch emerged from within, as Kathryn lifted her arms, deliberately and with power, until her fingertips reached skyward. In a commanding voice, she continued her supplication:

> *Cymryd i chi eich hun a rhoi i mi.*
> (Take for yourself and give to me)

She stood supremely, hands strained toward the ominous moon, eyes closed and lips still. She was omnipotent. *Now call to your protection, Kathryn,* the voice in her head commanded.

Awron Fi gorchymyn!
(Come forth the Seren!)

Her voice roared the summons, its fullness echoing across the deck of the entire ship.

Exploding from nowhere, a searing crimson stone shot out of the mist to Kathryn's outstretched hand. Lightning burst from around her and broke the foreboding calm with an ear-splitting crack. Fiery stone met the cool skin of her palm. She grasped the talisman securely and held it aloft.

Dianc Morrigan!
(Get thee hence, devil!)

Her voice commanded the evil permeating the ship, and as she did so, she held the Seren overhead, projecting the stone's sacred symbols upward toward the moon. The crimson glow from the stone illuminated the black sky, until it met the blood spots shadowing the moon.

Silver light melted into the florid incandescence that danced erratically over the *Revenge*. Its light covered the blood-washed deck with ruddy light.

Ar y domen.
(You are commanded)

Kathryn's voice permeated the bloodbath of light illuminating the ship. She held her hand toward the

Silver Moon. Slowly, she opened her eyes and lifted her empty hand skyward.

Y tafflu allan.
(You are expelled)

A low rumble sounded softly, then rolled quickly across the surface of the water in the direction of the ship. The sea responded, hurling spray in wild, vomit-like bursts that randomly matched the intensity of the sound. Closer and closer, it rumbled with a violently explosive sea spray that rained down over the ship and crew. The sound, amplified by erupting seawater, formed rhythmic patterns. Words emerged from the sonorous rumbling. A raspy voice whipped around the *Revenge*, whispering with a thunderous intonation that caused the pirates' very souls to vibrate in much the same way a cannon blast would force the heartiest gunner to quake.

"Stand fast, men!"

No one knew who'd dared to speak, and no one responded. A familiar icy chill ran along Kathryn's limbs as she recognized the ethereal voice from the sea. She'd heard it only once before as it spewed forth from this demon's sister.

Morrigan's voice.

As Kathryn raised her gaze to the topmost post of the mainsail, she saw the visage of a woman's face, sleek and pale. The woman's eyes were paler than her skin. They were yellow with slits for pupils, almost ser-pent-like in shape. Her skin was patterned with inky marks, the symbols of black magic and death. Morrigan looked into her eyes, and the young sorceress felt she was being appraised.

It rumbled again, and gnashed razor-sharp teeth as it spoke, an ancient tongue Kathryn did not rec-ognize, yet the meaning of the words magically were understood by everyone on the ship.

> *"My own I take, though dead not be.*
> *Beware, John Phillips, I come for thee."*

Raw fear bit her senses and spilled into icy steel resolve as Kathryn heard his name spoken by the evil entity hovering overhead. The Seren grew hot in her hand, and she knew the Sigel of Defense was the answer. Shifting the radiant stone from its lock on the moon, she swept her hand toward the top of the mast and directly at Morrigan's yellow eyes. With her other hand still open in supplication, she grasped at the air and clenched her fingers around invisible power. Snapping her fingers, she flung a spear of blue light toward the top of the mast. Lightning cracked as the blinding blue light met its target and pierced the sin-ister face that floated above the mast.

Kathryn's eyes locked on it as its features contorted wildly against the black sky—and then, she saw some-thing else. The silhouette of a man leapt gingerly across the taught lines. He was moving toward Morrigan. In one hand, he held a long spike made of crystal. Light danced in prisms from the length of it, and Kathryn gasped when she realized who it was that risked his life so.

"Seth!" she screamed out, but he did not hear her.

Morrigan's face contorted again and spit out flames that lashed fiercely at the ship. Seth clung to the base of the spike with both hands and swung the crystal in a low arc just as a column of fire stabbed toward the main mast.

"Take that, you motherless dog!" he shouted and batted the flame back into the face.

Morrigan let out a ferocious howl. With the power of the crystal spike deeply imbedded, the creature writhed in ghastly images against the blackened sky. Suddenly, the power of the Seren flared and Morrigan screeched just before she vanished altogether.

It was over.

The sea suddenly became still and silver moonlight washed over the blood-sodden deck once again. Kathryn glanced back at the mainmast where Seth had been, but he'd vanished. Without warning, her strength drained from her body, and Kathryn stumbled back, exhausted. A pair of strong arms appeared from nowhere and solid hands took hold of her waist to support her just as she was about to collapse. Looking up, she glimpsed the face of her rescuer. Seth's fear had been replaced by another emotion—triumph, she guessed. She was once again surprised by his strength and smiled.

"Thank you, Seth," she whispered as he helped her gain her balance.

"Aye, Kat," he said under his breath. "That was amazing, wasn't it?"

"I wouldn't call it that. Horrific, maybe. Terrifying, to be certain, but amazing? Likely not."

Kathryn leaned on Seth, grateful he held fast to her waist to keep her upright as her legs had certainly failed her. In truth, she was awed by his strength, which was that of a man well beyond his years.

"What would you call it, then?"

"The work of dark magic—a devil, methinks." Kathryn turned her attention to the deck.

Vaporous wisps lingered. The mist had all but evaporated, leaving behind the blood-soaked deck and what remained of the terrified crew.

Sade kicked a severed limb away from where he sat, then stood and vomited over the rails. Nutt pulled Skyrme to his feet, and Kathryn was grateful the sailing master lived. One by one, the survivors rose to their feet, pallid faces framing their horrified expressions as each man surveyed the ship. Gore and pieces of severed limbs lay scattered across the *Revenge*. It reminded the pirates that they had met with something other-worldly—something of legends and myths.

Out of the corner of her eye, Kathryn caught sight of the decapitated head that had rolled into Seth's boot.

She shuddered as she remembered its dull thud as he kicked it away. Revulsion soured the back of her throat.

"Where is he?" She could scarcely keep her focus as she scanned the remains for a particular face. The captain. She could barely tolerate the thought of it.

"Who?" Seth stared at the decapitated head, unable to peel his eyes from it.

"You know who...the captain!"

"I...I...haven't seen..." His voice failed him. "Is that Tate?"

"No! Help me find him, Seth."

They continued the search, although Seth's enthusiasm at the idea of inspecting body parts kept him staring at the back of Kathryn's head. Fortunately, no familiarity infused the body parts she surveyed.

"He's not one of those." Swallowing hard, she silently offered a prayer of thanks before she scanned the faces of those still alive.

The silver light of the moon was playing games with her as she strained to take in each face.

She watched as the crew slowly moved into little clusters. These men relied on one another for reassurance, particularly now that the nightmare had ended.

"Sure an' tha' be th' devil hisself!" a weak voice spoke in low tones.

"Aye, matey...such folly it has played on us. Oh, God 'ave mercy on our souls!" another replied.

Kathryn listened to their conversations. Sadly, she heard nothing about Captain Philips.

"Thar be no denyin' it. I saw wit' me own eyes, I did. The beast reached out its long tentacles an' snatch th' head right off poor ole Payne. Th' swab hollered as a wee lass a'fore he be cut an' sent to Davy Jones' locker."

"Well, wouldn't ye holler too if sommat that foul plucked your head clean off your shoulders?"

"Aye, mate. I suppose I would. It be nothin' but th' Kraken, it be."

The pirates nodded their heads in agreement.

"Nay…th' beast be surely the Blue Minch o' the Scots," a surly pirate stated boldly as he joined the others' conversation.

"Nay, it be Kelpies! Lots o' them, too!"

"Ah, methinks thar be Grindylows a hidin' along-side o' the ship. I saw them yon, o're by the fo'c's'le." McMead pointed a shaky hand to a point beyond the foremast.

Kathryn could bear their ignorance no longer. She glanced at where the pirate pointed and surveyed the forward part of the ship. Suddenly, her heart bounded. The outline of the man she had been seeking appeared at the fo'c's'le.

"Nay, men, you speak of folktales." She addressed the crew with authority. "The beast was naught but the Goddess of the Dead. You know her as Morrigan."

"…and we killed her!" Seth bragged.

Her eyes flashed. Seth pulled at her slightly, and she yielded. "Not now, Kathryn."

Together, they headed toward the bow. Out of the corner of her eye, on either side, she caught glimpses of the tormented pirates who were gathering up the remains of their crewmates. "They bury the dead at sea? A proper burial?"

"Not likely," Seth replied. "This way, and keep your thoughts to yourself for once."

Hushed voices floated by as they slipped past the men—all of them recounting personal moments of terror and trembling.

"Pathetic, if you ask me. Tragic and pathetic, at the same time."

"Ye'd best keep your mouth shut." Seth could feel the crew's eyes on him as they passed by. An occasional look of distrust, along with a new respect for her power, was becoming evident. Kathryn shook out her thick mane, a sign she was dismissing the whispered comments passing between the men.

Ahead of her stood the main mast, and just beyond that, the forecastle where he stood. Willing her legs to carry her, she moved one staggering step at a time. Kathryn drew on Seth's strength, grateful for it. He was allowing her to set the pace, she could tell.

"You hex a demon yet you cannot walk to the fo'c's'le?"

"Casting off evil is rather taxing work, Seth."

Still, his observation intrigued her. Where *did* her power come from? *Indeed, could I be a victim of the evil moon's power, as well?* Her thoughts whirled as her legs grew limp. Seth's grip tightened around her waist as she dragged her foot into the next step.

"I…Seth, help me," she whispered just before her legs gave way.

He took her arm, and she again noticed his strength. In that same instant, her vision narrowed, and she felt herself slipping down onto the deck and into darkness. Just then, strong arms drew her against a muscular body that felt warm and familiar. A voice spoke to her, low and deep.

"There, there, Kathryn…I have ye now, lass."

Her heart warmed at the rich tone, and she took a long breath. Saltwater and sandalwood. Again, she inhaled and felt her senses as they slowly returned. Her eyes fluttered open, and she looked into his face.

"Aye, me girl, that's it." His reassurance soothed her. "I have ye now, my Kathryn."

She blinked once more and this time her vision cleared. The emerald eyes glimmered slightly in the moonlight as they held her gaze. He smiled and tilted his head to the left, which matched the angle of his lopsided grin. She was safe, held not only by the man's strong arms encircling her. She could not look away. She felt warm, secure, and hungry for more of him.

As if he felt the same desire, he pressed his lips to hers.

Ten

"THE DEVIL CAME FOR YOU, John," she said weakly, not daring to take her eyes off him. He loosened his grip slightly, but he would not let her go.

"Ay, that be true, lass. But the seas took the demon back into its belly, and we are at peaceful waters now, don't ye fear."

"No…you don't understand. Morrigan came. She called for you!"

"I heard nothing, except the cries of my men as they were slaughtered by the beast. But it's withdrawn now and we are at peace, as ye should be."

She realized he did not possess the details surrounding Morrigan's sudden disappearance from the ship. Lacking the energy to carry the conversation further, she kept to herself and allowed him to lift her.

"Yes, we are at peace for now."

"Capt'n," Seth interjected. "You'd best listen to what she has to say. Methinks there's more to this demon than meets the eye."

Captain Phillips glanced up at him with a look that told him to hush. "Later, Seth. Now is not the time to discuss past events. We must get Kathryn to her feet before the men become suspicious."

"Aye," Seth said, taking hold of Kathryn's arm.

"Here we go…stand smartly, else the crew be thinkin' you're too weak for sailin'."

She stood slowly, supported by Seth's strong hands on one side and the loving arms of the captain on the other. Stars danced across her vision but cleared within moments. She sighed in relief as she held onto each man for just a bit longer. These were the men who brought her love and peace, the men who had her back and held her heart.

"Thank you." She spoke gently.

"I'll take my leave, then." Seth nodded before turning away and disappeared into a crowd of men clustered against the starboard rails. As she turned to face the captain, she eyed the carnage spilled over the deck of the ship. Men were somber as they mopped and scooped up the remains of their fellow crewmen. Her throat soured at the sight, and the feeling was accompanied by renewed urgency over the peril they faced.

"Capt'n." She faced him with sudden vigor, fueled by the memory of Morrigan's curse. Hers was the voice of a powerful sorceress.

"What is it, Kathryn?" His face was steady, although the flash in his eyes grew somber as he spoke. He had not missed the gravity of her tone.

"Morrigan was here, aboard the *Revenge*. She's the devil who swept the deck and killed the crew. Some speak of the Kraken, and others the Scottish Minch. Fortuitous for the poor blokes, they continue to think it was so—they'd likely crumple and fail at the thought of Morrigan on board. But, I am certain this...this..." She swept her hand toward the blood-stained deck, "...this is the work of the dark goddess." The captain said nothing, so she continued. "I cannot believe you did not hear her oath only moments before she was gone."

"I heard noises—sounds like the wind in a maelstrom. But nothing cursed, and if someone spoke, the words were strange to me, lass. I don't know what tongue the devil used, but methinks ye may have heard with ears that sailors cannot possess. It likely comes by magic."

"There's no magic in this, except for dark magic that is meant to annihilate a crew to get to its captain. You heard nothing, then?"

"Once I thought it called out a name before slitherin' off to the depths."

"Aye, Captain. A name it did speak. Did you recognize it?" She paused, not wanting to reveal it.

"Do not play games with me, Kathryn! My men have been slaughtered, and ye speak in riddles. If ye know of a name that the demon cursed, out with it so we can summon the wretch and do sommat about it!"

"John Phillips. It was 'John Phillips' she cried out."

His face blanched. The captain shifted from one foot to the other and narrowed his eyes slightly as he studied her. Finally, after a while, he pulled himself to his full height and glanced out at the sea.

"What were the exact words spoken, Kathryn?" His tone was low and unflinching.

"Morrigan wanted to take life from this ship and kill the crew to get to you, John."

"What else did she say...and spare nothing, savvy?"

"Morrigan spoke clearly when she said, 'John Phillips, I come for thee.'"

The muscles in his jaw clenched, and the stately captain turned his back to the sorceress as his gaze stayed to the sea. She could see his muscular back quivering as anger filled his body and his mind contemplated what the curse meant for them all. She waited, silently apprehensive about what would come next.

"This changes everything." He looked to the bow of the ship and the horizon beyond. The sea was still and offered no answer to the imposing captain's quandary.

Moonlight danced impassively on crests of seawater as they lifted the wooden hull. Kathryn raised her eyes to the moon—its bloody omen had been swept clean—as it cast its peaceful illumination into the night.

"It's the Silver Moon that tells of her comin', John. We watch for the Silver Moon and its bloody omen."

He looked at her. Clearly, he did not understand. The witch tossed her gaze upward to the moon in answer and then, shifted her focus back to him. He followed her and caught sight of the full silver sphere. Suddenly, he understood. They stood silent for a moment, the pirate's thoughts fixed on the moon and the woman beside him. Finally, he faced her again and spoke.

"Ay, then it be a Silver Moon we watch for. But ye must…" His eyes drifted to the Seren that hung about her neck as he searched for the words that would avoid emotion.

"The Sigel of Defense cannot protect the entire crew, Captain. You saw this for yourself this very night. I can only do my part, and it shall not be enough. You must find safer waters and stronger powers than I possess."

He said nothing. The idea of changing course was not a pleasant thought for any of them. Instead, he shifted his interests. Stepping forward, he closed the gap between them and reached out to her with one hand. He lifted a lock of her dark hair and let it slide down the length of his thumb and forefinger. Another step again brought them closer, and the pirate lowered his face just inches from hers, resting the warm skin of his cheek against hers. Gently, his arms encircled her and pulled her into his body. Tense muscles relaxed as the softness of a woman's body curved against his. She could feel him as their breath rose and fell in time with each other—in time with the sea. His heart beat steadily against hers—two hearts that beat as one. For the first time since she'd awakened, she felt peaceful and curled her arms around his waist and pulled him closer.

Nothing more was said. Their course was laid as the ship moved ahead in the calm waters. Kathryn and Captain Phillips held each other in silence as the gentle waves danced against the ship and filled each soul with the strength of the other.

Eleven

"Th' damage's more than we thought at first, Capt'n. You'd best take a look yerself." Gow's voice sounded unsteady, though he stared unblinkingly at Captain Phillips.

"Ay. Straight away, Mister Gow."

Kathryn was left to stand alone with her thoughts. An intense need for this man clouded her mind as she watched him stroll across the deck. The captain's duty to inspect damage to the port side took precedence. Duty always came first, that much Kathryn understood. In spite of any rational argument she might conjure up, her heart still ached. Such a sudden shift in his demeanor left her wondering just how easily she could trust his heart, as well. Always pressing upon John Phillips would be the call to answer the whims of his true love—the sea. A seductive lady of the sea, the *Revenge*, would always be between them, ready to take him from her in an instant.

"No wonder they call ships 'she,'" Kathryn said aloud, bitterly. "And you warn me about keeping secrets." She stomped her foot.

Before he left her, the captain had given her a solemn warning that deceit would not be tolerated. She had responded with the usual outburst, accompanied by a flare of her Celtic temper, but ultimately, she had assured Captain Phillips that she held no secrets. Indeed, what limited knowledge she had of Morrigan's magic had been completely disclosed.

"What need be done, then, lass?" he had asked at last, and she had heard angst spilling into his voice.

"I must visit the Obeah," she had responded. Try as she might, she was never able to mask her own fears of dark magic, especially that crafted by Obeah witches. Kathryn shivered involuntarily, though the night was balmy out.

He doesn't understand the power of the Obeah. But then, how could he? He's a pirate and cares for little else than the sea and her treasures. He'll soon find out...too soon, most likely. She shook her head at the thought. *He has yet to meet a true-blooded Obeah—a witch with the black blood of the Obayifo.* She pulled her shawl tighter around her shoulders.

The Obayifo were the damnable of the islands and hailed from a land filled with shadows. It was said they were witches, but Kathryn knew better. Tales from long ago told of the Obayifo who drank the blood of children. Unrecognized by commoners, they would often wear the skin of the living as a disguise when travelling at night. Some said they could be seen as glowing orbs. Frequently, these beings were spotted as they hovered in death houses and near solemn ground where the dead lay buried. Only twice, did Mariel make mention of the Dearg-dul who were buried with stones about their chests—their heads removed and turned to face downward within their deep graves. All of this was done to prevent the evil Obayifo spirits from rising in death to prey on the warm-blooded living.

No, the Obeah was not the same type of evil. Filled with malice, the black heart of an Obeah witch was not to be trifled with. These, indeed, were workers of the black arts, ancient sorcerers that played with the ancient island voodoo practices.

The women were especially dangerous and steeped in dark magic. Extremely powerful, Macha was one of Morrigan's two sisters. Kathryn had met her once before quite by accident when the *Revenge* had banked in a secluded cay to careen the hull on the Island of Tobago. The memory of the devilish sister caused Kathryn to shudder again. A reunion with the dark witch was not something she had ever intended to relive, but Kathryn knew the key to Morrigan's power lay within the black magic that her sister practiced. If discovering Macha's secrets was the only way, then that's what she had to do. Kathryn guessed the cost would be great—most likely, a higher price than imagined—and death would certainly be part of it. But, who would be sacrificed? Whose death would pay the toll?

She avoided the dreadful thought.

"So, what are your plans then Capt'n, if I may ask?" Her voice sounded peeved though she tried to hide it.

"We make for Tobago," Captain Phillips stated as if there were no doubts between them. Kathryn merely nodded, as her own courage had suddenly failed her. Again, the captain was hailed, and while almost grateful for her distraction, he dutifully turned away and walked back to his men in long, sure strides.

"Aye," she whispered. Fear bubbled up in her gut as she spoke. "Tobago it be, then."

* * * * *

The ship bustled with activity as the men set to repairing and cleaning up the damage left from Morrigan's attack. Purpose found its way on board as each of the crew resumed his duty. Apparently grateful to step back into familiar tasks, the crew busied themselves without orders. Kathryn remained where she was and watched the men as they brought the *Revenge* once again to her former self.

A soft golden shimmer danced over the lolling sea crests, replacing the moonlight on the water. Within hours, the sun would climb high into the horizon. This day promised to be sultry, a sticky heat found only in tropical waters.

"Ah, the Caribbean Sea." Kathryn moved to her left to find the portside rail and leaned her forearms on the damp, grainy wood. It felt cool and smooth on her skin—a welcome reassurance that would soon fade as the sun rose. "We have a love-hate relationship, don't we, Madame *Revenge*? Perhaps one day we will learn to share the same man without jealousy."

As if in answer, the ship supported her weight as she leaned on the rails, keeping her safe from the sea. Kathryn leaned forward a little further and felt the spray of saltwater misting her face as the waves lapped at the hull.

She exhaled slowly and allowed her muscles to relax. "Someday, I'll grow to love you as the others do… maybe even as much as our captain does." She patted the rail, then allowed herself to daydream of the strong hands that had gently held her earlier.

Something splashed in the still, darkened water below. She figured it must be a large yellowtail, or perhaps a dolphin that played nearby, and she smiled at the presumed innocence of the creature that danced in the swells. But the dorsal fin did not arc, something Kathryn had failed to notice. *Of course, the shark are feeding. A fine meal Morrigan has provided them.* She closed her eyes and allowed the thought to fade while a gentle lift of the bow matched her breath. In that same moment, she heard the crisp crack as the sails unfurled synchronously as the wind whipped them taut. The bosun called the orders to those at the sheets. Their efforts had gone unnoticed until the ship heaved, and the *Revenge* responded—once again at full sail.

"Well, look 'ere, men. What 'ave we got? Jes' lol-ly-gaggin' about th' deck while th' crew be a-workin' t' set sail? Methinks I see a witch!"

The raspy taunt was followed by a menacing hiss of a laugh. The surly pirate was soon joined by a small group of brusque men, all of whom approached her. She recognized the quartermaster's tone that hissed as he spoke. Unwillingly, Kathryn opened her eyes as her peace was suddenly replaced by disgust.

"Indeed, a witch!" Archer spat saliva with each word. Kathryn stepped forward to face him and the pack of pirates closing the gap to encircle her. She focused her attention upon her nemesis' black heart.

"Archer." The name burned sour on her tongue as she said it.

The quartermaster stood within a few feet, and she felt his icy stare drop to her neck.

He reached a grimy hand toward her throat, and with one finger, lifted a lock of her hair.

"You think you've won him over, don't you?" Archer mimicked the captain's movements from moments ago. He stared at her, sneering and hissing as he provoked her further. Kathryn refused to answer.

Suddenly, he seized a handful of ebony, wavy hair and yanked her to within inches of his face. His fetid breath rained down in sprays of spittle that caused her to choke.

"Witch! Thar be no need fer yer devilish ways aboard this ship!"

He jerked the sorceress backward and held her fiercely by the clump of hair in his hand. Her body contorted as she balanced precariously over the rail in such a way that she could barely keep herself upright. Below, the dark fins surfaced, then dropped, ready for whatever would be thrown next from the ship.

"You've tried to kill me before, Archer...and you failed then, just like you'll fail now." She struggled against the quartermaster's hold, attempting to regain her footing, but could not move. He sneered, and the cutthroats laughed out loud. Sea sprayed against her cheek, and she could hear the agitation of the sea creatures in the water below. Several black fins glimmered in the sunlight as they surfaced, then dipped below the water—predators seeking after their next meal. White shark, she figured, still feeding on the dead crew cast overboard.

"Thar be sommat waitin' to take ye to Davy Jones locker, witch! Piece by piece." His black eyes danced from the shark to Kathryn.

The pirates stepped closer, encouraged by Archer's provocation. They displayed their foul teeth, reminiscent of the predators below circling before their feeding frenzy.

Fury rose from fear, and she twisted against his hold. Her hand brushed past something hard tucked deep into the folds of her skirts. Instantly, she recognized the object and wound her fingers tightly around a modestly carved ivory hilt. Slowly, she pulled

MARTI MELVILLE

a seven-inch dirk from behind her back. For a brief instant, the silver blade flashed in the sunlight just before Kathryn made her move.

In a swift driving motion, the sorceress thrust the tip upward. The razor-sharp point found its mark and sank into the flesh just above the dark pirate's gullet. She felt bone beneath and pressed the tip deeper into the quartermaster's leathery skin. There she held it, with the blade threatening to pierce the pirate's foul windpipe.

"Think again, dog. Consider it wise ye make threats to take the life of a witch, Mister Archer?"

Archer's grip loosened slightly. *You've unnerved him.* Suddenly, she heard the ripping sounds of steel blades as they were pulled menacingly from leather scabbards, and Kathryn knew the bloodthirsty cutthroats would strike with little provocation. Out of the corner of her eye, she could see them poised with cutlasses raised and at the ready. Archer froze, the dirk's tip digging in deeper under his chin. He signaled to hold. The pirates did nothing, which gave her an advantage. Kathryn knew the pirates would typically hesitate just before a strike. She needed to act fast. In one fluid move, she swiped the blade of her dagger against the quartermaster's chin, raising beads of crimson in a long, clean line.

Archer cried out but held the signal for the others to stand down.

Blood dripped along the dirk's narrow surface and dropped through the tendrils of hair still held in

Archer's hand. She dropped the razor-sharp edge of the blade, slicing easily through her own hair and freeing her from the quartermaster's grip.

Before he'd realized what the sorceress had done, the unexpected sting of the dirk's tip landed just below Archer's temple. It pierced his leathery skin and left a crimson mark where it stuck. Archer stood dumbfounded as blood dripped from the line carved down to his chin, a clump of dark, wavy hair still grasped tightly in his outstretched hand.

Kathryn leaned into the pirate and hissed, "You'd best think again of your threats against me—against a witch, Mister Archer!" She raised her voice and cried out, "You'd all do well to withdraw. I have no compunction about destroying you all."

At this, Archer swung his free hand directly toward the sorceress and took hold of her throat. Kathryn could feel the heat of the Seren against her skin. The acrid stench of singed flesh rose in her nostrils, and she knew that its fire burned the pirate's skin. He screeched and was forced to release his grip on her. The ancient symbols inscribed upon the Sigel of Defense raised dark blisters over the palm of the pirate's hand.

Reflexively, he dropped the clutched mass of Kathryn's hair. It fell to the deck in a dark heap. He then grasped hold of his wrist to steady his blistering hand. As he moved, the tip of Kathryn's dirk fell across his cheek, leaving a deep slash. Blood oozed from Archer's face where the gash opened wider, then spilled in droplets along his neck and onto his dirty linen shirt.

"A curse I leave to you." As she spoke, she spun around to face the other pirates. All the while, she held the blade of her dirk upright, threateningly, while the men stared wide-eyed at her. The blade caught the sun's rays again and flashed ominously as it moved, stained with the quartermaster's blood. "Death is not a friend to you. It comes fiercely to each man who stands to rise against a witch. Those will be the ones who will be kissed by the reaper and greet the devil this night."

The pirates dared not move as she spoke.

"Now get thee from my sight." She spat out the last at the circle of men who backed away. As they did, they lowered their swords. Archer moved aft, still holding his blistering hand while blood dripped from his face, leaving a trail along the deck.

Kathryn instinctively crouched, dirk in hand, and waited for the pirates to withdraw. It wasn't until they were out of sight that she stood upright and bellowed. Finally, she lowered the dagger. Once the cutthroats had completely disappeared, and the area around her again was clear, she wiped the blade of her dirk on a burled piece of bulwark. She tucked the weapon into the folds of her skirt at her lower back and then, moved to the rail. Peering below, the water frothed, spotted with black fins that still danced hungrily on the surface, awaiting the next meaty slab to be tossed from the ship.

"I'll not be your fodder this day," she cursed, then spat.

Something lying on the polished deck not far from where she stood caught her eye. In that instant, her temper flared as she lifted the mound of hair that lay in a pile at her feet.

"A witch's mane, indeed."

Twelve

KATHRYN STUFFED THE WITCH'S MANE into the pocket of her skirt, then brushed her fingers through the uneven chunks of her hair. She could feel the different layers falling between her fingers, and she shook her head. Without thinking about it, Kathryn patted the dirk hidden carefully within its resting place between her skirt and the ebony sash she kept tied around her waist. She exhaled again and released the last of the fight-or-flight energy that always surfaced in Archer's presence. The quartermaster, her nemesis, would have to be dealt with eventually, but this was not that day.

Gathering her skirt, she tied a side knot that exposed the side of one thigh, freeing up her feet. This was something she did often as she moved between the pirate crew. Sadly, the men dismissed any thoughts of respect, their attention on her exposed flesh. Still, Kathryn could not risk tripping on her skirts in battle.

"Lower than pond scum," she said once while being reminded of her place aboard the ship. Ever since, she'd kept a respectful distance from the pirates unless invited to participate in one of their clandestine activities.

She turned from the rails and walked to the water barrel.

"Miss Kathryn." Skyrme bowed low as she passed.

"There's little water that's fit to drink here, but I've grog if ye're thirsty, miss." Davis shoved a leather colambre filled to the rim with mead.

"Thank you, Mister Davis." Kathryn took the leather pouch with both hands and drank heartily from it. She nodded at Skyrme, who kept his eyes on her from a distance.

It seemed that from the moment after she'd cast Morrigan from the ship, things had changed. The men treated her differently. Still, she only trusted maybe a few.

"Very welcome, ma'am," Davis said and tipped his brow. Kathryn turned from them and crossed to the opposite rails.

"Very interesting," she said aloud to no one. "Interesting, indeed!"

Just how the crew would accept or reject her was still unclear, so she made ready to fight or flee and kept her skirts tied high enough to avoid stumbling over the hem when that moment came. Out of the corner of her eye, Kathryn noted how the nearby pirates paused at their tasks to stare at her as she traipsed the length of the water-soaked deck. Kathryn lifted her chin indignantly, never moving her head, and kept her focus straight ahead.

Men on hands and knees worked their holy-stones against the smooth surface. They toiled in long strokes, washing out the bloodstains left behind by their dead comrades. Occasionally, they would peer upward, momentarily taking her in before returning to the rhythmic scrub of soft sandstone on oak. Kathryn watched the stubborn grain of the wood slowly relent-ing and transforming back to its light nutty color.

"A hellish way to go, methinks."

"Aye, Jasper, an' none deserved it." Cade stabbed at a stain and cursed.

"What scared the beast off? It's likely to come back, ye know, lest it was kilt."

"I suppose sommat otherworldly scared it off… sommat mystic." Cade looked up at Kathryn for a moment, then dropped back to his work.

"Ahem." Kathryn cleared her throat and stepped over the wet surface where they labored.

As she made her way aft to the quarterdeck, she heard agitated voices escalating. A small crowd had gathered. Standing at the head was the captain. The unexpected blast of a pistol roared above the fray and silenced the men. Kathryn stopped. The dull thud that accompanied the impact of a lifeless body falling to the deck's surface. Cautiously, she moved closer to the clustered pirates and witnessed with horror the captain's outstretched hand gripping the flintlock that still smoldered from its shot. In front of the barrel was a small gathering of pirates staring in silence at their dead comrade lying at Captain Phillips' feet. She recognized the dead man as one of Archer's cronies who had crossed her just minutes ago.

"There be yet another for any of ye thinkin' naught o're the Articles!" shouted the captain.

She approached the men and stopped just outside of the half circle they'd formed. Silently, she watched the blood pooling around the dead man's head and staining the deck in an uneven circle. The captain's eyes shifted to her briefly, but he did not acknowledge her presence.

"Ole' Bill only be watchin' out fer the Quart'm'ster, he be. Th' witch brought th' devil o' us, an…"

As if on cue, the captain turned on his heel and fired a second pistol pulled from a scarlet ribbon that was about his neck. The shot killed the pirate in cold blood before he could finish his sentence. Kathryn watched in horror. This, too, was one of Archer's henchmen who had threatened her. In fact, she realized, the entire group of men were the same bloodthirsty cutthroats who had surrounded her as Archer made his threats at the starboard rails only minutes earlier.

"If any of ye filthy blaggards seek to take this further, ye'll dance the hempen jig!" Captain Phillips roared. "Step forth and I'll be takin' ye before the mast meself!"

No one moved.

"Clean this here mess up and feed the sharks with it," he continued. Fury bit through his voice.

Archer stepped forward and Kathryn could see the gash that ran the length of his cheek still raised red but newly scabbed. *That will leave its mark!* The slight curl of her lips betrayed her thoughts.

"Capt'n," he said with eyes lowered. His balding head reflected the sun's rays. "If I may speak freely, Capt'n?"

"I see the young lass has left her gulliegaw mark on ye, Mister Archer."

Kathryn allowed the smirk to spread as she heard her own thoughts reflected in the captain's comment. The corner of the quartermaster's thin, dry lips twitched slightly. Archer shifted uncomfortably. He waited for permission to speak.

"Aye, Capt'n."

"Then sir, it be wise ye make note of the lady-healer's skill and keep to yerself. I will have none of this mischief aboard me vessel. And that be true for all o' ye…not just Mister Archer! Me orders be to each man here: Take leave of this ship's Physiks Indwaller, whom ye best begin addressin' as Miss Kathryn, or M'lady, else stand before the mast and answer to the Articles and your capt'n, savvy?"

Vivid scarlet rose across the captain's face, and Kathryn knew the men were in jeopardy of a good flogging…or worse. Rarely had the captain flushed with such a piqued temper, and, on the few occasions she had been privy to witness it, someone suffered a stout punishment as a result. Only a few times had Kathryn witnessed a public flogging during her voyage with the pirates. Without doubt, the recipient had been deserving of whatever the cat-o'-nine tails had bequeathed its victim. But the flogging was cruel, nonetheless. Because of it, Kathryn always looked away to the sea as the lashings commenced, particularly when the screams died to guttural moans.

Nothing from her peaceful life on the cliffs had prepared her for life at sea with pirates. It had been nearly a year since she'd been kidnapped. Life on board the *Revenge* had changed her, although no one seemed to notice. Throughout her captivity, she had never been assigned an official post…not until this moment. Her recent assignment as a "Physiks Indwaller" established her as the medical officer on board the ship. Still, Kathryn would rank low in status amongst the crew simply because their superstitious beliefs would not allow her to be viewed as anything but a witch.

"Aye," replied the quartermaster, eyes still downcast. But Kathryn could see the hatred seething as Archer reached up and tapped his gnarly index finger along the gash in his face.

Captain Phillips' face softened ever so slightly at this. "Get back to your duties, gentlemen." He stood with pistols still held aloft and aimed at the cluster of men.

Slowly, each man retreated. A few went aft to where they began hoisting the two dead bodies over the portside rails. The echoing splashes went unnoticed by most of the crew, but not by the sea creatures. Moments later, she heard a new sound—it was the frenzy as the shark fed again below the surface of the water.

"Was that necessary?" She regretted the comment as soon as she'd said it.

"You have no voice here, Madame. And I have a short temper, currently. Do not provoke me." He lowered his pistols. "Not now."

As soon as the deck had been tended to and the cleanup begun, the captain returned each pistol to its resting place. They dangled easily at the tail ends of a ribbon that bounced against his chest as he walked. He paused momentarily and faced her.

"Aye, sir," she said, curtseying as she lowered her eyes.

The captain responded with a commanding look that meant she was to follow him. Keeping herself a few paces behind, she trailed behind his long strides as he made his way across the ship.

Silently, she followed him into his quarters.

Thirteen

THE CHAIR CLATTERED ACROSS THE wooden floor.
Kathryn startled at the sound upon entering. He kicked
it again.

"Sit!"

She circled the upset chair, keeping an arm's
distance from him. Replacing the seat to its upright
position, she looked at him with Celtic defiance that
forced her to stand with one hand resting on the
chair's back.

"I'd rather stand, if you please," she said.

"No doubt." He clasped his hands behind his back
in an attempt to mask his growing irritation.

"This is not about me. Your displeasure lies elsewhere. What is it?"

He began to pace. "They'll say it was in cold blood,
they will, and I can't afford to lose more of me crew
o'er...insubordinate mischief!"

He spoke as if to no one in particular. Behind the
large table in the center of the room, a worn dirk was
set haphazardly off to one side. He marched over to it

and plucked it off the table, then held it ahead of him as if it were a military sword.

"I must keep the discipline aboard my ship! The *Revenge* shall not harbor miscreants for crewmen."

He flung the dirk to the tabletop where the tip of the blade pierced the bruised skin of an overripe plum and stuck there.

"And how do you propose to…?"

"I'll take any of them and see each and every one to Davy Jones, if need be. It's not difficult to build me a new crew. The men should know this…and fodder for the next vessel crossin' a'fore her. There'll be no quarter given at the next plunder, says I."

Kathryn shifted her weight uneasily as the captain formulated plans to seize the next ship spotted. She knew the entire crew was agitated after their encounter with Morrigan, and the captain was no exception. This was not the man who had kissed her just a short time ago. "Capt'n, you must realize that Morrigan's magic lingers as anger and malice in the hearts of the men."

"Ay, I'm well aware of the after-effects of murder. To overtake a prize and seize its treasure would definitely soothe on board tempers, methinks!"

Kathryn cleared her throat. This wouldn't be easy. "Take your prize, if you must, and slay the crew, as well. Allay your angst with whomever you will and I'll be fightin' alongside you. But, know this, Capt'n John Phillips, I'll not be fodder for the quartermaster or his pups."

"You're just as vulnerable as the rest of us, Kathryn. Do not think you've escaped the fallout from all of this."

"Perhaps not. But, be aware, Capt'n. I'll cut him down, if needs be, and I can do it. I will not be his folly, not while I breathe and walk aboard this ship!"

"Archer is not the problem!"

"He is my problem. Right now, he is all that stands in the way of my survival here...and be warned—survive I will!"

The captain watched in amazement as she spoke. He glanced at the Seren that lay quietly against her bare skin before returning to her face. He turned from her, then casually walked across the room and took a seat in one of the large chairs pulled up alongside the massive dining table. He reached out and skewered the dirk into the table, splitting the fruit with the dagger. As the pulp pushed up the length of the blade, amber juice dripped from the tempered steel.

Captain Phillips laughed.

"Are you threatening the quartermaster?"

"If needs be."

"Go on."

"In truth, Archer is but an annoyance to me. I will deal with him, if I must. That, you know for certain. It's Morrigan who brings danger to us both."

He seemed to ignore her, although his eyes never left her face.

She paused and waited for the message to sink in, then dragged the chair closer. Placing one foot on top of the seat, she lifted herself onto the edge of the table. Her skirt fell aside, which exposed the sun-kissed flesh of one leg. It dangled freely from the edge of the table while her other foot rested gently on the chair's base.

Indeed, she's become a pirate and uses her feminine weapons skillfully. The thought never left his lips.

Reaching across the table, she stooped to meet the captain's gaze. "This is not about Archer."

Encased within the deep green corset she wore, her bronzed skin and youthful breasts rose and fell with each breath. She teased him for a moment with a subtle scent of lavender and musk, but the captain's eyes never left hers as she did so. *Stubborn man, a true pirate!* The thought lifted the corners of her mouth.

"What, then, lass?"

"Consider what you would fight for, to the death if need be, Capt'n John Phillips."

She paused just long enough to provoke him a bit further until his attention shifted momentarily to her bosom. A victorious smile crossed her lips as she grasped the torn fruit from the dirk stuck in the burnished wood. The sorceress eyed the pirate seductively and sucked the juice from the fruit in her hand before biting into its tender skin. Slowly, she sat upright, just out of reach, and watched him.

"Ye are not so tame as ye make yourself out to be, Miss Kathryn." The huskiness of his voice revealed his desire for her. But his words were a warning, more to himself than to the young sorceress, and he unwillingly kept his distance, as a result.

"Aye, Capt'n. You would be wise to remember that truth." She teased him not so innocently.

The regal pirate eyed her and said nothing. She knew her tactics had worked soundly, a feminine spell cast over him to divert the pirate's bloodthirsty plans—thoughts of destroying his own crew in order to quench an unabated feeling of angst. There really was no purpose in it. Already, there had been blood-lust on board that had nearly overcome them both since Morrigan's attack. His plan to slay his own men at the least provocation would, indeed, backfire and create greater dissent. He was their captain and could not afford the appearance of weakness in any form—particularly the vulnerability that came with fear. She had done her job well, thanks to the magical power of feminine wiles, gifted to her at birth. This power was not an innate gift bequeathed to her from the white witches of her family.

"I come by my gifts, naturally, Capt'n."

"Indeed. You've bewitched many, methinks." The side of his mouth twitched.

Smiling, she realized how much this man needed her. She loved him for it. She bit into the fruit again, this time with genuine satisfaction, knowing she had distracted him, and possibly saved the life of some worthless swab above deck.

"Only you."

He watched her and thought of nothing else but the woman that sat before him. His crew was forgotten, his desire left unsatisfied, and his mouth thirsty for the taste of her lips. This was, indeed, a man who hungered.

"Kathryn, ye undo me, lass." As he spoke, he stood up and knocked the chair backwards. It hit the floorboards with a loud clatter. He dropped his head back, closed his eyes, and exhaled loudly. "I cannot be distracted by ye, or any other. Not now…not with the devil Morrigan upon me and my crew sailing directly into her path."

Kathryn moved from the edge of the table. She placed the remnants of the uneaten fruit on top of the place where she had been sitting and sauntered slowly over to him. Then, touching her lips to his, she kissed him, a woman's passionate kiss. His mouth reacted hungrily, feeding on her passion.

When they had parted, she moved to the large chair on the other end of the table. With grace, she lowered herself into its worn velvet cushion and comfortably positioned herself as she folded her hands across her lap—a proper lady, to be certain.

"Aye, Capt'n, that be true." Her voice was sugary. "The men need you, and the *Revenge* is surely lost, lest you take hold and stop the beast before she makes ruin of us all. There can be no distraction from that, to be certain, including the tomfoolery of silly sailors too long at sea.

Your men look to their capt'n for leadership, not brutality, as the English officers are known for.

Am I not right in this?"

He lowered his head in response. Slowly, he opened his eyes and rested his gaze on her, properly seated in the chair before him. She smiled, and it unsettled him further.

"You will be the death of many good men, lass," he uttered in exasperation. "Now go, before I can no longer contain myself. Ye best rest yourself. It has been at least three full moons since you met your end and saved me skin with your magic ways. I'm beholdin' to ye, and you know me heart's in it, as well." He smiled, and the left side of his mouth curled into a familiar, lopsided grin.

She stood and brushed out her skirt, pleased with the change in his temperament.

Without exception, John Phillips was one of the finest men Kathryn had ever laid eyes on. She paused to take in his fine features: the strong line of his jaw and the dark lashes that surrounded those emerald green eyes. Unable to help herself, she allowed affection to dance behind her eyes before she moved to him. Gently, she took his face into her hands, kissed his lips again, and lingered just long enough for him to know her heart. He lifted one hand to the nape of her neck and pulled her closer, then kissed the top of her head. It left him more than frustrated that he could not have her—not yet, anyway. His body ached for her, but the laws of the ship prevented their union. She felt him tremble. The pirate desperately wanted to take her.

Instead, he released her and turned to face the large stateroom window. "Goodnight, Kathryn."

She glided past the little cot she had slept on her first night aboard the ship. It lay undisturbed from when she had cowered in it so long ago, a memory left untouched. She glanced at it, grateful for that fateful night when she became a prisoner on board this pirate's ship.

"Until the morrow, Capt'n Phillips."

Fourteen

THE SUN ROSE HIGH IN a cloudless sky and beat a relentless fever over the sultry cerulean of the Caribbean
Sea. Dewy beads of sea spray met the sunrays in tiny
prisms that cast diamond droplets across the surface
of the water. A dazzling sunrise poured through the
negligible porthole used as a window in Kathryn's tiny
cabin. The interior was as hot as an oven, and the air
turned stagnant.

Kathryn awoke to blinding sunlight blanketing
her face, neck and arms. She could feel her hair matted
along the nape of her neck where her scalp met the
rumpled linen sack she used for a pillow. Shielding her
eyes with one hand, she leaned up on the other elbow
and glanced out through the open porthole.

Kathryn grimaced. The water churned with debris
scattered across the surface. Cannon fire exploded not
far off. The distant rumble caused her insides to tremble,
although the ship remained still. She could hear the
men calling out to one another, pirates—threatening
and ready to take a prize.

"No! Not this!" she breathed.

Scrambling to her feet, she collected her skirts about her and tied a side knot that exposed her legs from mid-thigh down to her bare feet. Then she fetched the dirk she'd used on Archer, fastened a long black sash around her waist, and shoved the dagger inside it within easy reach of her left hand. Next, she grasped the hilt of a long, curved sword and tucked the cutlass through the other side, where it rested against her left hip. Worn black boots had been tucked under her cot, and she quickly retrieved them and buried a foot in each one.

Turning to the writing desk on the opposite wall, she gently lifted the Scarlet Seren from its hiding place deep within a wooden compartment. Placing the talisman around her neck, she waited for the threads to magically loop and seal themselves together. When it was finished, the Seren rested in peace against her breastbone. She exhaled the ancient Celtic prayer that called for the Sigel of Defense to protect her.

"A spell…"

Kathryn pinched off a thick branch of sage tied tightly to a cluster of juniper boughs, and plucked the entire bundle from a beam in the ceiling. Striking a piece of flint, she lit the herbs on fire and set them carefully into an alabaster shell. With care, the sorceress lifted the smoldering shell with both hands and carried it just in front of her as she began to walk in circles around the room. Shouts from above-deck heightened, and Kathryn picked up the pace to complete the protective spell.

Hastily, she doused the embers with liquid from a pewter mug. She couldn't remember ever having used the mug and noted the telltale signs of neglect as dead fleas floated on the surface. The amber liquid quaked, stirred by a thick wand made from a branch that she dropped into the ale. She spread crushed herbs over the center of the table. With the index finger of her right hand, she drew three large rings, each one entwined with the other, forming the shape of a Welsh clover. Upon completion, she lifted her hands above her head and recited ancient Celtic prayers.

Ein nawdd, nawdd Duw.
(Our protection, the protection of God)

Gwasgu ar ei wynt.
(Bear this gift down upon me)

Sunlight flickered as the wind exhaled in unison with Kathryn, who cast dancing shadows over the grainy wood floor of her cabin. Element and witch entwined in enchantment for several moments in an ethereal tapestry, until suddenly Kathryn stopped. The sorceress opened her eyes and lowered her hands just as the bright light of the sun filtered back in through the tiny window. The small room was instantly illuminated and filled with stifling heat once again.

Kathryn grasped the hilt of her sword with her right hand and drew it from the sash tied about her waist. Her left hand moved mechanically up to the Seren and rested there as she bounded across the threshold to take the short stairwell with long, determined strides. As she approached the main deck, she paused to allow her eyes to focus in the blinding sunlight.

"Keep 'em in sight. Abaft the beam, Master Nutt! We must stay upwind an' keep the advantage."

"Aye, Capt'n. Ahead full sails!"

"Prime th' guns, scurvy dogs! Fire when ready!"

"Hard to port, Master Nutt!

"Aye!"

Male voices grew in intensity as they called out to a yet unseen foe, but Kathryn sensed their aggressiveness and knew the ship and crew were at battle. Dark smoke snaked across the ship in random ringlets that rose to meet the lacerated bands of slack sails. The ship was set ahull, and what little wind there was fanned the stench of smoke and burnt flesh out to sea. Debris cluttered the deck—bits of oak, metal and glass. Hunks of shattered hardwood still smoldered, occasionally threatening to ignite elements left as kindling.

The *Revenge* had taken a direct hit, and the damage was significant. Still, the ship remained seaworthy and rolled easily as she swayed over the current that shifted below the hull.

"Lay aft, Sykes, an' square up th' jigger-mast. Make haste o' it!"

Kathryn recognized Gow's deep, booming voice. He shouted orders with practiced efficiency that could only belong to the bosun. The ship's noticeable damage lay aft. A portion of the smaller mast had been blown away, and the beam that lay sideways formed a perfect square. The ship could still sail under these conditions, assuming no other destruction occurred.

"Aye, aye, sir!" A bare-chested, muscular crewman sprinted aft and took hold of the lines still attached to the fractured beam. Two others joined him as they worked feverishly to secure the damaged mast. Kathryn understood now why the *Revenge* had been refitted to remove all decking topside, leaving the main deck smooth and free of obstacles—potential lethal projectiles in battle. This was the custom for most pirate ships. Even though large ships, such as the *Revenge*, were not the preferred vessel of pirates, the merchantman had been a delicious prize when John Phillips had stolen her years ago at Petty Harbor.

Another cannon blast rang out on the starboard side.

"Who is that?" Kathryn shouted to anyone listening.

No one answered.

Men's voices pitched curses at one another. Death threats were bantered back and forth, soon accompanied by clashing steel as cutlasses crossed. The air popped, peppered with flintlock fire and dense smoke. Kathryn stepped forward, gripping the cutlass tighter. She knew she would not be tolerated as a woman—the scallywags on both sides would easily slit her throat, just like the rest of the crew.

In that moment, the Seren began to pulse. A compelling burst of electrical energy began pulsing, painfully prickly and fierce in its urgency. Kathryn's reflexes kicked in. She instantly crouched and swept the cutlass in a perfect arc toward the disagreeable sensation that rounded over her head. A deafening clang sounded as her blade deflected the forceful blow of an unknown assailant.

"*Prepart para attender o seu fim,*" the accompanying voice threatened.

Kathryn did not recognize the language of the foreign pirate. "*El* pirate," she said, and carved an arc with her cutlass.

His response held no meaning, sounding much like the staccato words spoken on the southern coast of Spain. Although the words were alien, the message was clear, and she glared at her assailant fiercely. His face was full and sweat spilled from tangled black hair that matched his hateful, hollow black eyes. Repulsion engulfed her, and the momentary thought of losing her life to this barbaric spume sent raw adrenaline rushing through her veins. *I will not die under your sword this day.* The thought propelled her advance.

"*Seren, diogelu mi a dod farwolaeth i'r rhai sy'n ceisio cymryd fy!*"

The Celtic call for protection sang from her lips, and the Seren glowed crimson. She felt her veins as they became electrified, pulsing with the same rhythm as the talisman around her neck. With strength that did not belong to her, she countered the foreign pirate's drive and overpowered his heavy sword. At the same time, the palm of her hand shone, illuminated with the same incandescent glow as the stone. Powerful energy formed itself within her cupped hand. Its intensity increased and prickled the surface of her skin. The electric ball grew heavy with its weight and turned a pale shade of indigo. Instinctively, she snapped her left wrist toward the pirate, who was still grinding his blade against hers. Blue-white light flew from her cupped hand and struck the foreigner directly in the chest.

"*Deus me ajude!*" He cried out, and his voice sounded metallic.

On impact, the light shattered into splayed lightning currents, which bonded together to form a giant prism of electrical energy. Its force lifted the pirate high off the ground before hurling his body backward through the air until it collided with a resounding thud against the masthead. His bones crunched as they shattered against the solid wood beam. His torso bent in half. Just as suddenly, the light disappeared, and the body fell limp to the surface of the deck below.

The stranger was dead.

Kathryn stood upright, deliberate in her movements as she studied the lifeless body from across the deck. Her left hand still tingled, and she glanced down at it in amazement.

Was that the power of the Seren? She questioned the thought the instant it crossed her mind. *No, something else.* The source of that power had come from something inside of her not linked to the stone that hung about her neck.

Am I no more than this? Are these hands filled with the same evil as that which allows Morrigan to take the souls of the dead? Do mine likewise take souls and leave death in its wake?

The thought sickened her, overwhelmed her. Kathryn shrank back at the power of her own hands. She watched as her crewmates banded together and cheered as the pirates deliberately overpowered at least a dozen or more men—all of whom spoke in the same foreign tongue as her assailant. Blades crossed and slashed ferociously at one another as they grew a darker shade of crimson by the moment. Eventually, strength found her once again, and she shifted the hilt in her right hand slightly, secured the grip, and circled to her right.

A study of the battle's momentum through dense smoke was not easy, but through it, Kathryn spotted the invading ship. It was smaller than the *Revenge*, with three masts, and what appeared to be only half the cannon power.

An easy foe, she surmised as she squinted against the sun's glare. She could barely see the deck, but noticed the foreign ship was endowed with a high, rounded stern that had suffered damage, likely from a direct hit sent from one of the *Revenge's* many cannons.

Interestingly, the foreign vessel had also been cleared and refitted for piracy. Her colors flew defiantly from the main mast—an intricate red, black, and yellow flag decorated with a painted skull in its center.

"There be no quarter given this day!" The familiar bass bellowed, breaking into her thoughts.

Kathryn's attention snapped to the captain, who stood to one side of the helm. Those that heard the captain's order cheered. Invigorated by the announcement of permissible slaughter, the crew bore down even harder on their foe. Many of the foreigners met a quick demise as they succumbed to the hearty blades that belonged to the crew of the *Revenge*.

Indeed, it'll be a blood bath.

Across a small gap of seawater separating the *Revenge* from the foreigners, she could make out the shadow of a rather tall bloke. He stood against the rails of the strangers' ship with one arm raised in gesture—offensive, no doubt, as he hollered back the response.

"*Nos nunca nos renderemos!*"

A crewman standing just off to the left translated for the captain. "They refuse to surrender an' I'll not be repeatin' th' rest o' his foul speech—Portuguese swine!"

The captain stared at him. "Do they understand they'll all be dead within the hour, at this rate?"

The crewman shrugged. "Likely they're as stubborn a bunch as we are, Capt'n."

Kathryn was a bit surprised by the foreigner's apparent lack of cooperation, even at the point of death. She looked from the captain to the smaller ship in hopes that one of them would give in. Another blast from the *Revenge* showered grapeshot over the Portuguese carrack, leaving no question that this battle would end badly. The meager foreign crew was soon left crumpled and defenseless.

Just then, Archer stepped forward and fired a large musket at the small ship. His aim was deadly accurate as the ball flew directly at the tall Portuguese captain, hitting him in the left breast. The man stiffened and heaved backwards slightly before toppling over the rails and into the agitated water.

They intend to kill them all.

The repulsive realization that Morrigan's toxic effects still lingered in the hearts of her own crew made her queasy. There seemed no way to stop the bloodshed.

The devil she is, that witch Morrigan, to turn the hearts of my crew to bloodthirsty bandits!

The thought had barely crossed her mind when a dry cackle whispered across the deck of the ship. Its breath rushed the length of Kathryn's spine. She raised her eyes to the heavens and encountered the unmerciful sun vibrating in streams and melting over her skin. She cocked her head sideways as she squinted against its blaring light.

Three rings formed in the swirling, golden rays, then separated into large, almond-shaped holes. The third separated again to expose teeth framed by a wide grin. Again, the cackle sounded, issued from a just-formed mouth. Two almond eyes mocked her as she stood isolated on the deck of the battling ship.

"Morrigan, you devil," Kathryn hissed at the amber face that stared down on her through the blaring sunlight. The ancient Celtic words rose to her tongue, and she cried out, her voice strong and clear: "*Dianc Morrigan*! Get thee hence!"

Peals of laughter billowed over the ship as the face lifted to the sky and disappeared into the rays of the sun. Kathryn remained steadfast. Without thinking, her right hand gripped the hilt of the cutlass, steel smelted by man, and her left hand encased the Seren, a talisman created with magic.

"I'll destroy you, devil. That is my promise, Morrigan."

Fifteen

OVERSIZED GRAPPLING HOOKS FLEW ACROSS the watery crevasse that separated the two ships.

Their barbs landed heavily on the inside rails of the Portuguese carrack and bit into the rotting wood. Brawny sailors secured the hasp into the smaller ship by yanking back suddenly on thick rope tied to the free end of the hook. The barbs dug easily into the damp Portuguese planking and refused to let go.

The "bitter end"—the opposite end of the large line—was held tightly by way of muscular bodies that leaned nearly backward as they looped the coarse line around the stanchions at the rail. Within moments, the carrack was rendered immobile and captive to the *Revenge*. A few of the longest lines were loosened from the topmast rigging, and several of the pirates used these to swing across the watery gap and onto the deck of the Portuguese ship. Seth led the first wave, sailing easily from line to deck.

Blood stained both decks from several fallen marauders. Kathryn watched in horror as her crew butchered the remaining Portuguese pirates, and then, one by one, cast their mutilated bodies over the rails and into the sea. The carnage continued until every last man from the Portuguese vessel had been dispatched.

And so, it happened that the captain's pledge had come true: No quarter was given.

"Divvy up her spoils, men, an' bring th' lot a'fore th' mast." Archer gave the command, then threw back his head and bellowed a devil's laugh.

A crewman delivered a last fatal blow to the one remaining Portuguese sailor still fighting on the *Revenge's* blood-washed deck. The bald, burly killer kicked the dead body over the rail while Archer laughed again.

"That'd be the end o' the wretched foreigners." Slade grinned and wiped his blade clean on the britches of a corpse.

"An' be certain to check th' cockroaches' pockets before castin' 'em o're. There be bounty a-hidden' in smugglers' hollows, says I."

Archer nodded as he watched the men pilfering the bodies. Kathryn's eyes paled to ice as she glared at Archer standing amidships. He laid the flat side of his cutlass against the rails, turned it over, and drew back the length of it in a mock effort to wipe the blood from the steel. With one foot resting just over the gunwale, his ebony stare shifted to Kathryn and his lips curled into a sneer. When he had finished cleaning his blade, he grinned through cracked lips, exposing yellowed teeth, and staring at her, began to sing. Archer's stare never left Kathryn.

"Oh, Sally be th' lass down in our alley.
 Now, Sally be th' lass that I spliced nearly…"
"So help me, Bob, I be bullyin' th' alley.
 So help me, lad, I be bullyin' th' alley."

Several of the men joined in, their voices full and hearty as they sang out and matched the rhythm of the shanty to the new task of hauling plunder from the small Portuguese ship. Forming two single lines, the men tossed crates and cloth from one to the other skillfully and without dropping a single object, all in time with the rhythm of the song.

The lyrics' double entendre had not gone unnoticed by Kathryn, and she glared back at the quartermaster. He only grinned wider and sang with gusto.

"I be leavin' me gal for t' go a-sailin'.
 I be leavin' me Sal for t' go a-piratin'."

A boisterous "whoop" sounded and one of the men slapped his raised leg with a free hand.

"So help me, lad, I be bullyin' th' alley.
 Aye, help me, lad, I be bullyin' th' alley."

The quartermaster's mockery continued while the men, oblivious to the underlying intent, sang. Kathryn's blood boiled. Archer's glare bored into hers, which she reciprocated with unfaltering contempt. This time, when he laughed, the scar along his cheek was stretched into a thin, jagged line. Kathryn's grip tightened on the cutlass. She moved it low and forward, and the subtle advance was not lost on Archer. His eyes widened, and he nodded his head, taunting her further, then dared her to make a move.

Kathryn tucked the free edge of her skirt into her waist sash, the other remaining firmly held in a knot. She widened her stance and crouched. Slowly, her left hand reached behind her back, and she pulled the dagger from its hiding place. Deliberately, she brought the dirk forward to match the defensive position of the cutlass. Here she remained, poised like a panther ready to spring.

"Oh, blessed day!" Archer spat and spun on his heels. "The witch wants to parry with a pirate."

A wolfish grin spread across her face, and she waved the blade, an invitation to accept her challenge.

"Archer!" she shouted. The singing stopped, and the crew began to take notice. "Dare ye cross blades with me now?"

Her taunts brought the sneer on his face to a full grin, and he roared with laughter. "Aye, lassie. I be right willin', at that." He touched the flat side of his blade to the top of his head in a mock salute, then took one step toward her.

Kathryn waited for him. Her muscles tensed, ready to spring, while she studied his every move. She could feel the Seren's heat on her skin matching the fire in her veins. Dancing through her subconscious, the warning sang in her mind:

Lo—A'dorned mid peace e're bondage ne'er cease.

She knew she had to draw Archer into the offense and coerce him into making the first move. If not, she'd suffer the same fate as the chubby pirate who'd been strangled to death by the Seren. Should her opponent aggravate her enough to make her strike first, Kathryn's fate would be sealed, and death would soon follow as the threads that held the sacred relic around her neck slowly crushed her throat. The first attack had to be from Archer.

"Come on, coward," she coerced him.

He hesitated. Somehow, she had to entice him into making the first move.

"Perhaps I should tell the others about your little visit to my quarters not long ago."

"Shut yer mouth, witch!"

She'd touched a nerve and had him now in a dance of betrayal—one that would mask her outward loathing and lure him into the power of the Seren.

"You remember, Archer. The sun hadn't quite risen yet, so no one could see you entering my cabin. Remember? Just a short time before, the captain was struck by the boom."

"I said shut it!" Still, Archer hesitated.

"Perhaps you planned it that way—to cut loose the yardarm and blame it on the storm?" She crept forward a few steps, her cat-like movements tense and controlled.

"Devil's tongue!" Archer screamed and leapt forward. His cutlass circled high overhead, and then he made an awkward pirouette and turned a full circle. The whole display looked ridiculous, but his strike was unexpected when it came. Kathryn rolled to one side, and the blow hit the deck. Archer laughed, which called for an audience as he turned to face the witch.

"She's an infant with a stick!" one of the pirates shouted. "Teach her sommat, Archer!"

"Aye…aye…behold the wretched doxy seeks yet to be in Davy's grip! Who then, vies yet to dispatch her?" He continued to turn in a wider circle and chuckled as several men gathered to form a larger audience.

Kathryn stayed motionless—her heart beating steadily while the anger that coursed through her veins shifted to a steely calm. She crouched, ready to destroy her worthy adversary. The vermillion stone strained her neck and seared the skin over her breastbone. Already, she could sense the silvery threads beginning to entwine themselves, which narrowed the trim that circled her throat. Unless the pirate attacked again, she would be dead within moments. She took another step forward, spread her arms outward, weapons raised, and bowed without taking her eyes off Archer.

"Do your best, unless the quartermaster's afraid to finish the deed himself…just like that night in my cabin."

Peals of laughter from the gathered crowd followed. The insult hit home and Archer turned on her. She dropped back into a counter stance and a younger crewman named Decker leapt forward while swinging a long, curved blade at her head. She ducked and sidestepped to the left as the tip of the pirate's cutlass fell short of her temple by only a fingerbreadth. Reversing her step, she dropped back into a crouch. By this time, the silver threads had grown tight around her throat, threatening to cut off air. A second lunge from the pirate sent steel toward her ribcage. She countered to the left as she slashed the cutlass downward to deflect the pirate's blow. Immediately, she felt the hair-like strands loosen about her neck, and she sucked in large breaths of salty air that filled her lungs and fed her muscles.

"Can't ye handle a little girl wit' a stick, Deck?" The pirates laughed again and Decker growled.

"This quarrel is not yours, Mister Decker," Kathryn sneered.

Decker shifted his weight from one foot to the other and waited for the young woman to make the next move. "I can handle her just fine. I'm playin' wit' her, that's all."

"Think again o're contending with a witch," she warned, but again, Decker ignored her and raised his sword.

"Go on, then, Decker!" Archer called out. "Finish th' dirty wench off an' be done wit' it."

"I'm warnin' you for the last time, man. This is not your engagement," Kathryn hissed through clenched teeth.

The pirate cross-stepped to his right, his sword held aloft. Still, he did not advance, and Kathryn sensed the man faltering.

"Yer nothin' but a dirty wench, an' I kills them who calls herself a witch!"

Kathryn countered to her right and as he spoke. The Seren cooled about her neck, and its heat was replaced with a familiar tingling sensation. She knew in that instant this man would not survive.

"I tell ye now, man. Raise your sword against me, and you'll be cut down by the powers that be this day. Sent to meet the devil, you'll be. Do not fight me!"

Another chorus of laughter peeled out from the onlookers, accompanied by a few slaps to each other's backs.

"Go on, Decker!" someone called from the crowd. It was quickly growing in size. "Ye cannot match a scrawny lass-of-a-wench in a fair fight, then?"

The taunt propelled Decker forward. He stood a single pace from Kathryn. Sunlight flashed on the gold loop that dangled from his left ear, and the fleeting thought passed through Kathryn's mind: *Before the sun sets, he'll use that gold to pay for his burial.*

Another flash caught her eye as the large blade sliced through the air, aimed at her throat.

Once again, Kathryn deflected the blow as she arched her cutlass to the right. Steel clashed, and she dropped her blade in a counter defense, warding off another lethal blow that would have taken off her right leg. She stabbed at the muscular bare belly but sliced through air as the pirate countered to his left. Her dirk only scratched the surface of his skin on one side. Blood welled up and drizzled down the rippled lines of his stomach, staining the wide leather belt fastened about his waist. He made no notice of the wound, took hold of his sword's hilt with two hands, and circled the weapon high above his head dramatically.

Before he dropped the razor-sharp edge, he gave a last "whoop" to the onlookers, then plunged the blade toward Kathryn's neck. Kathryn caught the edge once more with her blade and deflected the blow, the force bouncing her blade downward. She shifted her weight, and the angle of her cutlass shifted with her. In a back-handed slice, the razor-sharp edge of the English steel met with the pirate's abdomen. She jerked the hilt skyward and opened the man's belly wide—the gash gaping red and meaty beneath her blade.

Decker stumbled forward and cried out as Kathryn thrust the dirk deep into the pirate's right thigh. She paused for a moment and looked into the pirate's hollow eyes before she withdrew her dagger. "I warned you, Mister Decker. Now rest in peace."

He fell sideways as he clutched his gut and moaned. Several of the men rushed forward to lend a hand and dragged him off to the opposite side of the ship, away from the reach of Kathryn's sword.

The young witch stood tall, her weapons held outward with the points of each blade facing the heavens. Blood ran down the length of them both. Pivoting, she faced Archer. Her focus stayed keen, alert for any further advances from the crowd. No one moved as she lifted the flat end of the dagger deliberately before her face. Bloody steel touched her skin, and she smeared the dead pirate's blood along each cheekbone, leaving a lurid smudge pointing diagonally to her fixed jaw. At this, several of the pirates gasped, which brought a wicked smile to her lips.

With her eyes fixed on the quartermaster, she dropped the dagger to the Seren and smudged it in the same manner. The pirate's blood colored the now white stone with crimson. Black ringlets of smoke rose from the Seren as the blood hissed and sizzled against the stone before dropping to ash at Kathryn's feet. The curse was cast, and the pirate's blood boiled in his veins. His fate mirrored the bloody burning of the Seren.

Decker screamed.

Heads turned to look at Decker's agony, then snapped back to gape at the crazed sorceress. With great satisfaction, Kathryn noted the horror on the pirates' faces.

Archer, however, remained where he was, unmoved and visceral.

Kathryn threw her head back and laughed maniacally. The men's faces drained of color.

"Weak, superstitious fools, the lot of you!" She marveled at how easily they could be manipulated. "What say ye, Archer, you cockroach scruff? Dare ye now to cross blades with a witch?"

She suddenly stopped laughing and resumed her defensive crouch. She readied for him to strike.

"She-devil, ye be, says I. Get ye back to hell!"

Archer lunged at Kathryn with a fearsome thrust of steel, but she had become the panther again, lithe on her feet as she leapt to one side, and the blade missed her by an arm's length. The force of his attack sent him forward at a run. Kathryn pivoted to watch Archer stumble, barely catching himself from the fall. She cackled at him, mocked him, and then, taunted him further. All the while, the Seren stayed cool and silent about her neck.

Archer turned and charged again. His timing was accurate with one jab directed at Kathryn's heart, though it somehow missed. She dropped in a graceful *passata-soto*, then rolled to her left to avoid the lethal stab. The Seren had worked—she was somehow protected. Stunned, Archer recovered in an expert reprise and shifted to the right, then swung the cutlass down toward Kathryn, who still lay on her side. She saw the flash of Archer's steel and raised her own cutlass to intercept the blow just in time. The power of it knocked her sword to the deck, and she slid to the right, the hilt miraculously still gripped firmly in her hand.

"Quit playin' wit' her, Archer, an' send 'er to th' sharks!" one of the pirates called out.

Kathryn hopped back to her feet and faced Archer in a low crouch. She hissed at him, then laughed again, her icy eyes wild and lethal as they focused on her predator.

"Aye, Archer...let's finish this!" she spat.

The pirate held his sword steady ahead of him, the tip pointed at the crazed Kathryn. He held perfectly still despite his heaving chest. Fortunately, Archer was already winded, which played to Kathryn's youthful advantage. Still, he was stronger and had greater skill with the sword. She knew the slightest mistake would bring her doom.

Her left hand flipped the dagger, which she skillfully caught by the blade, a trick she had learned from Seth. She smiled at the memory of it: Seth had been rather pleased at how quickly Kathryn had picked up the trick and soon introduced her to an expert swordsman, named Wynn. She had quickly dubbed the man Wily Wynn, a nickname that was fitting for her "Master of Swordplay."

"You remember my mentor, Mr. Archer, don't you?"

"I know ye tricked Wynn into showin' a few moves wit' a blade, but it won' save ye this time. Wynn's grown old and slow."

The salty, silver-haired pirate was considered old by a cutthroat's standards, although Kathryn guessed he was only forty years of age. Most of the pirates had

ignored her, while Wynn had taken her under his wing—
at least in regards to swordplay. Mostly, they parried
during the dull days when the doldrums hit. Archer was
wrong—Wynn was keen and swift, and Kathryn felt
certain the lessons would prove a wise investment now.

Snapping her wrist, she flung the dagger at the
quartermaster, who easily leapt out of the way. The
dirk barely missed the upper part of his right arm. In
retaliation, he rounded with his sword arched in a perfect circle toward Kathryn's waist. No longer holding
the dagger, she blocked with her forearm and caught
the edge of Archer's steel against it, which split the
flesh, instantly staining the sleeve of her chemise a dark
scarlet. Kathryn howled against the pain that fueled
her to advance. Her cutlass sang as it sliced in reprise.
Archer countered with his own blow, but this time, did
not throw off her attack. She drew her wrist downward
to jab directly at Archer's abdomen. Her blade hit its
mark and sunk deep into the pirate's exposed belly. She
pulled through it, clutching the hilt with both hands,
but then, suddenly released the steel.

Archer growled and doubled over to wrap his left
arm around his midsection. In his right hand swung the
large cutlass. It flew out in front of him—a fierce pendu-
lum that cleaved the air with a great whooshing sound,
hunting for Kathryn. She pivoted on one foot, her blade
raised, ready for the next parry with the vicious pirate.

Abruptly, a loud crack sounded as wood split just
behind her, then suddenly, everything went black.

Sixteen

HE JERKED ON THE AXE handle two or three times before dislodging it from the large mizzenmast.

"I will not be havin' me crew butchered like herring on the block!" The captain's voice resonated from just aft of mid-ship. He stepped forward and scanned the gathered pirates. Order had to be restored on board the *Revenge*, and he was the one to do it. He lifted the handle and launched the axe deftly. The whole of it turned helve-over-head through the air until the sharp end wedged deep into the mainmast. The crew stared dumbstruck. "Now get to your duties 'fore I carve ye up meself!"

"Aye, Capt'n," sounded out as the crew dispersed into the depths of the ship and disappeared into their tasks. *That got those scurvy dogs' attention.* With satisfaction, he watched his men scatter. "Archer, get yourself to the sick bay and tend to your wounds. I won't be losin' the quartermaster *or* the chirurgeon over shipboard squabbles."

"Th' witch ought not to be th' ship's chirurgeon, Capt'n." Archer spat blood as he spoke. "She's nothin' but the devil's spawn and brings bad luck to us all!

She should be put away or hanged, says I!" Archer spat again, hunched over, holding his dissected belly. "Sure and I'm not the only crewman aboard this vessel what thinks so, Capt'n!"

"The lass be the only one aboard gifted in the art of physic, Mister Archer. Ye'll die soon."

"S'not so bad. I don't wish a witch's hands on me."

"You'll soon be findin' her value, especially when you're cryin' out for mercy o're your wounds there." He motioned to the crew. "Yer quartermaster will certainly go to the grave for arguin'. Fetch clean water, if there be any, and bandages. Quickly now!"

"Aye, aye." The voices sounded from the gathered crew.

"Archer, ye'd best find yourself a matey to stand by, as the lass, sure as I'm breathin', shan't be layin' willing hands on you for your healin'. As right well it might be after sufferin' such blows as you delivered against one another."

Captain Phillips stood with his imposing frame outlined against the burnished aft deck. The wood glared with the mid-afternoon sunlight against the pale blue sky, giving him a halo from behind. He remained so, realizing the power of the image he invoked.

"She provoked an' killed one of our men, Capt'n. Did ye expect me to sit idly by and watch?" Archer glanced up, eyeing the captain.

"I expected you to act as the officer you are. I will not have any more losses this day, Mister Archer." He turned to give orders to two crewmen lingering behind. "You there! Mister Evans, Mister Clipperton."

The two pirates looked up tentatively at their captain. "Aye, sir?"

"Take Mister Archer below and tend to his wounds as best ye can. Call for Seth to fetch additional supplies. I have business of my own to tend to."

"Aye, Capt'n."

Evans and Clipperton ambled over to Archer. Each one supported the quartermaster beneath an armpit and nearly dragged him to the front of the ship and into the crew's quarters. The gash in his midsection was long and superficial, and though it had bled profusely, the greatest damage was the stain that spread across the pirate's bedraggled clothing.

Archer would live.

The captain chewed the inside of his cheek and watched as the men hauled the ailing man away. "Insolent blaggards!" he breathed.

When they had finally disappeared, he turned his attention to a large bundle of sail that lay in disarray to one side. He shook his head and his tongue clicked in disapproval as he stepped next to it. The bundle lurched, and muffled cries erupted from within. Again, and again, it wobbled and pitched from one side to another. Something was caught and obviously trying to free itself from underneath the heavy sailcloth. A high-pitched voice cried out again—threats to anyone within hearing distance.

"Your thrashin' and carryin' on will not be freein' ye, lass." The captain crossed his arms and watched while the sailcloth bounced even more forcibly.

"Captain Phillips! I order you to release me from this mess at once!" the voice screeched. But the captain only threw his head back and laughed.

"You seem to be in a quandary and in no state to be barkin' orders at your capt'n."

With that, he bent over and scooped up the occupant, sail and all, and tossed it easily over his left shoulder. The cargo continued its pummeling from the inside, with curses thrown at the captain.

"You best cease your thrashin' about, miss, lest ye cause yourself some harm." He bit back a chuckle as he hauled his prize aft.

"I'm injured already, Capt'n Phillips! And if you were aware of it, you certainly would be moved to set me free!" came the response.

When he had reached the quarterdeck, he carefully set down the bundle and gently parted the free edges of sailcloth. Peering through the dark opening, she glared at him. Although he knew he would receive a tongue-lashing for it, he was unable to help himself—he let loose with an unbridled bout of laughter. Staring through the gaping course cloth, she cursed at him again.

Captain Phillip's lips curled into a lopsided smile. "Why, Miss Kathryn, it appears ye have run afoul o' this sail, ye have."

He extended one hand to help her to her feet. She swatted it away and rolled onto her hands and knees like an angry cat, then sprang upright rather awkwardly. So incensed was she that she could barely speak. In spite of her bleeding arm, she reached up and slapped an open palm across the pirate captain's jaw.

"How dare you, John Phillips! You cleaved that line to drop the sail." She stood to her full height and stomped her foot at the crumpled sailcloth. "You dropped the thing o're me when I was merely defendin' myself against that bilge scum, Archer!"

The grin on his face widened in spite of the sting that had spread along the side of his jaw. He forced himself to swallow and bit the inside of his cheek to stifle a rising chuckle. Stamped over her indignant display lay dark amusement—something pirates always found hysterical.

"And stop your grinnin' at me, ye bloody pirate!" she shouted at him.

The captain could no longer contain himself as Kathryn grew increasingly animated with each rebuke she spat. Frustrated, she raised her hand once again to slap him, but a muscular grip caught her by the wrist. Strong hands clutched hers firmly and pulled her forcibly against his chest. She fought against him while wringing her hands in a futile attempt to free herself. Captain Phillips held fast as she fought against his embrace. His gaze never left her fiery blue eyes, and the crooked smile he wore slowly softened with passion.

Kathryn looked up at him and felt her willpower fade. The warmth of his muscular arms caressed her and gradually dissolved her strength. Slowly, her resolve melted. Neither spoke. He leaned close, and she could smell the sweet musk of his skin. Deliberately, he brushed his lips against hers and kissed her passionately on the mouth. For just an instant, she fought against his advances. The last vestiges of Celtic temper welled up inside and sought release.

"Capt'n…"

"Shhhh." He kissed her again.

It was a dirty trick he'd played when he'd cut loose the smaller staysail and let it drop to trap her inside. But the act had prevented any further parrying between the young woman and the quartermaster, which had probably saved her life. She knew this was true, although she'd never admit it—or that's what she told herself as the pirate kissed her.

For an instant, she hesitated, then parted her lips against his open mouth. The warmth of his gentle lips soothed her heart and dissolved her will to resist. He felt her strength succumbing to his touch as he pulled her closer to him, then held her for a while. The steadfast beating of his heart matched the pulse that raced in her chest.

She clung to him. He reached one hand into her tangled black hair, pulled back on her tresses, and caressed her wavy locks with his fingers. As if to study her Celtic fire, he leaned back and looked deeply into her eyes.

"Ay, lass. It had to be stopped er'e Archer surely would have cut ye to ribbons. I cannot be losin' ye now."

This caught Kathryn off guard, but she managed to speak. "You robbed me of my pride, John Phillips, and the men surely will scoff. You can get yourself another chirurgeon in any port."

Against her will, her eyes welled up, and she dropped her cheek against his chest so he wouldn't see the tears.

"I need you, lass." His hand stroked her ebony locks as he kissed the top of her head.

"There are plenty of men who know physiks."

"It's for more than that, Kathryn," he whispered.

Blinking back tears, she stepped out of his arms to gaze at him. *This man's bewildering manner!* How could he kiss her so fiercely, then cast her aside like this? *Oh, but he is a scallywag. Indeed, I am in love with a pirate!* The thought gave her pause.

Could she allow a cutthroat to steal her heart? The man was a pirate, after all. Would he treasure her love as much as his precious ship? Such decisions were not easily made, and her fiery Celtic spirit reared its angry head again. She needed to see his intent, look deep into his soul. She wanted no confusion on this subject.

The pirate captain must have sensed this because he suddenly released her and dropped both hands to his sides to allow Kathryn to study him. This time his face showed no mirth, only the vestiges of pain left behind from a hard life at sea. Yet, there was something tender in his eyes, and she remembered the kindness hidden well behind the tough exterior of the pirate.

He merely nodded before he spoke again, as if he knew her thoughts. "You've stolen my heart, lass, and I can do naught but love you from a distance. My crew will not tolerate their capt'n bringin' a woman aboard for no less than service aboard the ship. It's a wretched thing that's been done to you, Kathryn, and I was filled with remorse the day you were taken from your home in the heather. Yet, the pirate within me praises God, with each sunrise, that He saw fit to bring you to me."

His sincerity pierced her heart and Kathryn wiped a cheek with the back of her hand. This man, torn between the life of a pirate captain and the guileless soul that drove his conscience, had captured her very soul.

"I can ne'er go back, John. I can ne'er leave you." She looked at a spot on some planking. "That's why I was strapped to the mast that night...so that your heart would beat again and bring life back to your broken body. A selfish act it was, actually. I cannot live without you, so I chose you to live...without me." Tears ran freely down her face as she spoke.

"Oh, Kathryn," he breathed. The pirate's gentle gaze settled on the young woman who had sacrificed her own life for his not long ago. His throat felt dry, and he swallowed hard, then prayed she would not think of him as weak.

"You have my heart, Capt'n John Phillips," she whispered.

He said no more.

Seventeen

"Where's my sword and short blade?" snapped Kathryn to no one in general.

With great fanfare, she gathered her skirts and marched to mid-ship with growing agitation, as she searched for her lost weapons. The wound in her forearm gaped open with each movement she made, adding to her ill temper. Not far behind, the captain kept several paces between himself and the raging woman. The tender moment that had passed between them was quickly cooled with the sudden loss of her blades. Whether from the throbbing injury or from her tender encounter with the captain, the reason for her irascibility was unclear, even to her.

Only a few of the deck hands took notice of her tromping around mid-ship. Frustrated, she kicked at the fallen sailcloth over and over again. "Bloody sails!" She cursed and kicked the tarpaulin again.

Captain Phillips wore an amused but tolerant expression. With hands clasped behind his back as he strolled, his air was one of disciplined self-control that contrasted smartly with her tantrum. She kicked at a barrel then let loose with tirades that flew in all directions. Those who noticed kept their sniggers well hidden behind tasks.

"You've a strong arm, lass…I'll give you that much," he said, catching sight of a shiny object that protruded from coiled rope piled alongside the quarterdeck. He strolled to its location, then stooped to retrieve the abandoned dirk. John Phillips cleared his throat.

The inflamed young woman turned on him. "Why now, John Phillips? You've never cared whether that bloody quartermaster of yours dispatched me before today. So why now?"

He faced her with arm extended and presented the dagger that lay flat on his outstretched hand. "Your short blade, m'lady." He bowed with great fanfare as he spoke, and the corners of his lips curled slightly. "Because I need a good chirurgeon onboard and you seem to be the only candidate available."

"That's why? You bloody, ungrateful, dirty scallywag…"

"Now hold there, Kathryn."

The tantrum that ensued caused even Slade to stop and stare wide-eyed. She stomped over to where Captain Phillips stood and snatched the dagger from him, then spun on her heels and stormed off. The outbursts continued as she kicked at anything in her path and cursed every cutthroat she'd come to know by name.

"And *you*! Call yourself Mister Davis...well, ye bloody well better find a new moniker, as you're no gentleman. Bloody yellow-livered cur!"

Davis dodged just in time as her fist sailed through the air, aimed for his jaw. Unable to contain himself any longer, Captain Phillips laughed out loud as he watched his men take great pains to avoid the maniacal wench aboard the ship.

"Watch it!" Reed shouted.

"Don't be tellin' me what to do, you filthy scum-sucker!" Kathryn hissed as she began the tedious process of locating her cutlass. The crew became less helpful, giving her a wide berth where she hunted. She'd lost her pride just trying to get out from under the sail, then faced a very satirical captain who, she was certain, had purposely kept the dirk under wraps.

"There's no need for name calling, Kathryn," Captain Phillips said, choking back another bout of laughter. She noticed.

"Bloody pirates!" she shouted. "I don't keep company with wretched dogs! Especially you, John Phillips! I had the situation in hand. You stopped my fight and caused me to lose my blades. It's a fine fix ye've gotten us into!"

Captain Phillips stared, even more captivated. As she searched the deck, she retraced her steps to where she had been just before the sail fell.

Exasperated, she turned her back on him. Clustered around the mainmast, a collection of pirates snooped through the newly acquired booty heaped into a large pile. Their interest in her was quickly replaced by the shiny gold and silver amassed there. Organized piles of sun-kissed gold bars were stacked in miniature pyramids and glistening mounds—where porcelain, silk, and gems had been scattered about. Shiny silver reales spilled from pots of brightly painted clay. Delicately shaded porcelain bowls, created to contain exotic liquids, had been cast to one side. Folded ornamental cloth rested to one side. On the other sat an array of personal commodities in no apparent order. Bronzed candelabras with fitted candles stood upright, waiting to be lit. Sacks of fragrant coffee and green bottles filled with spirits and stopped by unopened corks that had been sealed with wax lay in baskets set aside for the climatic end of the bidding. Tucked to one side in a large, lop-sided basket, well-worn from use, were bundles of herbs and vials of rainbow-hued glass. They had been abandoned alongside an enticing array of pearls, gold chains, and emerald crosses.

"Treasure, indeed." Kathryn stopped to eye the plunder. Everyone's attention danced from the pile of jewels to the coins, then to the bottled spirits…all except Kathryn. She walked up to the basket of dried plants and colored vials. Silent for the first time since her bandy with the quartermaster, she stared at the neglected basket's contents.

"Here." She hailed the pirates closest to her. They ignored her. "Jonas! What's this ship you've taken to prize?"

"Naught but a Port'guese shippin' vessel," Jonas answered. He quickly turned his attention back to the others.

"Where did she make berth, then?" Kathryn called out again.

"We can't be knowin' that," another pirate chimed in.

Someone added, "She was bound for Tortuga 'fore we caught an' took 'er as prize." The group seemed irritated by her constant interruptions.

"And the crew? Did it have a chirurgeon or a healer on board?" Kathryn interrupted again.

Jonas stared her down, "How should we know. Stop botherin' us, girly. We're busy here."

"Aye, an' likely as not, ye'll be getting' none o' it anyway, so stop starin' at it," Conroy chimed in.

"You can keep your silly doubloons," Kathryn snapped, her focus on the collection of herbs and vials.

Jonas shrugged his shoulders and turned his back on her, a clear signal he was finished with the conversation.

"Aye," she whispered to herself, "and why would any of you care? Your hearts were set to butcherin' the lot."

"There be no chirurgeon aboard that survived, Kathryn." The captain stepped forward to take in the treasure, as well. He glanced at the pile amassed at the foot of the mainmast.

She glared as he approached. "How would ye know?"

"Stop with the tongue-lashing, lass. You've got your dirk, and Slade seeks out your cutlass, even now.

There'll be more to this day than your little tantrum." He caught her by the wrist as she raised it.

"Think on it, Kathryn—the men don't take well to an obstinate woman on board. You're earning your place here and could jeopardize it quickly with that temper of yours."

She stared at him, and the muscles in her body relaxed a bit.

"Was the healer Obeah?" Her voice had dropped to hushed tones, as if speaking the name would curse them all. Her thoughts drifted momentarily to the witch, Macha, who dwelled on Tobago Island. The crone's dark power originated in the ancient voodoo practice. Captain Phillips tore his gaze away from the plunder and stared at Kathryn.

"Why do ye ask such questions?"

"There." Kathryn pointed to the basket of herbs and glass.

He saw nothing but bits of dried plant, strangely woven twigs, and cracked, dulled glass. However, her mood had changed, and the intensity in her voice warned of more than the trinkets. That alone gave him pause.

"Why? What is it?"

"Obeah trinkets."

"That belonged to the Portuguese. I don't see how that affects us when…"

"John, we must get to Tobago. I fear Morrigan intends to destroy the *Revenge* and seeks other ships at sea to carry out her purposes." She'd cut him off again and saw his irritation as he shifted his stance. "I'm sorry, Capt'n, but we're in grave danger. I fear I must speak again with the Obeah witch."

"That is impossible."

She looked to the water. "The brutal butcherin' of these foreigners by your men is proof enough she's workin' dark magic o're these seas."

The captain stared at the water and sighed. "You blame this on Morrigan?"

"I blame the butchery on her magic. Think on it, Capt'n…the men have never slaughtered like this."

"You've only been with us for a short while, lass."

"Aye, true. I have no idea how your crew behaved before my arrival, but since then, I've seen nothing to suggest such bloodlust until now."

The captain shifted his stance. "Ay, so be it. We're on a direct course for Tobago already, lass. Ye best pray Neptune guides us hence on swift winds."

"I have my own way to encourage stubborn sea breezes to fill slack sails, Capt'n," she said softly as her eyes met his.

The captain lifted his chin slightly in defiance, although it was clear he agreed with her. She turned her attention back to the basket.

"Should that lot be spared, I want to make claim to it."

Captain Phillips knitted his brows as he looked at the weathered basket and nodded. "I cannot understand why ye would want that refuse…" He waved a hand over the basket of trinkets, "…but if ye want it, it's yours to take, since no one else seems interested in dried weeds—particularly with such a bounteous plunder elsewhere."

In that moment, Seth traipsed forward, and brandishing the missing cutlass, presented it with a bow to Kathryn.

"Your wayward cutlass, Madame."

Clearly, he mocked her, but she didn't care and heaved a sigh of relief. "Thank you! But I thought Slade went after it," she said, more of a question than a statement.

"Aye, he did, and found it, too. He asked me to make certain you'd get it, seein' how he's busy with other things at the moment." Seth nodded to the mast where Slade knelt, thumbing through the booty.

"Ah," Kathryn said. Fortunately for her, it was the draw to treasure that kept most of the crew at bay.

"Ye best keep it where ye can find it." A thick pirate brogue had begun to worm its way into Seth's speech, and Kathryn wondered if he was really taking to these ruffians and their ill-gotten ways. Seth had proven himself a rather sly thief before being captured. But those were younger days in the village—or so she thought. She smiled at him, which he returned—their friendship intact in spite of the circumstances that had taken them to living amongst pirates.

Behind Seth, the twin pirates, Dobs and Jonesy, whispered between themselves, occasionally pointing to the plunder.

"Excuse me." Within moments, Seth had joined them, picking out treasures to bid upon.   Kathryn cast a sour look at him and dropped her hands to her hips. Seth shrugged, but his eyes sparkled. The three then disappeared behind the capstan, only to reappear atop the portside sheets. Kathryn gawked at them. All three were as agile as apes, but Seth had changed the most. Until now, Seth's sudden shift in attitude, as well as his brawny physique, had escaped her.

Kathryn studied the length of Seth's muscular back as he worked from the yardarm. It was browned from hours spent in the sun. *How has he grown so much taller without my notice?* She glanced at his strong hands and muscular arms. *Indeed, his limbs have likely strengthened from work with the sail and lines.* She watched him move with the grace of a panther as he maneuvered along the narrow boom. *How did I not see it before? Indeed, Seth is no young boy.* She looked at him askance. "He is a man."

"Excuse me?"

"Will ye be joinin' us, lass?" Gow asked, holding back a grin. Pieces of scattershot that had been collected in a rucksack was slung over his back.

"I…aye, Mister Gow, that I will," Kathryn stammered, surprised at the invitation.

Around the main mast, the number of men who waited to bid had grown considerably.

There would be shares divvied between them first. After that, the bidding would begin for the finest of the Portuguese treasure. The piles of confiscated goods had grown, heaped with stacks of fine Chinese silk cloth, spices from India, and Caribbean rum. Cook flagrantly helped himself to the baskets of limes, bananas, and salt pork, while two other men herded the livestock below. No one questioned Cook's actions, for everyone aboard knew his collection was prize enough. There would be food for every man…and woman. Savory meals without maggots and flies, figs, and plenty of grog, accompanied by song and dance, awaited the pirates tonight.

Kathryn surveyed the crew and stepped forward to assume her place amongst them. No one said a word, not even Archer. His roughly bandaged abdomen seeped as his cohorts literally dragged him to the front of the crowd. Gow walked ahead to join Sparks, who stood closest to the newly acquired weapons. His eyes gleamed as he surveyed the pistols and Portuguese swords. Most of those would soon be added to their arsenal. One-legged Taylor hobbled forward, as well. He hopped on his one remaining leg with a sawed-off oar propped under an arm as a crutch.

Kathryn watched him hobble and recalled the brutal amputation that had taken place the night Taylor had attempted mutiny by stealing a ship. Wood had been killed outright, Taylor's leg crushed, and Fern had been keelhauled as punishment. The two mutineers had survived, mainly due to Kathryn's skills with herbs and a bit of ancient magic.

"Waste of physiks!" she breathed.

The trio still whispered plans for mischief, as if no one knew. Nothing had changed, and Fern grew more irritable toward the quartermaster as the months wore on. This was a man she wished to avoid.

As Taylor hopped past the sorceress, the ship shifted and tossed the pirate into Kathryn's injured arm. She winced as the forgotten gash to her forearm opened up and blood ran fresh, staining her sleeve a bright, sticky maroon. In her rage, she had forgotten to tend to her own wounds. Taylor said nothing but dropped his gaze and moved on. Kathryn stared him down, repulsed by the man.

"Rudeness such as this cost you your leg, Mister Taylor. Has it cost you a tongue, as well?" she shouted after him as he quickly disappeared into the crowd.

"You best be gettin' that tended to, lass," a baritone voice breathed from behind into her ear. She jumped at the sound.

She'd forgotten the captain had remained on deck. Her face flushed as her temper rose to match the nagging wound on her arm. "It was fine until that scum, Taylor, bumped into it. I should never have wasted my time with him…and you should have let that leg fester! It was mutiny against you."

"It seems Taylor set off more than a gaping wound. Come, Kathryn. I'll tend to it meself."

"But the auction…"

"It will be a while yet before the plunder's divvied. You've got time to stop bleeding and calm your mood."

He spoke the truth, though she didn't want to admit it. Kathryn stomped her foot anyway then allowed him to lead her up to her quarters. As she opened the door, the captain released her arm and stepped backward into a narrow ray of sunlight. He rested his hands on his hips and paused, the look on his face stern. Kathryn spun on her heel and stared at him. Her expression went blank.

"What now? Tell me you're not taken with the same superstitions as your men."

"Nay, lass. Ye don't frighten me. Yet, it's prudent I do not step a foot inside your private quarters alone with ye."

"Pray tell me why?" Her face showed genuine amazement. "You're the capt'n. You can do anything you want. It's your ship, for heaven's sake!"

"The *Revenge* belongs to the entire crew. I'm bound by the same laws as the rest of 'em. As of late, the men have noticed my fondness for you, lass. They have the hearts of scallywags and lusty men. I'll not have them thinkin' I'm less than honorable…not with you. I won't allow ye to become folly for their lusty minds and evil thoughts, not whilst you're aboard my ship!"

Kathryn stared, speechless, not knowing how to respond. Her emotions danced between anger and amusement. The mere thought that a pirate carried such morals was beyond her comprehension.

"Fascinating!" Without restraint, she laughed and threw her hands to her hips as she stared at him in disbelief. "I don't believe it, John Phillips!"

He allowed a moment for the woman to collect her wits before he continued. "There be Articles aboard my ship, and my crew is bound to them, o'er the axe. I took that oath as well, Kathryn."

"Well, I didn't, Capt'n!" Color rose in her face. "You say I'm naught but a rule to be kept unbroken? Is that what I am to you, John Phillips?"

"Nay, lass. Ye know where me heart lies, and for that purpose alone, I cannot have my men thinkin' I'm having my way with ye. It's my duty as the capt'n…and the man who loves you…to protect your honor from these ruffians, lass."

Her heart suddenly ached, and she gathered his clasped hands with her own. "What did you say, Capt'n?"

"You heard me." He toed a loose plank, but did not withdraw from her touch. "You've bewitched me, sorceress."

She raised her face to his and parted her lips, then whispered, "Then you best take me as your own, Capt'n."

Gently, he lifted her chin with his forefinger, bent and kissed her tenderly, then traced the lines of her face with a finger. "I'll not be defilin' ye, lass. Rest assured, you certainly shall be mine to claim. But it will not be this way, m'lady."

He taunts me! She stepped back as both hands returned to her hips, which swayed as she shifted her weight from one foot to the other. Kathryn bit her tongue, obviously irritated.

"Such artfully crafted words. Are you so brazen to think you can have me at your whim? Such arrogance!" She stomped a foot and waved one hand in the air. "I will not be made a common madam by any man, particularly not by a pirate! You can take your scallywag bilge rat thoughts somewhere else, *says I*!"

Captain Phillips laughed aloud, his square jaw accentuating the fierce emerald eyes that danced as he regarded her. *Indeed, she's a fiery lass, this one.*

"Hold there, Kathryn." He stepped forward and took her by one arm as he spoke. "You misunderstand my intent and won't listen to what I'm *tryin'* to say. Even with your irascible disposition, I mean to take you for my wife. That be my claim on you, though God help the man who finally does claim you for his own, with that Celtic temper o' yours!"

She stared dumbfounded. Her hands remained stubbornly on her hips that continued to sway as she moved from one foot to the other nervously. He knew he had her, and the corner of his mouth curled triumphantly.

"I…I…" She stomped her foot again. "I won't be marryin' the likes of you, Capt'n Phillips! True, you've shown kindness to me, and my heart's cryin' out for you…but even if you're the last man on earth, I won't be marryin' you!"

"Are you so certain?"

"I couldn't be more so!" She stormed into the cabin and stared at him, but her voice gave her away. He smiled even broader to know she would one day be his.

"Ay, then, if that be your wish, lass. Now go fetch the chirurgeon's satchel and bring it to me so I can tend to your wound there."

She nodded once, rather unconvincingly, then disappeared deeper into the darkness of her tiny cabin. John Phillips sat on the edge of the steps that led to the deck and listened to his crewmen bartering as he waited for her return. Above, in the distance, the sounds of dividing plunder had begun. The captain knew he and the young healer would not be missed for a while. He smiled again to himself. He could wait for Kathryn, too.

Eighteen

WATER BLENDED INTO A PALE turquoise as the *Revenge* drew a frothy row behind her rudder.

The color was familiar to Kathryn, indicating they were bearing down on the Grenadines, a cluster of islands not far from Tobago. A chill ran up her spine, the shrill reminder of her last visit to the remote island and the black magic that dwelt there.

She drew a lavender merino tight about her shoulders. Despite the fabric's appearance, the wrap provided warmth. Smattered in pale patches along the ends where the damp sea air had encrusted salty grey stains, the fabric had begun to take on the same weathered look as the pirates' attire. It didn't matter. Kathryn felt secure against the constant sea spray and the private chill that accompanied thoughts of the Obeah witch from Tobago.

As the sun settled low in the sky, its vibrant coral and amber rays summoned a memory of the maple and yew trees that lay in the woodlands near her home at Mariel's cottage. The harvesters would be busy in their fields until nightfall, while the last of the little garden she had tended would be cleared of dead vines and plant stalks. Soon afterward, the produce would be dried and sealed in bottles for upcoming winter meals…and other mystical uses.

Kathryn's eyes welled as thoughts of home stung her heart. She allowed herself only a moment to long for the heather and lavender that meant home. She lifted her chin and inhaled the imaginary fragrances of the Celtic blossoms that lined the walkway leading to the cottage. Deep smoky aromas of musk and sweet flowers filled her nostrils, real bouquets that wafted in from somewhere across the sea. With a shake of her head, she dismissed her homesickness and wiped her cheeks with the back of her hand.

"Yer wound appears to be healin' right nicely." A bare-chested pirate stepped forward and leaned against the rails alongside her. He wore the weathered look of an old salty dog measured by a life at sea. Silver touched his temples and peppered his sparse beard. Although he wore his hair pulled back into a knot at the base of his skull, his scalp, bronzed and shiny, peeked through dark strands. All of this contrasted starkly against the ruddy handkerchief tied tightly about his crown.

He chipped away at an oval piece of fruit. The green skin peeled away easily from the orange, fleshy meat which clung to an abnormally large pit in the center. He hacked off a chunk, lifted it balanced on the edge of the long knife, then plopped it into his mouth. As he bit into the fruit, tawny liquid dribbled down his chin and dripped onto his chest.

"Aye, Mister Huggit." Inadvertently, she glanced down at the wound that circled her forearm like a withered snake. It was rather conspicuous and difficult to hide.

Without thought, she tugged the wrap to conceal the scar and looked seaward. The pirate sliced off another chunk of fruit and lifted it to his mouth. He also kept his eyes on the horizon.

"Word on board ship has it ye saved our necks from the Kraken," he said casually and paused to wait for her reply, but Kathryn said nothing. "I'd have ye know o' me gra'itude, miss."

He sounded genuinely appreciative, which caught her off guard. She cocked her head and gave the weathered sailor a sideways glance. They passed the next few moments in silence.   There was more to this conversation than mere thanks for staving off what he believed was the Kraken's attack, Kathryn could sense that much. It had been more than twice a fortnight since she had cast her magic and repelled Morrigan's evil from the ship. Most of the crew still believed it had been the legendary Kraken that had attacked them that day. However, her gut told her to stay attentive to the pirate who stood next to her. His attempt to probe her was obvious, though masked through casual conversation.

"Aye sir, go on."

"Well, lass, a few of us also thought it best ye be knowin' that there be some who meet in secret. They're not so thankful as the rest o' us. Ye best watch yer back, savvy?" She nodded. "We thought it best ye know of it…an' the Capt'n too."

"And who are these scallywags I best be watchin' my back after?"

The pirate shook his head and amber juice spread from the corners of his lips.

"Nay, lass, I cannot say. I have me own hide to watch out for. The lot o' 'em sure would cut out me tongue for warnin' as such. Jest keep a weathered eye out for those that be newly boarded, an' those they answer to, if ye understand my meanin'."

He cast a quick sideways glance at the young woman and winked, then tossed the peel into the clear water beneath. Turning from her, he added, "This is the last I'll say o' it, savvy?"

"Aye, Mister Huggit. I take in your meanin'."

He strolled away.

"…and will inform Captain Phillips forthwith," she replied aloud to the empty place where the old man once stood.

She watched him follow the length of the rails and caught a glimpse of his burley nod just before he flung another slice of pulpy skin into the water. Quickly, he popped another chunk of orange fruit into his mouth before he turned his back to the rails to disappear behind the forecastle.

"Thieving, murderous, conniving pirates!" She spat in exasperation as she turned back to face the water. Her mind reeled, filled with thoughts that surrounded Huggit's warning.

"And just who might these schemers be? Worse, just how do I break the news of a possible mutiny to the captain?" She shuddered. This was a conversation that would have to be planned carefully. Her place as chirurgeon remained privately undecided amongst most of the cutthroats, in spite of the captain's public announcement. She could not risk being the cause of dissent between crew and captain without losing John Phillips' confidence. The information would have to be delivered to him delicately, as if the man were discovering their mutinous plans on his own. Given the pirates' temperament of late, this would be tricky.

"Their spirits have settled little since Morrigan's visit. It's clear by the crew's constant hunger for plunder and blood." She shook her head.

Already, the *Revenge* had taken two sloops bound for Barbados since meeting with the Portuguese ship earlier. The unfortunate souls aboard the smaller ships were given a much better option to join the pirates or suffer whatever might befall them as captives. Most opted to join ranks and were willing to swear over the axe to the Articles of the ship. Once done, the crew then set to divvying the spoils amongst themselves, the newest members included, although their share was much less than their comrades. Still, Kathryn noted, the greedy glint in the new recruits' eyes looked the same as the seasoned pirates' when awarded share of the booty. "And from their own ship, no less."

They were all bloodthirsty and hungry for more.

"Scoundrels, the lot of 'em!"

Her mind drifted to the Portuguese prize and the bounty collected from its holds. The auction had been well underway by the time Captain Phillips finished bandaging her wounds and lead her topside. Her honor had remained intact that day, although she had hoped he would weaken. Given they had remained private and undisturbed in her tiny quarters, any show of passion could have easily gone unnoticed.

"He does have valor, I suppose…and honor as well, though he's still a pirate!" She glanced around to see if anyone had heard—but no one was near. She decided it best to make for her cabin and finish her monologue there. "He's as good as his word, Kathryn, remember that."

As if to apologize for his staunch morality, the captain had ensured the delivery of the basket filled with magic phylactery she had requested from the auction that day. It had been cast aside at the mast and brought to her quarters in secret. Kathryn had been delighted to discover it lying on the center table later that evening. Its trinkets and amulets were foreign, yet familiar enough for her to make magic, and she clapped her hands at the sight of it.

Kathryn breathed in the scent of dried sage and cinnamon. Smiling to herself, she rummaged through the basket's contents once more. She inhaled the foreign mix of fragrances that rose as she disturbed each bundle—a mesmerizing stew of alchemy that waited for her skill to bring its powers to life. Lifting her palms skyward, the witch gave thanks.

A sudden drop in her stomach brought her back to reality just as the ship lunged downward. *An aberrant swell, most likely. Indeed, this is powerful magic,* she thought and smiled cryptically.

At dusk, the sun dipped low toward the horizon—Kathryn's favorite time of day. Little remained of daylight, and she decided it best to move topside or miss the sunset, something she was not willing to do. Tucking her dirk into the small of her back, she rushed the causeway and made her way topside.

The *Revenge* was set on a steady course for Tobago, with the wind in their favor. Such fine drafts added speed as the ship accelerated through the water. Always, the ship would lift with the swells, then surge forward as her bow dipped. Kathryn stood at the mast, closed her eyes, and relished the cool spray of saltwater that showered the gunwale and dusted her skin each time the great vessel dropped. She inhaled the ocean air and breathed in the energy of the sea, ship, and the activity of the crew as they moved about their duties. Spirits were always high when the ship sailed this way—full and fast and free. It rejuvenated her and reminded her that this was the place she wanted to be. Above deck, with the wind in her face and the sunlight melting over her skin, the sea warmed her soul. Life aboard this magnificent vessel was fine indeed, even with the scallywags who crewed it, and especially, with their majestic captain.

Kathryn's lips softened into a gentle smile as she thought of those piercing green eyes.

"Land *ho*!"

A voice high above startled her as it called out from the crow's nest. Kathryn glanced skyward at the shadowy figure pointing to portside. She could see nothing ahead but deep turquoise water. Still, she knew his declaration was accurate. Land!

At this speed, she guessed they would make landfall before deep night. A familiar chill ran up her spine, reminding her of what waited in Tobago. Involuntarily, Kathryn shivered, then quickly gathered her skirts and moved below deck to her cabin.

She knew she would need something to present to the dark woman in exchange for information. Kathryn had very little by way of possessions, and anything she had obtained from her portion of the plunder would be of little value to an Obeah witch, even the strange Portuguese phylactery. As she entered her cabin, she scanned the walls and corners, searching for anything of value. Her disappointment turned to panic when she saw only dried herbs swaying in tightly woven bundles from the ceiling beams. Even the amulets, stashed on the small shelf tacked against one wall with the clusters of candles and burnt charms, offered nothing—mere artifacts tossed in a disheveled pile.

"Nothing? I have nothing of value?"

She glanced at the chirurgeon's satchel that rested upon the floor, but Kathryn was unwilling to part with that.

A fat wad of beeswax stood out so she lit the wick's stub that poked from the surface and placed it carefully inside a lantern that rested on the center table. The tiny room lit up to render its hidden crevices.

She pirouetted in slow motion in hopes of finding anything to trade. *Ahh, such inconvenience! Mariel would know for certain the fancy of an Obeah witch.* The thought danced through her head as she circled the room a third time.

"Mariel!"

Her eyes darted to a cotton rucksack hanging from a knot in the wood behind the cabin door. This obscure little bag was the very last thing Mariel had handed Kathryn just before the pirates forced her from the cottage. Inside, her grandmother had placed a number of charms, herbs, and other sundry talismans for use against ruffians. Hopefully, something inside was of use to her.

Kathryn rushed to where the faded bag hung, carried it to the center of the table and set it down next to the white light of the lantern. The candlelight danced over the woven cloth.

"Ah, my beloved Mariel, let there be somethin' here from you to bring me what I'll be needin' most," she whispered prayerfully.

Carefully, so as not to destroy its contents, she reached inside the bag and probed. She found nothing but decayed flakes of dried herbs and a few cotton rags left untouched.

"There's nothing here?" She was incredulous and flung it onto the table surface. "Worthless!"

Frustrated, she plopped down onto the chair with her hands cupped under her chin. A metallic thud sounded as the base of the woven bag hit the tabletop. Kathryn knitted her brows as she looked at the bag.

"What on God's blue sea…?" The question caught in her throat.

She squinted against the flickering candlelight. She had missed it in her search. Reaching across the table, she grasped the cloth. Something protruded from beneath the fabric. There it was—solid and hidden.

Kathryn hastily opened the bag and reached inside again, this time to one of the bottom corners. Her fingers grazed a cold, hard object threaded into the frayed seam. Deep within the folds of cotton, she grasped the item and pulled it from its encasement.

"*Bran Fendigiadd*," she whispered. Rotating it in front of the burning candle, its surface glistened in the flickering firelight. Ebony glinted off the rolling, uneven edges of the wings cut from rare onyx. A momentary flicker caught her attention as the lantern's flame responded to the object. Kathryn stared at the sputtering flame tucked behind glass panes. The ember shuddered briefly, then returned to a steady fire at the wick. She settled her attention back onto the onyx trinket poised between her thumb and forefinger.

"*Y gigfran*," Kathryn repeated, this time in her native Celtic tongue. "The Raven, indeed."

She turned the trinket around and slid it onto her finger. The silver and onyx ring moved as if alive, tucking its wings to rest snugly against her skin. It fit as if it had been created only for her. An intricately carved raven stared up at her with glistening sapphire eyes. Its wings lifted slightly from the black body, the whole of it peppered with knotted triskeles across its surface. Shiny, silver tips for feathers clustered into a trio of dagger-sharp points.

"Three…there are three." Kathryn felt a knot form at the base of her stomach. "*Bran*. The Raven. Three—as in three sisters. A Deity! Roane, Macha and Morrigan!"

Frantically, she tore the ring from her finger, placed the dark object onto the table, and stared at it.

"Why would Mariel…?"

She dared not take her attention off it, and struggled to hatch a plan for the ghastly object. Suddenly, she leapt forward, quickly gathering bunches of sage and lavender from the highest beams of the cabin's low ceiling. After she'd assembled the withered plants in symmetrical groupings, she crushed the herbs between her palms and scattered the powder over the top of the table. As the tabletop disappeared, she flicked her wrists to contort her hands into the ritualistic motions taught to her by Mariel. Her movements covered the ring in fine dust.

Near the lantern, she found a lint stick, which she used to light the tallow candle that rested on the center of the table. It burned until pale wax drooled down the sides and onto the table. Puddles of wax cooled to stillness in lopsided tentacles.

With a finger, she traced a five-pointed star into the crushed herbs that circled the perimeter of the candle. An ancient Celtic symbol emerged, encasing the ring inside the shape as the candle's flame danced to each point of the outlined pentacle.

Eneidiau uno gyda gigfran's allai
(Souls unite with raven's might)

Dirgelion cudd ar fin cael ei datgelu
(Mysteries hidden, soon to be revealed)

Ac yn dod unrhyw niwed ynddnyt.
(And bring no harm therein)

Kathryn waved her hands over the burning flame and fanned the herbs once more before stepping away from the table. The fire danced golden as it blessed the object lying beneath its light and did not move again until it had burnt itself to the base of the candle.

Rivulets of wax pushed through the edges of the powder before congealing cold and hard. The spell cast over the burnished oak tabletop was complete.

Kathryn snuffed out the ember that glowed atop the tiny wick and breathed a sigh of relief. *What was Mariel thinking to leave me such a thing as this?* The thought troubled her, but she knew there would be no answer—at least, not until she could raise the question with her grandmother in person.

She took up a small ivory napkin and laid it over the ring, gently so as not to disturb the spell. She then gathered her skirts and bolted through the doorway, taking the stairs two at a time as she made her way to the deck.

Nineteen

DARK GREEN FRONDS PAINTED WITH yellow dotted the beach behind tall grass and bamboo.

Eruptions of bright pink and purple bougainvillea cascaded in untamed mounds that burst from pocked cliffs in the distance. Ahead lay an embankment of snowy sand that sloped to meet the water as it lapped lazily against the strand.

Kathryn stood at the rails and reveled in the beauty of the shoreline. The island's rise to hilly mounds did not look familiar. Slender black birds with long gray necks that contrasted with their long orange beaks tipped their heads from side to side. Several types of fowl suddenly took to the air to glide just a foot above the glistening shallows. Falling suddenly, they tucked their wings just before they dove below the water's surface. Kathryn had never seen birds like that before. She knitted her brows, perplexed by their behavior.

"And where shall we make landfall, I wonder?"

"Dat be Gasparee Cove o' Trinidad, lady." A deep rumbling voice rolled from behind.

Kathryn jumped and spun on her heels to face a large pirate known simply as Pedro. His oily black skin glinted in the sunlight as thick, round muscles worked a massive cable against a worn cleat. He looked upward at her through long, dark lashes. Alabaster orbs encircled black pupils that never blinked. The pirate's head was covered with a vibrant russet headscarf tied in a large knot at the base of his skull. The ties trailed down his back in long, coppery streamers that fluttered in the sea breeze. His bare chest exposed a strange symbol branded to the left side.   Snaking along his back were raised, rope-like scars, which Kathryn knew had been inflicted not so long ago—the evidence that he'd once belonged to a cruel master, one that had been unable to tame this spirited man's will. Kathryn forced her attention back to the pirate's dark, chiseled face.

"But what of Tobago? The capt'n said we'd made way for Tobago."

"We na' be a-goin' da, lady." He pointed with a stout thumb to a smaller island barely visible ahead.

Kathryn squinted against the sun and lifted one hand to shield her eyes as she studied the tiny island. This was not the place they had planned to make port! There would be no Obeah on *this* tiny island, and no way to gather vital information about Morrigan. Without the Obeah's knowledge, they would remain vulnerable. Her mind grew cold. She turned back to face Pedro and involuntarily allowed her gaze to drift back to the strange inky mark branded over his massive chest.

"Where are you from, Pedro?" Perhaps he knew something of value, after all.

He stared in silence. It was risky to question anyone aboard the ship, except perhaps Seth or the captain—when he was in the proper spirit. The pirates were just as likely to slit a throat over mistaken inquiries as share a mug of rum, and Kathryn did not know Pedro's temperament. Still, it was a risk she was willing to take. With trepidation, judging her words, she pushed a little further.

"Pedro, you came from Tobago aboard this ship, yes?"

"Aye, lady." He dropped his eyes to the line in his hands. "What know ye o' dat Obeah woman livin' da?"

"You know of the Obeah?"

He stood and allowed the bulky line to go slack between his massive hands, as he studied her in silence. She could feel the heat of his stare and shifted her weight.

"Ye don' wan' be a-goin' to dat place, lady. De Obeah com' o' nothin' but black magic an' evil."

Kathryn met his gaze and forced herself to remain steady. "What do you know?"

"Da be sommat lyin' wait for any mon sailin' under de black flag at Tobago, see?" He lifted a large hand toward the smaller island again. Kathryn squinted at the tiny island. This time, she caught sight of something that moved around its perimeter. She shaded her eyes and was able to make out the shape of tiny sails that bobbed just offshore.

"Any vessel visible at this distance would be large and formidable, isn't that right, Mister Pedro? At least, one that the *Revenge* would best not reckon with, don't you think?"

Pedro nodded.

So that is the reason we make way for Trinidad, she thought to herself. Kathryn did not stifle the groan that followed. Her face soured—she would not be able to confront Macha.

"Wha' business make ye wit' de Obeah witch, lady?" Pedro broke into her thoughts.

Kathryn glanced at him. He'd resumed working the cable onto the wooden cleat and, though he appeared focused on his task, she realized his keen interest in their conversation proved otherwise.

"I need to know more about Morrigan."

Pedro made no indication he'd heard her and continued to wind the thick line, eyes lowered.

"I need to know what she wants of this ship and the crew," Kathryn continued. He still refused to look up at her, though his pace had slowed markedly. "She sent black magic to slaughter us all not long ago. Remember that night, Pedro?"

"Aye." Pedro sent a fleeting glance upward. There was no mistaking the restraint in his voice.

"The beast that night...some thought it was the Kraken, and others say the Blue Men of the Minch." Kathryn spoke boldly and noticed the slight twitch of his mouth. She was treading dangerous ground, and she knew it. She paused briefly to allow the pirate to take in her words, or perhaps plan his next move, lethal though it might be. A sharp warning flickered in his eyes.

Oho, this be a fearsome topic for ye, mate. Her mind was keen as intuition filled her thoughts. *Indeed, he holds his tongue silent when the dark goddess becomes the topic.* This man held knowledge about Morrigan that she desperately needed.

She took the risk again. "But you know better, Pedro."

Pedro stood upright. His full stature cast a shadow that spilled out onto the deck and blanketed the woman. He said nothing but moved one hand closer to his cutlass.

I cannot allow this man to see my fear or he will strike me down. Kathryn took one step toward him.

"Pedro, Morrigan came onto our ship to steal the souls of the crew. You witnessed the slaughter yourself."

He stared at Kathryn, intent on her every word. After what seemed like an interminable silence, Pedro finally spoke. "Da witch come for de men, de capt'n...an' you, lady. 'Tain't no mon to stop her now. We all be dead men walkin' aboard dis ship." His teeth clenched as he chewed out the last, then stared in silence once again.

He thinks I'm to blame for Morrigan's attack. The realization struck her suddenly. "Pedro, I have my own ways. The Celtic ways of the women in my family have their own...power. We call it the *Gift*." She lifted one hand to the white stone that rested against her chest.

"This is called the Seren. It has powers to protect me, and I have powers to protect this ship and crew. But I need to know what the secret of Morrigan is—what power can defeat her and her sisters."

"Tain't no power be defeatin' da black witch, lady."

Kathryn sensed the man's disquietude and feared that to argue her point would only cause him to turn away, so she changed course.

"Is that your island there, Pedro?" She pointed to the larger island that lay straight ahead of the bow.

"Nay, lady." He raised a large hand and pointed to the smaller island. "Dat be me island."

He aimed a finger at Tobago lying just behind the nearest island. Kathryn remembered the first time she'd laid eyes on the muscular black man. He was grouped with five or six others but stood out, obviously not a sailor by trade. The group of men had taken refuge on the quaint island. Pedro had snuck on board the *Revenge*, along with a few French fishermen, when the ship had put in to careen.

It was a well-hidden cay on the opposite side of Tobago. Somewhat remote and densely wooded with Kapok trees that lined the dense rise of the hills, pale pink flowers dripped from long branches feathered in vibrant green leaves. Its beauty gave no hint of the antics going on ashore. The island was a perfect place to careen a ship…or maroon an insolent sailor.

Pedro had been one of the many slaves who had been traded, and he had most likely escaped an abysmal fate. He had voluntarily signed the Articles once aboard the ship and joined the ranks of the pirates. Here he enjoyed an equal status with the new crew, something Kathryn still could not claim for herself.

"You know of the Obeah lady livin' there, do ye now?" The lilt in her voice thickened in an attempt to disguise her ravenous curiosity.

"Aye, lady. She be evil—nearly as bad as 'er sister. I say again, wha' do ye want wit' dat witch?"

"She's truly evil, Pedro, and has the answers I need to defeat Morrigan. You want me to send her away, now, don't you, mate?" Her voice was soothing as she spoke.

"Dar be da *vodouisaints* mon on dat islan'. He be a knowin' mon, lady."

Kathryn startled at the abrupt offering. *Why would voodoo be less ominous than the Obeah?* Her mind whirled. Ultimately, it didn't matter. She could still get some information, even if was from a Vodoun priest on Trinidad. She had to go ashore and speak with him.

"Pedro…you know this Vodoun man, personally, do you? You can take me to him, can you, now?"

"I can take ye, lady." He lowered his voice and his eyes narrowed. "It be costin' ye, though."

"Aye! Wait here, and I'll fetch…" She turned quickly to return to her cabin, intending to retrieve doubloon from her loot, but a large black hand seized her by the arm and stopped her in her tracks.

"No, lady." His voice dropped low and ominous. "It won' be me ye be payin'."

Twenty

KATHRYN WINCED AS THE RING bit into her skin. She twisted it in hopes that repositioning the ring would relieve her finger's discomfort. It helped a little.

She pulled hard against the current, and the wooden scull in her hand shuddered slightly. Latent muscles in her arms strained as she pulled again in time with the three other men who had taken up the oars in the eight-man skiff they'd boarded to go ashore. Trinidad's Gasparee Cove lay nearly a half cable ahead of the bow. She knew they would have to row another hour before they made landfall. Kathryn wondered if her strength would hold out. It was essential she hold her own with the crew, particularly as a woman—even more so, since most considered her bad luck on board the ship. Taking a turn at the oars was part of the crews' duties, which she would be required to do. Staving off the superstitious fools' minds about luck and women at sea would prove difficult.

The onyx ring stung the inside of her index finger as sharp, spear-tipped wings dug into her skin once again.

"Ow." She grasped the ring, and spun it again.

She felt the heat of his gaze upon her and turned her attention on him. He focused on her finger and the onyx ring there. The two did not speak, but Kathryn sensed his displeasure with her. Her quest to meet with the Vodoun, and Pedro's obvious angst over the ring, did not bode well. The crew's superstition was playing into this notion, as well.

Kathryn looked away. "Stop staring, Pedro. If you have something to say, out with it."

"Da's nothin' more to say."

She let it go. Pedro's natural aversion to her plan could only unsettle her further—something to consider. The idea of speaking with an island dark-arts priest was not an occasion she relished, anyway. Still, doing so was her only chance to discover Morrigan's weakness, if there was one—and she had to do it before the goddess found the *Revenge* and destroyed the crew. Kathryn felt sweat beading over the surface of her skin. Her clammy hands had not come from rowing the skiff.

To pass the time, her thoughts turned to dark magic and what she might find on the island. Suddenly, her thoughts were interrupted by the long drag of the hull against sand. She blinked a few times and focused on the crystal blue of the Caribbean ocean lapping at a narrow strip of almond-colored sand.

Tiny fish darted around her ankles as she stepped from the boat. Kathryn's feet sank in the cool water and into the soft sand beneath. She gathered her skirts, moved swiftly through the shallow water, and joined the men busy at anchor with the longboat. Two other skiffs were pulling onto shore just off to her right. She watched the pirates as they disembarked, then moved through the same routine task of tying off the skiffs for anchor.

Seth caught her attention and nodded at her briefly. He kept his hands busy, fastening the lines from his boat to a cluster of logs that jutted at an odd angle from a mass of dense ferns. Kathryn had little time left on the island, so she would have to move fast. The crew had a signal—two lanterns hung side by side—a warning that all skiffs should return at once to the *Revenge*.

She glanced back at the ship. A single lantern twinkled dimly in the twilight of the evening, the signal to all beached crewmen that the *Revenge* would stay at anchor, and the pirates could stay ashore. Her thoughts drifted momentarily to the captain.

"Why he didn't elect to go onshore this trip is beyond me." She voiced her thoughts to no one in particular.

"He felt it best, miss." The response came from Moody, who sniffed and rubbed a sleeve against his nose as he passed by.

Moody spoke the truth. Following a gut reaction, Captain Phillips had decided to remain on board and stay at the ready should they need to weigh anchor and take to the sea in haste. Kathryn felt a twinge of longing for the safety of the ship and the captain's presence, but dismissed it almost instantly as her focus turned back to the dense undergrowth with its pink blossoms and thick brush. Somewhere, hidden within this tropical beauty, nested a Vodoun priest who held the secret to Morrigan's downfall. Such evil encased within breath-taking resplendency was almost too difficult to comprehend, but comprehend it, she must.

"Our very lives depend upon it." Her comment was meant more for herself than anyone else.

She studied the pirates. A few had already made their way inland. Slow steps trudged through the undergrowth as the men hacked at tropical foliage with cutlasses.

The other skiffs had just reached the shoreline, and the men were eager to join their crewmates on land. She scanned each boat with hope she'd find a glimpse of Pedro. He knew the dark secrets this island held and would be useful about now.

"Pay-drow," she called out as she searched each man's face who passed by her.

"Thar," the familiar voice of the ship's gunner grunted as he pointed to the shadows in a cluster of trees to her right.

"Thank you, Mister Sparks," she responded, and made her way to where Pedro leaned against the long, curved trunk of a palm tree.

The dark-skinned pirate nearly disappeared into the sunset's shadows cast from the tree—a perfect chameleon—difficult to see even when one looked straight at him. This was one of his greatest assets, and he used it well.

Difficult to see, that is, unless you're a Celtic healer with a keen eye and clear purpose. She smiled at the thought. "Pedro." Kathryn walked up to the edge of the underbrush. "Which way to the Vodoun?"

Someone moved, and Kathryn's attention instantly shifted to him. The pirate cut long, precise chunks of pulpy fruit with a machete. He lifted it to his mouth with the edge of the blade as he watched Kathryn approach. He said nothing but stared at her, and the whites of his eyes glistened in the amber glow of sundown. She felt him examining her as he chewed with slow deliberation. He scanned the length of her body before returning to her face. She shifted her weight and planted both hands on her hips.

"We had an agreement, Mister Pedro."

He sliced off another hunk of fruit and bit into it without blinking. She had stuffed a gold doubloon into the leather belt strapped around her waist. She tossed the coin to the waiting pirate. A large hand swept in a perfect arc to catch the coin with the agility of a panther. Almost imperceptibly, he tucked the gold piece into the fold of his sash, then tossed the hacked fruit into the sand and began to walk.

"Da dark mon be through dis way."

He once again disappeared into the shadows as he strode past Kathryn. She scrambled to catch up to him and noted the fierce manner with which he hacked at the brush as they made their way through. How many souls had met their doom from that same savage strike with the machete? Would this be her fate as she wandered the unknown island? He was a fierce protector…or so she hoped.

"How much farther, Pedro? I didn't bring anything…I don't have a torch."

Night had stealthily crept up on them and Kathryn had forgotten the lantern. Pedro said nothing, but continued to hack at the underbrush.

She began to wonder if Pedro really intended to take her to the Vodoun. Again and again, she dismissed fearful thoughts of being hacked to pieces by her burly guide as swiftly and mercilessly as he hacked at the dense underbrush. *Your remains would be forgotten by the crew, and your absence would go unnoticed.* She shivered at the dark thoughts and stepped over a dense mound to put an arm's length of distance herself and the pirate.

Crickets chirped, and the low croak of unseen beasts rolled softly through the night air, pierced occasionally by the screech of a night bird that had been disturbed by things unseen. She jumped as something brushed across her foot. A momentary thought to give up the entire venture crossed her mind. Most certainly, the signal to return to the ship had already been given, and her overwhelming desire to return to the safety of the shoreline was warranted.

Suddenly, the dark pirate stopped. He tucked his machete against his left thigh and pulled aside a large, stalky plant to reveal a sparse clearing. Angry water gurgled from a brisk stream that ran along one side.

"Da it be," Pedro murmured.

His hushed voice dropped to silence as if he feared disturbing whatever dwelled out there. Kathryn scanned the seemingly innocent glade. All was still, devoid of movement or sound—an eerie silence like the gaping jaws of a predator, breathless. Abruptly, her focus concentrated on the far end of the clearing. A thatched shack stood upright, dark and ominous. The sight of it brought to mind memories of the Obeah's den she had visited almost a year ago on Tobago. Shivering uncontrollably, she swallowed hard and stepped around Pedro. Cautiously, Kathryn moved out into the clearing.

"Are you coming, as well?" she whispered.

Pedro said nothing and stayed put, tucked again in the shadows. Slowly, he shook his head, his eyes betraying the fear behind them.

"Nay, lady. Dis be as far as I go."

Kathryn shot him a look. The pirate only leaned farther back into the shadows.

"You be certain o' dis? I take you back now." His last offer.

She answered him with silence, and then stepped onto the path. Ahead, a black hut waited for her.

Twenty-One

A FRENZY OF FLIES DRONED, clustered around a bulky shadow as she passed it. Kathryn could not see what made the shadow, but she could tell it did not belong to the overgrowth. Its silhouette glinted moist and meaty in the moonlight as it swayed in a non-existent breeze beneath a knotty tree. Her eyes drifted briefly to the object before focusing on the black outline of a decayed shanty ahead.

The hollow chink of tiny bones strung from another tree caught her attention, and she instinctively lowered her hand to the hilt of the cutlass tucked at her hip. Beneath her feet, she could feel mounds and unfilled holes dug into the sandy earth. From beneath the pockmarked soil, strange jars and carved wooden dolls protruded. She had crossed an apparent graveyard of buried talismans and deceased phylactery. She stepped delicately around one of these to avoid the ashen skull of some unfortunate animal propped atop a carved totem. The ground beneath her feet shifted color as sand blended into a ruddy powder used to trace scrolls and lines—symbols of some sort. Kathryn forced her concentration away from the disturbing emblems and back to the hut. She looked up just in time to avoid running headlong into a clustered group of severed chicken feet tied with vines and hung from the roof of an unbalanced veranda. A dozen or more clawed talons dangled, their bottoms stained red where a frenzy of flies danced. She ducked her head and stepped aside.

"*Make byen kote ou steop,*" a deep voice growled from the darkness ahead.

Kathryn stopped short. Her heart was pounding in her ears, and she felt the breath catch in her throat. Her clammy palms gripped the silver hilt of her cutlass tighter. She steadied herself and called out to the voice.

"I speak the language of the Celtic witches and of the privateers in these waters."

A rustle of footsteps sounded only paces from where she stood. Odd spices and raw decay scented the breeze that blew past her. She wanted to run, but willed herself to stay.

"Be warned o' where ye be steppin'," the voice repeated, its accent thick with French and something else that reminded her of Pedro.

"I seek the counsel of the Vodoun priest."

Again, a faint rustle sounded, but only inches from her this time. Its swift movement unsettled the air. The foul scent grew stronger, much closer, and caused her to gag. She turned her head toward the sound, but saw nothing.

"Why you wan da Vodoun?" The voice echoed behind her now.

She spun around, but again, saw nothing except for the dark clearing behind her. Bile rose in her throat, and she swallowed it back, then addressed the unseen priest.

"I need to speak with the priest about the death goddess, Morrigan. I seek the Vodoun's assistance."

She heard movement behind her again. Something alive crept around within the hut. Turning slowly, she stared into the darkness just beyond the row of dangling clawed feet. The talons swung slowly on one side, obviously brushed into movement. As she inched forward, an obscure figure took shape. Faded beads were draped over sinewy dark skin. Brightly colored ribbon had been woven into knots throughout the matted hair that hung in slithering ropes as the priest stepped out of the shadows. He stood naked from his waist up, painted chalky white to give him the appearance of a demon. Deep scarlet encircled his eye sockets.

Shriveled lengths of leather swayed from a cable tied about his neck as he moved. When he stepped further into the moonlight, Kathryn could see they were tongues, nearly a dozen or more, pierced through and worn as tokens. She forced back the terror that threatened to overtake her. Tied around his waist, dangling nearly to his knees, a skirt made entirely of grass and leaves hung loosely. Feathers drooped from one side. His legs and feet, also painted, were barely visible.

Kathryn inhaled as the apparition moved closer. The devil eyes bored into her only a breath away from her face. She sucked in her breath—again, the stench of burned spice and dried blood assaulted her.

"It canno be done. Morrigan be da evil who take da souls of mon when dey die. She take your soul, too."

"I am the daughter of Celtic witches. I carry great power with me." Her voice failed her.

The painted Vodoun circled her, a predator eyeing its next kill. His icy stare cut deep into her skin, and she began to shiver. She averted her eyes, but was faced with the priest's hollow-eyed glare as he stepped in front of her.

"Wha powers belong to a wee thing as ye be?" He lifted a loose lock of her hair with the end of a long totem. "Ye have nothin' to match dat devil."

Kathryn grasped the Seren about her neck and lifted it with one hand, the other still clutching the cutlass. "I have this."

The Vodoun's dark eyes widened, and he jumped backward, maniacal laughter spitting from his black mouth.

"The Sigel of Defense!" He spun around and pounded the ground with his totem. "Aaahh, yessss. Tha' be very powerful, indeed." He paused, then pointed a bony finger at her. "But no' powerful enough!"

"I have me magic, born within my very soul and handed down from generations of the Celtic white priestesses."

Laughter peeled from his deranged mouth. "Ohhh-ho. *No!* Da be no white magic! No white witch to match da black Obeah magic o' da Morrigan. No mortal mon, excep' da..." His voice trailed away, and he dropped the totem.

In one swift move, a skeletal hand snatched hers from the cutlass. Startled, she dropped her grip on the Seren and reached to free herself from his grasp. With serpent-like agility, he clutched her by the wrists and turned both hands simultaneously, palms facing up. The priest bent forward to read the folds of her skin. She jerked, and he released one hand but held fast to the other, then slowly extended a bony finger to the center of her palm.

A painful burning sensation trailed along the path he traced with a razor-sharp, black fingernail along her palm. An odor of burnt flesh seared her nostrils. She dared not withdraw her hand, nor let on that it burned, and swallowed hard to control the reflex. But, through it all, her eyes never left the Vodoun priest.

"Tell me now, an' speak true...be there tha blind light o' tha skies from these hands?"

Kathryn hesitated, unable to understand him. *What fire comes from the sky?*

"I don't know what you mean."

He grasped her free hand once again and shook them both as if to jar some awareness from her. "Tha fire o' tha skies be in these hands. Whan did ye last use it, ahh?"

What is this demon speaking of? What does he mean "fire o' tha skies?" She searched her memory frantically to recall when her hands had met fire from the sky. *A light from the sky. Firelight from the sky? Lightning! Could that be what he means?* She looked into his crimson eyes, and then back to her hands.

"Lightning? Is that what you mean? Lightning from the sky?"

The demon nodded.

"There was one time," she admitted hesitantly. Kathryn watched the Vodoun. "How do you know this?"

The painted man lifted his hands to the stars and muttered something she could not understand. "Come...come...come," he insisted, grasping hold of her arm. He tugged and his nails dug into her skin, but she refused to flinch. Dragging her to the shack's doorway, she tried to resist, but couldn't. His voice cackled, and her fear mounted. "Come, I show..."

The interior danced in shadows, illuminated by clusters of candles of various sizes, each a different color. Earthen jars and glass vials were scattered over makeshift niches that pockmarked dilapidated walls.

Set apart, near the back of the hovel, an altar had been carved out of petrified wood thousands of years old. Secretive and serene, as if waiting to be awakened, a vibrantly painted green jar was centered upon its ancient surface. Bizarre symbols were written below a lid sealed with black wax. The Vodoun watched her, eyeing his prize.

"Da Jumbie." He cackled madly. "Do not look upon da Jumbie, or he take yo soul."

Kathryn blinked several times before she shifted her focus to the priest, who was crouched beside a large wooden tureen. He motioned for her to join him. Cautiously, she took one step toward the basin, but stopped abruptly when she caught sight of the contents within. Tiny bones the size of human fingers bobbed up and down in a pool of blood. The Vodoun priest dipped a finger into the crimson pool and stirred its contents.

"It happened on the ship. The crew was under attack by an unseen beast—The Eve of the Silver Moon Omen." She shifted her weight uneasily.

The priest did not look up, but plucked a long black feather from a dusty corner and used its tip to churn the gore. She seemed incapable of looking away.

"It appeared to be a beast of the sea, but I knew better," she said as a distraction.

He looked at her, then stared at the vile contents bubbling up from the basin.

"The spell was cast and I called for the powers of heaven to protect us. It was then that it happened…I never planned it. My hands bore light to match the lightning of the skies."

The Vodoun said nothing.

Pungent smells and grotesque images filled her thoughts and caused her head to spin.

She dabbed at beads of sweat on her forehead and looked around the room for relief, or a momentary distraction. Nothing. Just then, she glanced down and stared at the marks on her palms. *What is the significance of lightning?* Indeed, she'd used it to bring Captain Phillips back to life, but anyone could have done that… only no one else did. She needed this devil's knowledge to enlighten her mind on her inherited *Gift*.

"Come…see yo destiny." His eyes widened with excitement.

Kathryn shook the cobwebs from her mind and leaned in to look. The image paralyzed her as raw terror spread through her veins. Her heart pounded erratically, and she felt the room spin as she fought to hold onto consciousness.

"This cannot be for me, priest," she whispered.

His maniacal laugh filled the tiny shack. "Dis be fate. Dis be what waits for da *Mellt Sosye*."

Twenty-Two

BLACK SPUME BUBBLED FROM A blood-red surface to form a peculiar dark shape that almost resembled the outlined head of a bird. Bones crossed a trailing line of white froth to align themselves in uniform hash marks that tilted slightly to one side. Kathryn recognized the symbol.

"*Ogham craobh*," she whispered under her breath.

The Vodoun nodded and cackled. He kept his keen focus on her. "Ye know dis symbol?" he asked, anticipating the answer.

Kathryn fought against the dizziness that suddenly overtook her. "I…yes, I know this symbol." She stared at the image that foamed within the basin. "It's the writing of the druids. I've been taught some of these symbols."

"An' its meanin'?" He tested her.

"It's the mark of the ancient Sidhe…the blackthorn." Her voice trailed away, and she held onto the basin to stay upright.

The Vodoun smiled. She looked at him with bleary eyes. What remained of his black teeth disappeared into a nearly toothless grin. Its effect terrified her.

"Dat be true. Da be more for ye. Look deeper."

Kathryn strained to keep her focus while her vision shifted into a different dimension as she looked back into the basin. The image rose from the surface and spread dark wings. Crimson eyes glared at her.

The sign of The Raven.

Kathryn gasped, and the dark priest let out another high-pitched gurgle. "Da Raven be da sign o' da Morrigan," he sneered.

"Then there is no hope, indeed." Feeling defeated, she tore her gaze from the images.

"No so true as dat. Da be da last mark ye cannot see but through da Mamba." He grinned and slapped his open palms against his bare chest.

"Where can I find this Mamba?" she asked tentatively, fearful it might be a trap.

The Vodoun priest raised his bony finger and pointed to himself. "I be *vodounsaint*—da Mamba. I can give yo da third mark. Da last symbol." He paused, and she knew he wanted something in return. "But it will cost yo more dan yo can give at dis time."

She felt his fiery gaze burning through to her soul.

"What is it you want, Mamba? I have gold, if that be what you seek." Kathryn was tired of the game he had been playing. Still, she remained afraid to cross the powerful priest whose companion was black magic.

He dropped his gaze to the Seren that hung about her neck and ran a black tongue across his lips.

Kathryn took hold of the alabaster stone protectively. "This belongs to none but me. Take it and you shall not be spared the curse that befalls all who do."

"I be knowin' da powers o' the Seren. I be knowin' da power of da symbols, yes.

Payment must be made or wit'draw from Mamba." His tone was venomous.

Kathryn scrambled to think of anything of value she could leave him. She had nothing more than the gold doubloons tucked away in her skirts. She needed something equally as valuable as the precious stone about her neck. She clenched her hands in desperation. The sharp bite of the onyx ring dug into her hand to remind her of its presence.

"This! I have this for you, priest." She held out her left hand to display the raven ring.

The Vodoun gazed at it hungrily. He knew its worth, as well.

Since Mariel had never elected to tell her about it, Kathryn gambled on the idea that the thing was not meant for her. Perhaps Mariel had witnessed this moment in a vision and knew of its value to the Vodoun priest. Who knew, really? She stretched her hand out in offering to him "Give dat to me an' it be payment. Fair contract." His voice dripped with longing for the object.

In a swift move, he snatched the ring from her finger, then traced the curve of the black stone with the same bony finger. Kathryn felt the sting of her palm and rubbed at it with her free hand.

"Ye have the ring. Now, what is the meanin' of the symbols?" Her courage suddenly returned with the demand. The Mamba mulled over the onyx token for a bit longer before he spoke.

"Look da." He spat into the basin. Brine, blood, and spittle spread into bittersweet rings that surrounded the ghastly shape and pallid pieces of bone. The priest stirred the mixture again. Bone and a black substance burbled along the surface, and a new symbol took shape. Suddenly, a hazy blue light flashed from the concoction. Kathryn felt both hands burn simultaneously. She glanced at her seared palms and saw the same hazy blue light. Quickly, she stared again into the basin and watched as the light faded into ash that settled over the center of the florid mixture.

The Celtic symbol for a lightning bolt formed out of the ash. Just as suddenly, the contents settled and became still. She looked again at her palms, and the blue light faded at the exact same time. Slowly, she raised her eyes to the Vodoun.

"Da *Mellt Sosye* holds da power to confine Morrigan." He clapped his hands over hers. "Da power be in here." He patted her left hand. "An' it be in here." He clapped her right hand. "An' here." He cautiously touched the Seren that hung peacefully about her neck.

"Am I this *Mellt Sosye*, the Skyfyre Witch ye speak of?"

Kathryn had heard of the legend before. There was no possibility that she was the legend. It just couldn't be!

Kathryn closed her eyes. The answer already lay within her soul. She just couldn't bear to hear it spoken aloud.

The priest turned the corners of his mouth into a thin smile and said nothing, then turned his back on her. He dropped the onyx ring into a tiny box that rested on top of a narrow shelf. The Vodoun then moved back into the shadows.

"Three symbols be given for yo. Two be da symbols for da Morrigan. Ye cannot mistake her power. It be da Raven that come to you, no?"

Kathryn whispered, "Aye, I saw it."

"Yessss," he hissed from the shadows somewhere to her right. His voice rattled through the darkness. "Da Raven come for yo, an' another. Do ye know who dis be?"

"Aye," Kathryn answered meekly. Not willing to divulge anything further, she chose to say no more.

"Yessss. Dis be da first symbol, an' ye be warned. Da bones speak da druid language o' another. Da power be strong in da Sidhe. Dis be last. Yo must find a symbol of yo own—made from da same as da druid's mark."

The Raven was the symbol of Morrigan—of that, she was certain. But the oracles had also spelled out the name of a sacred tree in the ancient Ogham script—the druid's mark."

"Blackthorn? But where do I find a blackthorn tree on this island? They grow in the countryside throughout Britain. There is no possible way to find Blackthorn! This cannot be correct."

"Da bones do not lie."

"But I've seen none in these years at sea. I don't know where to find it."

The Vodoun priest stepped forward and stabbed a long wooden staff into the ground. The black grain was nearly invisible in the shadows. She could just make it out, gnarled and twisted along its length. The staff possessed great power. She could instantly feel it. He extended the shaft to her, an offering that she did not take at first.

Her eyes searched the object, and then darted back at the Vodoun. As if reading her thoughts, the priest began his explanation slowly.

"Dis be da Straif. It come from Blackthorn roots, an ancient tree wit' great power. Dis ye know. Da Straif can be used by da Morrigan, if she takes it. Dis ye know not."

"I don't understand," Kathryn replied.

"Ye be bound to da Morrigan. Da power o' da Blackthorn can be used for good o' evil. It can be used by da *Mellt Sosye*." He paused to eye her. "...o' da Morrigan. Both da same. Both not da same." A fiendish grin twisted his diabolical features. "Da choice belong to Mamba."

The Vodoun priest raised the staff and pounded it back into the sandy ground again.

"We have a bargain," Kathryn reminded him. Her eyes narrowed as she spoke. "You've taken the ring and we have an accord."

"Yessss, dat be true." He flashed a sinister grin. "Da Mamba must choose."

"Do not go back on your promise…" She paused, looking for the right words. "Do not dishonor a promise made to the *Mellt Sosye*!"

The Vodoun startled and his eyes flickered. The baleful grin returned, exposing his rotted teeth again. "Da Straif be passed from Mamba to yo."

"A good choice, methinks." Kathryn dropped her hands to her hips.

"But no' before da Mamba seal its power into da *Mellt Sosye*."

As he spoke, he reached for a black candle that sputtered atop the same narrow shelf as the box containing the ring. Carefully, he tipped it to one side, and the flame danced. Black wax oozed through the crevices of the intricately carved wood and dripped the length of the staff and into the sable grain.

"*Fè nwa sou pouvwa limyè a resptè a.*"

Strange intonations reverberated in time to the priest's chant. The syllables sounded foreign and frightening. His body twisted as he willed his gyrating limbs to pass over the totem. An eerie hum permeated the hut as if hundreds of forgotten spirits suddenly cried out in one voice. Candlelight danced in colors to the rhythm of his voice, and Kathryn felt her consciousness swimming once again.

"*Mellt Sosye se Bondye ki genyen nan Bondye a! Fòs yo rezurjan nan dimanch maten byen bonè nan maten, incorporée.*"

Suddenly, he stopped and stood still. All sound and color faded to stillness. Kathryn blinked to clear her head, and by that time, she realized the priest had finished his incantation and faced her. He offered the black staff to Kathryn.

In silence, she accepted the Straif, grasping the powerful totem with both hands for the first time.

"Yesssss."

She looked deep into his hollow eyes, her mind cleared, and her courage returned.

"You spoke of a third symbol." She caressed the blackthorn staff, pulling the Straif closer. "What symbol?"

The Vodoun crouched before the basin, once again poised over the bloody concoction. "Da symbol be wit' yo hands. It be here." He pointed to the basin as he spoke. "Da symbol be for da *Mellt Sosye*."

Kathryn looked briefly into the basin and caught a glimpse of the fading symbol cast from the floating ash. She looked down at her hands—no evidence of the blue light remained.

Suddenly, everything made sense.

"The power within me—the power of the *Mellt Sosye* is bound to Morrigan's."

"Yessss."

"Though not evil like the dark goddess, this power... my power...is equal to hers."

"Yessss. Yo eyes be opened."

Kathryn nodded. "I have the power of the skies within these hands. The Skyfyre Witch."

The Vodoun began to hop from one foot to the other, nodding and laughing hysterically.

"That I can withstand a lightning bolt cast from the skies to travel the length of a mast and run through my body is part of this power. No accident, as I see it."

"Yessss. Yo see, indeed. Da *Mellt Sosye* sees."

She glanced at the Straif and her powerful hands, which held it. Indeed, to withstand a lightning strike was miraculous enough. But, to have a bolt pass through her body and into the man she loved, bringing him back to life, was due in part to the *Gift*…but, mostly it was due to the power of the *Mellt Sosye*.

Kathryn now understood what the symbols meant. The priest's mark, singed into her skin, would remind her to never to forget her own remarkable *Gift*.

She stared tearfully at the priest. Then, without another word, the powerful *Mellt Sosye* turned from him and departed the *Vodounsaint's* hut, leaving the darkness behind her.

Twenty-Three

"YE CARRY DA MAMBA STICK!" Pedro stammered.

"Aye! And why were you not here waitin' for me, then, Pedro?" Kathryn exploded.

She thrust the Straif deep into the pristine sand for him to stare at. Then, suddenly, swept it back up again and strode toward the beach. Pedro trotted just to keep up with her.

"Where did ye get dat thing?" Pedro asked, incredulous at the sight of Kathryn in possession of the powerful totem.

She stopped mid-stride and turned on him. "You hide away like a young pup with his tail tucked tight between his legs. Then, you abandon me and run off to be with your mates, not mindin' what might have happened to me. Remember, I am a fair friend of the captain, too! What would you be sayin' to him then, eh, Pedro?"

Pedro stopped just in time to avoid a collision. He stood sheepishly as she berated him. "But dat's de Straif. No one touches it…'specially not a woman."

"Arrggh!" she growled, and once again stomped through the sand toward the longboats. Pedro resumed trailing behind the outraged Kathryn. It seemed his curiosity had overcome his fear of her Celtic temper.

"Da Vodoun mon give you da Mamba stick? He give it to you willingly?"

"The Mamba gave it to me in exchange for a ring. We had a fair exchange, an established accord."

He looked at the staff with large, dark eyes, the whites nearly the size of a full silver reale.

"He give it to ye? You made a deal wit' da Mamba?"

"Aye! Which is far more than you could muster… pirate!"

Kathryn marched directly into the water to the nearest skiff. Two other crewmen had made ready to cast off, and the boat was loaded with several men already.

"Make room, ye filthy cutthroats. I'm boardin' as well!" she barked, and the crew made way.

She stepped into the middle of the longboat, took her place on one of the cross-boards, and planted the base of the totem squarely in the center of the boat.

"Now take me to the ship!"

The two men cast off, then jumped aboard when the water deepened. She could see other crewmen scrambling to board the other skiffs. Pedro was running along the sand to one of the boats still tied off. Three men approached at the same time and worked feverishly to untie and cast off. There was anxiety about them, which Kathryn noticed for the first time. Something was amiss. The *Revenge*! She looked up at the great ship anchored not more than a furlong ahead and caught sight of the signal lanterns.

Bright light flickered from two pairs of lanterns set side-by-side. Two were swinging forward, while the other pair swung aft.

"What does it mean? The lanterns?"

"Th' signal's given. We've been summoned back, or be left behind. None o' us knows why." Tate glanced at the ship as he spoke and pulled on his oar.

Kathryn felt her gut clenching as she surveyed the ship.

"Pull, men! We've not much time left," Davis said, urging them to a more expeditious heave against the current.

Despite their skill with the oars, the ship still loomed ahead, several minutes away. In desperation, she scanned their surroundings for any signs of trouble, but there was none. The water stayed calm and skies clear. *At least the moon is at peace*, she thought to herself. *No omens tonight*. Kathryn sighed in relief. Still, she knew a clear night such as this would leave the *Revenge* exposed as a sitting target. Cutthroats and privateers occupied the waters. Escape would be nearly impossible, and she dared not think on what would happen should any ships in the King's Navy be nearby.

"What do the lanterns signal? Do any of you know?"

Cade, swayed slightly with each pull of the oars and Kathryn glared at him. "You're drunk, sir. Unfit to row, most likely."

"Aye, tha's true. But I still know wha' th' signal's for an' ye don'."

"Well then, share it with me, if you can spit the words out."

Cade grinned. "It be th' signal we needs to get back aboard th' ship." He raised a half-empty green bottle to his mouth.

"I am aware of that, ye drunkin' dog! I mean to find out from anyone here still possessed of his wits what calls us back with such haste."

A stout man named Simons sat directly in front of her. He pulled again on the well-worn scull, and the skiff moved closer to the *Revenge*. He lifted his head and looked at her. "No one knows for certain, lass. It be customary to light th' dual lanterns when men be ashore an' danger be o' th' waters."

"What kind of dangers, Mister Simons?"

"Could be anythin', but mostly, it be other ships."

Kathryn had no response and Simons pulled again on his oar. She looked up at the *Revenge* and noticed a few of the crewmen already boarding.

"Hopefully, we won't be the last to reach the *Revenge*."

"Aye. Once th' crew's on board, we'll put out to deep sea."

"Surely, they'll wait for us."

Simons and Davis shook their heads. "Not likely."
Davis glanced behind him at the *Revenge*. "No one
waits for laggards. It's the edict."

"Edict?"

"Law...th' code...rule o' the sea."

"Aye, the code..." Kathryn wished she were on deck,
side-by-side with the men. She'd certainly take her
place at the ropes until the sails were raised and had
taken hold of the wind. She clutched the Straif a little
tighter, as if its power would assure her arrival.

She, and any of the crew who had not made it on
board in time, would be left vulnerable and subject to
marooning. It was part of the pirates' code, and while
she didn't relish the idea of it, she knew it was a wise
rule kept mainly for survival.

Although the men rowed with vigor, the mood
was tense. She looked up to the top of the mainmast
where Duncan perched in the crow's nest. She could see
from his profile that he was intently studying the water
just aft of the ship. She turned to look off in the same
direction but could see nothing beyond the lip of the cay.

"Pull, men. Wit' all yer might, pull! We've an
urgency to get back to th' *Revenge,* else fall prey to
whatever awaits us."

"Thar be sails...an'..." Davis mumbled and leaned
back against the bow with his head cocked to the
portside.

"What colors be flyin'?" A pirate seated opposite
shifted his weight anxiously.

Davis strained to get a better look and nearly fell overboard. "I cannot see 'er colors, swab. Pull wit' haste, mateys! It be our lives ye be pullin' fer!"

Cade called out earnestly.

Rhythmically, the men pulled again and again, each time with greater strength that sent the skiff through the dark waters and closer to the safety of their ship.

Kathryn's eyes darted back to the large merchantman and the men who were scrambling on the deck with the rigging. Details came into view as they drew closer.

"We haven't much time! They're preparin' to cast off." Kathryn searched the deck for signs of delay. There were none. Only the sense of déjà vu. For just a moment, she was taken back to the first time she set eyes on the *Revenge*—to that night when she sat in a skiff surrounded by pirates. She had been terrified then of her imminent arrival on board the ship, and now, terrified of her fate should she not. It seemed like such a long time ago, although maybe only a year had passed.

"They're raisin' sail. We're sure to be left, mates. Pull!"

She could hear the voices of the crew on deck. They were calling the orders to cast off. "Is there word from the Capt'n?" Too late, she realized the question was useless.

"Nay," a few said in unison.

Kathryn turned back to face the ship. Slowly, the great square sails climbed the main mast. As they heaved the heavy sails, the crew's "Ho!" echoed out. The black flag had been lowered, and Kathryn knew the order to stow the colors had been given for a reason.

"The colors of England!" Gow stood at the bow, barking out orders. "It be one o' th' English fleet!" He pointed to the cay.

The pirates seated with Kathryn shifted in their seats, and terror crossed each weathered face. Even those who had been content to sip ale had suddenly sobered, their bottles tossed over the side.

"We be dead men, we be," Cade stated, no sign of drink in him now.

"The *Revenge* still waits," Kathryn responded. "We'll make it if you row for your lives, for all of our lives, men!"

The oarsmen pulled harder against the current, increasing their time as the distance narrowed between the skiff and the ship. Somehow, she'd motivated them. If she could only do the same for herself.

"Ho!" Their calls matched the shouts of the crew on deck working the lines. With each pull, the skiff was propelled forward. "Ho!" A chorus of deep male voices sounded, and the skiff glided further. Kathryn swallowed hard as the longboat cleared the lip of the cay. A massive ship sat there, flying the blue and red colors of England. It appeared to be a warship from the King's Navy—certain death for any vessel that met with her cannons. The *Revenge* was no match for her, and Kathryn knew the order to make sail, and leave them behind, was only moments away.

She could see the other skiffs rowing with the same urgency. Another pull from the oars centered the skiff within a few lengths of the ship. Kathryn could see the men on deck clearly. Her crewmates in the longboat called out to lower the ropes for boarding. Long, thick rigging fell from the gunwale, spaced in staggered lines along the side of the ship. The two on the skiff's bow stood upright and lunged for a rope with the next thrust of the oars. With the skill of sailors long at sea, they tied up the fore and aft ends of the skiff, then grabbed hold of the ropes and nimbly climbed one hand over the other. Their feet coiled in and out of the hemp as they lifted themselves to the ship's waiting deck.

Kathryn had no time to wait for assistance, and no one would hesitate to leave her behind, so she had to make the climb herself. She gathered her skirts and looped the edges into the leather belt around her waist. Unable to climb with the Straif in hand, she rested the long totem inside the edge of the skiff and secured it beneath the rough planking. She prayed it would stay put as the men hoisted the skiff aboard and secured her. It was a risk she had to take, even knowing it could be lost overboard in the process.

Each man fended for himself, so she was not alarmed that no one showed her the least bit of interest as she made to climb. Grabbing hold of the loose end, she wound it around one wrist for support. The course hemp bit into her flesh. She then slipped her ankles through the lower part as she pulled with her hands and rose nearly a foot up the line. As the force of her weight tugged her seared palm and stretched her injured forearm, the sting of those who had injured her brought back painful memories. She winced and reached up again, in spite of the biting pain, and took hold of the line, then pulled herself a little higher.

Bit by bit, she inched her way up the thick rope, praying her strength wouldn't give out. She raised another hand and crawled a few more inches, pleading with her body to hold out a little longer until she reached the top.

She lifted her gaze to gauge the distance. Above, she caught sight of a figure that hovered, apparently waiting for her. The captain reached out and took hold of the rope.

Twenty-Four

BROAD HANDS LIFTED HER ONTO the scrubbed deck and Kathryn sighed in relief. She was back where she belonged.

"Thank you."

"Foolish pander!" Though his voice sounded gruff, when their eyes met, she could see him relaxing a bit. Captain Phillips' irritation stayed coolly controlled as he shifted his focus aft.

He knitted his brows together as he lifted a spyglass to one eye. Suddenly, the captain shouted an order to the men still clamoring to board. The last skiff had made it, and not a moment too soon. Captain Phillips cursed and turned his focus again to the large British ship in the distance.

"What manner of ship is it?" Kathryn asked, feeling uneasy herself.

"Man-o'-war, and she's flyin' the British colors." He sounded vexed. "We've no time to lose."

Kathryn squinted, staring at the ship's colors. The war vessel was well-fitted with cannon along the gunwale, details that could be seen clearly, even from a distance.

"She's tacked a course dead astern o' us, Capt'n," a voice hollered from above.

Duncan was lookout and pointed frantically from the crow's nest to the British ship.

"Weigh anchor! Make haste men, or we needs cut weigh upon the yielding tide!" Captain Phillips barked. The tension in his voice matched the anxiety of the crewmen that darted about the ship.

"Aye, aye," sounded in unison as the men scattered about the deck.

James Sparks moved swiftly between the cannons with orders to make ready the guns.

Grapeshot stuffed into rucksack bags and iron balls the size of melons were piled alongside each middle tyre porthole, with leather pouches of gunpowder looped across the cannon's cascabel. Sparks smiled as he assisted the men, who scrambled about their duties to prepare the ammunition with expert precision. His position as the ship's gunner held tremendous responsibility when faced with battle, an assignment he relished at moments like this.

"Secure th' rigging an' set th' men to arms, Mister Sparks," Archer's voice rang out.

"Ye 'eard th' quartermaster, ye bilge swabs! Man th' guns! Prepare for battle!"

Sparks shouted across the deck as sheer adrenaline pushed every movement he executed.

The ship's gunner was made for battle and was gifted with motivating men for a pirates' fray. "See there, Mister Archer. Th' men be ready for a right bloody skirmish!" Sparks shouted loud enough for his words to reach the pirates' ears. The men's pace picked up at this and Sparks chuckled loudly as he witnessed it, slapping the nearest comrade on the back as he did so.

"It's a good day when pirates get to fight."

"Aye! An' it's nighttime…they're likely to be sleeping or drinking an' never'll know what hit 'em!"

Kathryn's gut wrenched. She listened to the men relishing the impending battle. Suddenly, she sensed the quartermaster was near and turned to see from which direction he approached. Archer leaned heavily upon a long pole that looked to her like a broken oar now being used for a crutch. She guessed he was still recovering from his wounds.

Without thought, her hand dropped to the small of her back. It was safely in place. Her palm smugly patted the dirk tucked into the leather belt there. Archer scanned the decks to monitor the crew's progress, then called out their statuses. Perhaps he hadn't seen her yet.

"Anchors aweigh!" he hollered.

He scanned the deck until, suddenly, he caught sight of her. His yellowed eyes narrowed to slits and rested on Kathryn. Deliberately, he walked in her direction, while heaving the oar underneath his arm for support. A holler from one of the men stopped him short, but his gaze never left Kathryn.

"You best stay where you are, Mister Archer." She hoped the filthy blaggard could feel her seething contempt for him. She hissed another warning, knowing he could not hear her. "Do not move…else you'll meet my blade again, and there'll be no Capt'n or sailcloth to save you from your fate this time, you filthy, wretched dog!" She kept her voice low, certain he could at least sense her intent.

For a while, the two stared each other down with silent threats, then Archer was summoned. He hesitated only a moment before he turned to the portside sheets where he bellowed another order. He soon transferred his irritation to the men suspended there. Dragging the crutch that scraped with a pugnacious grate along the deck, he moved toward the bow and did not look back again at Kathryn. She cursed him under her breath, but kept one hand set upon the dirk hidden behind her back.

"Her headin's changed, Capt'n." Kathryn heard the deep, gravelly voice of the sailing master resonating over the pandemonium on deck.

Captain Phillips set his gaze to the vessel on the other side of the jetty. John Nutt stepped up beside him and offered a brass spyglass that the captain accepted without looking away. He peered for a moment, then handed it back to Nutt.

"She's on a direct course dead astern—three, maybe four leagues—and sure to be ridin' our wake by midday.

Tell Sparks to keep the monkeys manned. We cannot lose a minute's fight should we come to battle." His eyes remained steady on the vessel following them.

"Aye, Capt'n. Th' men be at th' guns already."

"That's well, then." The captain nodded, still focused on the sea. "Take the helm, Master Nutt. Tack a headin' windward as soon as we be well underway in deep waters."

"Take 'er into th' wind? Blimey, sir! She'll be slow on the draft, an' th' English dogs be bearin' down on us."

"Ay, that be true, Master Nutt, but the man-o'-war be slower against the wind. We cannot win this fight, so we flee. That is our best course this day."

"Can we outrun 'er, Capt'n?" Nutt's voice gave way to fear as he glanced at the warship trailing behind.

Captain Phillips stroked his chin as he considered Nutt's suggestion. "Ay, that we can, with a good current and God's blessin's. Prepare to cut 'n run." He took a few steps toward the bow. Nutt followed. "Upon steering clear of the jetty, Master Nutt…steady now."

"Aye, aye, Captain." Nutt looked relieved.

Captain Phillips nodded his dismissal, and the sailing master sprinted across the deck and took his place at the helm of the *Revenge*.

The sea intensified to blending greens and blues into a richer turquoise as the ship moved out of Gasparee Cove and into the vast Caribbean ocean. With the skill of a seasoned seaman, Nutt watched the currents, noting the shoals off the starboard bow.

He quickly calculated the distance before he could tack to deeper waters. The man-o'-war had closed in nearly a full league already, and while she wasn't a fast ship, her cannon would be within range of the *Revenge* without any option for retaliation from the smaller pirate ship. The captain's advice to "cut and run" was, indeed, good counsel. Nutt fully intended to follow it.

And so, it was with great disquietude that Nutt estimated another thirty minutes would have to pass before the *Revenge* could be taken with full sail to the open sea. The crew, on edge, stared at the warship trailing along behind them.

Those who did not man the cannon anticipated the worst. With cutlasses bared and pistols at the ready, their frayed nerves stayed on edge as the *Revenge* struggled to outrun the man-o'-war that chased her.

Kathryn's thoughts had shifted from her recent encounter with the Vodoun to a fixation on the ships. Her eyes darted from the pursuing vessel to the captain, then to Nutt, and back again to the British ship. The man-o'-war was gaining on them. She had closed the distance at least a fathom, perhaps more. Terrified, Kathryn watched as the warship let out her cannon.

"Capt'n! She carries more than thirty cannons on one side alone."

Nutt overheard Gow's observation and prepared to change course.

"They intend to take us broadside," the captain called out. "Make your tack now, Master Nutt."

"Beggin' yer pardon, Capt'n." John Nutt stumbled for 0the proper words. "We'll surely meet the shoals just offshore an' we'll meet our Maker this day for certain."

"I'm ready to meet my Maker, Master Nutt! Should ye be disposed, and not able to face God, be it of your own accord! It's a coward who cannot face his own death. Indeed, I fear neither God nor the devil himself!"

The captain's eyes blazed. Faces lifted pensively to stare at the captain and Nutt. Tension increased in anticipation of what might happen if one of the men should cross their angry captain's orders.

"Aye, aye, Capt'n." He shouted to the waiting men, "Bring 'er about, hard tack to th' portside, ho!"

The *Revenge* heaved as she nosed to deeper waters. Just then, a large explosion erupted astern on the port side. There was a menacing glow from the warship's cannon in the distance.

"They're firin' on us! To battle stations!" Gow bellowed.

Sparks darted across the deck to the port side gunwales and leaned over the rails to peer at the possible damage. Spray dissipated where the cannon ball had disappeared. Nutt took advantage of the distraction and stayed behind the wheel while Captain Phillips stepped forward to face the attackers.

"Prepare to return fire!" Sparks shouted.

From the quarterdeck, Captain Phillips' voice carried above them all. "Belay the call to fire. Hold arms!"

All eyes shifted to the captain, who stood alongside John Nutt at the helm. One hand gripped the riggings, giving him the majestic presence Kathryn remembered from the first time she'd laid eyes upon him.

"Steady as she goes, Master Nutt!" Captain Phillips shouted loud enough for all aboard to hear.

"Aye," followed in response.

Another blast drenched the quarterdeck with sea spray. The crew responded by moving to battle stations. Many held their cutlasses and cursed the man-o'-war. Kathryn felt the hair on the back of her neck rise as she grabbed the hilt of her cutlass and drew the blade.

"Steady, men!" Gow shouted and eyed the captain with uncertainty, waiting for approval. "Steady…"

There was no response from Captain Phillips, who kept his focus on the water. Nutt turned the wheel again, and the *Revenge* lurched on a direct course into the open sea. The warship had suddenly realized the *Revenge* was widening the distance between them and fired several cannons simultaneously upon the smaller merchantman. Apparently, the English captain knew the pirates would escape in the vast waters ahead.

As the cannon shot fell short of the *Revenge*, the port side was bathed in salt water. The crew emerged undaunted from beneath the spray and cursed louder. Water glistened off the pirates' broad backs as cutlasses dripped to match the hair that dangled from their faces. Just to look at them gave the impression of menacing, dangerous cutthroats—true pirates.

Below their feet, the hull shuddered as the water beneath the ship was instantly peppered with cannon shot. The *Revenge* stayed intact and moved forward into the wind. Her sails luffed momentarily, giving the warship an advantage, gaining another fathom on the pirates.

"Steady, Master Nutt," Captain Phillips called out again.

The crew watched as the man-o'-war gained speed while the *Revenge* slowed against the wind.

"Capt'n, she's gainin' on us! Another blast from 'er cannons an' we all be sent to th' depths!" Gow stepped up to the helm and urged the captain to return fire.

"Ay, Mister Gow, that be true," Captain Phillips replied through clenched teeth.

Archer limped forward. Unease crossed his face. He was dripping from head to toe as he leaned on his crutch and eyed the captain with blatant disapproval. The captain refused to look at the terrified crew and kept his focus upon the sea.

"Stay the course Master Nutt," Captain Phillips repeated the order.

Suddenly, the man-o'-war tacked windward after the *Revenge*. As if on cue, her sails luffed and dropped, the large ship stalling. The British vessel bobbed, almost motionless, as her crew worked at bringing the sails to life again. Captain Phillips bellowed with laughter.

"That be me girl. She proved faithful once again! Our one true love, mateys—the *Revenge*!" He blew a kiss to the sails, patted the rails, then called out new orders to his men. "Hoist the colors!"

A cheer rose from the deck as the *Revenge* suddenly lifted on the current and bounded into strong wind. Kathryn felt a sharp pang of jealousy coursing through her heart as she watched the captain rallying over the ship. *Indeed, his one true love is this vessel, and your place is behind her.* A bitter thought. Kathryn swallowed it back.

Catcalls and taunts were hurled at the man-o'-war from the deck of the *Revenge* as the British warship faded to a miniature in their wake. All the while, John Phillips' black flag grinned down in mocking defiance as it climbed the mainmast.

Suddenly, Captain Phillips shifted his stance to face Archer and Gow directly. "Don't be questioning me orders again, savvy?"

Both men stammered, "Aye" just prior to being dismissed. They turned away, shame-faced, avoiding eye contact with their crewmates. None aboard the pirate ship stood tall after even the mildest of criticisms by a commanding officer—the quartermaster and bosun included.

Afterward, Captain Phillips slapped Nutt on the back. "Fine work on the wheel, Master Nutt." A rowdy laugh followed from the helm, and the pirates cheered as the ominous black flag reached the top of the stately mainmast. "Fine work, indeed!"

Twenty-Five

"Splice the main brace!"

The captain motioned for Seth to fetch spirits from the rum stores. Two other crewmen joined him as he scurried below deck while cheering, "Aye, *aye*! Capt'n!"

"Break out th' hogshead an' don't spare th' rum!" Archer repeated the order from somewhere mid-ship.

Beaten by the elements, the man-o'-war fell back and faded into the distance. It soon took on the appearance of a tiny toy ship that bobbed on the surface of the vast ocean before it disappeared into the vacant horizon altogether. As the *Revenge* made her way further into deep Caribbean waters, the crew made merry.

The cannon had been stowed, and the *Revenge* changed course, following a different heading and sailing north into a favorable wind. Pirate's laughter and sea shanties continued, growing wilder as the hours passed. Wind filled the sails as the breeze carried the pirates' rowdy melodies skyward.

Kathryn had returned her cutlass to its home against her hip and was standing where Seth and the other men had been not long ago. Three pirates flanked her on either side, firing pistols in the air at random.

"Perhaps it's time ye joined th' crew, Miss Kathryn." Wynn stared at the sea, though his comment was meant for her.

"Perhaps."

"Do ye have any idea what the cost o' battle be for some?"

Kathryn could feel her irritation rising. Did Wynn actually intend to talk with her about such a distasteful topic now? "What an odd question, Mister Wynn."

"Aye! Many a bloke pay heavily fer th' peg an' hook they wear." He smiled and glanced at her askance. "Do ye know what be the cost?"

"No, Mister Wynn, I do not. What is the cost of a hook or peg, then?"

"An arm an' a leg!" Wynn threw back his head and let out a roar at his own joke.

Kathryn tried to swallow back the chuckle that rose, but it was to no avail. She lifted her chin and laughed aloud with him. After a moment's hysterics, Wynn slapped her back and nodded toward the men. "Now, go join th' men, lass."

She glanced at the crew, smiling. Their voices had given way to a new shanty. The melody sounded familiar.

"Thank you, Mister Wynn. I believe I will."

Turning from him, she walked to a small cluster and joined their discordant song.

What shall we do with a drunken sailor?
What shall we do with a drunken sailor?
What shall we do with a drunken sailor?
Ear-la in the morning?

Pistols fired each time they sang "drunken." The pirates stomped their feet in time to the accordion being played vigorously by Pock-Eyed Pete, who danced a muddled jig as his hands fanned the instrument in and out.

Way-hay up she rises,
Way-hay up she rises,
Way-hay up she rises,
Ear-la in the morning.

Seth surfaced for the third time, brandishing three moss green bottles in each hand. The other two pirates did the same, carrying a large hogshead cask that they set down near the main mast. One of the bottles began passage from man to man, each taking a swig before transferring it to the next outstretched hand. Almost immediately, the crooning grew louder—bawdy songs from merry pirates.

"Come, Madame Kathryn." Seth's voice sounded above the fracas.

Kathryn turned on her heel to keep time with the melody just as Seth's strong hand grasped hold of her arm and dragged her to center deck. He pivoted gingerly and swung her in circles as he kicked his heels in time with the music. She threw her head back with throaty laughter and lifted her skirts to dance a Celtic Hornpipe. Her heels bounced as she moved her feet to match Seth's capers. They spun and turned under each other's arms, and the music grew louder. A large circle soon formed around the pair, several other crewmen joining them in dance.

Suddenly, the grip on her arm altered. Seth's strength had been replaced by a mature, rugged intensity. She looked to its source and found crystal eyes, the color of Caribbean Sea glass, gazing at her. A broad smile spread across John Phillips' face. He pulled her around him with graceful skill that became a polished danseuse.

"May I have the honors, m'lady?" His voice sounded husky as he pulled her toward him.

Kathryn met his gaze and smiled fondly, then coquettishly nodded. "Aye, sir, that ye may."

He spun her away, and she curtsied before he turned her under his arm. Their voices rose to meet the others. Captain Phillips let loose a full-bodied laugh that seemed to come from the depths of his soul. Kathryn joined in, skipping in a counter turn as she swished her skirt.

Well, a hundred years on the eastern shore
A hundred years ago,
Well, I thought I heard the first mate cry
That bleeding top main sheeve is dry.

Two more pirates had stepped forward to join the fray. One carried a drum-like bodhran that he pounded upon wildly, keeping time with the accordion. The other brandished a J-shaped buzzie that, true to its name, whistled and buzzed as the tubby man puffed on one end. The *Revenge* rollicked with music, and the pirates continued with their gaiety for hours.

Kathryn danced with the captain throughout the evening. Only when the men had taken their fill of rum, and dosed in blissful inebriation, did John Phillips pull her aside. With slow steps, he escorted her along the starboard rails to the quarterdeck, just above his cabin.

"Did ye find what ye were lookin' for, lass?" he asked and pulled her into him with one arm encircling her waist. Kathryn allowed his advance but did not meet his gaze.

"Aye, Capt'n, that I did." She shifted uneasily, unwilling to disclose her meeting with the Vodoun, and possibly tarnish a perfect evening.

"Go on."

She leaned against the taffrail with both elbows and gazed out at the sea. "I…I think it's a conversation for another day, Capt'n."

"I think ye'd best tell me what ye've been up to."

She sighed. If he wanted details, that's what he'd get. "I had an encounter with a Vodoun priest."

"You did what!"

Startled, he spun her around to face him. "Don't you know you could be cursed and bringin' it aboard me ship! Theirs be the black arts, Kathryn, and I will not be havin' ye put yerself or me crew in danger over it! Savvy?"

Kathryn stepped back and leveled a dark look at him. Her Celtic blood grew hot as indignation rose to her already flushed cheeks.

"Is *that* what you're concerned with? Your precious ship and crew?"

"It's my duty, an' you've possibly put us all in danger."

"You hardly know what you accuse me of, sir. A strong commander as yourself, still innocent in his assumptions!"

"Educate me, then, lass."

She looked into his eyes. "There's more at stake than you realize in this, and the Vodoun priest holds the key to the answers."

Captain Phillips cocked his head and studied her. "What is to be questioned, lass? The matter be plain enough to me! I will not bring black magic aboard my ship."

"How dare you presume to tell me my business and accuse me of bringing black magic to *my* ship and *my* crew! I am part of this." She waved her hands toward the deck. "There is, indeed, a dark secret, and many questions lie unanswered."

"Again, pray, educate me…an' lose the temper, else I may find mine. You're still under obligation to the capt'n o' this ship, Kathryn."

She took a deep breath. "All right, then. You ask me what they be. Let me ask you this…are you certain you want to know the answer, Capt'n?" She paused to allow him to respond, but he only stared at her.

Captain John Phillips had never been so reproved by a crewman before. Kathryn knew it was dangerous to show such insolence to a captain while at sea, but decided to take advantage of the moment...and his astonished state.

"There's great responsibility with knowledge such as this, knowledge that could affect your ship and crew. That includes me, of course." She eyed him as she spoke.

"If it involves me ship and me crew, then I best be let in on your little secret."

Kathryn swallowed back a biting comment and nodded instead. "Indeed, it involves the *Revenge*. Though, it's for you, John Phillips, that the Vodoun gave his warning."

This caught his attention. She watched the edge of his mouth flinch slightly, though his gaze never wavered. "Go on." He fought to keep his composure as one hand absently sought the hilt that lay next to his side.

"The priest spoke of dark magic and the power to conquer it. He marked my hand."

Slowly, she offered him her scarred palm. The captain merely glanced at it, then turned his focus back to her. His silence was her signal to go on.

"He told me of the Raven." She paused to watch for any sign of recognition of the symbolism, but again, there was none. "The Raven is the symbol for the Morrigan."

"Ay, go on, lass." Captain Phillips' mood darkened as she spoke.

"The Vodoun priest gave me a warnin'. He said the Morrigan 'come for another.'"

He gave no sign that he understood the significance of her story. "The priest spoke of you, John Phillips. He gave the admonition clearly. Morrigan comes for you."

The captain's face blanched. His eyes flashed and held her gaze. "How?"

"There is one who can stop the Morrigan, John. It's the chosen one. The Vodoun called her the *'Mellt Sosye.'*"

Kathryn lifted her outstretched palms upward. He took her hands in his and peered down at her palms. At first, there was nothing to see, but then suddenly, he saw the ragged mark scratched into her left palm. And, there was something else. He could faintly make out a blue iridescent light coming from the mark. He shot a look at her and shifted his weight.

"It's the Celtic name for Skyfyre Witch."

Gently, she brought both hands together. The palms met as if she were going to pray. As she separated her hands, the blue light trailed between her palms in a flickering line that danced mid-air between her palms. A tiny electric shock shot through the large pirate's body, and he hastily dropped her hands and jumped backwards.

"What is this, Kathryn? What…powers are these?"

"Don't be afraid, John." She lowered her hands and clasped them in front of herself. "This is the *Gift* bequeathed to me by my birthright."

"Is this the means by which ye cast off the creature? Th' one that nearly destroyed my ship and crew not a fortnight ago? Was it you, lass, that cast the monster from the *Revenge* that night?" His voice intensified along with his angst.

"Aye," she whispered.

She reached out to take him by the wrists, but the pirate stepped away from her, never taking his eyes from her.

"John, give me hold of your hands."

He stood fixed. "I witnessed the ungodly blue haze just before the beast departed."

She smiled tenderly and took hold of his hand. This time, she felt his muscles relax under her touch. "It is me, John. I am the same woman you've always known." She traced her fingers up the length of his bare forearms and watched as goose pimples followed her touch. Still, he did not withdraw. "This is the same lass you swept from the cliffs of Firth." She pulled his arms to her waist.

The sorceress moved closer to the pirate. Delicately, she plucked one of his powerful hands from her waist and lifted it to her temple. She lowered her cheek into his palm and closed her eyes. "This is the same skin ye have caressed."

Then, lifting his fingers to her lips, she brushed them against his fingertips and whispered, "These be the lips ye kissed."

She felt the muscles in his body contract as he pulled her into him, a carnal movement that held her fast against his body. She could feel his heart as it beat against her own.

"Kathryn…"

Silently, he tilted his face to hers and kissed her deeply.

Twenty-Six

"How will it be done?"

Captain Phillips draped a protective arm around her shoulders. Discussions of black magic unnerved them both, particularly on board a ship. Even more so, given they sailed in the mystical waters of the deep Caribbean Sea.

Both avoided direct eye contact with one another and, instead, kept their focus upon the moonlit water. Silver streaks rippled along the current, due to either the fresh peaks from the crest that formed deep within the ocean's tides or the unseen marine life that breached the surface to play under the cover of night.

Kathryn savored the security of the ship and its protection from the sea creatures. She watched as something splashed in the distance. It was a good thing—a living thing at play in the dark water. Something to help her ignore the gnawing panic that surfaced whenever she thought of the Obeah or Vodoun.

"The priest spoke of three symbols, three markers of power needed to overtake the dark Goddess. A warning was given to heed them all, and I was shown their signs."

"What are these symbols?"

Hope for the warmth of his body moved Kathryn closer. She nestled against his side to fight the chill that traveled along her spine in spite of the humid night air.

"The first you know already. I spoke of the Raven. This is the first symbol, the sign of the Morrigan."

John apparently noticed her use of the word "us" and shifted his weight uneasily.

"Ay, it comes for me. You've said that before. And the second?"

"Here within my hands, the sign of *Mellt Sosye*, the Skyfyre Witch. This is my destiny and power given at birth." She rubbed her hands together to warm them and gripped the rails for support.

"Ah." He looked down at her fingers as they dug into the rails. Her knuckles turned white as she curled her fingers around the smooth grain. Kathryn appeared just as distressed at the mention of her powers as he did, which added to the foreboding feeling creeping slowly over him. Reaching, he covered both of her clenched hands with one of his own. The heat of his skin blanketed her icy fingers and spread to every cell of her body, the touch instantly warming her spirit. She breathed in the salty night air and allowed herself a moment to feel secure at his touch.

"And the last?"

"Written in the language of the druids is the third…" She stopped mid-sentence, and her heart dropped into her gut as she realized what she had done.

"Continue, lass."

Kathryn stood mute, and her face turned as pale as her clenched hands had been.

"Kathryn…what is the last symbol?" His voice sounded urgent. He grasped her shoulders with both hands and turned her to face him.

Her voice failed her. She stared openmouthed at the beautiful man who stood before her, unable to speak. *Oh, what have I done?*

"Kathryn, are ye cursed, lass? Can you not speak of it?" His voice sounded frantic.

She shook her head in an attempt to shake herself free from whatever possessed her tongue. A new horror settled over her as she realized the depth of her error.

"The Straif! I've lost it…"

She bolted from his hold and darted across the deck to the opposite side of the ship. The longboat rested near one of the portside skiffs secured against belaying pins. Grasping hold of the side, she clambered over the edge and fell into the skiff with a thud.

"Kathryn, what are ye doing, lass?"

"Oh! It's not here! The Straif…it's vanished!"

She climbed from inside the skiff and looked over the edge in horror at the captain.

He stood with his hands in fists upon his waist. A fleeting hint of amusement crossed his lips as he stared at her.

"Climb down here this instant and tell me what in Adam's ale you're talkin' about!"

"I'm comin'," she said as one leg appeared over the edge, followed by the other. Her skirts bounced around her pantaloons. She pushed them down, casting an accusatory glance at the captain. His fight with an amusing smirk gave way to a crooked grin.

"Try to keep yourself modest while on my ship, will ye? Here, let me help you." He held out a hand that she swatted away.

"If I can get myself into the boat, I can surely get myself out!" Finally, she dropped the few feet to the deck and landed on her feet in front of him. "And I'm modest enough for pirates. Now…the Straif." She eyed him breathlessly. "The Straif is the third marker. The last symbol."

The captain dropped his arms to his side. The smirk disappeared into the straight lines of his face, and his eyes narrowed as he stared at her. Kathryn brushed salt and dust from her skirts with both hands and walked up to him.

"The druid writings tell of the dark powers of the blackthorn tree. It's the marker for black magic unless it falls into the hands of good, the *Mellt Sosye*…me, to be exact."

"And where is this Straif now?"

Fear coursed through her veins as she thought of the possibilities. "Oh, John! I am afraid it may have been stolen. Unless it fell overboard." She glanced at the water and shook her head. "No, it couldn't have. I watched the skiff loaded on board. Nothing fell out."

"How can you be sure someone stole it?"

"Because I cannot find it!" She stomped her foot.

He glanced at the skiff, then back to the young woman. "Did you have it upon leaving the island?"

"Aye. I had it with me as we made our way back. I carried it with me in this very longboat. We saw the beacon and knew you'd given the signal. We thought of nothing else but to return to the *Revenge*. I held it in my hands the entire time the men were rowin'!"

"It'll surface, lass."

"Oh, what have I done?" The horror of it would not leave her thoughts.

"You did wisely to return in haste." He tilted his head, looked at her askance, and shifted his weight, along with the subject. "I would have been forced to leave you behind, had the crew been aboard. You put the entire crew in danger! The lot o' you."

"Aye." Kathryn lowered her eyes.

"Still, I couldn't leave you, Kathryn. And yet, my men would have thought me weak for stayin', were it not for the other boats still makin' their way from land. I would have had to leave you, else face the mocking dictum of my crew…and right by it, they would be. It's the Code!"

Captain Phillips studied her. He could not remain angry with her for long. He loved her, though he tried over and over again to be indifferent, he could not.

"I'm truly sorry." She bent over to pick up a discarded bottle. Sandalwood and lavender carried on a sudden, salty breeze and caught him unawares as she moved. He drank in her scent and his heart softened. She offered the rum to him, but he refused, so she drained it. He cocked his head and watched her graceful movements as she set the bottle inside a barrel filled with empty, discarded casks.

"This Straif must be considerable to your charge."

"Aye, it is. The Straif holds the key to dispatching Morrigan. It will set you free, John…you and your crew."

He drummed his fingers along his jaw while considering her words. "It seems to me that you've a penchant for coming up with solutions. I'm sure this Straif isn't as irreplaceable it seems."

"You don't understand how dangerous it can be."

He exhaled loudly, then turned from her to look over the drunken crew scattered about the deck. Several slept where they'd fallen, while others had taken up their duties until the rest were sober enough to manage the ship. The men were diplomatic as they handled the duties aboard the *Revenge*, though greedy with her spoils.

"I fear it will most certainly be lost without a hefty reward. Ye'd best avoid swordplay, my dear. Ye're likely to get yourself killt, at best. Are ye prepared to pay for its return?"

She lowered her eyes. Arguing about her skill with a blade seemed futile, and she'd given the last of her gold to Pedro. The weight of her error settled over her anew.

"If that's the toll, then all is lost," she said.

An air of defeat followed her as she walked to the nearest intoxicated pirate. She carefully pulled a moss-colored bottle from his flaccid hands, then lifted the brim to her lips. Warm, savory liquid swam down her throat and sent soothing heat to every nerve of her body. She gulped heartily and allowed the amber elixir to melt her senses into the relief of dull awareness. If she couldn't lose her guilt, the least she could do was drown herself in rum.

She could feel the captain's presence next to her and smiled at the mellow sensuality of his aura, gold and rose—the colors of power and love. Finally, she lowered her head and allowed the bottle to fall from her lips. Again, she extended the bottle to him. This time, he reached for it and brushed her hand as he did so. The warmth of his touch radiated along her arm and into her heart. Suddenly, she forgot her despair, forgot the threat of Morrigan, and forgot the gift given to her by the Vodoun priest. The amber liquid acted like truth serum.

"You know I love you." She closed her eyes, basking in her feelings.

"Kathryn, look at me."

Smiling, she opened her eyes, gazing at his strong, angular face and enticing green eyes. He lifted her chin and kissed her, then buried his face into her hair and inhaled her intoxicating scent once again. It was the act of a man held captive by a woman…and she loved him even more for it. He looked at her again, and she focused on Captain Phillips' face.

In that moment, a shadowy figure appeared behind him. Kathryn blinked, and the smile fell abruptly from her lips. Her vision cleared to reveal the identity of the dark silhouette.

Alone in the shadows, an opaque figure stepped forward, and in one hand, held the Straif.

Twenty-Seven

THE APPARITION STOOD, JUST OUT of sight, and shadowed the Blackthorn totem. The Straif literally floated ahead in the darkness of the sticky night air. Two or three moments passed in silence as Kathryn stared at the image standing just behind Captain Phillips. Sensing it, he spun around and faced the same dark image hidden within shadows.

"Make yerself known, else suffer the consequences."

Slowly, Pedro stepped out into the moonlight, holding the powerful Straif clutched in his left hand.

"Pedro!" Kathryn shrieked. "What are you doin' with that?"

She swaggered toward him. Each step echoed against the burnished planking and marked a commanding presence. Not until she stood within a few inches of the black man's face did she stop moving. Her eyes bored into Pedro's, and she widened her stance with both hands resting on her slender waist. She said nothing but thrust her right hand out and waited for him to hand over the totem.

"I be findin' da Straif left alone in da longboat, Lady." He cleared his throat, raised his chin. Looking down at her through ebony pupils, the whites of his eyes took on a ghostly glint. "Ye cannot neglect da tasks be given ye fro' da Mamba. Ye surely bring bad luck o' us all, Lady."

He pushed the Straif into her outstretched hand. There was an air of certainty about him. He was confident he had berated her enough for the moment.

"Aye, Pedro. That's true, and you're right to tell me so. It shan't happen again." Kathryn tossed out a half-hearted curtsy while clutching the totem tightly. "Indeed, I am indebted to you, sir, for findin' it for me."

Pedro nodded, accepting her apology, then glanced at the captain and nodded again out of respect. Captain Phillips touched his brow with fingertips in response. Almost immediately, the muscular black man melted back into the shadows and was gone.

Kathryn exhaled.

"Ye show your true character, offerin' amends to the man, lass." His voice was low as he spoke.

She faced Captain Phillips and smiled. "I gather I owe him at least that."

"I take it that be your lost stick, eh?" It was clearly not a question.

Kathryn sighed and waited while the muscles that ran the length of her neck finally loosened. She held the totem overhead as she sauntered back to mid-ship, then laughed aloud.

"Aye." She pushed the totem forward for him to see. "The Straif of the Blackthorns. There's talk of it in the '*Ogma's Tale of the Trees*.'"

He shook his head. "I've not heard of it."

"Ancient Celtic writings I learned long ago when I was but a wee girl. Mariel spoke frequently of the powers of the mighty Blackthorn tree. Some thought it was a fool's tale or an evil omen, but Mariel said it brings an awakenin'."

Her eyes wandered the length of the staff, noting each mark on its surface. Her mood grew somber. With both hands, she offered the Straif to the captain.

"Keep it." He shook his head again.

"The priest spoke of the Morrigan. He said the Straif can be used both for good and for evil. He said the Mamba would choose its rightful owner. Then, the priest chose the Skyfyre Witch, the *Mellt Sosye*. I suppose, the Straif listens to the language of the Vodoun." She paused momentarily before continuing. "The Vodoun chose me." She looked back to Captain Phillips and smiled, then pointed a finger at herself. "Me!"

"Don't be so proud, Kathryn." Still, he bowed and touched his forehead, a formal act toward Kathryn. "Respect is due, I suppose."

What an odd thing to say…to do, Kathryn thought. *He really doesn't understand the significance of it, indeed.*

"Well then, what's to be done with the thing?" he asked, confirming her suspicions.

She sighed. At least the pirate within Captain Phillips had not grown annoyed with her. "That's something I'm not certain about as yet. I guess we'll find out, won't we?"

"Indeed."

"Truthfully, I don't know exactly how it works. My hope lies in the marks etched in the grain, here." She pointed to one side of the Straif. "And here." She pointed to the opposite side. "I need to find someone who can read these strange symbols."

"Symbols, ye say? Is that the language of the Vodoun written there?" He eyed the odd bands struck deep into the dark wood.

"It's the ancient marks of the druids—Ogham writing found in my homeland."

"Then ye should be able to read it." He waved a hand toward the Straif.

"Sadly, I've only been told tales of the Straif. Ogham writing is far too ancient for my eyes."

"Ye were never schooled in readin' and writin', then, lass?"

"I was schooled well, sir. In Mariel's cottage, I learned far more than most. Within that place lies unseen conjury, powerful for healin' and prophecy. Some call it 'heresy'…even 'witchcraft.'" She paused as the bitter word rolled past her tongue. "Such talk is the rants of fearful tongues and ignorant fools!"

Kathryn focused on nothing as her mind wandered. She stomped one foot in agitation at the thought of what had been done to her grandmothers.

"Sorcery is against God's will."

"You cannot be serious, John Phillips." She glared at him, and he shrugged. "Oh, granted, the women in my family were highly regarded whenever someone was taken with the fever or required treatment for wounds or broken bones. 'God's messengers', they were called… and those in need certainly paid well for their skills.

However, the loyalty of those who sought my family's powerful skills quickly became lost when the afflicted soul was overcome by whatever malady had befallen them. Indeed, my grandmothers were not gods and certainly did not hold the power of life over certain death. But that was something soon forgotten when the patient took a turn for the worst…"

She began to pace and Captain Phillips decided to give her a wide berth.

"Fear, Kathryn. That's what drove them to use the stake."

Kathryn shot him a look. "Perhaps, although my grandmothers were diligent in using the rare *Gift* passed down, not all could be healed and made whole. This led to accusations of false pretenses and the lethal moniker, *Witch*!"

Captain Phillips eyed her. He knew well the consequences that followed an accusation of witchcraft: a swift hanging, or death by fire.

"Those foolish enough to believe it quickly tied the innocent healer to the stake and let her burn to death." Kathryn's voice dropped to a whisper. "Many of my ancestors have met their Maker that way."

"Kathryn…" He reached for her, but she stood and looked him in the eye. "The *Gift* would be taken from amongst the colony for a short while until the next of my kin had been properly groomed and prepared for its use. I supposed I am one of those."

Kathryn knew at an early age the importance of keeping her *Gift* a secret or else suffer the worst from those who did not understand. *He won't understand, either.* She blinked back tears but refused to look away.

"Can ye read any of it, lass?" Captain Phillips broke into her thoughts.

She dropped her gaze to the strange markings on the totem. "Aye, some of it. Yet, these marks are from times long ago. The language of the druids is very old. I cannot be sure of its meanin' without knowin' all the symbols. Perhaps that was something known by the Vodoun when he chose me."

The pirate stared at her in silence. *Indeed, there is more to this woman than meets the eye.*

Behind them, one of the drunken crewmen moaned and dropped a half-empty bottle from his languid hand. The last of the amber liquid drained from its open rim and spilled in a dark puddle, which spread around the drunken man's knees. The couple glanced at him briefly, a sudden awareness of the presence of others in the vicinity. Kathryn tossed her head in dismissal, spilling long, dark hair down her back, and looked back to the captain.

"The sun's soon to awaken, John. Methinks it best we part ways forthwith and hold fondly to the events of this night." As she spoke, she curtseyed deeply.

"Ay, then, love...*adieu*," he whispered and lifted her hand to his lips.

Kathryn stepped forward and kissed his dark tresses, then paused to lay her cheek against the crown of his head.

"G'night, my sweet capt'n." And, turning from him, she moved gracefully across the deck and made her way below to her quarters.

Once inside her cabin, she leaned the long blackthorn totem in a far corner. It stood taller than her height, even at an angle, and she marveled momentarily at its majestic beauty. The ebony wax filled each crevice etched into the grain, accenting the grooves and symbols there. She knew this would not be an easy task to accomplish—not aboard a pirate ship. But search it out, she must, if she intended to decipher the code that lay inscribed upon it. This became her new resolve.

She fell back and settled onto her bed, her mind filled with hazy thoughts of the heather, the ancient people of her homeland, and statuesque ruins—all monuments of prophecy. She rolled over on the cot, pulled the worn coverlet to her chin, and dozed as she remembered the land of her birth and the verdant vegetation that blanketed the endless rolling hills and cliffs.

So green they were. As vibrant as the Caribbean waters she sailed upon…as clear as emerald eyes.

His emerald eyes.

Twenty-Eight

Most aboard the *Revenge* slept through the next day and the following night. The ship seemed to sleep, as well, as it bobbed on top of placid seas that rocked the crew on gentle currents. At random, a pirate would scurry across the deck to secure a free line. Usually, he'd tack their course, always hailing the barrel man before scrambling below deck to whatever berth waited to lull him back to sleep. Fortunately, the sea remained tranquil and, for a day and a night, peace settled over the pirate ship.

Too soon, it seemed, the sunrise appeared. Its golden light bathed Kathryn in transparent amber, warming her with its caress. She raised her arms above her head and stretched, letting out a heavy sigh as she yawned and willed herself to wake. The rocking ship lulled her back to sleep, but she fought the temptation to yield.

Unusual for the morning, the ship sounded strangely quiet. She craned her head toward the ceiling and listened for sounds of ordinary activity, but heard none. *Strange*, she thought and rolled to one side. Her head pounded, so she closed her eyes and allowed the sway of the *Revenge* to soothe the ache inside her skull.

Wind hummed through the tiny open porthole that sent puffs of sea air swirling over her sun-kissed skin. She inhaled deeply and tasted the salty breeze in the back of her throat. Inwardly smiling, she recalled the familiar scents of sea spray and lavender from her childhood home in the Scottish firth.

I wonder what Mariel would do, she thought and opened her eyes slowly to focus upon the dark stave that leaned against the wall. She studied the hatch marks one by one, and her thoughts wandered. *I wonder if she could read these.*

"Of course, she could," Kathryn answered out loud. "Mariel…once again, where can you be found when you're needed the most?"

Over the edge of her cot, a blanket had fallen to the floor. *It must have been a fitful night*, she thought and dropped her feet to the floorboards. Her head pounded, and she rubbed stiff hands through her hair. So as not to anger the ache in her joints, she moved slowly to the center of her cabin. Poised on the edge of the oak table rested an abandoned flask. She lifted it to her lips and drained the last of the grog before returning the emptied bottle to the table.

"Mariel, sweet Mum," she droned as she sauntered across the room to where the totem rested. "What would you be thinkin' now?"

Kathryn smiled to herself as she imagined her grandmother's face, steel grey-blue eyes wide in amazement at the sight of each intricate carving inscribed into the blackthorn staff. The emblems would not be foreign to Mariel. She'd interpret them. A familiar sadness rose and Kathryn swallowed hard.

She turned back to the table where she took hold of a pomegranate that had been set into a large wooden bowl. The mere presence of the fruit meant Seth had snuck into her cabin while she lay vulnerable and asleep.

"Thank you, Seth," she whispered to an empty room. "Your calling-card."

She smiled gratefully at the gesture—leaving food for her the way he had done so many times. She bit into the pulp and savored it with eyes closed. Suddenly, behind her in the doorway, she heard the faint rustle of someone watching her. Spinning on her heels, she saw a large, muscular shape filling her doorframe.

"Pedro!" Kathryn startled and nearly choked on the fruit in her mouth. The man stood motionless and said nothing. "You gave me a fright, ye did." She swallowed hard, and the fruit slid down while her heart pounded. "What would ye have of me at this hour, Pedro?"

He lifted his finger and pointed to the corner where the totem rested, then stepped across the threshold and entered the young woman's cabin. "Dis be very powaful magic, lady," he said, his voice a warning.

"Yes, I know this, Pedro...and I'm deeply beholdin' to you for findin' it and returnin' it to me!"

The pirate narrowed his eyes to slits as he studied her. It dawned on Kathryn that Pedro may be expecting compensation, and so she moved quickly to a small box set carelessly against the opposite wall. There, a satchel overflowed with herbs and charms. Some of its contents spilled out and onto the floor as she lifted it. Pedro eyed the contents as they scattered at her feet, but said nothing. He waited in cadaverous silence.

She turned her back for privacy as she lifted the lid from the tiny teak box and pulled from it a tarnished coin. "Here," she said as she handed it to him. "Here's the reward I owe you for deliverin' the totem to me last eve." He hesitated for a moment, so she pushed the pieces-of-eight a little closer to him. "Take it. You've earned it sure enough!"

He tucked it into the sash tied snugly around his thick waist. "Ye don know its power, now do ye, lady?"

Kathryn sighed and took a seat next to the table. Then, remembering her uneaten breakfast, she bit off another hunk of the ruby fruit. She looked at him as she chewed, and the seeds popped in her ears as she bit each one separately. It provided a tiny distraction from the gnawing feeling that clawed at her gut.

There was not much known about Pedro, only that he had abandoned his own crew of fishermen, and willingly joined the pirates in Tobago, when last they had careened the *Revenge*. He kept to himself, but was well liked among the men. A hard worker, to be sure. The captain had always shown a little more respect for the man than usual. Kathryn assumed she could do no less and decided to confide in him.

"I know it's blackthorn, most powerful in the black arts. I also know the Vodoun priest chose the *Mellt Sosye* to be its keeper." Pedro's eyes widened. "Ah, apparently you've heard of the *Mellt Sosye* before." She had his attention, perhaps some respect, too. Whatever it was, he was definitely showing apprehension for her—something she could use to her advantage. "The priest did, indeed, bequeath the Straif to me, the *Mellt Sosye*."

Pedro's full lips parted and his eyes expanded. "Yo?"

"The Skyfyre Witch. It's me the priest chose, Pedro. 'Tis true whether either of us likes it or not. There's mysteries surroundin' the Straif, to be certain, and its purpose is kept secret, only to myself. But, know this, Pedro, the Vodoun did give it to me by choice."

Pedro nodded and spoke in barely a whisper before he turned to leave. "Then ye best be fulfillin' th' callin' Mamba give yo, an' mark me words, ye don' wan' be careless again wit' dat dark magic stick."

The weight of his warning hit hard. He turned to leave. As she watched him, it suddenly dawned on her the significance of his words. If Pedro knew the importance of the Straif, perhaps he also knew the meaning of the symbols. It was worth a try. She jumped up just as he stepped onto the stairway leading to the deck above.

"Pedro! Wait!"

The large man stopped and turned to look at her through the doorway. Kathryn rushed across the room, tossing the peel to the floor. Gently, so as not to startle him further, she touched his massive bicep. "Pedro…do you know about the markings carved into the Straif?"

He nodded and glanced again to the corner where the totem rested. His eyes darted back to hers. "Aye, it be th' marks o' th' *Ogoun Iwa*. Th' marks come from the Vodoun in my homeland."

"Will you tell me their meanin', Pedro? I will pay you well for it, I will."

"I can only read da symbols. Da meanin' ye must figure out for yerself."

Kathryn nearly danced. Taking hold of his massive arm, she led him to the Straif. Gently, the sorceress lifted the totem from its corner and held it in the light for him to see.

"Look closely there. Tell me what you see. What does it mean?"

"I see symbols. Dey grouped like dat for a reason."

"Aye! What do they mean, grouped together like that?"

"Dey be a warnin' an' a curse. Together wit' dis mark, it say…"

Suddenly, cannon fire sounded from above and crewmen began to shout.

"All hands on deck! All hoay!"

Pedro turned from her. "I must go now, lady." He darted out the door, up the stairs, and disappeared a moment later. Kathryn was alone, the blackthorn totem still clutched in one hand.

Another cannon blast sounded, and the ship shuddered. Kathryn stumbled backward, losing her balance. Quickly, she returned the staff to its corner and snatched her cutlass from the hook near her bed. Hastily, she tied the weapon to her waist, slid her dagger through the sash, and rested it against the small of her back. She then darted across the room, pulled a cluster of juniper and Adder's Tongue from her sack of herbs, and then, darted up the companionway onto the bright, sunlit deck.

"Sails to starboard, ho!"

Kathryn lifted her free hand to shade her eyes. She tucked the herbs inside a pocket, then dropped her hand to the hilt of her cutlass. Crewmen ducked in and out of the rigging—the majority of them dressed for battle with cutlasses freed of scabbards and pistols dangling from brightly colored ribbons hanging about their necks. She raised her eyes to the top of the mainmast and watched the black flag thrashing against the wind. The *Revenge* had raised a warning to the oncoming vessel a few fathoms off. The ship had no choice but to surrender, or else be destroyed by pirates.

"No quarter!" was shouted from somewhere near the ship's bow, and the men echoed the threat across the waters as the vessel neared. Kathryn felt a curious surge of energy as she thought of an impending fight with the smaller ship. It was obvious from the chants and calls from the men aboard that they likewise felt the same anticipation at the prospect of a new prize.

Am I becoming one of them truly? Unsettling thoughts swam in her head as she watched the *Revenge* close in upon its prey. She pulled the cutlass from its sheath, stepped to the starboard rails, and took her place alongside Gow and Seth. Gow nodded in her direction, and Seth offered a smile. This time, she hadn't been sent below decks. This time, she had a place next to the pirates, her mates, and she would fight alongside them as one of the crew.

"Ye'll be viewed as no less than any o' the rest o' us," Gow said, eyes on the prize.

"A pirate who sails under the black flag, you say, Mister Gow?"

Seth nodded, and she responded with a smile for them both. She set her stance and stared at the oncoming ship.

"So be it!"

Twenty-Nine

BLUE AND RED, THE COLOR of the British flag, flew from the main mast of the sloop.

"It be but a fishin' vessel, Capt'n. Thar be no spoils fit to divide among us, surely, says I." Seymore stood near the helm alongside John Phillips.

"That may be true, but she deserves the chance to impress us, still," the captain replied, his lopsided grin spreading across his lips. Both men chuckled as they watched the crew from the sloop scrambling at their approach. "Mister Archer, we give no quarter. Make certain these fishermen are appraised, will ye, sir?"

The quartermaster leaned against the quarterdeck rails, spyglass in hand. "Aye, Capt'n!" He handed the spyglass to Seymore, then faced the sloop and shouted. "Ahoy thar, English dogs! Whar be yer captain?"

A beefy man with mutton-chops and thick arms stepped forward and replied boldly from the smaller ship. "My name is Captain Haskill, and I am the captain of this fishing vessel."

"Aye, Mister Haskill, an' so ye be. Likely thar be nothin' in yer stores save fishes and nets, eh?" Archer called back.

"Aye. We carry nothing but our supplies and the catch we bring in. Who captains your vessel, sir? I would have a word with him and beg he let us pass in peace."

Archer rocked with laughter and a few of the crew joined him.

John Phillips stepped forward. "I am the capt'n of the *Revenge*. State your destination, sir?"

Captain Haskill consulted one of his men, then faced them again. "The *Dolphin* is naught but a mere fishing boat, sir. Our course hails to the north, near Antigua."

Captain Phillips considered the fishing boat momentarily, one hand raised to his chin. "What do you make of it, Mister Seymore?"

"I'd say he's lyin'."

The men shouted threats while Archer called for no quarter to be given. Just then, William White joined them. "Capt'n, I know that fellow…the one standing aside, there."

John Phillips glanced at his crewman, then turned his attention back to the *Dolphin's* crew. "Which one, Mister White? They're all standin' aside."

White lifted a finger and pointed at a tall, young fisherman. "That one, sir. We apprenticed together 'fore I joined th' crew. His name be Filamore. He's skilled with th' sailcloth."

"He's but a lad, Mister White!"

"He's my age, sir!" White sounded indignant.

Captain Phillips raised the spyglass and studied the young fisherman for a moment. "Will ye vouch for him, Mister White?"

"Aye, Capt'n. That I will," White replied without faltering and snapped to attention to make his point.

Captain Phillips shouted again to the *Dolphin*. "Do ye know of us, Captain Haskill?"

"Aye. You be nothing but bloodthirsty pirates and filthy criminals, the lot of you!"

Curses rose, and the crew of the *Revenge* raised their blades as they bellowed threats and mocked the fisherman.

However, Captain Phillips, amused, tipped his tricorn in response. "Ay, true enough and the *Dolphin* be our prize this day, sir. There be no quarter given, so ye best be showin' me men your respect, else suffer their fury at your own expense."

"There's surely nothing aboard this vessel, save bait and fish, and that we have in poor reserve as it is, with the waters being greedy this whole month!" Captain Haskill shouted back.

"Ay, but there be great treasure aboard your vessel, indeed, sir." Captain Phillips paused to allow the fishermen a moment before he continued. "Ye have a crewman that surely befits my needs for a tailor and sails man."

Haskill turned his gaze upon the young lad who had shrunk back in horror and was shaking his head.

He turned back to Captain Phillips and shouted. "Nay, the lad belongs with us. Surely, you cannot expect a youth such as this to make company with pirates! The answer is *no!*"

"How unfortunate for the *Dolphin* and her crew." Captain Phillips clicked his tongue and shook his head. "Ye will certainly force my men to move upon ye with our guns, lest ye make the trade."

"Trade? What trade is that, sir? You speak of kidnapping, sir, and a youth, at that. Forced into the service of pirates."

"We live a hearty life, free of encumbrances. We'd be doin' the lad a favor."

"Hardly befitting the gentleman his mum intended he be. I shall not trade wit' ye, pirate!"

Kathryn flinched the moment he said "kidnap" with the memories of her own abduction still too fresh. She watched the captain carefully. The crew waited, ready for the signal to attack.

Captain Phillips turned aside to Archer and gave orders under his breath. "Take young Filamore alive or dead, it matters not to me. But, keep in mind, our diligent tailor, Mister White, deserves a companion to help him work the sails. And so, for the tailor's sake, spare the lad's life."

Archer responded, "Aye, aye, sir," and strode the length of the deck to where the gangplank was stowed. He instructed the men who stood nearby to let down the plank, then shouted across to the *Dolphin*.

"Prepare to be boarded!"

Several of the pirates grasped hold of lines released from the mid-ship cleats and swung out over the water, dirks clenched between their teeth. With the agility of feral cats, they leapt onto the begrimed deck of the *Dolphin*. Haskill looked on incredulously at the *Revenge* and shook his fist at Captain Phillips, who smiled in response.

"This is a friendly meeting, sir. How dare you send your men to my vessel without invitation?"

"We're not your friends, sir. We're pirates."

Swiftly, the four pirates surrounded the fishermen and held them at bay while the remaining cutthroats combed the vessel for valuables. Slade moved forward, the ring through his ear swinging as he moved upon the lad. He grabbed hold of him with a beefy hand and held him apart from the rest.

"We be makin' a fair trade wit' ye, fisherman," taunted Archer from mid-ship. "The men will leave ye in peace. In exchange, ye be giftin' us wit' a young tailor."

The pirates roared with laughter, and the brute with the earring held his cutlass over the young boy's head. The lad cast a desperate glance at his captain. Haskill stood apart from his crew, Cuddy's long dirk held to his throat. He stared helplessly at his men.

A significant clatter from below deck sounded as three pirates surfaced from the hold, carrying large crates filled with yellow fin and lobster. Their appearance brought triumphant grins from the pirates.

"An' we be takin' sommat to feed the growin' boy wit', as well," Archer announced.

The pirates bellowed at this. Haskill looked up with hatred at Captain Phillips, who shrugged and joined in, laughing from the rails of the *Revenge*.

Slade hauled the youth roughly off the deck and up the gangplank by the nape of his neck. He was dragged, kicking and screaming, from the vessel he called home to the pirate ship. As he stumbled onto the deck of the *Revenge*, Haskill shouted out to Captain Phillips, "You have what you want. Now let me and my men go free!"

Young Filamore shrieked, "You can't leave me here, Capt'n! You cannot leave me in the hands of the pirates, sir!" Filamore fell to his knees and plead with his captain and crewmates.

At this, Slade released him, and the youth immediately scrambled to one side, cowering with eyes closed and head bowed.

"It appears we have an accord, Captain Haskill." John Phillips saluted. He then turned from the rails, moved back to the helm, and took hold of the wheel. "Leave 'em be."

The pirates still aboard the *Dolphin* let go of the fishermen and snatched whatever they could carry before retreating to the *Revenge*. Terrified fishermen stood by and helplessly watched as the pirates ransacked their vessel. Still, none dared cross the pirates for fear they'd lose their lives.

Captain Haskill stayed on deck, his eyes fixed on the young Filamore, who now stood at the rails of the *Revenge* with tears streaming down his cheeks as he pled for someone to rescue him.

"Set a course ten degrees Nor-Norwest, Mister White," Captain Phillips ordered as he stepped from the helm.

"Aye, aye, Capt'n." White took hold of the wheel.

"Pinch hard to larboard, then come up close haul to wind. Set the sails and choke a block, blokes. Take her deeper and put distance 'tween the bloody fishin' boat and me girl, the *Revenge*!" Captain Phillips patted the rails affectionately as he spoke.

"Aye, aye" rang out across the deck as the men scrambled to set the sails and move away from the *Dolphin*.

Kathryn watched him. *Perhaps one day "me girl" will be used for you, Kathryn.* She shook the thought away. *He'll never love you that much.*

She kept her eyes on the captain as he strode across the deck and made his way to the new recruit. When he finally reached Filamore, the youth stood up and bravely looked the pirate captain in the eye.

"Welcome aboard the *Revenge*, young Master Filamore," Captain Phillips said, holding his gaze. "You're now in my charge and will make assignment with an ol' matey of yours, Mister White." Phillips tipped his head toward the helm and Filamore followed. His youthful face betrayed a fleeting moment of relief as he caught sight of his old friend standing firm at the helm. Filamore lifted a hand in greeting, but thought better of it and wiped dry a glistening cheek, instead.

"This be a kidnapping, it be." Filamore puffed his chest out defiantly. Tears flooded his eyes once again, but he did not wipe them away. "What right 'ave ye to enact foul deeds amongst honest men?"

"I'm known as John Phillips. You may call me Capt'n." Ignoring the insolence, he turned from the young man. "Take him below, Mister Gow, and introduce the lad to his new quarters."

"I've got this," Seth volunteered and leapt from the yardarm. Gow stepped forward,

Seth joined him, and they led young John Filamore below. As they passed by the helm, Filamore glanced up at his comrade, who tapped his brow with a free hand. Moments later, John Filamore disappeared below deck.

Kathryn stood transfixed as she watched the men's interplay. Her conscience pricked. She turned back to the rails and watched as the *Dolphin* faded into the distance. *He will be forced into service with pirates, just as they had done with Seth…just as they had done with me.*

Their treatment of her brought back memories of the terror she felt when dragged on board. *This very ship.* She traced her fingers over the weathered wood rail and felt a rush of awe for the magnificent vessel she now called home. *Aye, but you're a fickle lass,* she scolded the *Revenge*. "You're nothing more than a pirate yourself, takin' whatever you please and holding everyone and everything captive…includin' the heart of your captain…even his plunder."

She sighed, unable to fight against the feelings she'd developed for the *Revenge*. "It's a bittersweet love we have, isn't it? I'm jealous of you, and yet love you at the same time. I suppose it's not your fault, though. You are a beauty." She ran her eyes down the length of the polished brightwork with its multicolored grain— evidence of years of wear by saltwater and battle. "Very beautiful, indeed."

The *Revenge* was a magnificent vessel, beautifully created by skilled hands. Directly below the rails, intricate carvings decorated the upper portion of the gunwale. Deep within, the innermost etchings had been stained grey from accumulated salt and battle wear, giving it a wise and weathered appearance. It reminded her of the snow tuffs that would settle over the cottage on rare occasions, sparkling in the sunlight just before they melted.

Shattered fragments where cannon or other shot had made contact broke up the elaborate detailing and glinted with the same snowy stain as the intact ornamentation. Along the interior of the taffrail, the same intricate carvings lined the quarterdeck. Truly, the *Revenge* was a magnificent ship. To Kathryn, it was something else. She ran her fingers along the rail and softly whispered, "Home."

Kathryn admittedly felt safe aboard the *Revenge*. Inwardly, she hoped the young lad just brought aboard would one day find the same affection for the majestic merchantman as she had. Should he not, however, it would be of his own choosing. The life of a pirate, though difficult, offered rewards in company and camaraderie—something he most likely had not experienced on board the fishing vessel. *Obviously*, she thought, *as his captain had no qualms about leavin' the boy!*

"Stowed and sobbin'." Seth's voice rang out and woke her from her reverie. She made her way to him.

"I guess your duty with Filamore is completed?'

He turned to greet her with an enthusiastic smile. "Good day, Miss Kathryn." He tapped his brow with two fingers. "Yup. The pup is below decks, meetin' new friends and bawlin' like a baby about it." Seth grinned.

"Oh, poor lad." She shook her head. "Uh, may I have a word?"

Seth bowed, nearly touching his nose to his knees. "How may I be of service, Madame?" The grin spreading over his face made him more attractive than Kathryn remembered. She tossed her head back and chuckled. "You're really a fine sight to see this day. You know that now, don't you?"

"Perhaps the day will come when it'll be your eye I'll be catchin'." He wriggled his eyebrows as he said this.

"Unlikely…but then, you never know a woman's heart, do you?" she teased back. In truth, she had hoped not to encourage him further. "Actually, Seth…I need to ask a favor."

"Go on, then."

"When the crew brought us both aboard, you showed me a bit of decency and stood up for me against the pirates for both of our sakes. Although to snatch a young lad such as yourself is common, to kidnap a young lass just beyond eighteen…" Kathryn stamped her foot absently.

"That's also common, Kathryn."

"Well…it shouldn't be."

"You're talkin' about pirates, Kat."

"I know, I know. It's just that I don't see any reason…"

"What would you have me do?" he asked, cutting her off.

She glanced up at his large brown eyes framed with long black lashes. Her heart pounded. He must have sensed her disquiet, and he stepped forward to narrow the gap between them. Kathryn cleared her throat and rested her hands on her hips.

"I ask you to show the Filamore lad the same kindness you showed me." She stepped back to catch her breath. "I've grown fond of this ship and the crew…"

"And the capt'n," Seth snapped and moved away.

"That's none of your business, Seth!" She tried to sound stern, but her cheeks flushed nonetheless. "The crew needs all hands behind the capt'n. That one's a strapping, strong arm who would go against us all in a foul wind."

"What makes you think so?"

Kathryn motioned to the space young Filamore had just occupied. Her voice sounded almost matronly as she spoke, though she did not intend it, so she cleared her throat again. This time, her Celtic will seethed. "Perhaps it's woman's intuition."

"There are many strapping sailors aboard this vessel, Kat."

She stomped her foot again. "The lad needs to be taught loyalty to the ship and the crew.

He would best find his devotion for the captain quickly aboard a pirate ship, savvy?"

"You're talkin' irrational, lettin' your mood dictate your mouth, and you're going to get yourself into trouble again."

"Seth! There is more to this than a mood. How dare you say that!" Kathryn took a deep breath to calm herself and continued with measured words. "You know that I have more than just a gut feelin' about things. This runs deep, and I need you to do this one favor for me. Help Filamore find his loyalty to Capt'n Phillips and the *Revenge*. Please?"

Seth nodded. "Aye, then. I'll be speakin' with him as you wish. But, I cannot promise his allegiance to us all. William White and he are mateys from earlier days—apprentices together on another ship. William has already beseeched the lad to swear o'er the axe and join the crew, but Filamore refused outright, sayin' he 'will not be part of any such wicked manner, takin' up ranks with a crew of pirates!' Stubborn bloke, that one."

"Just as I feared." Kathryn looked away as worry spread into thin lines across her face. She had noticed a pale glow of dusky light about him. This, she knew from her grandmother's Celtic teachings, was a foreshadowing of his spirit—a slate aura that surrounded the boy. Kathryn knew it meant he carried dark intentions, which she had hoped was merely a reflection of the fear that came with being kidnapped by pirates.

"I'll talk to him," Seth said and shrugged. "But, I don't think it will do any good."

"Not yet maybe, but with time, let's hope." She smiled at Seth, but dread passed behind her eyes. "At the very least, Filamore will have to be watched, Seth."

He nodded. "Whatever you suggest."

"Aye, then. I'm beholdin' to you once again, Seth." She smiled and half curtsied, then turned to walk away.

"He's in his quarters as we speak."

Kathryn did not stop but touched the crown of her head in an off-hand salute to the bold remark. How did he know she intended to see the captain?

"Bold of you, Seth," she said aloud. "Bold, indeed!"

Thirty

WHEN KATHRYN REACHED THE OVERSIZED door of the captain's quarters, she hesitated and wondered whether an unannounced visit would be problematic. Still, she couldn't risk silence.

Filamore's aura had smoldered far too menacingly, and no one but Kathryn had seen it. She lifted a fist and rapped on the oak.

"Enter," bellowed the bass voice on the other side.

She struggled against the heavy door but refused to let on that it was too much for her. Truth be told, she would do poorly in the eyes of the crew if she could not carry her weight aboard the ship—opening a door was the least of those tasks.

"Do you need help?" the voice sounded from inside.

"Hardly." She grunted and pushed against it with her shoulder, nearly stumbling inside as it gave way. Then, collecting herself, she strode into the room using long strides. "Something's wrong with the hinges on your bloody door."

She paused as usual and waited for her eyes to focus in the dim light. Captain Phillips sat behind a writing desk, a huge grin plastered across his face. A leather-bound book lay open, illuminated by the flicker of a single candle's flame. A quill, suspended from his right hand, moved only slightly.

"M'lady." He gestured to an empty chair near the center table. "Please, sit. I'm in need of your company."

"Grateful for that, I am truly, John, but I must speak urgently with you."

He set down the quill, and the boyish grin fell with his mood. He knitted his brows together as she settled into the empty chair. "What it is, Kathryn? Has the crew been offensive to you?"

"No, nothing like that. The crew is most dear to me…all but the bloody quartermaster—a yellow dog I still say you should have let me cut down!"

He chuckled, relieved there had been no improper courtesies from his crew. He could not afford to lose a single soul to the consequences that would follow a break to the oaths made o're the axe—not while he had a new prize on board the vessel.

"Spoken like a true pirate!" he stated.

"Be that as it may, Archer is nothing but trouble for you and your crew, and I don't trust him!"

"Aye, I be well aware of your lack of affection for the man, but he has proved himself a worthy seaman and loyal to his capt'n."

It seemed obvious that this topic would go nowhere, so Kathryn decided to leave it.

"I hope his loyalty is deep enough to protect those under the capt'n's affections."

"Your comeback's a riddle, Kathryn. Either ye hold your tongue, and with it, some secret, or you're in the mood for an argument."

"No such thing! I approach you genuinely, as a member of the crew."

Captain Phillips cleared his throat. She pushed a bit too far for his comfort but he would not give into a quarrel with her. Time would not permit it. "What's botherin' you, lass?"

She looked into his eyes. Her clasped hands fell to her lap as she organized her thoughts. "Well…" She sighed and forced her gaze to match his. "The boy brought aboard the ship today…I fear he has a dark heart filled with foul intentions for the ship, crew, and their capt'n."

A grin broke through the lines of his face. Laughing aloud, he stood up from the desk and walked over to her. "That is your great concern?" He chuckled as he spoke. "My sweet woman, your frettin' is wasted…although greatly appreciated."

She glared. "Your light-hearted reception to bad news is rather unsettling, Capt'n." She remained seated in spite of an itch to stomp an angry foot.

Captain Phillips took her hands in his and gently urged her fingers to relax as he propped himself against the table next to her.

"Hardly, ma'am. Perhaps a bit more level-headed than you realize, is all."

"Don't be so arrogant, John. Did you not hear what I said? It's more than just concern for you. The lad has maleficence about him. I sense it. I beseech you to take caution, not only for yourself, but the crew…for me!"

"Ah, then ye would have him watched?"

"Aye. He cannot be trusted."

"As you wish."

He nodded, bent down, and kissed her once upon her forehead, then dismissed her and turned his thoughts back to the matters at hand. He positioned himself behind the cluttered desk and studied her in the awkward moment of silence that followed.

A wise look settled across her face, and she wrung her hands in her lap. It was evident she was alarmed. The thought nagged him. "Indeed, Kathryn, you've always proved accurate in the past…mostly."

She couldn't decide whether to be angry or relieved. "What will you do about it, then?"

It was obvious she would not let the matter go, a sign he should take her warning seriously.

Sighing, Captain Phillips relented. "I will have Mister Harridon stay with the boy to observe his actions. Should anything appear of a foul nature, I will act upon it with utmost swiftness."

"You're word?"

"This I promise you!"

That was all that the captain would concede on the matter, but it brought reassurance, and she thanked him. She turned to leave.

Waving an arm over the book, he continued. "But what can be done about today's business?"

"Beg pardon?" She turned back to face him again.

"How can I log this with accuracy? Speak to that, will you?"

"Sir?" she stated, confused.

"Should this come to pass and I log the events of young Filamore's consignment to this ship, my legacy will be viewed as cutthroat an' myself as a foul commander, indeed." He wrung his hands, spilling ink over the desktop. "Damn!"

"Let me help you." She snatched a napkin that lay discarded on the center table and began to blot. "There, now. It's not so bad…just a little stain on the grain, but that gives the desk character. Don't you think?"

"Not at all! See what the affair has done to my wits! I'm a ruined man. It'll prove so in the books."

"How so, John?" She shook her head. "Surely people will know your actions were just and fair with the lad."

"Nay, Kathryn. I'm a pirate, and that's all that will be remembered. History will prove me a foul and wicked capt'n on either account. To take young Filamore unwillingly fares poorly in the eyes of those who don't know of the mercy given by the act."

"An act of mercy."

"Ay! I exchanged his service for the lives of the fishermen! My men would have cut them down to ribbons, otherwise."

"But why be so concerned? What does it matter to anyone but you?" She was more confused than ever.

"It always matters, lass. History will be written again and again in these logs. The tale of the *Revenge* lies within this quill, and I cannot foul her name with poor accuracy. This log is the only record we have—save for the tales of the men, and you know how tainted their stories grow taller with time…and rum."

"Indeed, I do." She nodded.

"It shall never be known that the *Dolphin* lay in peril of my men, riled as they were to battle. Had Filamore not been brought aboard, the crew surely would have set the fishin' vessel to flame, destroyin' her and the crew alike. My act of piracy, to kidnap the boy, as it were, mercifully saved the lives of all those aboard the *Dolphin*. Yet, no one will recognize it as such."

"So, tell the tale truthfully, John. Write your intent in the log, along with the facts, and let history be. Perhaps fate will cast a foul lot your way, and your honor may die as you go to meet your Maker, but those who know you know better."

She walked to the desk and glanced down at the elegant script that laced the page. Her eyes drifted affectionately to his face as he stared down at the open book. Kneeling beside him, Kathryn reached up and touched his cheek gently, then stroked his ebony hair.

"I know you, Capt'n Phillips. I know your heart beats true."

He looked at her. With delicateness unbefitting a pirate, he lifted her chin and brushed her mouth with his lips…which was met with a woman's kiss.

Thirty-One

"Avast, ho! Ship ahoy to th' larboard bow!"

The clatter of men pounded across the deck as the crew dashed about the ship, making ready for another confrontation.

"All hands, hoay!"

Archer's voice roared above the cacophony on deck. "Step to, blaggards! It's a fine prize that awaits th' heartiest o' swab, says I."

The captain, still seated at his desk, leapt to his feet and bounded up the companionway two steps at a time. Kathryn followed, hand on cutlass.

"She's tacked a hard course directly for us, Capt'n." Archer didn't bother to hide his anxiety. Would ye 'ave a shot across th' bows in warnin', sir?"

The captain cleared the deck with long strides, dashed up to the helm, and took his place next to the portside rails. He did not answer right away but lifted a brass spyglass to one eye and studied the advancing ship. Their colors were foreign, and though he could not be sure, the vessel looked fitted for piracy.

"Nay, Mister Archer. We'll bring her within reach of the long guns and see what her capt'n intends. She's flying colors I have not seen before, yet she looks ready for battle. Methinks they be pirates lookin' for a prize."

He handed the spyglass to the quartermaster, who looked long and hard through the eyepiece before handing it back.

"I'll tell Sparks t' get th' men ready at arms," Archer announced, then hobbled off with the crutch dragging under one arm.

Kathryn stared, fascinated with the speed at which Archer could move, given his ever-present disability. She doubted he would improve much. Shouts from the crow's nest snapped her attention back to the foreign vessel. She quickly made her way across the deck to the portside quarterdeck, where she took a place just below the helm, close enough to listen in on the conversations. She lifted a hand to shield her eyes from the shimmer of sunlight on water and peered across the ocean. In the distance, tiny white sails dotted the blue horizon and marked the passage of a vessel she recognized as being much larger than the fishing sloop they had just plundered. The glare from the water made it difficult for her to make out anything else. Only time would bring the object into better view.

"Bring Master Nutt to the helm." Captain Phillips shouted the order at Seth as he crossed the quarterdeck.

Seth glanced up at the captain and tapped a finger to his brow. "Aye, aye, sir!" he shouted back without breaking stride.

Kathryn watched him pick up his pace, disappearing to where the sailing master would be working the rigging. She scanned the deck, watching the midshipmen who were busy at their tasks. The powder monkeys made ready the guns while a handful stood by to wait for the call to fire. At the masts, other men scrambled up the shrouds as gracefully as spiders scaling a web. The *Revenge* would be ready when the vessel drew near.

She gathered up her skirts and tied the hem into a knot, then secured it under the leather belt around her waist. With the cutlass in one hand, she tightened her grip on its hilt, then shifted her weight and felt a solid mass of steel pressing into the curve of her back. Instantly, a rush of confidence accompanied the presence of her dagger hidden there. Kathryn then faced the sea to focus on the ship in the distance… and waited.

Moments passed into hours as the crew aboard the *Revenge* waited.

"The seas seem unusually calm." Seth's voice was nearly a whisper.

"Aye, an' so is th' crew." Dobbs kept his attention glued to the ship in the distance.

All eyes were fixed on the ivory sails that expanded as the ship closed in upon them with each passing moment.

"Three masts an' far too many guns over a vacant deck." Jonesy pointed to the ship.

"Aye, an' enough crew to match. Look at 'em. Runnin' around like ants on a sand hill." Dobbs began to chuckle, but was cut off by a stern look from Jonesy.

"The water's too still." Seth shifted his weight and looked aft. "Far too still. It's not right."

"Still, that ship's been refitted…for battle, methinks. That much I see."

None of those details went unnoticed by any man watching the vessel's approach from aboard the *Revenge*. The ship was ready to fight.

"Not military either. Look there!"

As the sun lifted to its peak just off the starboard bow, a tiny, distinct flag atop the vessel's mainmast came in to view.

"Avast to colors," rippled from the crow's nest.

Captain Phillips stood motionless, the spyglass once again fixed against his eye.

"She flies European colors. Red, white, and green. Where hails this vessel, Master Nutt?" The captain addressed the sail master from the helm.

"It be Roman colors, Capt'n. She be an Italian Brig, she be." Nutt looked wide-eyed at Captain Phillips. "What's Italians sailin' these waters for?"

Silence ensued as the two men stared at the ship on a course headed directly for them.

"I don't trust the vessel is honorable," the captain stated and gave new orders to Archer. "Hoist the colors!"

Kathryn watched as the black flag climbed the mast. The ghostly form holding a blood-red, spear-pierced, heart danced in the wind as it rose—a warning the *Revenge* promised piracy.

The ship sailed within easy view of the crew and Kathryn counted at least fifteen guns that lined the length of her portside gunwale. She would be a formidable adversary for the *Revenge*. The rest of the crew likely noticed her armament, as well, as their moods changed abruptly.

"Black flag, ho!" The call came from the crow's nest.

Kathryn lifted a hand to shade the fierce sunlight from her brow and squinted.

"Whose colors be flown?" Sam, standing next to her, said under his breath to no one.

As the ship tacked leeward, the flag came into view. The profile of a skull flanked by a sword and snake whipped in the wind. Beneath, in black script, were scrolled the words: *Morte ai Nostri Nemici.*

"*Morte.*" While Kathryn did not know its full meaning, she recognized the first word written in Italian.

"What's it mean?" Cuddy scratched his head.

"Means death."

She shuddered and watched the vessel tacking back on course, now within range of the *Revenge's* long-guns.

"Send them our greeting, Mister Sparks," Captain Phillips called out to the gunner, who immediately placed one hand alongside his mouth and repeated the order.

"Fire!"

With the welcome directive received, the men responded and fired the nearest set of long guns at once. All those aboard waited with bated breath for the vessel's response. Moments later, the answer came with return cannon fire, a near miss to the larboard bow.

"Hard to starboard!" the captain shouted. "We'll pull up abreast and fire on her abeam!

Guns at the ready!"

"Ho!" The response came scattered from several men quickly reloading.

Another blast lit up the portside cannon on the foreign vessel. Moments later, the cannon ball made contact and blew apart the uppermost gunwale at the third gun. Lethal fragments splintered from the side of the ship and transformed into deadly projectiles that peppered the mid-ship surface. The cries of pirates impaled with foreign bodies suddenly sounded, and Kathryn instinctively crouched. The captain leapt behind the wheel, took hold, and pulled it forcefully to starboard.

"Return fire! We have the weather gauge, we do!" he shouted, cursing under his breath.

"The hairless scum be naught for Davy's grip before I'm done with 'em! *Fire*!" Sparks ducked and lit another fuse.

The deck shuddered as several of the remaining guns fired at once. Smoke filled the air and Kathryn struggled to see beyond the haze. She could hear the

SILVER MOON

cries of the injured men filtering across the water and knew they had hit their mark. Too slow, the smoke cleared, but she could see the *Revenge* had pulled up alongside the ship. Several gaping holes stretched across its side, and the foreign ship was taking on water. It would not be a lengthy fight, though blood would wash both decks before it was finished. Of that, she was certain.

"Fire another round! Make haste, else we'll be baitin' the waters 'fore sundown!"

"Aye, Capt'n."

"They're boardin'!" Archer rushed to the rails, cutlass raised.

"Let 'em come. We'll cut 'em down where they stand." Captain Phillips pulled his pistols from the ribbons around his neck. "Steady men!"

Kathryn grasped the hilt of her cutlass and drew it from her waist. Ready to dispatch any man within reach, she crouched and waited for boarding. As she squatted, she felt a sharp barb digging into her thigh. Reaching down, she grasped hold of a dried stalk tucked deep into her pocket. Suddenly, she recalled the powerful herbs, juniper and Adder's Tongue, which she'd hastily tucked out of sight earlier.

"Protect and healin'," she whispered.

Flintlocks popped as the crew began to fire across the narrowed gap. She heard the blast of cannon fire from a distance, followed by the sickening crack of a forward mast. Quickly, she tucked the Adder's Tongue back into her pocket and crushed the juniper into tiny bits within her palm. The floorboards beneath her feet shuddered again as the brilliant flash from the nearest long gun blinded her momentarily.

Beyond, the captain cursed and fired his pistols as the sound of shattered wood echoed from across the narrow gap. Another direct hit, and she glanced out at the large brigantine to see the scattershot dropping several of their crew mid-ship before the main mast. Just then, the Italian flag attached to the bow disintegrated in another explosion. The brig was nearly disabled, but it continued to fire on the *Revenge* mercilessly.

Kathryn lifted her hand to her lips, then uncurled her fingers, ready to scatter its contents. The moment she intended to execute the spell, an alarming electrical sensation ran up her spine, accompanied by a loud command: "*Passata-soto.*" Instinctively, she dropped her hand to the deck, and her body followed as she thrust her cutlass overhead defensively. A resounding clang sounded only inches from her right ear. Turning to face her attacker, she realized she stood alone against the assailant.

The air whistled. She leapt to her left and nearly tripped over the body of one of her crewmen as she dodged the next lethal strike by a hairbreadth. The herbs lay spilled in a heap next to a body. Occasional bits blew at random from gusts of sea air and disappeared into the hazy smoke that hovered over the deck of the ship. *My spell!* Another zing hit her spine and Kathryn lost interest in the scattered herbs.

Behind her, the pirate sliced at her, and the air hissed as his blade just missed her again. She rolled to her left and broke away, facing her assailant. He dropped his sword slightly and Kathryn thrust her blade at the pirate's gut. He sidestepped and slashed at her throat, but sliced only air as she ducked and circled her blade around in a full arc aimed at the man's thick ribcage. She felt the steel in her hand pierce the pirate's leathery skin and carve a long gash along his torso. He arched backward and wailed in pain, which gave Kathryn a moment's reprise. Her lips mouthed the Celtic spell that intended for the abandoned herbs. The rhythmic chant matched the movement of her blade.

Deuses du mar,
Deuses du aire.

She lunged again, this time for the man's sternum, but missed. Instead, the blade sank deep into the soft tissue beneath. The pirate gurgled and lashed out blindly at the young woman, then fell face forward to the deck.

Amddiffyn fy gymdiethion,
Yn fy amyddiffyn.

Kathryn stood upright to catch her breath. Panting, she slowly withdrew the cutlass from the brute's torso. Staring at him for a moment, she dropped her cutlass to one side. Something caused her to look to the helm.

There she watched as Captain John Phillips slashed fiercely at a large pirate. The man staggered backward, his hands clutched at his own gaping throat. The captain kicked at the gasping pirate, sending him over the rails of the ship. He paused momentarily to look at Kathryn, who nodded in assurance that she had not been injured.

In that instant, her skin prickled again, and she spun on the balls of her feet. Her cutlass flew outward, as well. Without warning, she awarded her new assailant with death. He crumpled at her feet.

"As you deserve." She spat and looked away from the body.

Mid-ship, the clash of metal against metal rang through the hazy smoke as the crew fought wildly against the foreign pirates. An occasional groan sounded as another man fell to his death, but the chaos was devoid of cannon fire.

Kathryn paused long enough to peer over the rails at the Brig. Fire had broken out near its bow and water was pouring in through the freeboards. It would be an hour or two at the most before the foreign vessel sank.

She began to chant once again, this time aloud.

Pwer yn y more,
Rym yn y lleuad,
Dewch pwer I mi.

Kathryn shifted her focus across the deck and through the clearing smoke, glimpsing her crew at battle. Blades glinted as steel met tempered steel—a shattering explosion of weapons that sang with the bedlam of pirates in combat. In the distance, she caught sight of Seth crouched low, one hand behind him as he balanced on the planks for support. In a defensive move, he swung at an enormous man dressed elaborately in colorful plumes and gold earrings. Havoc shone in his eyes. The pirate slashed again and again at Seth, who fended off each blow with weakening strength.

Instinctively, Kathryn raised her hand and willed an unseen energy toward the foreigner. With her palm facing outward, she hurled a dagger-like bolt of blue light directly into the pirate's spine. The man stiffened, then fell to the deck face forward.

Seth's cutlass found its mark, and the pirate breathed his last. As Seth stood upright, he turned to look toward the bolt of light's origin and saw Kathryn standing with her hand outstretched, eyes locked on him.

"Kathryn?"

She nodded and Seth tipped his head in thanks to her, then leapt forward to aide a mate in battle. A tingling sensation in her palm was all that remained. It gradually subsided, and she dropped it to her side. In that instant, electricity shot down her back, and the Seren flared. She ducked, not knowing where her unseen assailant stood. At the same time, the air above her sang as she felt the sting of something slicing into her right shoulder.

She cried out and dropped her cutlass. Eyes wide, she searched for her assailant. Black boots skirted the deck, and she caught a glimpse of scuffed leather out of the corner of her eye. As quickly as the boots appeared, they disappeared, and another gust hissed next to her cheek. There was a dull thud immediately to her left, and she jerked her head to one side just in time to see the assailant falling backward, his arm still poised for a strike.

Suspended from his chest was a dagger, the one that had cut her from a fallen sail. She looked the other way and caught sight of its owner. His green eyes blazed. She locked eyes with him for a moment.

"A man to love and to fight for."

No one heard her, but no one else needed to. From the look on his face, it was apparent that his concern for her was greater than for himself. Suddenly, the clatter of weapons against wood broke them apart.

"Relinquish yer weapons, ye scurvy bilge scum." Archer's deep voice bellowed over the fracas. "It be by God's mercy ye find quarters this day. By me capt'n's orders, so be it."

Kathryn looked mid-ship and saw the smoky haze rising to the tops of the intact masts. The main teetered precariously to one side. Archer stood against the capstan, his sword held high overhead, the need for his crutch momentarily eliminated by a burst of fighting energy.

One by one, the foreign pirates dropped their swords and held their hands overhead—a sign of surrender. Three or four of the crew, including Seth, stepped forward and clapped their hands along the backs and torsos of each foreigner before running a hand inside their boots.

Once deemed clean of weapons, the prisoners were kicked behind the knees or forcibly shoved by the head into a kneeling position. The cluster of foreigners looked to be praying, but Kathryn knew their fate was sealed. God didn't answer prayers on a pirate ship.

"Ye be naught but foul dross aboard this vessel, an' be it by me own choosin', I'm sendin' ye to Davy Jones' locker meself…th' filthy lot o' ye. What say ye, men?" Archer shook his sword over his head.

"Aye! Cast 'em over t' call upon th' devil o' th' deep, hisself," a voice called out from behind, and a collective "Aye!" resonated in approval.

Archer lifted a lanky pirate by the scuff of his neck and dragged him to the rails. He pressed the tip of a long dagger against the man's throat. There was no resistance from the foreign pirate as they forced him to lean over the edge, poised and ready to drop into the current. Kathryn held her tongue as she watched Archer taunt the pirate. Thunderous laughter poured from the watching crew.

"The order's not been given. He hasn't the authority to dispatch captives." Her distain for the quartermaster mounted. "Rather arrogant of the quartermaster to execute him, methinks."

"Archer don't need orders for that." McMead sniffed and wiped blood from his blade. He glanced at Kathryn. "No quarter given stands."

"That's heartless."

"That's the way o' pirates, lass." McMead tucked his cutlass into its sheath and crossed his arms.

Behind them, the captain stood on the quarter-deck, observing their folly. Still, she anticipated he'd give a command from the helm, but he remained still and impassive.

"You wait, Mister McMead—within moments all will hear Capt'n John Phillip's commanding voice."

But the captain said nothing.

Suddenly, gunfire exploded—a single shot. Someone had fired a weapon, and Kathryn instinctively ducked, reaching for her cutlass. She sensed the outbreak of another battle and scanned the ship for the perpetrator. Just then, a voice rang out.

"Why don' ye take 'im to kiss th' gunner's daughter, aye?" Silence crept across the *Revenge* as all eyes turned to see from where the voice had come. "Or be it yer scared to pull a trigger on the pup?" The tone was deep, full and feminine.

A woman's voice.

Thirty-Two

REMNANTS OF GUNPOWDER CURLED IN long, wispy ribbons that climbed the foresails. It lingered slightly, encircling a curvy figure crowned with henna and russet curls that cascaded down in lazy waves over bronzed shoulders. The tip of an ornate blunderbuss still smoked. The hammer and frizzen glistened with etched gold, and the butt appeared to be carved ivory. Full, coppery lips puckered and blew at the last thread of smoke before looking up at the pirates. The men stirred at the sight of it.

"This man's a coward an' best be done away wit'," her full alto sang out, mesmerizing those who heard it. A lilt to her words indicated she was from somewhere in the most southern part of the Caribbean.

Brown eyes framed by long, thick lashes glanced sideways at the wretched pirate still under Archer's blade. She smiled with the corner of her mouth, a wickedly beautiful smile that caused even Kathryn to catch her breath. This woman was like none she had ever seen before. A true beauty with striking features and a svelte body that suggested many years at sea. Her clothing looked as ornate as her weapons. An intricately embroidered corset, crafted with gold bro- cade, was secured about her tiny waist and draped with leather holsters and a fine silk sash. As she stepped forward, she moved with a swagger that suggested great power and raw sexuality.

Seth leaned in, his jaw slack and eyes wide as he stared at her.

"Close your trap, Seth. You look like a blowfish!" Kathryn snarled. Seth snapped his mouth shut, but try as he might, he couldn't peel his eyes off the woman.

"What call yerself, missy?" Archer jerked back on the prisoner, a gesture intended to intimidate him. The man winced, and the woman's deep, throaty laugh unsettled a few.

"Ye can call me 'Back from th' Dead Red'," she jeered.

Murmurs rippled across the deck, but Archer stayed silent, his eyes wide as he examined this creature who approached with panther-like stealth. Sultry cin- namon and jasmine scented the air as she moved—an aphrodisiac that froze the men in place with its aroma.

"I say ye meet th' rope's end, ye cowardly bilge rat!" she bellowed at the captive pirate. She swung a cutlass that deftly sliced the right side of the pirate's head. Archer released his hold and jumped backward, barely missing the steel edge of her blade. The pirate howled in pain, clasped his hands to the bloody spot where his ear had once been and screeched in a flurry of foreign curses. She lifted the elaborate pistol, aimed it directly at the pirate, and cocked the hammer.

A loud click sounded from the helm.

"Drop your weapons, Madame!"

The woman froze with the gun, ready to fire on her crewman. She shifted her gaze to the helm and grinned at Captain Phillips, who stood with his own flintlock poised and ready to fire.

"An' who might ye be, to order me about so?"

"I am Captain John Phillips and this be my ship. Now drop your weapon or I will certainly shoot you."

She tipped her head, opened her hand with her arm still outstretched, and dropped the pistol onto the deck. With great pretense, she did the same with her cutlass, and the metal rattled across the deck. She then faced the captain and curtsied deeply, her eyes never leaving him. As she rose, she bellowed another throaty laugh.

"You, sir, may call me Jacquotte Delahaye, for that be me given name."

Captain Phillips aimed his pistol at the breathtaking woman. No one else moved. Everyone watched the interplay between the stunning redhead and Captain Phillips.

"Where be your capt'n, Madame?"

"Dead. Yer cannon fire made quite a mess o' my ship, an' the capt'n caught shot blowin' the mast in twain. He lay dead on board, if ye want to see the corpse."

Captain Phillips narrowed his eyes and studied the woman as she spoke. His weapon stayed aimed directly at her heart. Kathryn glanced back and caught the woman staring at her. Their gazes locked. Kathryn raised her hands to her hips and sauntered a few steps toward the brazen woman. As she moved, the sting from her shoulder reminded her that the injury from her last challenge was still fresh, and its raw edges still needed to be sewn. It would have to wait. Kathryn hid the pain well, and except for the bloodstain on her sleeve, no one knew she guarded a wound.

"An' so, ye have yer own bawdy prize aboard wit' ye, aye? She be but a waif. Has th' lass skill with th' blade, or does she carry th' cutlass for sport?" the redhead sneered.

Kathryn's cheeks blazed, and she instinctively lifted her cutlass while dismissing the burn in her shoulder. The captain had stepped down from the helm and was already positioned between Kathryn and Madame Delahaye. He extended his free hand and held it in front of Kathryn, a warning to be still.

"Not now, Kathryn." Captain Phillips whispered while keeping his eyes on the female pirate.

"Ah, she has a name, has she? Simperin' Snit would fit her just fine, methinks."

Fury rose to color Kathryn's cheeks as Delahaye's heady scent raised bile to the back of her throat.

"You are my prisoner, Madame. Ye best curtail yer tongue, else the crew'll cut it out." He turned to face his men. "Secure this foul lot to the capstan. The Madame to be handled with her crew equally."

A few hearty pirates dragged the unarmed for-eigners to the ship's center and tied their wrists and feet together, then secured each one, evenly spaced, to the capstan to ensure no one could escape. Madame Delahaye's eyes never left Captain Phillips as she saun-tered to where her crewmen sat and willingly joined them. An inviting grin spread across her full lips as she planted her brown eyes on Cuddy, who trembled ever so slightly as he fastened the line around her waist.

"Mister Gow, amass the booty and divvy the spoils handsomely," Captain Phillips ordered. "Alight the brig and send her to the briny deep. We shall not leave any telltale testament of our efforts this day. Make haste, Mister Sparks! I wish to see her sails afire within' the hour!"

"Pitch th' torches an' ignite 'em."

"Aye!" shouted a few men, who hurled the lit torches across the narrow gap to the brigantine.

"Make swift work an' strip the ship of everything valuable a'fore the fire takes it all, including th' spirits."

"Aye." The men quickly hauled hogshead casks filled with European wine and Jamaican rum onto the *Revenge*.

"Don't leave anything behind, mates." Archer snatched a small chest and threw it onto one shoulder. "Davis an' Reed be on the livestock."

"Aye," Davis replied. Both men steered goats with the barrels of their muskets, while others hauled crates with hens, their nests heartily filled with cackle fruit.

"Take it all below deck."

"Aye!" Pock-eyed Pete turned to the causeway, carrying a large, lidless hamper filled with vials of oriental spices and herbs. Perched in the middle of the basket was a large, slate-colored cat. It stared at Kathryn as she studied the contents of each basket hoisted on board. She glanced at it and whispered something in Gaelic, then looked back to the baskets.

Most of the herbs she recognized, but a few were foreign, and she hoped Cook would be willing to part with some of the precious plants. Her small stock had diminished, and the plants would be a welcome addition to her dwindling supply.

Pete caught her staring and shifted his load out of view to hide the cat sitting there.

"She'll bring us luck," he stammered, and picked up his pace as he passed by.

Kathryn shook her head. *Apparently, pirates relish pets, as well as plunder.* The thought made her chuckle. She smirked and waved him on. To her left, she watched as half a dozen pirates marched from the foreign ship, carrying items to be used or auctioned at the mast. As the last man stepped off the gangplank, the mainsail ignited. The darkened sky flared orange and red as pieces of blazing sailcloth broke free and floated heavenward. Flames danced along the boom and hopped to the shattered mast.

Within moments, the entire topside of the brigantine was ablaze, illuminating the surface of the *Revenge* with an eerie glow. Kathryn noted the faces of the prisoners, eyes wide as they watched their ship burn.

A familiar laugh broke the tension, and Kathryn's focus darted to the newcomer tied up with the rest of her crew. Her skin glistened in the firelight, which made her only slightly more breathtaking, especially when she tossed her head back and laughed.

The captain stepped forward, circled the captives, and with his weapon outstretched, aimed it at no one in particular. His eyes never left the woman. *How could her beauty not take him aback, as well?* Something inside Kathryn turned dark and pensive, as the thought took hold. Fortunately, in that moment, a breath of briny sea air swept all remnants of Delahaye's sultry scent overboard. Kathryn inhaled and hoped her crew would do the same to clear their heads of this vixen's enchantment.

Finally, Captain Phillips spoke—again to no one in particular—his gait even and regal as he circled the captives. "What be the name of your ship?"

"*Il Potente*," a tremulous voice said.

"Where does she hail from?" The captain cornered the man and pointed the barrel of a pistol directly at the captive's heart. The pirate said nothing, just stared mutely at the weapon, his eyes wider than before.

"Just shoot him an' be done wit' it, Capt'n o' this ship." Sarcasm rippled through Delahaye's voice like the currents of a riptide. She eyed him from the opposite side of the capstan.

Captain Phillips' gaze narrowed, never shifting from the woman. His stride spoke louder than his words as he crossed to where she sat. He deliberately lowered the barrel of his weapon at her forehead. She stared up at him with soft brown eyes and smiled.

"This ship be naught for wasted bloodshed, wench!" Captain Phillips spat and stepped closer to her, touching the tip of his flintlock to her left temple. "We kill men that need killin' aboard this ship. That's sommat ye'll never decide.

"Aye, an' it be plain to see ye be no malingerer, Capt'n Phillips." She smiled broader, exposing alarmingly alabaster teeth that contrasted with her bronzed skin.

He cocked the flintlock. Silence settled across the *Revenge*, disrupted only by the crack of timber ablaze in the distance. All eyes were on the captain. Perhaps there'd be bloodshed, after all. The pirates waited, hoping to witness the execution of Madame Delahaye.

"I will shoot you, lass," Captain Phillips hissed between clenched teeth.

Jacquotte snickered. "*Il Potente* makes berth in th' port o' Genoa."

"You're far from home in these waters." He paced as he spoke.

"Aye." She tossed another reckless smile at him. "But it seems th' voyage be not for loss. Perhaps it's fate I meet up wit' th' Capt'n o' th' *Revenge*, aye?"

Captain Phillips held his tongue, and instead, turned to face the quartermaster. "Mister Archer, bring the axe."

She did not flinch.

"Aye, aye, sir!" The quartermaster bolted.

Archer's agility had much improved and only a slight limp remained, something not lost on Kathryn. *Perhaps we will soon meet again at the sword*, she thought, and her eyes narrowed as she watched his movements. *And yet, one more threatens. This foreign woman, this new intruder, will certainly pose additional menace and require my cutlass to resolve it.* Kathryn felt a twinge of uneasiness as she counted the enemies she had quickly amassed.

She glanced back at the prisoners and the female pirate held captive with them. *She's cunning, this one.* Kathryn sensed it and knew she would need to keep close watch on her. As if to confirm her fears, a heady dose of cinnamon and jasmine blew across the deck—the aroma spared no one.

Archer returned with the axe and assumed a wide-legged stance of authority. He posed before the mast with the axe's head in one hand and the grip in the other. This was obviously a timeworn ceremony executed with fluid precision—something Kathryn had not witnessed first-hand during her sojourn aboard the *Revenge*. Crewmen began to gather around the main mast, forming a tight semi-circle near Archer. Just behind them, the foreigners watched, still lashed together against the capstan.

"There be no quarter given this day!" the captain shouted to all on board. The crewmen cheered, and cutlasses were raised in salute. Kathryn stood apart, her cutlass held at her side, and watched as fear drained the color from the prisoners' faces. A few cast defeated glances to the deck.

"Your ship sailed o're Caribbean waters where ye be marked the enemy. In the wake of justice, she met her penance. You see her skeleton ablaze for retribution." Captain Phillips turned on the captives. "By all accounts," his voice boomed, "ye be accused of piracy against this vessel and her crew! For this, you face the sentence of death as foreigners and foes. Prepare to dance the hempen jig!"

Gasps and protests sounded from the captives and blended with shouts of approval from the *Revenge's* crew. Kathryn watched as a dubious look crossed Delahaye's face. Her brown eyes flashed to match the glow of the last embers of their ship.

She's hatching something in her pretty little head. Kathryn could see it in her eyes.

"Who be ye to make judgment o're th' laws o' the sea? What powers possess ye to condemn us so?" Jacquotte Delahaye sneered.

Color flooded the captain's cheeks. He drew nearer the woman and leaned into her until he was but inches from her face. "I am the capt'n of this ship, and there be my prize." He pointed to the flaming main mast without looking away. "The remains of which are sent to the devil himself. See it sink, even now!"

She flinched as he spoke of the brig and glanced momentarily at the port bow while it burned. With fire in her eyes, she addressed him. "If ye be lord an' master o're me crew an' mates, then grant us justice by th' Code. Offer a choice to join yer crew or wear th' hempen halter."

John Phillips stepped back. "Daring of ye to suggest such a bargain, Madame. But, certainly, it's not an unreasonable proposition." He cocked his head and glanced at Archer, who nodded enthusiastically. Several of the men also nodded approval. "We'll put it to vote." He turned to face the crew. "What say ye? Shall we bring on crewmen or hang them from the mast? What is the vote?"

The cry sounded, "Bring 'em to crew!"

Thirty-Three

KATHRYN'S JAW DROPPED. "THE VOTE'S unanimous? We're bringin' on additional men?"

"Aye, we need more hands." Matthias had stepped up beside her without her noticing. The smell of fried pork and wine accompanied him.

"But it's been their habit to vote for a robust hanging."

"Aye, true. The *Revenge* requires many hands, particularly during rough seas. We be rather short-handed, presently."

"Won't it be burdensome to feed so many mouths?" Kathryn looked at the cook, who shook his head.

"Hardly, given the stores just acquired."

In fact, the whole of it had come from the Italian ship and unfortunately, most would rot and be filled with maggots.

"Aye, perhaps it's a good idea, then."

Still, there was Madame Jacquotte Delahaye.

"It appears to be settled, then," Captain Phillips stated. "Bring each prisoner, in turn, before the mast.

Let him swear o're the axe to the Articles of this ship. He…or she…who refuses such shall be hanged."

The men cheered and Archer handed the axe to Nutt, who assumed the same wide stance, a mark of authority, by all accounts. Archer made his way to the capstan and cut free the first prisoner. The young foreigner was dragged to the main mast and positioned in front of the men.

"What be yer name, pup?" Archer growled loud enough for the crew to hear.

The captive man looked directly at Archer and shrugged his shoulders, then began to rant in strange, staccato syllables.

"He cannot speak yer English tongue, Quartermaster," Jacquotte's voice rang out.

"What manner o' speak be this?" Archer roared back at her, and held his dagger against the pirate's throat.

The man fell silent. His hands were still tied at the wrist, and his inability to understand Archer's demands left him defenseless. His eyes, as wild as a caged animal, searched the crowd for sympathy. There was none to be found.

"Jacquotte, *lei parla questo linguaggio barbaro. Che cosa vuole da noi?*"

(Jacquotte, you speak this barbarian's language. What does he want of us?)

Her dark eyes darted from the captive man to the quartermaster. "Th' coward wants to know what manner of dyin' ye plan for him." She made a gesture with her hand toward the pirate with the knife at his neck.

Immediately, the other captives protested. The same strange staccato language ricocheted in all directions. One man's expletives sounded familiar. The captain stepped forward, scanned the cluster of captives, and spotted him. He looked rather like a sailor who would have been part of His Majesty's Royal Navy, blue-eyed, with brightly colored feathers tucked into his tousled, auburn hair.

Captain Phillips motioned with his pistol. "You there, with the plumes—step forward!"

The man struggled to his feet, prodded forward by a crewmen Kathryn recognized as one of the barrel men. He snapped the line at the man's waist and pushed him to the main mast.

"Ye'll be the first," Archer announced.

"Do ye, by penalty of death, swear loyalty to this ship and company, thereby joining of your own free will the life of piracy aboard the *Revenge*? Place your hand o're the axe and swear by it, man, or you shall surely meet the devil this day." Captain Phillips clenched his teeth as he waited for the prisoner's response.

The man stared hard at the captain for a moment, then glanced at the men gathered in front of him. He reached out his hand and grasped hold of the steel head.

"Aye, I swear by it!"

"Cut him loose," Captain Phillips stated. "What's your name, man?"

"Francois Santos, sir."

"That's French, is it not? Yet your crew speaks a foreign tongue to my ears. Your colors be European. Still, you be English by my eyes."

"Aye, 'tis all true. Th' ship be Italian, as Madame Jacquotte attested. We put into port near Hispaniola, where me an' a few o' th' men joined 'er crew." He spoke with the rounded dialect typical for the French island settlers. "Me name's from th' island, taken a'fore I set to sea. I was born Thomas Middleton of Bideford."

The pirate stood upright, in spite of new wounds sustained in the recent battle. He looked Captain Phillips in the eye as he spoke.

"Take your place with the crew, Mister Santos." The captain nodded in salute as the man stepped forward and into the circle of pirates. "Your wounds shall be attended to forthwith."

As he took his place, Captain Phillips turned to Delahaye and faced her with hands on hips. Archer shifted his weight, and the captive man still under his blade winced.

"Now, Madame, it would be most agreeable should ye be inclined to translate for your crewmates."

"An' what exactly would ye have me say to my crew, John Phillips?"

The vixen makes her way with him! Kathryn's blood boiled, and her grip tightened on the hilt of her sword. She stepped forward. Seth quickly crossed to where she stood and placed a strong hand on her forearm. "Stay out of it."

She shot him a seething look and shook off his hold.

John Phillips was losing patience. He leaned forward until his clenched teeth nearly reached Delahaye's throat. "Swear the oath or die!" he hissed.

Apparently, Madame Delahaye's scent did not affect the captain in the same manner it affected his crew. The woman batted her eyes at him and nodded before rattling off fluent Italian. The crew was captivated, and Kathryn felt more than disgust for their enamored interest. *Madame Jacquotte certainly has a commanding way about her—something carnal that adds to her provocativeness.* Kathryn's mouth soured as she thought of it. When Jacquotte finished giving instructions to the other captives, she glanced back at Captain Phillips with a look that twinkled amusement. Heads nodded, accompanied by declarations of refusal in their native tongue.

"*Mai! Noi moriremo prima!*"

The captain looked impatiently to Jacquotte for translation.

"They would 'ave ye kill 'em, Capt'n Phillips," she stated.

Captain Phillips snorted and turned to face Archer. Kathryn's temper rose as she stepped forward, and once again, Seth reached out and grasped hold of her arm.

"Not now, Kat," he whispered. "This is not a fight you should go lookin' for, savvy?"

She looked at him and saw wisdom behind his eyes. His face was strong, aristocratic.

Gone were the traces of youthful innocence, most likely wiped clean from hard months of service aboard a pirate ship—like herself.

"Aye. But one more…" She shifted her weight. "I won't stand by and watch this much longer, Seth."

"Hush, Kathryn." Seth fingers dug into her skin.

"Mister Archer," the captain's commanding voice boomed. "Bring each of the prisoners and let him swear o're the axe. Should a fool refuse the privilege, tie him up by the ankles and douse him o'er the rails until he swear or be dead, savvy?"

"Gladly, Capt'n," Archer responded.

"Who'll do th' speakin' for 'em, sir? Th' bawdy wench sees to 'er own ends an' cannot be trusted," Santos piped up, shooting Jacquotte a dark look.

"Traitor!" she screeched.

"Hold!" John Phillips barked and moved to the center of his crew. He took Santos by the shoulder and shoved him hard toward the main mast. The pirate stumbled and looked backward at his new captain in confusion. "Mister Santos will speak for the prisoners."

"He's losing patience," Kathryn said to Seth.

He gripped her shoulder a little tighter. "Aye, and he'll likely lose patience with anyone else who interferes. Pick your battles wisely, Kat."

"This is my battle."

"No, it's not. Soon, blades will cross, and the blood of a female will be shed as easily as the rest. This is not your moment."

Kathryn glanced at Jacquotte Delahaye, who stared at her with mischief in her eyes. "She calls me out, Seth."

"She is but a woman—you are the *Mellt Sosye*, remember?"

"How did you know...?" Behind Delahaye rose a cinnamon aura—the color of survival.

"Not this battle, Kathryn."

Thirty-Four

"BE CAUTIOUS WITH THAT ONE, John," Kathryn warned as he stood next to her.

All eyes remained on Jacquotte Delahaye. She glanced at Seth, Captain Phillips nodded, and Seth relaxed his hold on her arm. It still hurt from his grip, and she shot an irritated look at him, then reached up to rub the spot where his fingers had left marks.

"Thank you, Seth," she said sarcastically.

Seth ignored her and kept his focus on the main mast, where another pirate had stepped forward and laid his hand over the axe. Santos stood just in front of him and spoke rapidly, while Nutt steadied the large cutting tool. The whole affair looked very official.

"She's trouble, that one. I'm tellin' you true, John," Kathryn pressed.

Captain Phillips seemed oblivious to what she had said. "Then you'd best keep your distance from her, lass." He kept his voice low.

"Oho! You protect the likes of her?" Kathryn snapped.

"I'm merely protectin' you. She's a weathered pirate, albeit female, and I will not have you crossin' blades with her."

Kathryn's cheeks grew hot. "Are you givin' me an order, Capt'n?" She looked from Captain Phillips to Seth, who merely shook his head.

"Nay, lass, just a request." Phillips turned to look at her, and his emerald eyes stopped her heart for an instant. "Please, Kathryn. Leave her be."

Kathryn paused and glanced back at Seth, who feigned interest in the ceremony. It was obvious he could hear their bantering but chose to distance himself. *Wise decision, Seth. Ye do not wish to meet the other end of my temperament this day.* Ignoring him, she turned back to the captain. His incessant stubbornness meant he would not budge on the issue. This was a battle of wills, one she would not win, but her temper required a release, so she turned on Madame Delahaye.

"Aye, then, for you I'll do it, Capt'n, but only for that," she stated.

He smiled, but his eyes never left the activities at the mast. A strong hand took hold of hers and gave it an affectionate squeeze. *Oh, how this man infuriates me!* The thought caused her to raise her foot slightly, ready to strike the deck below it. His fingers entwined with hers and a warm sensation spread from her fingertips to her heart. *How can such contrary willfulness suddenly turn itself onto such indomitable carnality? Indeed, this is a man most lasses only dream of. How can I be willful?*

How can I do less than crave him? She shook her head against her thoughts, but did not pull away.

"It's a right bad omen, bringin' a woman aboard a ship such as this," she muttered.

Incredulous, he stepped back in disbelief. Seth snickered, then caught himself, cleared his throat, and shifted his weight, feigning renewed interest in the proceedings.

"You're aboard this ship, Madame! What say ye to that? I suppose your gender bears no relevance on this account?" The captain dropped her fingers and set both hands on his waist.

"Well, it's different on my account."

Seth could contain himself no longer and laughed out loud, then slapped a hand over his mouth, and fabricated a cough. Kathryn looked at him indignantly. "Seth! Do you have somethin' caught in your throat? Don't you have somewhere to be?"

"Aye," Seth blurted, and trotted off. Once out of range, he threw back his head and let loose a riotous belly laugh.

Kathryn stomped the readied foot as he howled, then turned to face the captain, who stifled his own chuckle, which only served to infuriate her further. She stomped her foot a second time.

"Why be so smug, Capt'n Phillips?"

Captain Phillips could only chuckle in response, then leaned over and kissed the top of her head. Lavender filled his senses as he did so. "Ay, my Kathryn. I'll keep a watchful eye on the Madame as you request."

Clamor from mid-ship brought their attention to the mainmast. Archer was dragging a scrawny pirate to the rails. The man bellowed protests in Italian, shaking his head vehemently while the redheaded lady laughed. Shouts of "*Pirata!*" and "*Cani!*" from the last few prisoners brought a few to their feet. Enthusiastically, two of the crewmen started tying knots into unused lines. The ropes, fastened onto an empty hogshead barrel, were then tied to the pirate. The entire bulk could, then, be thrown overboard to bob like a cork and left trailing behind the ship until the traitor was dead.

Kathryn had never witnessed "a corker" in person, but she'd heard talk of it on long complacent nights when the men gathered around the scuttlebutt and told tall tales.

"Let th' scurvy dog take a bob in th' drink," one of the crew called out.

"Aye! A corker, he be!"

Within minutes, the barrel-laden man was tossed overboard. He dipped underneath the water's crests for only a moment before bouncing back to the surface. One end of a long line had been tied to the unfortunate's feet, and the other end was anchored to a portside cleat. The coil unwound as the bobbing barrel floated alongside the ship, and then held fast while the man and barrel was towed behind the ship.

Cries for help, muffled by the slap of each swell that pounded him to silence, soon grew weak. A pistol fired from the stern, and all eyes moved to find its agent. With one foot resting on the taffrail, Jacquotte Delahaye took aim again and fired a second time at her crewmate trailing in the ship's wake. Splinters flew into the air as the barrel cracked, and the man cried out again. She tossed her head, and red locks rippled in the breeze as she called out to the bobbing man.

"Vivere e morire come un codardo, è feccia romana!"

Stepping up to Jacquotte's side, Santos took aim and fired. Within moments, three additional pirates had joined the firing squad and simultaneously discharged their flintlocks. The barrel splintered as the man fell limp.

"He called us Roman scum…sounds like a threat to me, don' it, mateys?" Madame Delahaye called out to the crew.

Wild laughter exploded from the sharpshooters. They walloped each other's backsides victoriously as they watched the barrel bound with the body flopping over it.

Captain Phillips stepped forward, his face flushed—not from the heat of the sun. "That will do, gentlemen… and that includes you, Madame. Cut it free."

Archer stepped to the rail, severing the line with a single blow. A deep gash in the wood remained the only memorial. The body floated free while sea birds circled above it.

"Who's next?" Archer sneered as he turned his pistol on the remaining two pirates still tied to the capstan.

"I don't recall that bawdy little wench swearin' her oath," a female voice hailed from behind them.

Kathryn sauntered forward, her hands on her hips, and tossed her head in the direction of the redhead. Captain Phillips glared at Kathryn, who avoided his gaze. Her attention was on Delahaye and Archer. "Perhaps she'd rather strap herself to a barrel. I'll take the first shot!" Kathryn stopped and glared at Jacquotte.

"She speaks!" Delahaye smirked at Kathryn in response.

"Aye! Th' lass be owin' 'er pledge o're th' axe!" Wynn shouted.

Several crewmen offered a hearty "Aye!" in agreement. Archer pivoted and aimed the barrel of his pistol at Kathryn, a sure warning she had overstepped her bounds. Kathryn met it with a firm, unflinching stance and some sass.

"You know the Articles yourselves, you who sail on board the *Revenge*. Do you intend to break the officer's code and swear in your chirurgeon?" Kathryn shouted.

Archer flinched. Kathryn spoke the truth. The ship's surgeon was not required to swear to the ship's Articles and take the oath o're the axe. In fact, it was discouraged on most vessels to prevent preferential treatment toward the infirm. Most chirurgeon's filled other duties, sometimes even manning the helm.

Kathryn was not to be trifled with on this issue, and Archer knew they were surrounded by a bad audience, should another battle ensue between quartermaster and witch. Slowly, Archer aimed his weapon at the piratess. Jacquotte Delahaye stepped down from the taffrail and sauntered toward him, her hips full and seductive as she walked. All eyes were drawn to her as she moved, and the men fell silent.

"Aye, sir. Methinks yer capt'n would soon be lively indeed, havin' himself a real woman aboard." She leaned forward to expose the surface of a plump bronzed bosom. As she did so, she cast a crusty look at Kathryn.

Kathryn stepped forward and drew her cutlass. *Insults from an established crewman is barely tolerable, but to have this foreign strumpet mock me so will certainly win the wench a meeting with the sharp edge of my blade.* Kathryn's thoughts raged as she leapt forward. Instantly, the captain moved in between the two women.

"You have no business aboard this ship, Madame, and be granted opportunity to join only by the grace of this crew, including the chirurgeon."

Kathryn glanced at him in amazement. She had never been formerly designated as the surgical officer of the ship, though her role as the healer had been clear the day she'd been brought aboard. Such gall as she had just displayed, to title herself as chirurgeon, was brazen enough. The risk of doing so could have bought her the powder ball that waited inside Archer's pistol. But that risk fled with Kathryn's rebuttal to Jacquotte's insults.

Now it was official, made so publicly by the captain, and none could refute her title.

Kathryn scanned the unruly crew's faces for disapproval, but found none. Seth stood off to one side, grinning from ear to ear. As he caught her eye, he lifted his cutlass aloft, a silent "Huzzah!" meant only for her. A designation as the ship's surgeon put her third in line, directly behind the quartermaster. She knew the captain's announcement was more for her crew than for the Madame pirate.

Inwardly, she savored a feeling of triumph, knowing she would receive a greater share of the spoils heaped about the mast for auction. With renewed confidence, she lifted her chin and peered at Delahaye with venom.

"Surely ye jest! That waif be yer chirurgeon?" Jacquotte spat. "Th' little mouse hasn't th' strength to lift a physik's scalpel."

Kathryn lunged forward, her cutlass ready to strike. This time it was the captain who seized her. "Hold, Kathryn!"

"Let loose of me!"

"That be an order," Captain Phillips added, but let her go.

The sorceress stood down with her cutlass still poised. So agitated she couldn't contain it, Kathryn shifted her weight from one foot to the other in anticipation of the next opportunity to strike. She eyed Jacquotte with fire in her icy blue eyes.

Captain Phillips broke in before she could respond. His voice dropped again, a lethal whisper she had heard only once before, long ago, when he spoke of Morrigan. "Think again, pirate, o're crossin' blades with a witch!"

Jacquotte's eyes widened when she looked at Kathryn with disbelief. There was a subtle flicker of hesitation behind the velvety brown eyes, which did not go unnoticed. Kathryn dropped into a curtsy. Behind her, the crew crossed themselves and spat.

"Aye, aye, sir," Jacquotte uttered. She bowed and remained there much longer than necessary.

Kathryn knew this was not a sign of respect, but she sheathed her cutlass anyway and folded her arms. Captain Phillips glanced a warning at Kathryn.

He suddenly turned to address his men. "Mister Archer, ye best finish swearin' in the rest of these miserable prisoners and make haste of it! We've got plunder to divvy."

A cheer rose from the crew, and as it grew louder, the next prisoner was brought forward. The captain then turned to his chirurgeon, the tone of his voice severe.

"And you have the wounded to tend to…"

Kathryn nodded, grateful the captain had been charitable with her once again. Most likely, her temper would have found her standing in front of a pistol or dangling from a hangman's noose. *You'd best get control of it, Kathryn. After all, there are the Articles to uphold, and as captain, he is bound by them just as the crew is.*

"Kathryn...you've crossed into uncharted waters now."

"I beg your pardon?" She looked up at the captain who stood with hands clasped behind his back, eyes forward.

"You've been accepted as part of the crew and now have the unusual prestige as the ship's chirurgeon... and without approval from the crew. Don't abuse the privilege."

"We could always put it up for a vote. Maybe Cuddy'd be better with a scalpel, aye?"

"Kathryn, do not press this!"

She sighed, "Aye, Capt'n." She'd grown weary of arguing and decided she'd best watch her outbursts, particularly in regard to issues belonging to the captain. Kathryn swallowed her pride and felt the pang of humility hit again.

"Good. Now please tend to the injured. I want to be back to full sail before nightfall."

"Aye, aye, Capt'n."

His mouth let slip a smile before he turned from her and strode with a seafarer's gait back to the main mast. Jacquotte Delahaye stood before the axe and faced the Articles tacked to the mast. As she placed her hand over the axe, she tossed a seductive look to the captain, then swore the oath. Her demeanor was aloof and impassive, but conniving thoughts swam behind her eyes.

The Madame pirate had joined his crew.

Thirty-Five

Swearing in the last two prisoners, neither of whom understood the words, happened quickly. Santos was not employed, as time was of the essence, given the numerous battle injuries taking a toll on the wounded. Besides, the lively sport of dispatching an oppositionist and using him for target practice was not an activity either prisoner was willing to participate in. As a result, no interpreter was needed, and both pirates gladly grasped hold of the axe head and swore vehemently.

"*Lascio la mia fedelta a questa nave, il capitano, e l'equipaggio…si!*"

"Accepted herewith yer pledge o' loyalty to the ship, the Capt'n, an' crew. Take yer place as a duly sworn seaman o' the *Revenge!*" Archer shouted.

Kathryn turned to leave, but the plunder held her captive. She kept her eyes on the whole proceedings and watched as Gow stepped up to assume his position for the auction.

"Ye'd best get below," Seth stated, catching her standing there.

"In just a moment."

As the last prisoner took his place among the crew, Archer swiftly moved back behind the mast and began to direct placement of the newly acquired booty. A large cask was rolled forward, and Archer laid the same dirk that had been used against Kathryn on top of it.

As the stash was moved into plain view, Archer picked up a polished coffer and gently lifted its lid. Inside, Spanish doubloons and silver reales sparkled under the light of the flickering lantern suspended overhead. Archer grinned and immediately set out to count coins. As he did so, Gow dragged another chest forward, this one larger than the first. All eyes moved to the bosun as he hacked the lock from it with his cutlass.

"Shares be made a'fore th' biddin' begins," Archer called out ceremoniously. "Capt'n,

one an' half. Master, gunner, bosun"—he paused and glanced at Kathryn sourly—"an' th'

chirurgeon be one an' quarter. Th' rest be a share each, includin' th' prisoners who be th' newest members o' th' crew."

"Huzzah!" sounded from the gathered men, their greedy eyes on the coins. Two pirates joined Archer on one side and spread out a large sailcloth. Piles of shiny reales and gold doubloons were separated as the quartermaster counted and then placed each on the cloth. Archer raised his dirk, and with the adept skill of a pirate who had done so many times, hacked a chunk off from a silver coin, then pushed the piece into one of the piles. He said something to Cade, standing nearest to him, who quickly lifted the coins and set them apart from the others.

Archer repeated the process. "Pieces of eight" had a new meaning for Kathryn, who smiled as she waited for her share, along with the rest.

"Capt'n," a stocky pirate said as he lifted a basket filled with coins and carried it to John Phillips.

The captain stepped forward. "Mister Smythe." He tipped his tricorn in salute. Smythe poured the coins into a pouch. Captain Phillips retrieved it and commanded him in a low voice to collect another basket directly.

"Yer welcome, sir." Smythe grinned.

"I will be deliverin' the chirurgeon's share." His voice was but a whisper and his eyes shifted to Archer in warning.

The quartermaster wisely said nothing but nodded to Smythe to collect the pile set at the edge of the cloth. Smythe began to load coins into his basket as John Phillips tied the pouch and dropped it down the waist of his trousers.

"There will be no lack of assurances that the total share be true, will there, Mister Archer?" Captain Phillips' query was laced with caution.

"Aye, th' full share be there, Capt'n," Archer replied without looking up from the count.

With the declaration made and accounting verified, Archer proceeded to divvy the remaining wealth.

"Don't crowd me, swabs. I'm likely to lose count an' it'll be yours that goes short!"

"Back off, Jonesy."

"Ye back off, ye bloody, greedy cur." Jonesy balled his fists as he squared off with Tate.

"Hold, mates! There's enough for everyone!"

Smythe handed the basket to the captain, who quickly surveyed the pile of coins. He then spun on his heels and spotted Kathryn where he'd left her on the quarterdeck and motioned for her to join him. Realizing that she carried no pouch, she gathered her skirt to one side.

"The chirurgeon's share," he said and poured the coins into the folds of her skirt.

When he had finished, she tied a knot around the loot and held it with one hand. The captain looked sternly at her, and she recognized the warning. Her time was up—she needed to tend to the sick bay.

"Now, lass, you best mind the infirm as is your duty aboard this ship, and the accountability you've been paid for."

"Aye, Capt'n." Gathering her effects, she withdrew from the crowd.

As she moved toward her cabin, she could hear as each man was called forward to collect his share. An impenitent smile crossed her face, and she fingered the coins against her thigh.

"Music!" she said, listening to the jangling of doubloons above the rumble of pirates bartering. "This belongs to me. The spoils of a new plunder—sweet and satisfying. Perhaps the life of a pirate suits me better than Celtic cliffs and heather."

She smiled at the thought, and entered the chirurgeon's cabin buried deep within the heart of the *Revenge*.

Thirty-Six

A TRAIL OF WOUNDED SAILORS lined up along the starboard rail, waiting for their turn. Kathryn sighed as she looked at them. Each man had onerous injuries that needed attending to by the chirurgeon. Out of desperation, and because of the large number of injured, Kathryn had designated the forecastle as a temporary sick bay.

"You're not to enter without visible blood or broken bones, says I."

"But this hurts me severely." The pirate held out an arm peppered with shrapnel and splinters. "See there… it's blood, to be certain."

"Get in line." She pointed to the end of a string of bruised and broken pirates. "You'll wait your turn like the others!"

The entire sick bay was already occupied with groaning men and supplies. Several had been forced to find sleeping space elsewhere on the ship. What few hammocks and cots were available remained designated for the infirm. A constant, almost overwhelming, flood of men petitioned for her skill.

"It's a blessin' that Mariel acquainted me with her unusual practices. Growing up as a young girl, guided in ancient Celtic alchemy—you'd best be grateful for it! Now settle yourself over that barrel and let your arm drop limp." He did as instructed, wincing as he allowed his arm to dangle. She yanked on it, and the dislocated shoulder snapped back into place. The pirate yelped, but it was over quickly enough, though her patience seethed.

"I'm much obliged, ma'am. Just please be a bit more gentile, if ye could."

"It's a *Gift* bequeathed through my lineage." She slipped the dressing around his arm, looping it over his neck, and pulled it tight. "I'm sorry this hurt, but it's the only way for proper healin'. Still, pain reminds you that you're alive, doesn't it, now? That's somethin' to be grateful for. That's all I'm sayin'."

She smiled at him, which he returned, then hobbled off under the care of a matey, glad to be leaving the attention of the newly appointed chirurgeon while still breathing. Seth pushed past them, carrying a bundle with both hands.

"I heard what you said."

"Well, then you understand my frustration. They're lucky to be alive. This is a brutal business. Sometimes, I think no one realizes that."

"Some do, Kathryn."

"How would you know, Seth? You're so busy swingin' from yardarms and snitchin' rum with your mates there. You're as bad as the rest." She chuckled and looked at him out of the corner of her eye.

"You're gifted here…" Seth touched her hands. "…and here." He touched her forehead. "They may not see just how gifted you are, but I do."

Kathryn softened and looked up at Seth. It didn't matter, really, that anyone else understood, only that she did.

"Thank you, Seth. I suppose what I offer is better than what they've had in the past, aye?" She wrinkled her nose as she thought of a physik's modern medicine and the landlubber surgeon's methods of treatment, particularly for injuries from pirating.

"Aye, they cut and bleed a man." Seth shook his head and dropped a pile of folded sailcloth at her feet. "These are for you."

Kathryn sighed and nodded, then watched as Seth bounded out of sight. "Bleeding, indeed!" she muttered under her breath. The mere thought made her cringe, although she did have great uses for leeches and hoped some could be found before the pirates' wounds festered further.

The young tailor, William White, stepped forward. He was the next in line and presented a swollen ankle that had been bludgeoned by flying timber, along with his forearm that was lacerated with crisscrossed marks from wrist to elbow.

"How did you come by these wounds, Mister White?" she asked and smiled reassuringly.

"I…it…" He stammered and looked at his black and blue ankle. "I fell over a cannon thrown loose by th' damage."

"And these?" she asked and lifted his arm by the wrist to eye level.

"Caused by th' blade when I was lying on me back. Fortune be mine, as th' scallywag took scattershot that finished 'im off 'fore he cut me down."

Kathryn listened to his tale, all the while wrapping arnica and white willow leaves against his bluish skin. The torn strips of sailcloth brought in by Seth were welcomed and relatively clean. She sighed, grateful for the rags, especially now.

Kathryn gently placed a poultice of calendula petals and herbs against the oozing gashes. After the lacerations were covered, she tied it in place with wrappings that spiraled up his forearm all the way to the elbow.

"Ye best keep off that foot," she said matter-of-factly. Brushing her hands together, she shook off bits of the herbs into the cracks of the flooring. "The cuts, though deep, don't require stitchin' this time, but mind them well, else you'll be back here to stay, you'll be. Oh, and Mister White," she called after him, "you best be savin' some of the sail for the others. I'll be needin' more before mornin'."

"Aye, Madame." The young tailor nodded his thanks and hustled out of the sick bay.

Deep night had crept upon the ship, and the crew had long taken to their berths on deck.

The ship resonated with the pirates' snores, a sure sign the crew was fast asleep.

Kathryn knew morning would be upon them soon, and she would begin the day devoid of proper sleep. She hoped there had been sufficient merrymaking among the crew following the auction for most to avail themselves of a late day slumber. That would give her the only chance to find a vacant cot and steal a few hours' sleep for herself.

But that wouldn't happen for a while yet. The line of men continued on, and so did her duties. "Bring the next one forward," she said, dipping her bloodied hands into a basin of grog.

Two crewmen lifted up another pirate and brought him forward. She waved them off, and they bolted from the cramped sick bay. The man could barely talk, and when he did, he muttered only slurred, staccato syllables. *One of Madame Delahaye's crew!*

"Well, I won't be mindin' that jilt!" she stated, not realizing she had voiced her thoughts aloud. "She can rot in…"

"Lady, he be from th''talian ship."

"Oh! Pedro! You startled me."

Strong, dark arms lifted the man's broken body and gently placed the foreigner at her feet. Kathryn looked up at the source of the deep Caribbean voice.

"Pedro! Are you hurt, man?" She jumped up, ignoring the pirate laid out on the floor in front of her.

"Not bad, lady," he replied, "but dis man be bad hurt. Dey give 'im th' whole bottle o' rum for da pain."

"Yes, yes, I see," she said. "Help me get him to the cot there, Pedro. You, too!" She barked the order at another pirate who was casually observing them from a distance.

The startled pirate stepped out of line and jogged over to where the injured man lay. But, before he could lend a hand, Pedro had scooped up the foreigner and placed him onto an empty cot. His glance said enough. He did not require assistance, and Kathryn uttered a silent apology as he stepped back into line.

"I suppose a cot is appropriate, even though there aren't enough for everyone, Pedro."

He eyed her, and she decided not to push him. Bending over the injured man, Kathryn peeled away his bloodied shirt. Protruding from his abdomen were several large pieces of splintered wood. She looked back at Pedro.

"I saw this man take the oath o're the axe. How came he by these wounds?"

The muscular pirate stepped forward and peered down at the impaled stakes. He shrugged his shoulders, then answered matter-of-factly. "Da' oath be taken. He injured, but he still swear o're da axe. I guess he choose to join de crew an' not on da barrel. Those wounds be not so much pain as a shark bite be."

"How could he not notice, Pedro? This is…" She broke off as the man groaned. "You'd best have a seat topside or get yourself comfortable there." She motioned with her head toward the far wall as she directed the pirates who stood in line. "I've sommat to do here, and it won't be swift work." She then turned to Pedro and asked, "Where lie your injuries, Pedro? And be truthful about it, man. I'll find out soon enough, so you may as well show me now."

He lifted his shirt.

"Bloody hell! Pedro!" She stared at the skin of his muscular torso, torn the length of his ribcage, sagging and bloodied. "How can it be you do not faint from such a wound as this?"

"It's not deep, lady. I wait for 'im." Pedro nodded his head toward the cot with the groaning pirate.

Kathryn had almost forgotten about him and glanced at the injured foreigner, bewildered. Quickly, she snatched up some fresh cloth from the pile. Handing it to Pedro, she instructed him to press it over his gaping wound. Then, turning to the basin, she ladled fresh grog water over her hands and shook them dry. From the top of a small table, she retrieved several dulled instruments from the old surgeon's satchel and moved back to the cot.

The man's eyes had glassed over, and the only sounds he emitted were barely audible. She shook her head, knowing her efforts were futile and a waste of time.

"So many still need to be seen. His wounds are mortal, and his breath grows irregular," she said aloud to no one.

With a silver clamp, she took hold of one end of the largest chunk of wood and pulled. The thick sliver slid free from the man's protuberant belly and released a dam of bloody ooze. The pirate shuddered, then fell still. She laid the palm of her free hand on his chest and felt no movement. She then slid her fingers to the side of his neck to count his pulse.

There was none.

"He's dead." She tossed the dangling stake into a basket filled with refuse. "Take the body topside and inform the capt'n of his losses."

Pedro and another pirate stepped out of line and crossed to either side of the cot.

"Hold there, Pedro." Her outstretched hand, still holding the bloodied clamp, stopped him dead in his tracks. Once more, she dipped the clamp, and her hands, into the grog. The process was mechanical, almost ritualistic. When she'd finished, she lifted a lantern from its hook and motioned for Pedro to follow to a wooden crate. "Now then, show me again, Pedro."

He lifted his shirt to expose the gash once more.

She held the lantern close to his chest and shook her head. "This will have to be sewn, Pedro."

He did nothing but stare straight ahead. "Do it." Kathryn noticed his chin twitched as he forced a swallow.

She reached into the satchel again and pulled out a long, curved needle, the same one she had used on the captain the first time she had laid eyes on him. Next, Kathryn dumped rum-laced water over the gaping wound. Pedro flinched but did not move otherwise.

Finally, she began the arduous process of suturing the edges of the thick skin together. Pedro winced only once, but never made a sound as the sharp needle pierced his flesh again and again. A long black spiral of coarse thread wound its way across the muscular torso.

"You're fortunate, indeed, Pedro. The bone has stayed intact and your musculature appears only slightly damaged."

His eyes remained unemotional, staring forward without blinking.

She finished the last stitch and cut the thread with a scalpel, then inspected her handiwork. Satisfied, she smeared a poultice along the length of the sutures and wrapped his entire chest with sailcloth.

"One more gash. It'll be finished soon."

"Aye, lady."

She kept her eyes focused on her work. "We need to speak of the Straif, Pedro. I need to know what the symbols mean." She paused, and he glanced to the needle in her hand, but said nothing. "I need you to tell me all that you know about it." She shot him a steely look before dropping her eyes to the needle that pierced his skin again.

"Aye," he replied, then grimaced for only a moment before speaking. "Th' symbols speak o' th' Morrigan. Th' symbols tell of ways to confine th' evil one, and th' Straif be th' tool to do it." He looked down on her with dark pupils accentuated by the whites of his eyes. It was not a friendly look, but instead, one of warning. "It be a dangerous venture, it be. Not many 'ave survived its attempt." Pedro's voice sounded grave.

Kathryn nodded, her eyes fixed on his as she digested the meaning behind what he'd just said. Her skin crawled as she thought of what lay ahead with the dark goddess. As the image of Morrigan crept into her mind, her voice failed.

Instead, she nodded, then dressed the wound in the cleanest bandage she could find. He would live. Satisfied, she clasped her hands together and waited. Pedro dropped his shirt and expressed his thanks to her, then bounded up the stairway to the deck.

Kathryn sat, paralyzed by her own thoughts, as she thought about Pedro's warning. The pirates who waited for their turn with the chirurgeon remained patiently silent, apprehensive about being on the receiving end of the surgeon's tools.

Meanwhile, the dead pirate's body had been removed from the cot. Kathryn barely noticed as the next man stepped forward and offered her a dismembered, waxy hand…then held out the bloody, bandaged stump that had once been attached to it.

Thirty-Seven

TWILIGHT PAINTED THE CRESTS OF the turquoise sea a glittering salmon and gold, matching the colors splashing outward from where the half sun rested on the horizon.

"Bloody sun!" Kathryn cursed and raised a hand to shield her eyes, as if it would help.

That was the image that greeted her fatigued eyes as she stepped above deck for the first time in over eighteen hours. Her body ached from stooping over injured crewmen throughout the night, and her mind was dull from lack of sleep. Her duties as the ship's chirurgeon were taking their toll, and she knew she would need to rest soon or face the possibility of becoming ill herself.

"They'd look on things a bit differently should I be unable to perform the surgical duties assigned here." She blinked a few times and looked around for something to drink.

Truthfully, the consequence of that was not something she was willing to face. Her safety aboard this ship remained precarious, at best, given that she was a woman and unsworn to the Articles. Her newly granted title of "Chirurgeon" was all that stood between distant tolerance and the foul play doled out by the pirates. Of utmost importance was the need to protect her title, particularly now.

"With injuries added to a cutthroats' sour temperament, there'd be no knowin' what they'd do to me." She forced her body to move, pausing atop the causeway to take in fresh air. "This is beautiful," she said, glancing to her right. The delicate gold and sienna of sundown painted itself over the surface of the ocean as the sun advanced toward nightfall.

She inhaled once more and willed her weary footsteps to carry her to the portside rails, where she gratefully rested her aching forearms and gently clasped her hands together in relief. She emptied her mind as she took in the panorama ahead. A feeling of contentment settled in as she rested.

"Take this." The balmy baritone resonated behind her. "Some libation for ye."

She glanced back and met eyes the color of the Caribbean Sea. Smiling, she accepted his offering. "Thank you, John." She sighed and cradled the mug in both hands. "It's been tedious of late."

She sipped and felt the warm liquid trickling down her throat, and suddenly realized she hadn't taken food or drink for nearly a full day. Instinctively, she rubbed her grumbling stomach.

"Have ye eaten, lass?" he asked her.

"No. The men kept comin' at me with their wounds. It seemed there was no end to it.

My heart wouldn't allow me to evade the incessant need of so many injured, so I continued on, as best I could. But they're dyin' in the sick bay, even now, as I stand here." She made a feeble attempt to wipe her grimy hands against a bloodstained apron tied about her waist.

"Men die, Kathryn. That's the way of the sea, and these men know it. There's nothin'

you can do when God wills a soul return to Him." Kathryn blinked back unwanted tears. John Phillips' voice softened. "It's not your fault."

He placed his hand over hers, urging the mug to her lips.

"I'm exhausted," she said, unable to keep the tears at bay.

"You've been stalwart and brave."

"I can't fight the fatigue." The tears rose.

"Drink. You'll feel better." This time, she let them wet her cheeks as she dutifully drank. The amber liquid burned her parched tongue, but soon warmed her belly and soothed her nerves. "Drink up and I'll get us sommat to eat," he said and disappeared into the encroaching darkness.

Obediently, she lifted the mug to her lips again and felt the contents slide easily down her throat, this time warming her soul. She watched the last moments of sunset until the amber orb finally dipped below the horizon and disappeared. A weary smile crossed her lips, and she closed her eyes, then inhaled the salty breeze once more.

"This—the best loved hour," she breathed, grateful for the interim when the sun would melt and the moon ascend. The earth's transition, blended with soothing drink, made her feel satiated and secure.

Within moments, the captain had returned with strips of crispy bread, a pungent hunk of cheese, figs, and an oddly shaped green vial. He motioned for her to join him, which she willingly did as her stomach protested again its neglect.

"What have you here, John?" Seating herself next to him on the edge of a rise, she stared at the morsels he carried. He smiled slightly, the glint in his eye youthfully mischievous, and began laying the food out in front of them on a sideways crate. He took a small porcelain bowl and filled it with dark green oil from the vial, then tore off a crackling chunk of bread. He silently lifted it to her mouth, and she accepted, amused as she watched him pull his dirk from beneath his coat and slice off several pieces of cheese. Its pungent smell teased her senses, and she smiled.

"Dip it so," he directed and plopped a piece of crust into the green oil. "Then…" He lifted the saturated bread to his mouth and smiled as he chewed.

He tore off another ragged piece of bread and dipped it, then lifted it again to Kathryn's mouth. Obediently, she opened her mouth and bit into the soggy bread—slick and filled with the flavor of olives, a delicacy, to be certain.

"I've seen this once before."

"Have ye now?"

"Aye! Mariel was once paid richly for using her *Gift* to heal with a sack of rare fruit. It happened one summer eve. I remembered how much everyone enjoyed the spoils of her labor."

"Take this slowly, Kat. The flavor be potent an' meant for those able to savor its rich peculiarity."

Kathryn recalled Mariel's warning and thought it best to heed such counsel, even now. The bread tasted sweet in her mouth, imbued as it was with the heavy, exotic substance. She did not want to give into the urge to swallow, but could not help herself. Her eyes lit up as she savored the unusual flavor. The captain sat back and watched her with great pleasure.

"Oh, John, what do they call this?" she asked him breathlessly when she had finally swallowed.

He chuckled and shrugged his shoulders in response.

"I don't know for certain, but Cook said he watched the crew from the Italian ship eatin'

it, dipping their bread, like so." He dowsed another piece, and she watched him press it into his mouth. She licked her own lips and felt her soul stir.

"I…what did you say?"

He glanced at her but failed to notice the blush in her cheeks. "Cook said this comes from olive trees."

"Olive trees? Oh, yes." She cleared her throat. "I tasted the wee fruit once as a child, but did not know they grew upon trees."

"Ay, they're grown in the ruffian's homeland and traded or sold in foreign ports. We came away with a true prize on that ship, we did. She was loaded down heavy. An odd booty, true, but much to benefit the entire crew…and this oil for tradin'. The stuff brings many a doubloon in English ports."

"So, we're eatin' gold, Capt'n Phillips."

"Ay, all of it." He grinned. "Have as ye will, it's ours for th' takin'."

She glanced at him sideways and knitted her brows.

"It's an old pirate sayin', lass."

He drained his cup, pulled a long glass bottle from under his coat, then stabbed the top with his dirk. As he did so, he loosened the wax seal, pried the cork from the rim, and carefully filled his mug with the deep maroon liquid. Closing his eyes, he lifted it to take in the aroma—a hint of oak blended with cherry—and then, sipped.

"Wine found in the hull of their ship." He opened his eyes and looked at her again, drinking in the curves of her body.

Her breath caught, and she nervously dropped her eyes to a handful of figs. She took up one and let her lips slide seductively over the fruit. Within moments, she felt masculine heat as he watched her bite down. A low moan escaped his throat, and she glanced up at him through long, dark lashes.

The food energized her, and his company quickened her heart. She eyed him sideways, awed at his beauty. Rough seas and hard living had weathered his skin, but youth still played behind his eyes, made brighter by the tanned skin and laugh lines that surrounded them. His dark hair hung loosely tied with wisps dancing about his chiseled jaw as the sea breeze kissed him. His lips were fuller than most men's, glistening in the moonlight with the traces of the oil. In the light, it accented their fullness.

She ached to kiss those lips. Swallowing hard, she dropped her eyes and governed a warm feeling of desire that rose up from deep inside. He must have sensed she hungered for more than the exotic cuisine. His mouth parted as he watched her delicate skin flushing slightly.

"This is good," she whispered.

"Precious beyond measure." The meaning was not lost on her.

He lifted a tiny piece of cheese and placed it on her lips, which she gratefully accepted, unable to meet his eyes for the moment.

His voice dropped to a whisper. "Cheese found hidden away in barrels next to the wine."

She savored a new flavor once again and droned a guttural "hmmm." He watched her mouth as it moved, her lips perfectly shaped, her lower lip giving her a sultry pout. Watching her in the moonlight, he felt his loins stir, wanting her more now than ever. It made him feel weak and vulnerable, a state he was most unaccustomed to. *Irresistible, especially in the moonlight. To taste her mouth, touch her skin, and take her as my own.* He shook his head to clear it and heard his own voice escape.

"There's no evidence it's spoilt, though it reeks boldly. Cook said the Italians ate it in spite of the smell and gave it to me, along with the bread and wine. I suspect I was the first on board to try it, just to be certain it was safe." Immediately, he regretted opening his mouth. *What a foolish thing to say. Better to have kissed her.*

Kathryn chuckled. "You've never tasted cheese before?" He shrugged. "Nice parry, Captain Phillips." Chuckling, she lifted a piece and sniffed. Her nose wrinkled. Then, handing it back to him, she stated, "After you, sir."

He opened his mouth, but waited as she placed it on his tongue. She did not let go and he closed his lips around her fingers, taking them into his mouth, warm, moist, delicious. She shuddered as she lifted her gaze to meet his. It burned with the heat of passion—intense, vibrant, and dangerous.

His mouth released her fingers, and she dropped her hand. The heat of his stare warmed her with his passion. In one fluid motion, he drained his mug, then reached through her hair, grasped the back of her neck, and pulled her face to his. She felt the warmth of his lips brushing hers and tasted the deep flavors of the Italian delicacies still lingering on his tongue.

His body tensed against hers as he pulled her into him and kissed her deeply. Her mind reeled as her body responded, arching closer to his muscular chest. She reached her fingers through his hair and clung to him. Time stood still, and the sea ceased to rock as the pirate fell under the spell cast over him by this sorceress. This kiss was tender, heated, binding their souls together with a spiritual feast of pirate to witch, woman to man.

Suddenly, glass crashed behind them, and the deep snorts of a startled crewman resonated, breaking into their intensity. Captain Phillips turned and cast a warning look at the sleeping man sprawled out behind them. The pirate simply rolled over and snorted again. The bottle he'd been holding was shattered. Tiny slate fragments lay in a deep ruby liquid.

"Alas, the timing," Captain Phillips said, then laughed out loud at the folly of it. She chuckled nervously.

"This will help." Kathryn handed him the bottle, filled with what remained of the rich wine. Kathryn turned from him and helped herself to the forgotten food lying on the crate.

"It's delightful! I never knew there were such delicacies!"

He glanced at her and drained the bottle.

"Truly, you've bloody spoilt me now, John Phillips. A fine plunder, says I."

She had once again changed the subject, but the pirate did not miss its double meaning. "'Tis but a small sample of what awaits, my dear. Where did ye learn to use such dross verbiage? Methinks you're turning pirate, indeed!"

She blushed. "Aye, of that I have no doubt, and such words have been heard to cross your lips, sir. Point your accusations elsewhere! In the meantime, you must be careful o're dishing out such delicacies to a Celt. I'll be wantin' more, most likely."

"Then more ye shall have…when the time is right. Until then, we have this."

He chuckled and gestured to the food that rested upon the crate. "And savor it, we shall. What say ye to that, me lady?"

"Likely as not, you'll not find me eatin' grog-soaked hardtack again, Capt'n Phillips."

He roared with laughter at this, rolled back, and slapped his knee. She took another piece of the cheese, laid it on the bread, and dipped both into the olive oil, then bit into all greedily. Glistening droplets threatened to drizzle from the edges of her full lips as she relished each flavor.

She's delicious! The captain gently dabbed the corners of her mouth with his thumb, then placed it into his mouth and sucked. He gazed at her face and his heart swelled.

"Come sit here with me, Kathryn," he whispered, and she moved to sit alongside him.

He draped his arms around her shoulders as he pulled her back against him. She relished the warmth of his caress and felt at home in his arms. Nestling her head against his chest, she listened to his breathing in time with his heartbeat. It soothed her, and her tense muscles relaxed into the rhythm of his breathing.

They sat in silence and stared at the moon, full and radiant, as its light cascaded over the water, thousands of sparkling lights rollicking with the movement of the sea.

"Are ye happy here…aboard the *Revenge*, Kathryn?"

The unexpected change of topic broke the silence… and her comfort. She sat up and stared at him. "What an odd question, Capt'n Phillips." Never before had she been asked that question. "Are you taunting me?"

"Nay. Why would I do that?"

Bewildered, she plucked a fig from the basket and bit into it. His mood had changed. "Perhaps you feel you've settled."

"Settled for what? For you?"

She avoided his eyes. Perhaps he felt love—she couldn't tell. "Can a pirate truly love a woman? I mean, really love a woman…more than the sea?"

His face softened, but there was a glint in his eyes. She placed the other half of the fig in his opened mouth, then laid her head against his chest again. The luxury of feeling the heartbeat beneath his muscular chest soothed her.

"You don't have to answer if it's discomforting to do so, John."

"Ay, I'll answer. Of course, a man can love a woman. Why ask such a thing?"

"Hmmm," was the response. "It's a subject that troubles my mind of late."

She scanned the ship's inner landscape painted in moonlight. *He'll never give you a truthful answer, Kathryn. Stop pressing the issue.* She sighed and listened to the rhythm of his heart. "Well, it's a senseless question, John Phillips."

"It's said a ship captures its crews' hearts as prisoners, then carries them off to freedom."

His voice was a whisper as he tossed a bit of crust into his mouth.

The pirate captain has also captured your heart, Kathryn. She dared not look at him, even now. "Am I a part of the crew, then? Because this ship suits me well."

"Ye're the ship's chirurgeon."

"Aye, then." The current lifted the bow, reminding her that they were at sail over a vast ocean, warming her soul. The love of the ship's captain would keep her bound to the pirate ship forevermore. "This is my home now, John, and I belong to the sea…to you."

Instinctively, he began stroking her hair tenderly, lovingly. Each stared in silence at the glittering moonlight that danced atop the water crests as nightfall flourished. The ship lifted and dropped, rocking them nearly to sleep. A gentle touch swept the hair out of her eyes, and she felt his lips brushing the crown of her head. Her body relaxed, and while he knew the food and drink had nourished her, he also knew his love for her was sustaining her, protecting her. "Sleep lass," he whispered.

She closed her eyes and allowed herself to drift off. As she slept, he stroked her hair, lost in the moment. He raised another bottle and drank deeply of the rich contents, then returned his gaze to the sea he loved almost as dearly as the woman in his arms. The moon smiled downward, and the deep night embraced them both.

"Love from a pirate is never certain," he whispered, and closed his eyes.

Thirty-Eight

MOONLIGHT FADED AS GOLDEN RAYS vaulted from the east. Kathryn opened her eyes, blinked, and looked around. Her surroundings looked unfamiliar.

"Where am I?"

The effort to reorient herself appeared futile. Droning and rhythmic, Captain Phillips' breath reverberated against her back. She craned her neck and spotted dark wavy hair cascading over a bronzed, muscular neck.

"Could it be the majestic capt'n snores whilst sleeping?" She laughed as she sat upright and scanned the still, dim sea.

Clouds of fine mist, typical of early mornings, had settled over the water. She reached for the mug that rested next to the basket. The pungent aromas of fragrant cheese and exotic oil from the night before scented the air. Silently, so as not to wake the sleeping pirate at her side, she lifted the mug to her lips and sipped. He stirred but did not wake.

The morning air smelled fresh in spite of the balmy haze that settled over the water. Kathryn drew in a long, deep breath, closed her eyes, and listened to the sounds of the ship coming to life.

Muffled voices sounded from a distance, indicating that only a handful of sailors had risen for the day. A soft, low growl sounded just beyond her feet. Her eyes widened at the unnerving rumble just in time to see Pock-eye's cat leaping into a stack of coiled rigging. The cat growled again and Kathryn caught a glimpse of a long, tapered tail disappearing around the base.

"Ah, then there's more than one predator gone to huntin' aboard this ship. I hope a larger mouse escapes so easily the outstretched claws waitin' to ensnare him," she whispered, her thoughts momentarily drifting to Morrigan and omens.

The cat crawled out of the coil's center, no longer the hunter, and promenaded in front of Kathryn, then paused to rub its back against her feet.

"A good omen, you are, methinks. Black cats are rumored to be good luck onboard a ship. I hope you prove as much." She smiled and tossed the crust's end to the creature. It flicked its tail before disappearing around the smoke funnel.

In that moment, soothing fingers wrapped around her shoulders and gently pulled her back to lie against his chest. She gave in and rested her head against tawny muscles. Her own breath matched the rhythmic rise and fall of his, her life force matching the distinct pulse of his heartbeat.

"Ship's in repose for all but the mornin' watch, and the bell's not been struck. Rest a while longer, Kathryn," he whispered with his eyes closed.

"Aye, John, but I've the sick bay to attend to before the heat sets in and turns it foul below."

He pulled her closer to him, said nothing, and then faded into still desperately needed sleep. Around them, the ship slowly woke as the sun rose higher into a clear blue sky. Another two hours passed and the couple slept peacefully despite the clamor materializing around them.

When Kathryn finally awoke, it was to the sound of Seth's voice jarring her awake.

Captain Phillips had already arisen and was fastening his belt about his waist. She lifted herself to one elbow and shaded her eyes with the other hand as she watched them.

"...th' men are in arms o're it, Capt'n. I fear there'll be bloodshed a'fore noon."

"Ay, then, I'll come shortly," Captain Phillips responded, and slipped a worn, leather tricorn over his head.

Kathryn clamored to her feet and began picking up remnants of their meal from the night before. She stared, bewildered, at the captain and Seth, who quickly took leave. Captain Phillips glanced at her briefly with worry knitting his brows, then tucked his dirk into the side of his trousers.

"I must withdraw myself, lass. There's trouble brewin' astern," he stated, then bent over and kissed her atop her head. "What be the state of the injured?"

"I haven't seen to them yet this mornin'…" Kathryn dropped her gaze to the deck.

His temperament had shifted along with the urgency of the crew's, and she knew he now addressed the chirurgeon as captain. "Ye'd best be at it, then."

She nodded to show respect, and her reply was the same. "The sick bay fills with foul air by full sun and we can scarce breathe below deck. The heat adds to the men's fevers, which I fear will be greater today. I'm low on tinctures, but young Will White keeps fresh cloth for bandages aplenty."

He nodded as he mulled over her report. "Ay, then."

"The fester will surely set in for most soon, perhaps this day. Have we leeches aboard?"

He stroked his chin and shook his head. "Nay. You can inquire of Cook whether he's found any hidden in the scuttle barrels. The water already tastes foul by my likings."

"Aye, Capt'n. That's where I'll seek," she said and bowed slightly in respect.

"No need to be so formal, Kathryn. We share more than a simple accord betwixt us." One side of his mouth curled as he spoke. "I'll call for the carpenter to drill holes to let in some fresh air below." He proceeded to make his way toward the rear of the ship, but stopped. "And you best take care of yourself amidst your ministerin'. There's no one left to care for ye, should ye fall ill, as well."

She smiled at him. "Aye, sir." Then, gathering the basket, along with her few effects,

She made for her quarters and the fresh clusters of healing herbs that waited inside.

* * * * *

Thick sea air assaulted Kathryn as she stepped into her cabin. It had been almost two full days since she had been inside, and a twinge of neglectful remorse pricked at her.

"Oh, how I've missed you," she said and immediately crossed to the single port hole, nudging it open. Salty breezes pushed their way into the tiny opening. She inhaled deeply before resuming her tasks. She carried a basket that she tossed onto the center table, secretly grateful it still contained the bits and pieces left over from their meal the night before. Her stomach rumbled. She snatched a dried mombin and meandered to the tiny porthole, where she urged it all the way open. Crisp sea air brushed against her face as it swung on rusted hinges that groaned, as always, when disturbed.

Poised with her nose directly centered in the opening, she stood for a moment and inhaled fresh air into her lungs as it seeped into the room. Kathryn nibbled on bread and thought of nothing in particular as she stared at the clear blue sky and vibrant sea.

"Would you have me take the scraps?" A voice interrupted her solitude.

She spun to see who had spoken and noticed Seth picking at the contents in the basket.

"I didn't see you come in, Seth."

He lifted a fig from underneath a discarded piece of cheese and popped it into his mouth. She smiled at his lack of stealth as he plundered her scant food supply.

"Help yourself."

He lifted a chunk of the milky cheese between two fingers and wrinkled his nose.

"The foreigners sure eat foul smellin' provisions, don't they? I guess you can cure 'em when they all fall ill o're putrid stuff such as this." He pinched his nose with a thumb and forefinger.

Kathryn laughed out loud, propped her hands on both hips, and watched him. "Ho there, Seth! Bite into it and see for yourself. The stench is foul but the flavor is pleasing. Go on…taste it."

"Oh, no. Not I." He pushed the basket away.

"Lily-livered, are you, Seth? You leap from yardarm to mast, but you're afraid of a piece of cheese?" She laughed again.

"You'll likely pester me until I eat sommat."

"Aye, that I will."

Seth closed his eyes and, extending his arm overhead, opened his mouth wide and dropped a piece into his mouth. As he bit down on the soft, waxy wedge, he stared at her with apprehension.

"Chew...swallow! Aye, Seth," she said with amusement behind her eyes.

He did as directed, and chewed hesitantly at first, then as his eyes popped open, with more gusto. A smile crossed his face.

"Aye." She grinned triumphantly. "It's better with a drop of rum." She took hold of the pitcher and handed it to him. "Wash it down with this, Seth, and see how it tastes, then!"

She watched him discover the rich flavors introduced to her only a few hours earlier. He drank from the rim, then lowered the pitcher back to the table and wiped his mouth with the edge of one sleeve. "Blimey! I never would have thought I'd like it."

"Me, neither, until last night when I tasted it for myself. It's foreign, and a rich plunder, methinks."

"Aye, the delicacies of the Italians."

Kathryn snickered again and moved off to an obscure corner, where she began to gather clusters of shaded vials. Seth watched her with large eyes as he pecked at a fig. She decided this was as good an opportunity as any to bring up his earlier conversation with the captain.

"Seth." Her voice was honey. "What's this I heard brewin' this mornin'? Is the crew in strife once again?"

She handed him another piece of dipped crust as she spoke, which he gladly accepted. He waved it in the air as if to brush off the topic, then answered her rather nonchalantly. "There's trouble with the crew and the bawdy lady from the Italian ship."

"What trouble is that, Seth? Tell me!"

He popped another fig into his mouth as he casually recounted the events thus far as if it meant nothing to anyone who listened. "Madame Delahaye sent one of her own mateys off to meet Davy Jones."

"What?" Her astonishment had gotten the best of her.

"Aye, 'tis true. Shot him clean through the heart and tossed him overboard this very mornin'," he replied in between bites.

"Why?

Seth shrugged, and the look he gave warned her not to pressure him on the subject. Kathryn decided to drop it for fear she'd raise Seth's suspicions. Most likely, he'd already disclosed more than was fitting. She crossed the floor and took hold of a half-spent candle, then placed it next to the bundled herbs. Seth's eyes stared uneasily at the array.

"For the sick bay," she stated.

Seth must have sensed his error. He suddenly grew quiet as his appetite failed him. His eyes settled on a strange object leaning against the wall. She paused, keeping a wary eye on him. Suddenly, his expression changed. It was obvious he didn't recognize the object, but was well aware of its power.

"Superstitions at sea are well known, Seth, and you're no exception. Fear can easily overtake logic at any moment, which seems odd applied to you, as I've watched you fight bravely in battle."

"Perhaps the overwhelming fear of the unknown has greater power than the sword."

Shocked, she shot a look at Seth. Kathryn would remember that for future reference. In the meantime, Seth stared at her and bristled.

"I don't get you, Seth," she said. "I've watched you all this time—no fear of heights or fighting…and your skill with a weapon is beyond comprehension."

"I'll take that as a compliment." Seth stood a little taller.

She ignored him, marched to the corner, and took hold of the staff. "But, when it comes to the water or big sticks…" She held out the Straif.

"Those things are different, Kat. There's the unknown about them both," he said and paused only for a moment. "Weapons are real. You can handle them with your hands."

"So is the water…"

"But water sifts through your fingers even with the tightest fist," he countered. "And dark creatures reside therein. Beasts that appear to be still until just before they eat or destroy you…just like the dark magic of that stick you're holding."

He's still innocent. The thought moved her, and compassion overrode curiosity as she stepped in to rescue him from his own anxiety. "It's called a Straif…bequeathed to me by the Vodoun priest on Trinidad Island."

Seth moved toward the door, then motioned to the dull green bottle and dried meats he'd set on the center table on his arrival.

"There's your morning sup, Kathryn. I'll take my leave." He backed toward the doorway.

"Look at it for a moment, Seth. It's harmless in my hands." He shook his head in a sporadic tremble as he crossed his chest and the threshold at the same time. "Seth, it's just a stick! Seth…" She called after him as he darted up the short staircase in two leaps and disappeared out of sight.

Kathryn carried the Straif back to its resting place, mumbling in annoyance at Seth's reaction. "Worthless bloody pirate's superstitious ignorance!"

Carefully, she placed the remedies in the center of a cloth satchel. She gathered them up, snatched the untouched grog, and raced up the causeway into the bright sunlight on deck.

Thirty-Nine

A MALODOROUS STENCH OF FERMENTING sepsis and bile assaulted her nostrils as she entered the hatchway leading to the sick bay. She gagged at the smell and stopped halfway down the narrow steps.

"Bloody hell," she breathed.

Unable to move farther, she glanced around to find some useful item to stave off the stench. Nothing presented itself, so she set her supplies on the step next to her and tore a length of her top skirt at the hem. Tying the long, green strip of fabric around her face, she entered the interior chamber designated for the injured and dying.

"Ahoy, mateys!" She attempted a cheerful salute from behind the facemask. Anguished moans met her ears, the plea from the suffering. A sinking feeling hit the pit of her stomach.

"Hello, Miss Kat'ryn." The bedraggled voice sounded from her left.

She set her supplies on the small table near the stairway, took an abandoned cup from the top of a crate, emptied, then refilled it with fresh grog from the bottle she'd brought with her. She walked in the direction of the voice and found old Billy One-Hand propped up on an elbow. His face burst into a rosy, toothless grin at her approach, though she was sure it was the grog in her hand, and not her presence, that caused his enthusiasm. He gratefully accepted the cup and guzzled the sweetened rum greedily.

"How are you this day, Mister Billy?" she asked playfully.

"Not so bad as yestern, lass. Me leg surely be fine for walkin' upon today, methinks."

As he spoke, Billy One-Hand kicked back the canvass covering his right leg to expose stained bandages wrapped snugly there.

Kathryn unwrapped the dressing and was pleased to see that septic poisoning had not yet set in. Scattershot usually brought gangrenous infection from bone shards and splinters, but Billy seemed spared of that. Perhaps he would, indeed, keep his leg, unlike his hand. Kathryn was relieved and smiled at him.

"See it here." He obviously wanted to escape the sick bay as badly as his caregiver did.

"Let me take a closer look." She leaned in to inspect the injury and was pleased to find there was no odor.

"Jes wrap it back up an' I be on me way, lass." Billy grabbed for the discarded bandages.

"Oh, no." Kathryn stopped him cold. "You won't be usin' these again, mate."

She dumped the soiled dressing into the refuse bin, crossed to her table, and ladled water over her hands. Then Kathryn sorted through her remedies, picked out a long silver leaf, and carried it back to Billy, who watched her with wide eyes.

"Why, that be right wasteful o' ye! We don' carry enough sailcloth fer ye to go tossin' it off like so. Luther never tossed off what still had good use left in it," he stated with impertinence.

She bent over Billy's injured leg and dumped a portion of the rum from the bottle onto it. Billy hollered as the liquor burned the raw edges of his flesh, but he held still and allowed her to place the leaf gently over the open wound. She then gently wrapped the fresh strips of sailcloth snugly around his leg.

"Luther was the ship's chirurgeon before I came aboard, then?" she asked, her curiosity getting the best of her.

Billy nodded. "Aye, that he be, God rest 'is soul."

Kathryn finished and stood upright, placing her hands on her hips. She stared at the stump.

"Aye, and so I see how he left you, pilferin' the supplies meant for his patients. Your previous wounds could certainly have caught you the fevers. You were lucky, indeed." She motioned to his extended stump.

Billy's mouth snapped shut as he stared at the place where his hand had once been.

"Now then, Billy," she continued. "We'll be doin' things my way from here on out…and you can keep your limb and be free of this dungeon at the same time. I'll give you a clean bill of health as soon as those dressings come off for good."

Billy grinned and showed the hollow spaces between his gums. "Thank ye, ma'am!"

"In the meantime, you're free to go topside, but no seawater, and keep that leg above your belly, savvy?"

"Aye! Leg above the gut!" He leapt from the cot and grabbed hold of his effects, gave a little bow to the chirurgeon, and thanked her as he darted up the stairs. She watched him leave, stalling until the last moment before turning back to the dark stench of the sick bay.

In the farthest corner of the room, the sound of something stirring caught her attention.

She took a lantern from off a long nail stuck haphazardly into the nearest beam, lifted it toward the noise, and slowly made her way forward. The lantern sputtered, and the light flickered, nearly spent of its oil from use through the night. She cursed under her breath, unable to peer farther into the darkness as a result.

"Who goes there? And what's your business in my hold?"

A stout figure stepped forward into the flickering light. He was cumbersome, dressed in an overcoat that was much too warm for the heat. His bald head shone in the flickering light, and what little hair he had was pulled back into a tight knot. Tufts fell loose, trailing the length of his back. In his ear dangled a gold ring—his burial bounty, as was the custom of many seasoned pirates.

"It's me, Miss Kathryn," he called out casually. "Henry Barnes."

The figure then stepped back into the shadows, intent on some business there.

Kathryn inched her way forward with the lantern held high, its flame sputtering light in a thousand different directions. She could see the wide-eyed crewmen lying in hammocks and on top of cots or beds made from old linen and blankets stacked upon the damp floor. All but a few watched her as she approached the pirate. He was bent over a far cot, while his hands stuffed something into one of the long coat pockets.

"What in Neptune's blue sea are you doin', Mister Barnes?" Her temper flared as she watched Barnes rifling through a pair of trouser pockets while its owner lay motionless atop the cot. She lifted the lantern a little higher, casting dim light over the cot.

"Well, I figure 'e won' be needin' it any longer, an' I'd 'ate to see it all go to waste," Barnes chortled.

From the shadows, guttural laughter joined Barnes' own peals. Kathryn spun to her right and peered in the direction of the second laugh. In the dancing light, she caught sight of a tall but thin, and rather meagerly dressed fellow she recognized as one of the lookouts.

"Jonas Tate! Tell me you're not part of these black deeds, sir!" She stomped her foot as color rushed to her cheeks.

The wiry pirate glanced at her, then dropped something from his hands to the floor as he snapped to attention. The object clattered and rolled behind him as the *Revenge* shifted leeward.

"I...I...figured he won' be needin' it, ma'am," Tate stammered and motioned to the heap lying on the cot.

"Hold there whilst I check my patient," she ordered.

Neither moved as she bent over the first cot. The dim light flickered to expose ashen skin and glaring eyes fixed in a death's stare. The stench coming from the body was almost more than she could tolerate without gagging, even with the cloth tied about her nose and mouth.

"Dead," she said flatly. He'd obviously been so for most of the night.

His body lay half-naked and sprawled stiffly across the cot. All but his trousers had been pilfered, and Kathryn guessed the over-sized coat now donned by Barnes had once adorned the body on the cot.

"We figured..."

"The least you can do is close the poor bloke's eyes, Mister Barnes," she snapped.

She waited as Barnes pulled two large silver coins out of the dead man's britches to place one over each of the open eyes. She bent over the body and held the lantern over the dead man's face, illuminating the exposed eyeballs. Kathryn gasped. "Wait!"

Barnes froze in place, the coins in his hands glinting in the lantern light. Kathryn pointed. The whites of his eyes were bloody—the pupils glared like black ebony swimming in crimson.

"What is it?" Barnes asked and leaned in to get a better look.

"Cover them and make haste of it, man!"

He quickly closed the eyelids and placed the coins, then crossed himself, clutching the coat tightly around his torso. "It be th' devil's eyes," Barnes bellowed and backed away from the cot. His face contorted with terror, and he crossed himself again.

Kathryn floated the lantern down the length of the dead man's torso, then hovered just above the corpse's belly. Bubbling just beneath the surface of the skin were large black pustules, still intact, though ready to erupt underneath the smooth, pasty skin. Kathryn swallowed hard and bent down to examine the flooring just beneath the cot. Glimmering pools of yellow and black lay sticky on the planking.

Her realization of what now plagued the ship caused panic to spread from her lungs to her gut. Reflexes kicked in as she froze and held the lantern directly in front of her. Its light cast an uneven glow that illuminated the terrified Barnes standing directly in front of her. She studied his face, paying particular attention to his eyes. She was relieved to find them only mildly yellowed—the telltale sign of rum's most ardent lover.

"Where'd you come by that greatcoat, Mister Barnes?" she asked, her voice grave.

He lifted a thick finger and pointed it directly at the cot. The man's knees trembled.

Kathryn clenched her teeth and swallowed again, her mouth dry.

"Take this body and bedding and cast the lot overboard. Make haste! I need this bed for the livin'!"

"Aye!" The man jumped and began the task of clearing the cot of its occupant.

"You!" She pointed at Tate. "You stay where you are." Kathryn walked briskly to where Tate stood, anchored next to the heaped body on the floor at his feet. "And get rid of that coat, Barnes!"

"What's the botheration, ma'am?" Tate asked, wringing his hands.

She scowled at the pirate before lowering the lantern. Its light danced just above the bundle piled on the floor. Kathryn clicked her tongue and shook her head as she examined the bulk. She moved the lantern up and down as she searched for several moments before snapping back to face Tate.

"This one's eyes are clear. You have luck on your heels, Mister Tate." She tossed him a sour look. "Take this body topside and cast him overboard, same as the other. You'd best do the same with the bedding, just to be cautious."

"Aye, aye, ma'am," Jonas Tate stammered and joined Barnes in collecting the pile of linen and blankets around the dead man's body.

Haste did not warrant delicacy as they handled the corpses, or the effects, and within moments, both pirates had scurried topside and had flung the bundled contents over the rails.

Kathryn cast one last disgusted look at the two pirates. She glanced at the empty cots one last time and shuddered. Then, turning from her duties in the dank sick back, she set the lantern back on its nail and announced loudly, "I need to speak with the capt'n!"

With that, she darted up the steep stairwell and out of sight.

Forty

BRILLIANT SUNLIGHT PLAGUED KATHRYN'S ICY blue eyes as she surfaced into the midday sun.

She raised a hand to her forehead, shading her eyes, as she advanced toward the quarterdeck. Only a handful of skillful crewmen worked the sails that kept the ship on a straight tack against the brisk wind. Their time, working the sails, was going to double as manpower dwindled. Several of their comrades had already expired from wounds sustained in battle. Able-bodied crewmen were becoming fewer in number, so those with less severe injuries were bandaged and sent back to their duties—prematurely, in most cases.

Kathryn moved across the deck with agility befitting a seasoned salty dog. She caught Seth's eye as she crossed to the opposite side of the ship. Nodding the appropriate greeting between crewmen, she accompanied the gesture with an affectionate smile reserved for those she considered friends. Seth returned in kind, tapped two fingers to his brow, and grinned broadly, a salutation for mateys.

Voices were piqued to a thunderous pitch as she approached the causeway that lead below to the captain's quarters. Captain Phillips' vexed baritone the loudest as she stepped up to the arched doorway.

"This is my ship, and they be the Articles o're the crew, not to be expounded by a single creature! Most certainly not by a woman!"

A familiar, throaty laugh met the captain's declaration, and Kathryn's spine was chilled at the sound of it. She pushed against the solid oak door, loudly protesting by way of a forced entry. Heads turned in her direction as she stepped across the threshold.

Pausing briefly, she allowed her eyes to adjust before she advanced further. The hairs on her neck stood on end as a woman's voluptuous accent rolled from somewhere near the back of the room.

"Yer own Art'cles set forth th' punishment for breakin' th' laws of this ship! How dare ye presume to judge this pirate any less than yer own crewmen, especially as I be a woman. Th'

cur made off to have his way with me and met me pistol as th' ninth Art'cle directs." The redhead stood indignantly and continued. "I shot th' filthy dog, clean through his black heart, I did." With pomp, she drew her cutlass from its sheath and studied it as she spoke. "T'would surely have been sweeter with th' blade. Alas, yer written laws speak to riddin' th' world of scoundrels as such by pistol shot." She broke into Italian and stared fondly at the cutlass. "*Solo colpo*! *Come un codardo's.*"

"She dares to call our laws cowardly! One shot be th' Code! Let me cut 'er down, Capt'n, an' be done wit' 'er," Archer hissed.

Dull, scabrous chafing hissed from the steel as three blades scraped against leather scabbards. The cutlasses were brandished *en garde*—all of them glinting in the window's light.

"Avast, Madame!" Captain Phillips kept his voice low and lethal. "Ye have no voice here and best be mindin' your tongue, else the quartermaster's got leave to cut it from your pretty, little throat!"

The woman returned her sword to its scabbard and perched atop a nearby chair. The bosun and quartermaster lowered their blades but kept them unsheathed and held ready at their sides. Captain Phillips dropped the tip of his cutlass, as well, and tucked the curved blade loosely against his thigh, as was his custom when faced with threats.

Kathryn's eyes darted from the captain to Archer, and finally, to Jacquotte Delahaye, where they narrowed. The woman's gaze found her.

"An' so th' mouse crawls forth from her carrion den an' creeps meekly to th' capt'n for cover," Jacquotte mocked.

Kathryn reached for her cutlass but found only empty space where her hilt should have been. She growled at the woman in frustration, realizing she stood defenseless.

"Disarm the wench," Captain Phillips ordered.

The two officers stepped forward, and the elaborate cutlass clattered to the deck in front of them, tossed defiantly by Jacquotte, still perched atop the chair back. Without pause, and perhaps a little too eagerly, both pirates ran their hands down the length of her curvaceous body, supposedly scanning for hidden weapons. She smiled provocatively, amused as their calloused hands searched her.

"Thar be none else, Capt'n," Archer announced as Gow tucked the Italian cutlass into his belt for safekeeping.

Both men looked flushed, and Kathryn growled again, disgusted by the carnal stirrings Jacquotte was able to raise. "Performing their duty. Bah! Lusty dogs, the lot of 'em! Would that I could inspect the tart. 'Tis the end of my dirk that'd do the exploring!"

The bawdy female pirate sneered at Kathryn, then cocked her head and hooted.

"That be the very reason the quartermaster and bosun be given the job." Captain Phillips stated, eyeing her. "It's apparent there's no trusting a snarling woman."

She gritted her teeth. *Dimwitted, fatherless dogs!* Kathryn's thoughts floated to the tip of her tongue, but stopped as the captain stepped forward to stare at the discarded cutlass.

He nodded his approval and directed his officers to keep watch over Jacquotte. "She's chosen to act unlawfully an' remains our prisoner."

"Aye, Capt'n." Archer approached her as her mild protestations in Italian fell upon deaf ears.

"Exasperating!" Kathryn could barely contain herself.

Jacquotte spat out a string of profanities in Italian.

"An honest observation given by our chirurgeon." Gow glanced at Kathryn, and while he did not smile, she thought she saw his eyes twinkle.

Finally, the woman fell silent, and Kathryn breathed a sigh of relief. With her head cocked to one side, she glared at Kathryn, and in a disturbingly calm voice, spoke to no one in particular.

"Why do ye all protect th' waif so? Why not let we lasses cross blades? Ye can take fancy in th' sport o' it all. What say ye, mouse?"

"Because she's a witch!" Gow blurted before Kathryn could answer.

Jacquotte's eyes grew wide. The idea that such a puny thing could possess the power of a real witch was playfully enticing to her.

"A witch, ye say? An' yet ye protect her? She must be an ineffectual little vixen to be needin' so many coming to her defense."

Kathryn stepped forward. The stealth with which she moved gave a warning as deafening as her lethal stare—all of it directed at the cinnamon-skinned Madame Delahaye. Captain Phillips tried to position himself between the women, but the witch held her hand up and stopped him.

Kathryn breathed a word of caution to the curvaceous pirate. "Think well on what utterance spews forth from your mouth, Madame. You'd best not be threatenin' me or my crew. There's black magic awaitin' the likes of you."

"Don't threaten me, mouse."

"A pirate, indeed. The totality of a witch's wrath you may invite with your careless deeds disguised as innocent acts."

Kathryn lifted both hands in a slow arc, raised them above her head, and began to chant in the ancient Celtic tongue of the white witches.

> *"Bwriad cael ei ddatgelu.*
> *Diben cael ei nodi.*
> *Evil yn cymryd ei hun."*

Archer and Gow withdrew a pace and moved to the edge of the room as Kathryn cast her spell.

"Intent be revealed…"

The captain stood, rooted in place with eyes fixed upon Kathryn as she lowered her hands to just before her lips.

"Purpose be known…"

With a deep sigh, she closed her eyes and blew heavily between her cupped palms.

"Evil takes its own."

Instantly, a warm gust of air circled the room, a ghostly hiss that echoed as it passed each inhabitant within the room. The dark corners burst into light as every candle and lantern simultaneously ignited.

> *"Dod â golau i cysgodion,*
> *A galw am yr hyn sy'n cael ei guddio."*

Her voice rose as she discharged the spell.

> "Bring light to shadows,
> And summon that which is hidden."

From across the room, something rattled. Drawing up her right hand, she cast toward the shadows, expelled evil, and called for light to arm her with power. A long white bolt flashed from her outstretched palm, and in that instant, a curved blade flew overhead that cut through the air and moved directly toward her. Jacquotte Delahaye's cutlass landed in her outstretched hand, and she grasped the ornate hilt.

"You'd best think on your conduct, Madame Delahaye," Kathryn hissed, low and menacingly. She held the ornate cutlass up before the startled woman's face. The captain stared, speechless, as his eyes shifted to the pirate. Archer crouched and waited in the farthest corner. Gow was unable to move, terrified from all he'd just witnessed.

Delahaye merely nodded and dropped her head submissively for the first time since boarding the ship. Kathryn half-smiled, satisfied, and tossed the cutlass back to Gow, who made no attempt to retrieve it as it clattered to the floorboards at his feet.

"Enough!" Captain Phillips' voice broke the silence. "The wench will stay here till it be determined otherwise."

Kathryn cast a startled look at him, then glanced at the two pirates on the opposite sides of the cabin. "What! Surely…" she stammered, not wanting to betray her sudden disquiet at his decision. "I…I need speak with you about your injured crew, Capt'n."

The captain gave directions to Archer, who responded with nods and near-silent "Ayes." He then took hold of Kathryn's arm and escorted her forcefully through the doorway and out of the cabin. Once they were away from his quarters, the captain turned her around to face him. Still holding her arm, he lowered his eyes before speaking.

"That was quite a display, lass. What were ye thinkin', acting so?" His face flushed, though he held his temper at bay.

Indignantly, she pulled her arm from his grip and placed both hands on her hips. "What do you mean? What's your purpose invitin' the wench to be your cabin-mate?"

He shot her a stern look, but Kathryn would not budge. "I don't trust her!" He pronounced each word as if doing so would give it proper emphasis.

"I don't either!" Kathryn snapped back.

"The wench killed one of her own men, Kathryn," he said, exasperated. "She won't mind killin' any of my crew either, savvy? I cannot be losin' any more men. The ship's down too many already from injury. Your sick bay is full, and there's barely enough hands able to work the sails in strong wind."

Kathryn dropped her arms to her side and shifted her weight uncomfortably, then cocked her head to one side. "Why did the wench kill her own man?"

"You heard her below. She claims he would have had his way with her—clearly against the Articles. She was correct about that. Still, methinks she's up to some mischief of sorts, shot him for it, then dumped the wretch to the sea. There's nothing to show for it, so it's her word against a corpse!"

Kathryn's blood boiled. "Then the issue is not so much that a pirate from the *Il Potente* has been murdered, but rather, because the Madame has run rogue?"

"Nay, mostly she's tried to corrupt the Articles of the ship. True enough, Article IX gives leave to put to death any man who meddles with any woman without consent, but she presses the law…presses my authority!"

"I highly doubt that is Madame Delahaye's case."

"Why do you constantly question me, Kathryn?" This time, it was Captain Phillips who stomped his foot.

"Because she is known as '"Back from the Dead Red.' She's a meddler, and up to no good. There's a dead pirate who now lies at the bottom of the sea, and no one really knows why the bloke was shot in the first place."

"Exactly my point!"

"She runs rogue, that one." Kathryn shook her head. "I fear you will be next, John Phillips." He snorted and waved her off with a "Bah!" but she continued anyway. "The mere thought of that woman lyin' in your own quarters in the very bed you gave to me on my first night…well, it's not right! Worse, you're not impervious from the woman's mischief!"

He stepped forward, took Kathryn by the shoulders, and gazed directly into her sky blue eyes. "Now listen to me, Kathryn! My character is above reproach on this measure, which you, of all people, know to be true!"

"I know that's so, John, but it's that tart I'm so aggrieved o're. She'll be havin' her way with you, John…I know it!"

He shook his head in frustration and released her shoulders, then turned away to gaze at the sea. Kathryn folded her arm as she waited for him to collect his thoughts. Her aggravation with the lady pirate mounted by the minute. Suddenly pivoting on his heels, he faced her with an austere expression that matched his voice.

"Where was my bed last night, then, lass?" He paused to allow her to recall their evening together just hours ago. "And where shall it be this night?" He paused as if he had considered the answer. "For now, I don't know, but it shan't be in my own quarters where Jacquotte Delahaye lays her head. Me men will have guards o're her throughout the night while I'll sleep elsewhere. She'll be put to shore soon enough. Your conjurin' brought enough fear to everyone to keep the woman, and my men, at bay. So, I've naught o're that issue to worry about for now."

"It's a good plan, and will keep you safe, John. But you put your men at risk, even still."

He turned his back to Kathryn and peered vacantly at the sea. "The men can take care of themselves. There'll be vexations elsewhere aboard this ship, and my diligence is needed for more important matters. The state of Madame Delahaye is moot, and this be the last ye'll hear me speak of it!"

Kathryn was not entirely convinced the temptress could be contained, but knew their conversation had ended. She dropped her eyes and conceded. Then, remembering the purpose for the visit in the first place, she cleared her throat, interrupting his thoughts. "Capt'n, I have grievous news I fear may burden the crew and yourself."

"Go on."

"I cannot speak to the back of your head. Please face me, John."

He turned slowly to face her and looked directly into her eyes. There was a fire that simmered behind his look, which Kathryn hoped would soon die out. She noticed the captain shifting his broad stance into the one used when he commanded the crew. She cleared her throat again, this time because her mouth had gone dry.

"One of the captives…" She struggled with the words. "…one of the prisoners, who had joined the crew, died last night. His body was covered with dark marks under the skin. I'm certain it was the Black Pox."

The captain lifted his chin and inhaled slowly. He stared at her without blinking.

She continued. "I'm almost certain one of the men—calls himself Barnes, by name—came in direct contact with the infected body. He was wearin' the dead man's coat when I saw him last."

"Barnes be a half-witted squiffy!" the captain blurted.

"Aye, that may be true, but your crew has all made companionship with the pox, as a result. I had the fool throw the body overboard, along with the dead man's bedding, just for good measure. Still, they'll all be exposed."

Captain Phillips paced, his hands clasped behind his back, as he wore a path in front of her. She watched the lines deepen in his forehead with each step. This conversation would not go favorably, just as the previous one had not. Still, she could not make light of it. Kathryn hesitated and watched him struggle with the announcement of Black Pox aboard his vessel.

"This is hard news, Captain." She shifted her weight and watched him. *Truly, this man carries great responsibilities at sea, consumed with the task of commanding a now ill-afflicted ship.*

Her heart softened as his resolve hardened. After a moment, he broke off his pacing and faced the sea.

"I've lost too many men, Kathryn. Do what must be done to save my crew. You'll have the accord of the men, that I assure you, lass."

Kathryn stepped up beside him, slipped one hand through his arm, and joined his focused attention over the sea. The current lifted the scorched bow of the ship, blackened from the cannon blasts it had received earlier this week. The crew had patched the main mast, and it held sturdy against the fair winds that blew against its sails. However, no one manned the crow's nest. The colors had been lowered, and the topmost point swayed precariously. The crew was working non-stop through the daylight hours to repair the damage inflicted by the recent battle.

She thought of the *Revenge*, crippled and wounded, nurtured by skilled hands laboring feverishly to repair her. The scene mirrored Kathryn's own efforts below deck. A twinge rippled through her, a pressing feeling of urgency. Kathryn glanced down at her own hands and thought of the sick bay that waited for her return.

"I need additional shafts drilled into the floor-boards for fresh air below deck…in the sick bay."

He nodded and kept his eyes glued to the sea, so she continued.

"Any man showin' the black mark is to be confined. And all men should be ordered to bathe."

He looked at her, puzzled. "What's the reason for that, lass? Our stalwart sails be few, and drawin' them seaside for bathin' will use up the resources we have."

"There's prudence in this."

Her stern look sent the message that she would offer no further explanation. It was a minor request. So, shrugging his shoulders, he relented on this point.

"Anything else?"

"There's one more request, Capt'n." Kathryn hesitated.

"Ay?"

"My fore-mothers have a certain practice for healin' the pox. Your crew needs to be given the remedy, though it be risky."

The captain's expression shifted to one of misgiving. Just then, a school of dolphin surfaced to dive playfully in and out of the swells alongside the ship. Kathryn gasped at the sight of them and whispered under her breath.

"A sign! Surely it's a sign."

The captain glanced at the dolphin arcing in and out of the water, then turned his attention back to her. "What do you mean, 'a sign?' And what's this risky business ye propose? Your list of demands grows lengthy, Kathryn, and wearies me sommat."

Kathryn moved to the side and leaned on the rails to watch the dolphins with interest. The captain joined her and stared at them with skepticism.

"The dolphin is the Celtic symbol for protection over sacred water. Where do we sail now, John? What is this water?" she asked urgently.

"It's the waters of El Caribe, lass. We've been sailin' o're these waters for years," he replied. Confusion crossed the lines etched around his crystal green eyes.

"Their pattern's straight, and methinks I see five abreast. The number of the Pentacle."

She turned to face him enthusiastically.

"What are ye sayin', lass? What do you mean 'of the pentacle?' Honestly, Kathryn, my patience with this conversation wanes. I have little time for your sorcery, and even less for your superstitions." He waved a hand at the dolphins swimming alongside the ship.

She stomped her foot indignantly and faced him.

"Yet you have plenty of time for your silly salty dog traditions? Don't speak to me of patience with such things, John. The Celtic ways are truthful ways. You've seen it for yourself."

She held up her hands, and he remembered the power they possessed. The pirate heaved a stiff breath. "Your demands exasperate me, Kathryn."

"It's the sign of the women in my clan, the ancient symbol for well-being and magic.

The dolphin bring protection over the water when in a group of five, a number for the pentacle…for wellness of the body and soul!"

"Celtic superstitions."

Kathryn grasped hold of the captain's forearms and held his gaze. Her ardor, something the captain knew was rare and meaningful, and a sign of urgency, held his attention as she spoke.

"It has meaning! John, this means I must move forward with the remedy. All aboard must receive it, but the men won't listen to me, even though I'm the chirurgeon. This order needs to be given by their capt'n."

He glanced back to the water to watch the dolphins as they leapt in time with the ship.

Five dorsal fins arced in time with the ship's movement.

"What is this remedy, Kathryn?"

She hesitated, knowing he would object initially, but the signs were visible—signs he had witnessed himself. Surely, he would agree and order the crew to yield.

"The skin is sliced and a slight measure of the pox itself placed inside the opened body."

"What? What did ye say? Have you lost your mind, woman?"

"Capt'n." She opted to address him formally. "As the ship's chirurgeon, I am petitioning the capt'n with hopes of gaining credence…and approval for a very risky proposal. I know this sounds foolhardy. Alas, it's true." She reached a hand out and touched him on the arm. "My mum and grandmothers gave this remedy to an entire village once plagued with the pox. Those who received the stuff survived."

He could hear the earnestness within her treatise but had no response.

"It's true, John. I can save these men upon your word, else I fear the entire crew will be lost."

His shoulders dropped, and she knew this was yet one more encumbrance heaped upon him. For what seem like an eternity, the captain stared at the ocean, lost deep in thought. She had all but given up, when he spoke, his attention still upon the sea but his message intended for her.

"All right, lass I'll give the order. But their lives be in your hands. Mind you, tend to the crew well. I will not have my men slaughtered by a witch's remedy," he warned.

She smiled and nodded her head. "Aye, Capt'n. Your men will survive. Send me Barnes first. He's a dead man anyway, and he will be the proof you need. The remedy favors this vessel. The signs speak of it."

She pointed at the sign of the pentacle, and the dolphins responded on cue, arcing once again—five black fins dancing alongside the *Revenge*. She smiled and kissed him lightly on the cheek.

Just then, a voice called from the bow.

"Sails ahead, *ho*!

Forty-One

SALLOW, TRIMMED SAILS APPEARED ON the horizon, barely visible in the glare of the late-day sun. Both Kathryn and Captain Phillips scurried along the waist to the forward part of the ship, joining Archer and several other men on the bow.

"Can ye see her colors?"

Heads craned to view the tiny ship as it bobbed in the distance.

"Nay."

Several of the crewmen watched from the front of the ship as a self-appointed lookout straddled the bowsprit. Another crewman stood precariously on the slippery plank.

"Nay, too far off in the distance," the pirate called from the bowsprit.

Kathryn watched, amazed at the agility of both sailors, neither of whom ever faltered as the long beam lifted, then fell forcefully against the ocean swells. Archer handed a spyglass to the captain, who accepted it and instantly lifted it to one eye. He remained ominously silent and peered at the sails.

"What manner of vessel is it?" Captain Phillips asked as he gazed through the long eyepiece.

"I can't be certain, Capt'n. It appears she's not flyin' her colors," Archer responded.

Captain Phillips lowered the spyglass and handed it back to Archer.

"Assume it be foe. Keep watch and let me know when her sails lie within a league of this ship," the captain ordered and turned to leave. "I'll be on the helm."

He glanced up at the empty crow's nest and stepped from the assemblage. Seth passed mid-ship, just before the mast, as he carried a bundle of powder bags. The captain hailed him and ordered him to meet him at the helm. Seth nodded and hollered the usual, "Aye, aye" as he made his way to the starboard cannon.

Kathryn remained where she stood, though her attention shifted from the oncoming ship to the captain. She could not decide which demanded greater urgency. Suddenly, as if he'd read her thoughts, Captain Phillips stopped to address her.

"You'd best secure the sick bay, lass. I'll be needin' every available hand at arms should we engage these interlopers in battle." The captain nodded toward the sea, then turned on his heels and made for the back of the ship.

Kathryn cast one last glance at the open water and squinted at the approaching ship. A shudder ran down her spine, and she involuntarily began to shiver in spite of the muggy weather setting in. *What is it?* Shaking it off, she scooted down the causeway and back to the sick bay where her patients awaited her.

Moody and Wynn threaded their way between injured men, handing out hardtack, the foreign cheese, salted fish, and grog to outstretched hands. On the far side of the cabin,

streams of sunshine cut through the ceiling planks, allowing gleaming shafts of daylight and fresh air into the dimly lit chamber. Above, she could hear wood splintering as someone gouged and bored with a hand-drill. Kathryn smiled to herself, pleased the captain had sent his crew to her aid so quickly.

The viridian cloth still hung from her neck, ready to cover her face. She adjusted it in place before she moved deeper into the room. Her eyes grew quickly accustomed to the gloomy light, aided by the emerging shafts of sunlight.

"Much better," she said, watching newly drilled dust particles glittering as they float in and out of the sunlight. "And now for the rest of you."

Scattered shadows rose from obscure lumps perched atop cots and bedding stacked on the floor. As Kathryn moved deeper inside, the ambiguous shapes became human bodies possessing the familiar faces of her crew. Sitting upright were those who awaited a clean bill of health. Most played dice, while others kept busy, telling tales between nips from doled-out rations and guzzled grog. Still others remained far too motionless, sprawled atop their beds.

As Kathryn made her way toward them, she calculated the approximate number of injured and fit. "There'll be no way to inspect each of you—at least, not soon enough, given the menace that looms on the horizon."

"What menace, ma'am?" Wynn stopped at the foot of a cot and stared at her.

"A ship approaches and is sure to be within range of the guns inside of the hour."

Dusk had claimed the skies already and time was running out. She had to sift quickly through her patients and send those able to bear arms topside to stand, ready to fight.

"Has the captain given orders?" Moody asked.

"In a way. Stand by…" With that, she hopped on top of an empty cot and shouted. "Avast, men! We face a station of utmost urgency. A vessel has appeared upon the horizon little more than a league off. All able bodies stand forth and be inspected, a clean bill of health awaits every man with pure intent, solely to take up your weapons, should the call to arms be made. Those who cannot stand upright shall be deemed infirm and remain confined to the sick bay."

"Aye, aye!" sounded enthusiastically from all corners of the chamber. Men jumped upright from their beds, renewed with the hope they'd be awarded a clean bill of health and allowed to escape their confinement in the dismal sick bay.

"Mind you, your appointment above deck is strictly my own to assign. Should you be declared unfit to bear arms, remain below here with your comrades, as the capt'n shan't be tolerating weak men topside. Savvy?"

Her warning sounded stern enough to be acknowledged aloud.

Moody and Wynn seemed less shocked by her brazen decision than the risk of a topside battle with the rest of the crew. As she hopped back to the floor, the two pirates dropped their commodities and bolted up the causeway, taking the stairs two at a time.

"Blaggards!" Kathryn watched them run off. She was secretly pleased with herself for having sent two able-bodied crewmen to the captain's assistance, despite their motives in abandoning duties below deck.

As she approached her first patient, she recognized the boyish face belonging to John Evans. He stood at proper attention. Indeed, the man truly befitted a sailor of His Majesty's Royal Navy. She removed the wrappings and could see the wounds at both lower extremities and across both wrists had healed nicely.

"Can you wield a sword, man?"

"Aye," he responded enthusiastically. Almost before she had finished, he bent in half and pulled a long, straight sword from beneath his disheveled cot. He brandished it proudly. With the skill of a seasoned Welshman, he cut the air on either side of her to show her his skill—all done without a grimace.

"So be it, Mister Evans. You're cleared of your infirmities and declared fit for duty. Tell Mister Sparks the chirurgeon declares it so, and should anyone question it,

MARTI MELVILLE

they need only seek me out. I haven't the time to draft a bill of health, so Sparks will have to take my word on it."

"Aye, aye, ma'am…I'm sore' obliged!" He gathered up his meager effects.

Kathryn nodded, moved aside to allow the man to pass, and then, walked to the next crewman in line. His agitation had caused him to literally dance in place. She gave the pirate clearance and watched as his meager attempt to cover an emerging limp failed.

"Good enough, Simpkins," she whispered.

"He's still limpin'," a voice said behind her. She waived the comment off.

"I'm fully aware, sir. He'll heal faster with rest, I know. Still, he's free to go, as he's likely to fight well enough with or without a limp." The memory of Archer's disabled agility had prompted her decision, even though she was a bit wary.

She sighed and moved to the next man, who stood as she approached. Kathryn went through the same process with each of them, clearing each man who could pull himself upright. She pronounced a clean bill of health, and watched as pirate after pirate took his place among those who stood topside.

Privately, she hoped the captain—or, more importantly, Archer—wouldn't notice their condition. If it became obvious these men were cleared while still somewhat infirm, her abilities would be questioned. Kathryn did not wish to cross blades again with the quartermaster, at least not at this moment.

418

The sick bay had been cleared of nearly half its occupants. Kathryn fixed her hands on her hips and sighed as she scanned those who remained.

Most expressed dismay at their fate, but she ignored it, and kept one ear cocked to the cacophony rumbling from above as she moved about her tasks. Footsteps pounded in scattered patterns directly overhead, knocking trapped debris from between the floorboards. Floating particulate danced boldly in a glimmering whirl to hover in streamlets of bleeding light. She glanced at the light and wished she were above.

"She makes t' breech t' larboard, Capt'n." Slade's burly voice sounded directly overhead.

Kathryn quickly finished bandaging an unconscious pirate's disfigurement and walked over to the basin of water that had been propped on top of the makeshift table. She dipped her hands into the murky water, dried them on her skirt, and hurried to the ladder that led above deck.

"Miss Kathryn," a feeble voice called out to her right, "we need be takin' arms wit' th' rest' o' th' men."

The voice trailed off, followed by bursts of rattling, wet coughs. She halted mid-step and turned to face the voice in the now dark room. Wide eyes peered at her through dim light, the shadows unable to conceal dark, raised wheals peppering the pirate's strained face. Kathryn felt a wave of compassion for the poor fellow. He would be dead before morning. She tugged the face cloth tighter about her nose and mouth and stepped forward.

"Honorable, you certainly have proven yourself to be, Mister Powell, true enough. And you know best what lies ahead for us all, should the ship be breached and boarded by our enemies."

The injured man nodded enthusiastically.

"These men are far too infirm for fightin' this day and need a champion." She paused to study his eyes. The outside sclera had already turned crimson. The man coughed, a death rattle, then nodded again. Kathryn smiled and waited for him to stop.

"I'd volunteer." He coughed again.

"Indeed. I cannot clear your bill of health. Your skin's pocked and too apparent for the crew above deck. Yet, you seem fit and ready to bear arms. Alas, I cannot do it myself," she lied.

Powell straightened up, inhaled weakly, and puffed out his chest in response. "I'll do it, lass."

"And so, we're all beholdin' to you, Mister Powell. Defend these quarters and your mates, as infirm as they be. This is your charge, and an honorable one, indeed!"

"Aye, ma'am. There'll be no blaggard's dog makin' his way past me blade, else meet 'is Maker, he will."

Kathryn smiled and fought the urge to pat the man on his shoulder. Instead, she touched her brow with the highest salute used for those who've fought with valor. Powell nodded again and returned to the darkness to retrieve his cutlass and pistol.

Above deck, the footsteps of crewmen rushing about grew more pronounced. She could hear cannon balls being dragged across the deck and secured next to the long-guns. Kathryn glanced upward instinctively as an anxious voice called out the enemy's approach.

Without a second thought, she turned from the sick bay, dashed up the short flight of stairs, and into the deep evening that had already settled over the *Revenge*.

Forty-Two

"JOLLY ROGER!"

The cry came from the crow's nest. Billowing black sails crossed the horizon just ahead of the *Revenge's* bow. Atop the main mast, the ominous smaller black flag shuddered. Vacant eyes, set within a chalky skull that floated above two crossed cutlasses, stared at nothing.

Kathryn's breath stuck in her throat as she caught sight of the pirate ship not more than a league off the starboard bow. "Surely, we cannot face another battle," she whispered to no one.

"Aye. It be folly to engage such a magnificent vessel, given 'er Capt'n," a chafing voice responded, and Kathryn turned toward it. Sparks' had commented as he passed her, arms loaded with grapeshot and gunpowder pouches.

She had nothing to say in response, so she merely watched him advance dutifully to the guns. Suddenly, a familiar chill plagued her veins again. She wrapped her arms around herself a bit tighter and allowed her teeth to chatter. Lined against the bow's rails, most of the able-bodied crewmen waited. Several had been released from the sick bay only hours earlier.

A fleeting sense of relief gripped her. She had made the decision to give a clean bill of health to most, even if doing do was suspect. *At least there will be men enough for a fair fight, even if half of them are peaked.* The thought was fleeting but noted.

As she turned to the quarterdeck, she saw a familiar cluster of men huddled about the helm. Sunlight glinted off the spyglass the captain held to his eye, causing her to blink. She gathered her skirt and bounded toward the rear of the ship, then made her way to where the men stood.

"There be no evidence of adverse action, that I can make out. No cannon alit, none bearing arms unfavorably. I cannot make sense of it."

The captain lowered the spyglass and handed it to Archer, who held it to one eye as the other squinted tightly. The whole of his face twisted into a ghastly grimace. The captain's gaze darted to her as she approached. She assumed an uninvited position alongside the men. No one voiced concern, seemingly untroubled by her presence.

She dropped her skirt and met the captain with a silent look of concern. Her stare demanded information—the kind that would reveal what their collective minds had schemed.

Once again, as if hearing her thoughts, Captain Phillips addressed her. "They be pirates, surely seeking plunder, as do we. I cannot make out their intent."

"Do ye know the ship?"

"Ay," Captain Phillips answered, shifting his focus back to the black ship. It had advanced rather quickly. "The *William*. It's Jack Rackham's sloop."

"Calico Jack?" Kathryn asked. She focused on the dark vessel.

"The same. See, his colors fly atop the main mast. There be none but Jack Rackham who flies the skull and cutlass, as such."

Kathryn eyes shifted to the black flag that waved violently atop the main mast. Involuntarily, she glanced at the large mast in the center of her own ship and noted the black flag had not yet been raised over the *Revenge*.

"Why do you not meet his colors with your own?" she asked.

"Prudence dictates we watch for first shot. I need to know if Capt'n Rackham intends to take the *Revenge* for plunder. He does not recognize our ship, or her Capt'n, yet."

Kathryn looked back to the *William* and waited for the first guns to fire. But the ship remained silent. She shuddered as another chill ran along her spine. There was something about this ship that conveyed more than the threat of the powerful Calico Jack and crew.

His crew.

She trembled as she thought of the pirate crew lined up against black rails, ready to fire on the *Revenge*. The captain stared at her.

"Are you well, lass?"

"Aye." She shivered again, and her teeth began to chatter involuntarily. "There's somethin' about that ship that bothers me."

He studied her for a moment, then suddenly, turned to face his own crew. "Hoist the colors!" he ordered. "Let's see what Capt'n Rackham does."

The black flag began to climb the mast. A ghostly figure was painted across a black field. In its hand was a spear with a tip that had pierced a bleeding heart. She shuddered again.

"Hoist th' colors, ho!" came the affirmation.

The young woman wrapped her arms around herself in an effort to squelch the shiver and watched in silence as their own flag reached the top of the large central mast. Glancing back to the water, she watched as the inky craft navigated its way closer. Within minutes, the ships were within shouting distance of each other. Even though deciphering the actual words hollered between crews would be difficult, it would only be moments before some sort of discourse took place. The pirates understood one another, even without words. The black flags guaranteed that.

Will Calico Jack view the colors as a sign of aggression? The thought crossed her mind as she watched the bold Jolly Rogers shuddering in silent defiance of one other.

"Man the guns, Mister Sparks," Captain Phillips' voice thundered and broke into her thoughts.

"Aye, aye, Capt'n," sounded from somewhere ahead.

It was evident, the captain feared the same threat of aggression and planned to be at arms,

just in case. Just then, a familiar figure stepped to the starboard bow. The sheen from an ivory handle glimmered in the amber rays of the setting sun as she propped one foot upon the bow's rails. The lean, bronzed arm extended ever so slowly to take aim at the opposing ship.

"Hold your fire!" The order thundered from the helm.

Jacquotte Delahaye's elbow dropped, and the pistol pointed skyward instead. "We best be done wit' all this waitin', Capt'n Phillips. Let's get on wit' it, then," she hooted. "There be two...nay, three good shots ahead o' me!"

"I said *hold*!"

Shouts carried from across the water, and a voice befitting a man obviously seasoned by laughter, roared. All eyes shifted to its source. Mid-ship, against the gunwale, stood the most elaborately decorated man Kathryn had ever laid eyes on. His hair spilled down in dark curls that rolled in a rather disorderly fashion over narrow shoulders. His air was one of grandeur and flamboyance. Atop his head, sat a pristine black tricorn tipped with bronze stitching, the back of which bobbed with enormous ostrich feathers dyed in various colors of red and yellow. But, the object most impressive was the man's coat. Navy blue velvet draped with brocade the color of spun gold, rubies, and emeralds—the whole of which rustled about his breeches as he pranced back and forth. In one hand, the pirate brandished an elaborate sword, no doubt taken from Spanish plunder. He waved the blade about ceremoniously in salute.

"Capt'n Phillips! Is this th' manner by which ye greet yer comrades?" His voice sounded jovial.

"Fair winds to ye, Capt'n John Rackham." John Phillips saluted, then tipped his head toward Jacquotte Delahaye. "She be nothin' but trouble to me, she be. You can take her, if you'd like, and do with her as you please."

Jacquotte shot a venomous look toward the helm but remained atypically silent. Kathryn shuddered again, but this time, her chest filled with warmth while her teeth rattled. The boisterous laugh sounded again as the ships bobbed side by side now. Despite the façade of joviality between captains, both crews hovered, alert at the guns and ready for the command to attack.

"Nay, she be yer own fine booty. I have but two o' me own fair to look after!" Rackham shouted.

At that, two rather small pirates stepped forward, each brandishing well-used flintlock pistols in hand. One stood slightly taller than the other and walked with an unsettling swagger.

The pirates stepped forward and took a place on either side of Calico Jack. Kathryn felt her heart pound, and her breath caught in her throat. In that instant, she leapt forward and grasped hold of the rail just off the starboard helm. Captain Phillips darted after her and caught hold of the back of her skirt just as she lurched forward.

"Kathryn! Be careful," he whispered. "The water's dark here."

She ignored him, and another bellow rolled from the flamboyant Captain Rackham.

"I see ye 'ave yer hands full thar, Capt'n Phillips," Rackham jeered.

One of Rackham's sidekicks stepped away and ran alongside the very spot where Kathryn perched, just opposite her. Captain Phillips kept firm hold of Kathryn by the back of her corset as she teetered there.

"*Winne*!" she screamed. "Winne! Is it you?"

"Kathryn!"

The voice sang out, high and feminine. Their interplay spanned the watery gap as both shouted salutations back and forth from the rails of their respective ships. All eyes rested on the women.

Flaxen curls cascaded mindlessly from underneath a battered tricorn as Winne lifted it from her head. Underneath, the face revealed the unmistakably large, round eyes and very full lips of a woman. Despite being dressed in men's clothing, with britches visibly too large and belted about the waist, the pirate's full, womanly figure was obvious.

Waving the tricorn in one hand, her raspy voice called out across the divide, "Kathryn! It's you! Oh,

Kat! So long since we've seen one another, and Mum's so worried o're you!"

Kathryn turned and faced Captain Phillips, cheeks wet with tears. "It's my kin…my cousin, Winne, who was raised with me in the same cottage your men snatched me from." Urgency filled Kathryn's voice as she relayed their secret. "Let me go to her, or bring her here to me."

The captain's eyes darted from Kathryn, who literally bounced with anticipation, to Winne. He let loose of her skirt and shook his head in disbelief.

"Please, Capt'n."

"Ay. Bring the lass aboard, with her Capt'n's permission, of course." He looked to the flamboyant Captain Rackham.

"What say you, Mary?" The ornate Calico Jack chuckled and posed with one foot perched pompously on an elaborately carved precipice and an arm draped over the shoulders of the other crewman at his side. In his other hand, he loosely gripped an ornate cutlass.

"By your leave, of course." Captain Phillips nodded in salute to the garish Captain Rackham, who returned the salute by tapping the cutlass against his hat. Meanwhile, his companion shifted her weight to the other foot. Keeping her focus on Winne, Mary Reed seemed uninterested in the interplay between captains. As she moved, her leather vest gaped open to expose the delicate shape of a woman's breast, which did not go unnoticed by John Phillips. Ever so slightly, one corner of his mouth lifted, and a smirk spread across his face.

"Welcome aboard the *Revenge*, Capt'n Rackham. You and your…er, companions." His voice bellowed across the water to the *William*.

Once again, Calico Jack tapped his tricorn hat in salute, then whispered into the ear of the pirate still clutched to him under his arm. Almost reactively, Reed stepped out of Rackham's grasp and sauntered over to where Winne stood. Winne kept one hand hooked through the coarse lines attached to the forward sails and wrapped the other about Reed's shoulders. Balancing precariously on the narrow strip of railing that ran the length of the great ship, Kathryn smiled, impressed with her cousin's agility despite the movements of the ship and sea.

Kathryn returned to the gunwale edge as she shouted to her cousin across the water. Within seconds, the sultry Reed stood ready to disembark the vessel, as well, taking a place alongside Winne at the rails.

"Avast! Capt'n Rackham an' party be boardin' anon. Make ready for the safe transfer o' passengers." Archer relayed the order to the men, followed by scattered "Ayes" on deck.

With the ease of a dancer, Winne leapt from the rails and rushed to the gangway just as the board was lowered onto the polished surface of the dark sloop. Curls bounced against her shoulders as she paced back and forth, impatiently waiting for the gangplank to be lowered.

"Tedious task to make it secure. Ye're grating against my already fragile supply of patience." Winne cursed as the men fortified the board to the deck. "Bloody incompetents!" she barked, and lunged for a stout line fasted to the aft rigging.

Winne gripped the line with both hands, leapt from the rail, and swung in a wide arc across the water. Landing gracefully on the deck of the *Revenge*, she bounded to her cousin.

"Kathryn!"

Forty-Three

"WHERE BE TH' RUM?" THE call came from one of the
William's crew.

Methodically, as if boarding a strange pirate ship
was standard practice for pirates, several of the *William's*
crew made their way onto the deck of the *Revenge* in a
rather orderly fashion. Little more than the hereabouts
of the rum accompanied their conversations.

The flamboyant Calico Jack Rackham and the
sultry Mary Reed, were among the men. With great
pretense, the garish Captain Rackham waved his hand
in choreographed circles and bowed deeply to Captain
Phillips, who waited near the helm to welcome him.
The spectacle, with which Calico Jack presented himself did not go unnoticed by the crew, either. Most
gawked with eyes wide and mouths hanging open.

Once on board, Calico Jack bowed and remained
there for a moment longer than would be customary.
He waved to his sultry cohort to do the same. A half-
hearted tap to her forehead indicated her insincere
salute. Instead, Mary stood in a wide stance with one

hand planted on her hip. Captain Phillips fought back the urge to smile while watching the pair. He reflected on her momentarily exposed womanly figure and the smile found its way to his lips.

Captain Phillips cleared his throat and touched the rim of his own tricorn. "Ahoy, Capt'n Rackham." An air of placation, intermingled with respect, colored his voice. "Indeed, welcome aboard, sir! You and your crew be welcome aboard my ship, and to me best rum." He nodded to Seth, who responded immediately and darted off toward the galley below where the stores of Caribbean rum lay hidden.

"Aye, Capt'n Phillips, ye do me well, indeed, an' I be honorin' ye wit' me own company, as it were."

Pompous, malevolent ass! John Phillips did not stifle the thought as it raced through his mind. "Please join me here, Capt'n Rackham. Your…er…mates can find company with the chirurgeon." His voice trailed off as he motioned to Mary, but she had already made her way to where Winne and Kathryn stood, chatting at the starboard rails.

"Lo, an' it appears me Mary has made 'er way there already." Calico Jack laughed his now familiar bellow. "So, Capt'n Phillips, it appears we have an accord betwixt our lassies, aye?"

"So it seems," Captain Phillips replied, mesmerized by the three women.

Just then, a sultry alto shattered their reverie. All chatter stopped as everyone turned toward Madame Delahaye.

She sauntered aft, holding her pistol, aimed skyward, and threw her head back as she spoke in a deep-throated rasp.

"Now what 'ave we 'ere? Why, it appears a fine gatherin' o' bawdy gossips, it do."

The three women inclined their heads to take in the cinnamon-skinned Jacquotte, who responded by cocking the hammer of her pistol. With lightning speed, the two women from Rackham's crew spun to face the dark-skinned beauty with their cutlasses held en garde. Jacquotte merely tossed her head and hooted at their display.

"Ho, ladies." Jack Rackham stepped forward. "Capt'n Phillips, let me introduce ye to me best at th' sword, an' the one beholdin' to me heart—me Annie, an' me mistress, Mary."

Winne and Reed simultaneously glanced at Captain Phillips, then turned their attention back to the pirate, Delahaye, whose ornate ivory pistol stayed cocked and pointed at Winne's left breast.

Captain Phillips responded in kind, stepping alongside the women. He shot a warning look at Jacquotte. "Truly, an honor, ladies," he said and bowed low. He didn't take his eyes off Jacquotte the entire time. "And this be Madame Jacquotte Delahaye, who is sharin' our passage north. Apparently, she is not aware of civil buccaneers' customs." He straightened and spoke through clenched teeth. "Methinks she'll be learnin' manners quick enough, else soon she'll be keeping company with rats in the brig."

Jacquotte lowered her pistol and dropped into a makeshift curtsey. Mary lowered her cutlass, as Calico Jack placed a gentle hand on Winne's outstretched arm.

"Lower yer weapon, Anne," Captain Rackham whispered. Reluctantly, she complied, although neither women sheathed their blades. Both remained poised and ready to strike, if need be.

As if on cue, Kathryn stepped sideways and gently lifted a finger toward Jacquotte.

Imperceptible light radiated in powerful waves and slammed into the ivory pistol, causing it to fly from Jacquotte's strong grip. The weapon landed several feet behind her. No one spoke. Kathryn tipped her head at one of the crewmen, and he instantly retrieved it. He held the pistol under the lantern light, inspecting the ornate detail carved along its length. He then handed the weapon over to Captain Phillips.

"Madame Delahaye be naught but a gentlelady in the presence of such honored guests,

methinks." The sarcasm in Kathryn's voice was biting.

Kathryn stepped up to Calico Jack and offered him the top of her hand. He met her advance and planted a gentle kiss upon her hand. "I don' believe I've made th' pleasure o' yer acquaintance, M'lady."

"Kathryn of Manannan Mac Lir at your service, sir." Kathryn curtsied as she spoke.

John Phillips shot her a withering look and rolled his eyes, to which she returned a sheepish smile and shrugged. *Truly, Captain Rackham won't have heard the tales of the fabled sea god, Manannan Mac Lir. 'Tis but a Scots tall tale, and this Calico Jack is not so learned, indeed.* Kathryn waited for any acknowledgement to cross behind Calico Jack's eyes, but nothing registered, and he bowed deeper and kissed her hand once again, a little too fervently.

"Ay, please forgive me, Jack. This is the ship's chirurgeon." Captain Phillips stepped forward and placed one hand on Kathryn's shoulder, then leaned his weight against her so that his mouth was next to her ear. "And the love of me heart, though she be impish in her ways."

Kathryn smiled wryly at Calico Jack and nodded the appropriate greeting reserved for nobility. An imperceptible warning crept into his expression, even as he smiled. Indeed, Captain Phillips would keep an eye on Calico Jack, particularly around the fairer sex.

Jack dropped Kathryn's hand and returned John Phillips' salute. Though pleasant, it became clear the two captains had squared off.

Kathryn stepped forward. "Aye, Capt'n, it's my pleasure to serve you and the crew, indeed." She glanced sideways at Captain Phillips and smiled affectionately, then nodding, turned her attention to the pretentious Calico Jack. "An honor to serve your crew in the capacity of healin' and physiks, sir."

Both men relaxed their stances and gazed at the dark-haired chirurgeon. All the while, Calico Jack beamed and nearly danced forward, hand extended to John Phillips, a sign of their accord.

Kathryn continued the preliminaries. "May I introduce you to my kin, Winne…" She caught herself midsentence and cleared her throat. "…me hearty, Anne Bonny."

Winne shot Kathryn a startled look at the slip, but no one seemed to notice. Captain Phillips glanced from Kathryn to Winne, who stepped forward and bowed low.

An alias? Indeed, her name is Winne, we all have them. Your secret is safe with me, Anne Bonny. He smiled at the thought and held the bow long enough for suitable propriety.

"The pleasure's mine, Capt'n Phillips." Blonde curls bobbed as Winne curtsied sideways, her hips swaying suggestively as she grinned a rather seductive smile. Lips full and inviting, Winne had a way with men, but as Anne Bonny, she had even greater skill with the sword.

Kathryn watched her cousin flirting with the captain, shook her head, and laughed silently to herself at Winne's dallying.

"And this be Mary." Winne gestured to the provocative woman who stood behind her. As Mary stepped forward, her auburn hair caught glints of gold from the lanterns, and her deep-set eyes illuminated the wide smile that crossed her face. Indeed, Mary was striking as she made eye contact with Captain Phillips.

"Capt'n," was all she said, but it was enough.

Several of the crewmen shifted uneasily, unsettled as they were by the stunning women who had just boarded their ship. Captain Phillips cleared his throat and nodded in the direction of each of the women.

"Ladies!" Calico Jack clapped his hands enthusiastically, shattering the salacious greeting between Winne and Kathryn. "Now that we all be well acquainted, what say ye to a trifle o' yer best rum, sir?"

"Ay, and a good way that be, Capt'n Rackham!" Captain Phillips turned away, searching his crew. "Seth! Spice the main brace, me boy. Rum for all, says I."

John Phillips stepped forward, clapped Calico Jack on the back, and escorted him mid-ship as the three women followed. Jacquotte Delahaye watched as they neared her, hands on her hips.

Captain Phillips paused and his eyes narrowed to slits. "This is your last warnin', Madame. We have guests aboard, savvy?" He emptied the ivory pistol of shot and tossed it to her.

With cat-like reflexes, she caught the object and turned away. "At least it looks fetching, even though it's chamber be barren." She replaced the pistol securely at her side.

"Madame Delahaye," Kathryn called as she approached. "You're welcome to join us, provided you mind your place and know there'll be none here who'll think naught of cuttin' you down for want of provocation."

Kathryn wrapped her arm around the waist of her cousin.

"What are you doin', Kat?" Winne asked in a whisper.

"I'll keep my friends close…" Kathryn squeezed Winne's waist. "…and my enemies even closer."

"Good plan." Winne snickered, then shouted over her shoulder. "Aye, come join us, Jacquotte."

Madame Delahaye stared at the women as they walked away, then thought better of refusing an offer of rum. She hopped forward and took a place alongside Mary with a stride that matched the others.

"Th' name's Mary," the sultry brunette said matter-of-factly, and offered her hand to Jacquotte, who accepted it.

"Back from the Dead Red…but you best call me Jacquotte Delahaye," she replied with a grin.

Forty-Four

PEALS OF LAUGHTER, ACCOMPANIED BY song and grog, sailed across the decks of both vessels.

Harmonious blends of a lute and the bombard lightened the muggy night air, along with Cajun rhythms.

I took that maid upon my knee
Mark well what I do say!
I took that maid upon my knee
Cried she, "Young man, you're much too free!"

A crewman warbled the lyrics and winked at Mary. She lifted a bottle and blew him a kiss. Within moments, she was comfortably seated on his lap, singing along with the rest of them.

I'll go no more rovin' with thee, fair maid,
A rovin', a rovin', since rovin's been me ruin!

Both crew celebrated and forged a strong friendship as the pirates hopped back and forth from ship to ship. With time and freely flowing spirits, they became increasingly more uproarious as they shared wild tales of the sea and bottles of island rum.

The unchecked levity escalated throughout the evening and deep into the night. As the moon smiled its toothless grin, barely illuminating the surface of the water, the stars danced in time to the Caribbean music.

Both captains sat side by side as they watched the celebration and raised toasts to fair winds and fine weather, brimming booty, and buxom beauties.

"Join me here, Mary, me darlin'." Calico Jack patted his leg, and Mary moved to sit there. He kissed her cheek, and together, they toasted the evening.

Boisterous laughter shattered the night air in staccato bursts that sounded randomly from hidden sections of the ship. Heels pounded the decks in bumbling time to the rhythm of the sea and music.

The *Revenge* celebrated.

"To ye an' yer crew!" Calico Jack's garbled decree rose portside above the noise. "An' this lassie be me best prize, mind ye."

Jack's broad hand swatted Mary's derriere affectionately. She nestled herself on Jack's knee and lifted her mug in salute before draining it. He wrapped an arm around Jacquotte, seated on the other knee, and gave her tiny waist an affectionate squeeze.

"An' ye, Madame Delahaye," he muttered not so silently into her auburn mane. "Ye be right fittin' fer me crew, be ye willin'…or perhaps not willin'…as ye would have it!"

Calico Jack threw back his head and roared at his own joke, then squeezed both women heartily. Watching the ostentatious display, Captain Phillips couldn't help but chuckle and take another swig from a stout-necked bottle. Jacquotte planted a kiss atop Calico Jack's head and Mary hiccupped, unconcerned about anything else other than rum. Jack groped both woman and handed Mary another bottle. She smiled lazily and nestled further into his lap while Jacquotte let loose a throaty laugh.

"Aye, methinks I've found a frolicsome fellow th' likes o' which be offerin' pleasantries to parlay with, indeed!" She chuckled and kissed the pirate full on the mouth. Mary watched,

bleary-eyed, and absently reached for her sword.

"Let me be of assistance, Madame." Captain Phillips leaned forward to distract her and poured generously from his bottle in order to fill Mary's mug again. By now, she was drinking with both hands—in one, she held the mug, while the other gripped the bottle.

"Thank ye, kind sir," she slurred, and lifted the rim to her lips. All thoughts of Calico Jack's indiscretion had apparently been forgotten, along with her sword.

Not far from them, sitting upon two firkins that pushed against the port rails, Kathryn and Winne were deep in conversation. Both women spoke in low tones, oblivious to the chaos going on around them.

"…and you kept it secret for so long, Winne? How, ever, did you pull it off?" Kathryn's eyes locked on her cousin's, which were sparkling with mischief as she tossed her blonde curls and laughed.

"The crew never suspected for a moment that I was anything other than a full-bodied sailor, albeit a few thought me a trifle weak for my size. I'm quite small for an adult seaman, of course. Still, they accepted me, and their respect flourished for my skill with the sword."

"And Mary?"

"Ahhh…Jack stayed wary of Mary from the first moment she boarded. Indeed, she stole aboard and none thought of it, except Capt'n Rackham, who eyed her from the first moment. He apparently became jealous of our friendship. Of course, I knew the moment she stepped aboard that she was a woman, but none else knew it."

"Not one suspected?" Kathryn glanced at Mary.

"No one. Many treated us as if we were lovers, all the while knowin' I belonged to Capt'n Rackham. Still, it's been most favorable, havin' a female companion on board."

"How'd he find out she was a woman and not a man?"

"For a brief moment, when I thought certain he'd toss her overboard, jealous as he was, Mary boldly pulled aside her blouse and showed the old fool her ample doppelgangers!"

Winne tossed her head back and let loose another throaty laugh, then wiped her eyes as she finished.

Kathryn chuckled at the sound of her cousin's laughter and squeezed her hand affectionately. "Doppelgangers!" Kathryn repeated.

"Mary was taken in as one o' the crew immediately. Her fierce way with the blade and her stubbornness of heart fit in nicely with a crew of cutthroats." Winne's infectious laughter escaped again. "As I said before, I'm most fond of havin' companionship with Mary. The capt'n treats us both well."

"He appears rather pretentious, does he not?" Kathryn squinted involuntarily while she studied the pirate a few paces off.

"Aye, but it's his way. There be few at sea who dare confront him, so aghast at the show he presents. Fortunately, there is seldom thought of battle, as a result. What little conflict there be, Jack's silver tongue quickly settles it. More skilled at discourse than with the sword, he is!"

Winne's glance followed Kathryn's to the pirate captain.

"You mean, he talks his way out of battle."

"Aye. It bodes well for him that he has me and Mary aboard, defendin' the ship as we do."

"A task that hardly seems fit for a woman." Kathryn's expression dropped.

"Somebody's got to do it, and Jack won't."

"Is this Mary so skilled with the blade?"

"Aye, that she is…yet I'm stronger, methinks." Winne seemed to be boasting—the persona of her alias, Anne.

Kathryn eyed her cousin sideways. She thought it was a clever muse for Winne to assume the name *Anne Bonny* before hopping onto Calico Jack's ship. *She is rather bonny, Winne is. An excellent disguise, indeed. John Phillips Buchanon did the same, changing his name before going pirating.* For a moment, she wished she had been as clever—to present an assumed name that fateful day she had been kidnapped and brought aboard the *Revenge*. The thought unsettled her.

"Would that I'd been as clever as you, the day these blaggards took me from the cottage."

"Not so clever, Kathryn. Mostly, I wanted to flee— to find you and escape my betrothed. It was a wretched match, that was. Bad marriage from my vantage point, anyway."

"It wasn't meant to be, it seems."

Winne shook her head. "There are always forces at work outside of our own plans for life. You know that, as well—forces that placed you on the pirate ship and into the arms of your beloved Captain Phillips."

Kathryn couldn't help but smile. For nearly an hour, Winne continued to brag. Kathryn listened intently, never doubting Winne's skill for a single moment. The *Gift* they shared, though similar, remained tailored apiece. Each possessed her own innate talents, and the power of the *Gift* flourished in both because of it.

"No disputin' your ability to read the past and future as ye do, Winne," Kathryn said and glanced down at the palms of her own hands. The title, *Skyfyre Witch,* filled her thoughts.

"Aye, and I saw you, Kat. You're very powerful on your own, cousin. There's a totem ye possess, no?"

Kathryn shot a look at Winne, unable to hide the astonishment that crossed her face. "What did you say?"

"Oh, don't be so startled, Kat. You said it yourself. I am strong with the *Gift* of prophecy. I saw that totem in your hands, as sure as I see you sittin' here with me on this godforsaken ship!"

Kathryn sighed and dropped her gaze back to her palms. "The *Revenge* is home to me now, Winne, and the capt'n…" She trailed off and cleared her throat uneasily, then changed the subject. "Made of the black-thorn. The Straif was given to me by the Vodoun priest, though he called it a 'Mamba Stick.'"

Winne gasped, and Kathryn's eyes darted back to her cousin's face. The buoyancy drained from Winne's countenance as she clutched Kathryn's forearm. Kathryn flinched under her cousin's grasp, sharp nails digging into her skin.

"You? In the presence of a Vodoun? Kat, what are you thinkin', cousin? The Vodoun possess dark alchemy used to overcome those with the *Gift*. Have ye for-gotten Morrigan's powers?" Kathryn's head shot up again as she stared at her cousin with disbelief. Winne simply waved her hand and continued. "Aye, I know of Morrigan and her fetish o're your beloved capt'n."

"How? How could you know that?"

"The Morrigan has black intentions for Capt'n Phillips…and for you, as well, Kat. She means to seek you out and destroy you both. You'll be safe only through your own powers. Use them wisely, cousin! Flirtin' with the presence of a Vodoun priest is not wise, mind me on that!"

Kathryn dropped her gaze and peeled her cousin's grip from her arm, then lifted Winne's hand to her cheek and held it there. "I've much to learn, Winne." She kissed the back of Winne's hand. "I know that well enough…much to learn."

"Aye, that ye have, my Kat. But, we are here now, and you will surely be safer with us aboard, though we won't be with you for much longer. Jack means to sail back to Jamaica, and I'll be goin' with him."

"You love the man, don't you, Winne?"

"Aye, that I do. Mary does, too, though I am his favorite, for certain." Winne laughed, forgetting they chatted in private. Then, winking at Kathryn, she continued, "There is much to tell."

"I can imagine."

Winne's tone suddenly grew somber. "Aye, and my life is not what I thought it would be back when we were both younger, in Mariel's garden."

Winne stared off at the dark ocean, unable to see more than an occasional crown as the water crested with the tide. It was evident her thoughts had drifted elsewhere, to another time and place.

"We both took paths we did not plan for, Winne. It was our fate, I suppose. Though, I often wonder what would have been, had we lived our lives out in the *pentref gan glogwyni*. If you had not gone to sail aboard the *William* with Calico Jack, of all people."

"It's not obvious? I set after you, Kat. Not long after you were taken by those scoundrels, I put my back to Mariel's cottage and stole aboard a fishin' vessel bound for the south of Wales."

"Foolish decision, Winne."

"I couldn't leave you in the hands of pirates. Mostly, I couldn't leave myself in the hands of that bungling blighter, John Bonny."

"But you took his name, still?" Kathryn stared at Winne, intrigued.

"It seemed a good alias, so I changed mine and left as Anne Bonny. Those who searched me out, found Anne Bonny in the arms of Calico Jack Rackham."

"What of your given name?"

"I could not allow Winne to be tainted, attached to that lubber. Winne Bonny?" She looked at Kathryn and shook her head. "Oh, no. Winne was Mariel's great-grandmother's name, as well, a powerful white witch. The name was passed to me. I could not bear to see it dishonored by joining it with the surname the likes of John Bonny!"

"I understand, Winne." Kathryn looked up at the night sky and stared at the moon. "Anne fits you well."

"Aye, true enough." Winne glanced upward. "The night was moonless…a good omen…the night I left with Jack." Winne's lips curled gently, then dropped.

"Mariel knew my intentions, though she kept it to herself. She was most distressed the last time I stayed with her, but she said nothing, only gave me this." Winne held her hand outward for Kathryn to see. "She counseled me of its magic."

Kathryn gasped.

Positioned snugly over her first finger was the onyx ring, its wings folded back—a mirror image to the one Kathryn had given to the Vodoun priest. She clapped a hand over her mouth.

"Oh, Winne, this is the same piece she hid in my bag. I had no inkling just what it was for and thought it but a token to barter with. I assumed Mariel had sent it for that purpose."

Winne tossed her curls as she lifted her chin. Her signature raspy chuckle bubbled out.

"A token? Kat, you know better than to think our Mariel gives out mindless tokens, particularly to those possessed with the *Gift*." Winne's laughter melted to a faint whisper, then silence, as she glimpsed Kathryn's face.

"What is it, Kat? What's wrong?"

"Winne, I've done something terrible!" Kathryn replied, barely able to speak. "I gave the Mamba priest the match to this ring…to your ring. I bartered my own ring to the Vodoun."

Winne fell silent, and the color drained from her face. Her eyes bored into Kathryn's as she delved deep into thought. The scattered pop of pistols peppered the evening air, only mildly disturbing the silence between them. A celebration still carried with the breezes fanning the *Revenge* along on the balmy evening air—a gift to the women seated against the rails. But neither shared the merriment.

Kathryn watched as Winne's eyes shifted focus and changed into a glassy doll's gaze, instead. She remembered seeing the same look when Winne divined images of past or future events. Of course, Kathryn could not see them herself, but she recognized when something vital was being revealed to Winne. Kathryn remained silent but observant.

As if the flicker of a candle had been suddenly blown cold, Winne snapped her eyelids shut, then blinked several times until her focus was once again upon Kathryn.

"I cannot see what lies ahead for the ring you gave away, Kat. The Vodoun priest has it hidden deep within his stock of talismans and dark treasures. One can only hope he forgets its purpose and leaves it there. For now, it is safe."

Kathryn's face twisted slightly, unable to hide the horror she felt. "It was foolish of me, Winne, to think the item a worthless trinket...particularly because it came from Mariel. She never bequeaths an item without intent, and I know this!"

Silently, Kathryn berated herself while waiting for Winne to respond, but she held her tongue. Kathryn's inner battle was apparent to Winne, who finally answered the question that had lodged in Kathryn's mind.

"The purpose, cousin, is to join souls. Both rings are the mirror image of each other. This joins both rings with inseparable destiny. The raven is the sign of healing, vision, prophecy, and great power. Morrigan is ruler o're the ancient Samhain that takes the form of the raven." Winne paused and hoped Kathryn would understand the symbolism, but she was met with a blank stare, instead.

"I still don't understand how Morrigan is tied to the rings, or why Mariel would have possession of them. Why would she give us each one in secret?" Kathryn blinked back tears as she spoke.

Winne sighed, pulled the ring from her index finger, and held it up for Kathryn to see. Kathryn leaned forward, eyes intent on the menacing black form with wings tucked over the ring.

Winne's voice was no more than a whisper. "The Morrigan seeks power…dark power, 'tis certain. The rings are bound together in purpose. It ties she who possesses it to the other. Each shares the other's fate. This power, should it be captured by Morrigan, surely ties her to the one possessed of the other ring."

"But you possess one ring, and I the other, Winne. How could Morrigan…?" Kathryn's voice caught as realization hit home.

"Aye, now you understand," Winne said. Her eyes glinted. "Morrigan stole the ring belongin' to you and will use it to destroy whoever possesses the onyx raven's mate. I suspect Morrigan had hoped you would bequeath yours to Capt'n Phillips. Extermination of those who oppose her is the dark Goddess' plan, and carnage the effects. You won't be spared, Kathryn...

nay, nor your Capt'n Phillips."

"So, Mariel gave each of the rings to us in the hopes that Morrigan would never find one. You and I would be tied together inseparably."

"Aye."

"But now, the Vodoun has mine, and you are tied to him?"

Winne nodded.

Kathryn dropped her head into her hands as the full understanding of Winne's message weighed on her. "I've endangered us all." She sat with pleading eyes fixed on Winne. Her cousin shrugged. "Then you must rid yourself of the ring, Winne. Surely, it isn't safe for you to be keepin' it."

Winne grew distant. Her face relaxed, and her breath slowed and deepened. Kathryn knew to wait while Winne forced her mind into a trance-like state, allowing it to be filled with images of the past or future. Another ricochet of pistol fire sounded, and Kathryn turned her head in its direction. Emerald green eyes locked onto hers.

Her heart leapt, and she forced a warm smile at the man. A corner of his mouth curled in response. Chaos melted into silence as Kathryn's and John's gazes lingered just a moment longer than usual. She felt her heart skip in its rhythm, then strike again to match his. Their souls united momentarily—a silent witness to the union she sensed they shared from before her birth.

"How strangely comforting," Kathryn whispered, and Winne's eyes snapped open.

"Aye, you need not worry!" Winne's elation was vibrant and unchecked. "The priest's intent is to hold the ring for his own. Greedy, but fortuitous for our purposes…'tis true, very comforting." Winne grinned and caught sight of her cousin's interest. She glanced back and forth from her cousin to the regal pirate captain, smiled knowingly, and tucked the onyx ring into the pocket of her trousers.

For the moment, the threat of Morrigan was displaced by deep, predestined love.

Forty-Five

BY THE NEXT AFTERNOON, THE celebration had settled into a drunken wake. Only a handful of pirates had been shot and thrown overboard. Their personal effects had been divided before the victims even hit the water.

"A rather indiscriminate loss," Calico Jack said as one of his crewmen was tossed overboard. Most agreed.

All in all, it proved a very joyous celebration of cutthroats and buccaneers from two prominent ships.

Kathryn had parted ways with Winne not long after their conversation ended. Calico Jack had sought his companion around the same time Kathryn had locked eyes on Captain Phillips. As Jack whisked his Anne away, Mary on his other arm, Kathryn stepped alongside John Phillips.

She chuckled as Jack danced with both women. "How does he keep up?"

As if on cue, Captain Phillips bowed with one hand extended. "I think it's about time ye honor me with your presence, Lady Kathryn." He displayed a gentleman's offer and bowed lower.

She took his hand and smiled. In that moment, the night's moonlight caught her in its luster and cast a silvered brilliance over her sun-bronzed skin. Indeed, she was breathtaking in that light, and the pirate's heart leapt as his gaze settled upon her.

"Aye, I'll dance with you. Perhaps, though, it's wise to consider which lass you be makin' such an offer to, Capt'n Phillips," she teased back. "There's many a fine, robust lass aboard this ship. Certainly, most will be countin' on time with the capt'n." She tossed her head, chuckled, and her gaze darted to Jacquotte Delahaye.

Captain Phillips did not miss the subtle gesture and followed her glance to the pirate, encircled by lusty, drunken crewmen all vying for her affections. "You need not be thinkin' that way, Kathryn." His baritone was sticky in his throat, more like a guttural whisper. In truth, he couldn't take his eyes off Kathryn.

A strong hand led her aft and stopped just short of the taffrail. Gently, the captain pulled her to his chest. She leaned against him to allow her skin to tingle against the taught muscles beneath his smock.

"The day soon comes I'll be askin' you to be me wife."

Kathryn shuddered as the smile that had begun in her heart crept its way to her face. She nestled deeper into his broad torso. "That may be, Capt'n, though I'll be the one replyin' to your proposal. Don't forget it… should you ask, and should I answer, 'aye.'" She teased him further, brushing her lips against his cheek as she whispered against his skin, "Perhaps…perhaps no."

He leaned in, and she lifted her face and kissed his mouth tenderly. Pirate hands gently found their way to the small of her back and pulled her body into his. A strong sensation of icy fire ignited deep within to cloud her thoughts as her body responded. She pressed herself against him. They remained, united in souls, as their bodies gave in to passion.

"A-hem." The deep voice interrupted. "The rum's 'bout out, Capt'n. Wit' yer permission, I say we best fetch one o' the barrels kept in hold."

As the couple parted, a corner of the captain's mouth lifted involuntarily. "Ay, do as ye will and be gone." His eyes never left Kathryn's as the intruder briskly made off.

Neither Captain Phillips nor Kathryn spoke again of their plans for a legal union between pirate and witch. The few remaining hours of twilight were filled with talk of superficial things, and the unspoken unity between them, until both fell into silence. The *Revenge* lifted and fell as the currents carried them forward. Darkness would soon escape as morning gave birth to a new day.

As she lay against his chest, she traced a finger along the scar that brought back memories of the day his life had been taken with a single blow from the massive boom. Her eyes drifted up to the heavy yardarm overhead, and the night sky beyond. *Indeed, that was a dark night*, she thought, and allowed her gaze to wander up to the half-moon still bright in the fading darkness. She sighed, grateful this man was alive.

"*Bendigedig fyddo Duw, diolch iddo fod yn,*" she whispered the ancient prayer of thanks and closed her eyes, content to be one with a pirate.

As the dawn washed the darkness off the endless expanse of ocean, drizzles of golden light trickled across the deck in long, finger-like beams that crawled with flecks of dust and sea spray. Kathryn allowed her mind to wander as she followed the sunlight that crept steadily along the polished deck. Tiny particles shimmered, and her stare grew fixed, mesmerized by the glittering objects that floated in the sun's rays. It reminded her of something—something she had seen before—sunlight that danced through holes in a dark room.

The sick bay!

She bolted upright and stared. Her mind suddenly became aware of the men below deck. The captain felt her shift in his arms. He opened his eyes and blinked against the sunlight.

"What's wrong, lass?" he asked, his voice scratchy as he spoke.

"The sick bay. John, there are men down below needin' my attention, and I still have the black pox to deal with. Capt'n Rackham does not know about the pox amongst the crew and will be sorely vexed, should he be findin' out what ills we're harborin' aboard this vessel." The captain nodded and rubbed one eye as he sat upright beside her. "Does this pox need your attention this very instant? The sun's barely risen," he protested.

Her answer was a silent scowl. Feeling her tension, he shifted position and opened one bleary eye after the other in an attempt to grant her his full attention— which was what she wanted, apparently.

"It cannot wait! Do you intend to turn from the needs of your crew and sleep the mornin'

away, or stand forth as their capt'n?" she snapped. "I walk a fine line, as it is. If I shirk my duties as chirurgeon, I'll surely be at the mercy of the men—regardless of your position as leader."

"Your point's made. True enough. What do you suggest o're this grave predicament then?" he asked and reached for a bottle discarded to one side.

"Winne, er…Anne…knows of the ways of the healer. She's as *Gifted* as I, with powers to heal sick men. I'll seek her assistance and we'll inoculate the entire ship against this infestation. You must stand behind me on this, John." Her eyes pleaded stronger than her words. He would not be able to refuse her.

"Ay, then, so be it. But keep me apprised of your progress. I'd best have a word with the good Capt'n Rackham." He stood upright, bottle in one hand, while the other reached overhead to stretch against the warm, sunlit morning.

Kathryn was already on her feet, gathering her effects. She wrapped both arms around him from behind and gave his waist an affectionate squeeze before rushing off to find Winne. The captain watched the woman he loved disappear into the depths of his ship.

Winne was precariously perched against the starboard rails as she balanced a steaming cup in one hand and plucked a hunk of heavy bread from a tray with the other.

This was how Kathryn found her.

"Typical, Winne. Calm while at risk doing the most mundane tasks."

"Good morning, Kat." Winne's ruby lips parted to reveal an infectious smile that Kathryn returned.

"Where is Mary?" Kathryn asked.

"She's still asleep, as far as I know." Winne hopped down to the deck.

The cousins moved to one side, and Kathryn launched into the details of the sick bay and her plans to inoculate the crew. Winne listened intently but said nothing—only nodded occasionally. The flush to her cheeks soon paled as she learned of the pox.

"Well, this isn't favorable news, now is it, Kathryn?"

"No. Captain Phillips is letting Calico Jack in on it now."

Winne shook her head in dismay, then set her resolve. "So be it, Kat. Gather your necessaries, and I'll meet you below deck." Winne glanced behind Kathryn. Her eyes scanned the length of the ship. "I need to find Mary, first. She should know of this before talk finds its way to the crew. You should have told me when we boarded."

"I should have done a lot of things differently, Winne."

"Aye. 'Tis in the past."

Kathryn nodded and thanked Winne. The two women clasped hands reassuringly before parting ways. Kathryn kept her eyes forward, not wanting to make eye contact with any of the pirates, as she moved quickly toward the bow of the ship. Her cabin lay just ahead. Just as she was about to descend the causeway, she caught sight of the captains in deep discussion out of the corner of her eye.

Calico Jack proved just as flamboyant in gesture as in attire. It was obvious the topic they were deliberating on was the sick bay's malady, and in spite of the exaggerated gesticulations from Captain Rackham, he appeared to be receiving the information well.

Let's hope the rest follow suit. I don't want rioting from drunken pirates. Kathryn heaved a sigh of relief. *At least I was spared partnership in that conversation.*

Kathryn scurried around the corner, reaching the doorframe of her quarters. Abruptly, a sharp bite pierced the side of her ribcage. Something pinned her right arm to her side, and a strange pressure encircled her throat.

The foul stench of fetid salt pork and stale rum filled her nostrils as a deep rasp whispered in her right ear. "Ye won' be killin' me men aboard this ship, witch! I 'eard what ye said to Anne jes' now."

Kathryn recognized the grating voice as belonging to Archer and strained against the Grip, which only tightened about her neck as she struggled. "Let me loose, dog!"

"I won' let ye do it, daughter o' th' devil! I won' let ye destroy th' crew wit' yer hexes an' mischief. Ye won' be stickin' me wit' yer malady, ye won'. Not me, nor me mates!"

She felt his calloused fingers dig deeper into her throat and knew he meant to crush her windpipe—to silence her, once and for all. "You won't get away with it, Archer." Kathryn inched her left hand closer to the small of her back and felt the rigid surface of the dirk hidden there. She firmly grasped the hilt and pulled it from within the folds of her skirt.

Unaware, Archer's threats had grown more brazen as the grip on her throat tightened. "Th' men don' trust ye, either, witch! Th' entire crew would see ye sent back to hell!" Spittle scattered as he spoke, and she fought the urge to gag.

Kathryn lifted the blade almost imperceptibly, tracing the length of her own torso, the tip aimed for Archer's gullet. "And how do you think the capt'n will be takin' to your plan?" She choked as she spoke.

"Oh, he'll be thankin' me for certain. Most likely be rewardin' me for riddin' his prize ship o' vermin such as yerself!" he hissed.

She felt her blade hit its mark.

"Drop your blade, Mister Archer." Kathryn pressed the tip of her dagger into the soft flesh under his chin.

The quartermaster froze but did not loosen his grip. She waited. Just then, the cock of a pistol hammer sounded behind her. Archer's eyes darted to the sound.

"Ye heard th' woman. Drop yer blade, ye foul, motherless git!"

Kathryn recognized Mary Reed's clear, commanding alto and pressed her dirk deeper into the soft tissue. A second clap sounded.

"I'd be mindful of your warnin', pirate. This is the last, and if ye think we're women too timid to cut ye to ribbons, think again," Winne stated.

Archer withdrew his hand from Kathryn's throat but held his blade firmly against her ribs. She met his gaze and pressed the point of her dirk deeper into his throat. Blood drizzled down the steel, and she watched him swallow with difficulty.

"*Marwolaeth yn aros bwriad budr, diflastod tragwyddol i ddilyn*." Kathryn chanted.

Winne's eyes darted to Kathryn, and her infectious grin soon followed. "Death awaits foul intent, eternal misery to follow." Winne recited the ancient curse with her cousin.

"What's that? What's she sayin'?" Archer spat.

"Aye, dog, even now you're blessed with your own curse." Winne tossed her head back and chuckled. "You're married to your doom now and surely be givin' your soul to the devil."

Mary smiled at Winne's answer. She chuckled again, her raspy laughter filling the small space they occupied. Slowly, Archer withdrew the blade, and Kathryn felt the skin smarting where it had been. Her own dagger remained against the pirate's gullet, forcing Archer to retreat.

Once free, he lifted a free hand to the bottom of his chin and wiped the warm crimson ooze from it. "Ye be devils yerself, an' he can take th' lot o' ye." He cussed out the three women and spat at their feet. Then he turned his gaze upon Kathryn. "Sleep lightly, witch, an' keep one eye vigilant. This won't be th' end."

Laughter peeled from Winne and Mary as the quartermaster spun on his heels and leapt up the causeway and out of sight.

"Well, well, Kat…"Winne mused as she un-cocked her pistol and returned it to her side. "That was most enlightening, and a rather merry way to greet the day."

Kathryn lowered her dirk and wiped the bloody dribble on the edge of a stair. "The dog and his antics are no stranger to me. Archer's mostly an irritation and a nuisance to me, although the git seeks to catch me unawares. Certainly, he could do me in, then."

"Well, today is not that day," Mary said, and set both hands on her waist.

"Aye, and I have you to thank for it, Mary." Kathryn smiled at her new friend, who returned the gesture.

Kathryn was grateful Winne had found her way to Mary. It would be a sad day when Kathryn was forced to part ways with these powerful women. Her thoughts jumped back to the sick bay and the men trapped there.

"I'll be needin' your assistance below." Kathryn's voice was weak.

"Aye, for the pox?" Winne's response sounded more like a statement than a question.

Both women glanced up at Mary, who remained silent, though her eyes darted between Winne and Kathryn. Kathryn moved deeper into her cabin and began gathering bundles strewn across the ceiling. Winne joined her, helping herself to sprigs of dried herbs and stones, as she circled the tiny room. Near the farthest corner, she stopped abruptly and stood as rigid as stone. Her stare was fixed on a dark recess. Kathryn noticed her cousin and paused. Without asking, she recognized the dark look on Winne's face.

"It's called a blackthorn totem...the Straif," Kathryn responded.

Winne glanced briefly at her cousin before returning her attention to the dark totem. Winne crouched and traced a finger along its surface, lingering for a moment over the carved black symbols. "And do you know the meaning?" Winne asked matter-of-factly. Her eyes never left the intricate staff.

"No," Kathryn said. "Not at present, but there's a crewman aboard who claims he does."

Mary stepped up behind Winne and bent down to study the ornate symbols, her head inches from Winne's. Kathryn waited. "So, ye keep a Vodoun stick in your sleepin' quarters, and ye know not wherein lay its powers?" Mary asked incredulously.

She stood upright and placed her hands on her hips as she stared at Kathryn in disbelief. Winne's focus stayed fixed on the Straif.

"Aye, I suppose it seems reckless of me, not knowin' what the symbols mean," Kathryn admitted and sighed loudly.

Winne glanced at Mary and shook her head in frustration, then stood upright and spoke in measured words. "You'd best be learnin' what these markings mean, Kat. There's dark power in the blackthorn, and it's meant for you…savvy?" Winne lifted her eyes to meet Kathryn's as she bit off the last syllable.

Kathryn nodded. "I've other, more urgent, tasks at hand, as you can see." She began to gather the herbs and amulets from off the center table.

"Have ye now?" Winne had managed to get in the last word once again.

Kathryn refused to answer, and Winne dropped the subject for the time being. Mary and Winne also filled their pockets with objects they could use on the crew below deck.

"This way," Kathryn said, heading to the causeway. "And, close the door behind you."

As they made their way across the ship, Kathryn explained the precarious situation they faced with the black pox now on board the *Revenge*. Both women listened intently as Kathryn spoke. Winne nodded occasionally, knowing she and Kathryn would draw on the magical arts taught by Mariel. Every now and then, Kathryn would lock eyes with Winne, and the two shared a dark look.

"How shall th' crew be given remedy for th' pox, then?" Mary asked frankly.

Kathryn swallowed hard before continuing with the explanation. "A tiny slice will be made in the flesh and a small bit of the excretion placed in the open wound."

Mary fell silent, and Kathryn could see her face blanching slightly in spite of the permanent blush that came from years at sea under a bright Caribbean sun. "So you're tellin' me we cut th' bloody skin an' infect th' open wound wit' th' oozin' spew bubblin' from th' bloody pox itself?"

"Now, Mary...it's not like we're hackin' a limb off to do the deed," Winne replied. Mary set her hands on her hips and shook her head. "Oh, no! Not me, ye won't. Ye bloody won't be pokin' th' bloody pox into my arm. Oh, no!"

Winne waved a hand in dismissal and marched across the deck ahead of them. "Aye, you will, Mary. You and me both!"

"I hear ye clearly, Anne...and I'm tellin' ye, ye'll have to kill me first!" Mary shouted after her, but was met with only a quick toss of blonde curls.

"That can be arranged, Mary. Stop frettin'...you don't know anything about the remedies, so hush your mouth about it!"

"Yer plannin' to gouge sommat th' bloody pox into th' men's raw flesh, be all. That's what yer bloody plannin' to do!" Mary stopped in her tracks before suddenly lunging forward again to keep up with Kathryn. "I heard what you're sayin'!" she muttered to herself.

"The remedies will stave off most of the infection and become the antidote, should we be needin' it," Kathryn said, motioning to the herbs she clutched in the folds of her skirt.

"Aye, an' that makes me bloody feel so much better about it," Mary countered, the sarcasm in her voice unchecked.

"It's the right course of action, Mary, and you'd best get onboard with it yourself, else suffer the pox forthright. That, my dearie, you'll be doin' for certain!" Winne grunted as she and Mary caught up with Kathryn. "Such stubbornness…"

Nothing more was said as the three women walked to the short stairwell that led below to the sick bay. Kathryn and Winne made their silent way between the few men who remained confined within the dimly lit chamber. Mary sat on the edge of a sagging step and watched as Winne and Kathryn wielded their daggers and skillfully collected pus from the seeping pustules of two infected men.

"This one's gone to meet his Maker," Winne barked from the opposite side of the room.

Mary clenched her teeth as Winne spoke and reached through the support beams for a discarded bottle lying on the edge of a barrel not far from where she sat. She figured this was the rum used to wash instruments, or some poor fool's wounds, but wasted no additional thoughts on it as she lifted the dusty rim to her lips and drank the hot liquid in large gulps.

"The body should be cast overboard, and the linen and clothing burned," Kathryn answered.

"Aye, then ye best get someone onto it. The body reeks," Winne replied.

Within moments, they had summoned two unfortunate volunteers, who, upon hearing about the task, abruptly disappeared. Winne and Kathryn moved back to the stairwell, where they found Mary still guzzling rum.

"There you sit while we do the dirty work, then, Mary?" Winne said.

Mary ignored her as she set the bottle down gently next to her.

"No mind." Kathryn waived them both off with one hand. "I'll let the capt'n know we're ready to begin."

"Aye, do that, and send someone down to fetch these wretched bodies…and bring Mary more rum!" Winne called out, then plopped down on the step next to Mary, who grinned.

"An' me bloody lass, Tooth-less Annie," Mary added as Winne broke into her grin, a perfect row of teeth flashing behind her infectious smile.

Kathryn ran topside and scurried across the deck to find the captain. "Time to deliver the bad news… and infect the crew with pox."

Forty-Six

"I've WARNED YE FOR THE last time! These be foul plans you've hatched. My crew best come out without loss, else you'll be held accountable. There'll be naught I can do on your behalf, then. Mind me well on this, Kathryn." Captain Phillips' green eyes blazed fiercely as he spoke.

"Aye, I'm fully aware of my position," Kathryn snapped. "Mister Archer has surely made his intentions clear with one hand at my throat, and the tip of his blade against my ribs here." She pointed to her right side as she spoke.

The captain's eyes darted to her side. "And yet you're still alive." His face twisted, lost in thought. "I'm not sure of what must be done. It seems too risky."

"Aye, this is risky, John. But there's no other option I can think of. There's another two bodies below deck since just this morning. I dare not wait any longer, else you'll face an entire crew with the black pox sendin' them to their grave."

Captain Phillips nodded silently. "I'll call the men topside, and you can begin your work. Capt'n Rackham

MARTI MELVILLE

will make up his own mind about what his crew will do about it."

He brushed past her and made way for the quarter-master. Kathryn wondered if anything would be done about Archer's latest attempt to kill her. Her gut told her otherwise, and she anticipated harsh words, instead, would soon pass between Captain Phillips and Archer.

She turned her back on the men and returned to the sick bay. As she passed mid-ship, she spotted Seth working the lines next to the capstan. She veered toward him and hailed him from across the deck. "Seth! Here, Seth."

He paused to shade his eyes and watched her advance. He waved. "Hoy, Miss Kathryn."

When she finally reached him, she was surprised to find herself out of breath, and paused momentarily to catch it. He studied her, patiently waiting for her to speak. A look of concern crossed his features, and she feared inwardly that she must appear more fatigued than she realized.

The inoculations will have to be done quickly, or suffering the ill effects of too many patients will certainly be my lot. She grinned and waved at him.

"Seth, there's a body below deck…actually, two men died of the pox in the sick bay last night. They need to be retrieved, stripped of clothes, which must be burned, and the bodies thrown overboard without ceremony. Can you arrange for this?"

"I'll tend to it," he answered.

She caught hold of his shirt and shook her head. "No, Seth, someone else must do it."

"Why?" He gave her a doubtful look but said nothing.

"I have my reasons. See to it you do not touch them. Do not even go near them! This is work for another... savvy?" She spoke with a voice that trembled, and her eyes sent the warning her words could not.

"Aye, I understand," he replied. His voice matched hers.

Kathryn nodded and turned from Seth, who immediately set off in the opposite direction toward a small group of newly claimed prisoners clustered near the port side guns. She watched him for a moment, curious to see who the ill-fated chosen would be. A satisfied smile crossed her lips. The lad had chosen well. Prisoners were disposable, and none would miss them should they fall prey to the pox.

As she reached the stairs leading to the sick bay, she heard the quartermaster bellowing orders. Immediately, men began the arduous process of assembling themselves topside. Faced with the difficult task of maintaining a cool, calm control, Kathryn swallowed hard and faced the men. *This will not be easy.* The thought made her stomach turn.

Winne and Mary had seated themselves at the top of the companionway. She waved them over.

"Th' crew's assembled, per th' capt'n's orders," Archer said.

"Thank you," she replied, then turned to Winne. "Bring the amulets and vials, and I'll gather the contagion."

Winne retrieved the bundles of herbs and vials they had brought with them from Kathryn's quarters. Kathryn cautiously lifted a glass bowl filled with purulent, yellow pus that had settled at the bottom of it. Just as carefully, she took up both daggers from beside the glass and carried them, held outward in an awkward grip, so as not to accidently brush her own skin with the contaminated tips. Mary stood, looked around, and snatched the nearly empty rum bottle before following Kathryn across the deck.

All eyes shifted to the three women as they approached the assembly. Captain Phillips paced uneasily in front of his men. It was obvious his words of encouragement were not wholly believed—even by himself.

"Just so there be no dispute o're the matter, these be me orders. Each and every man will step up to take his remedy, else be set adrift in one of the longboats…and may God have mercy on your soul, either way, says I!"

Protests rose from the gathered men. Everyone fell silent as the blast of a pistol rang out from behind. A pale grey cloud snaked skyward that parted abruptly as Jacquotte Delahaye stepped through. Her elaborately carved pistol still spewed smoke from the end of the barrel.

"Ye yellow-bellied dogs cower amongst yerselves as drownin' rats do." She sauntered forward and faced

Kathryn. "Here be me arm, an' ye can start wit' it first. Th' not so courageous can follow."

Jacquotte rolled one sleeve up and extended her bare arm to Kathryn. Smiling, Kathryn took hold of Jacquotte's wrist and lifted one of the tainted daggers.

"Aye, you're, indeed, most brave, Madame Delahaye. I'm beholdin' to you—bein' the first volunteer, as it were," Kathryn said warmly.

"I'm doin' it for yer benefit, waif."

Winne shot her a severe look, stepped forward, and wiped the bare skin with a rag saturated in rum. She then handed the bottle to Jacquotte, who took a long swig. When she was finished, Winne retrieved the bottle, stepped back, and waited with a long sprig of dried green leaves clutched in one hand.

Quickly, Kathryn placed the tip of the dagger over the damp skin and pierced the flesh. Crimson welled up around the silver blade and ran down both sides of Jacquotte's forearm. Kathryn pressed one side of the blade against the open wound as she withdrew it, then wiped the black pox pus against the inside gaping tissue.

That same moment, Winne stepped forward and pinched the sliced flesh together between her thumb and forefinger. Biting the tip from one leaf, she drizzled clear fluid from its stem directly over the pinched skin and paused before releasing the injured site. Magically, the incision closed.

"Don't be fussin' o're that, Jacquotte. It best be left alone for two full days. And drink this when the fevers begin," Winne said, and poured a capful of amber serum from a delicate vial into a half-filled mug of grog.

Jacquotte accepted the mug and lifted it in salute to the crew. "Cheers, men! We'll see ye gathered 'round th' devils' capstan 'fore sunrise." Then, laughing her deep, full alto, Jacquotte drained it and rolled her sleeve back down over her exposed forearm, covering the ghastly incision. "Aye," she said and stepped away to face the gawking stares of the clustered men. "Bloody cowards!" she blurted and walked toward Mary, who handed her the bottle.

Jacquotte drank greedily and took up her place next to Mary. In that instant, a muscular forearm thrust out, in front of her. Kathryn glanced up to see who had bravely stepped forward. Her eyes met the captain's penetrating gaze. He stared at her while she began preparations. Fighting back tears, she gently took his wrist in her hand and held it as Winne dabbed the saturated cloth over his forearm. Kathryn hesitated while trying to hide the tremble that seized her hands.

"Go on and do what you must, lass." His voice was a whisper.

She swallowed, repeated the same process, and inoculated the captain with the contagion. Winne dressed the fresh wound in the same manner as she'd done with Madame Delahaye. Kathryn's heart pounded as she gazed at his face, knowing she might have impregnated his flesh with a cursed disease that had the power to take him from her.

He smiled at her reassuringly, stepped back to his men, and clapped the burly Pedro on the back as he passed.

Kathryn wiped her eyes with the back of her hand and grasped hold of the next arm presented to her. Its hand still gripped the neck of a half-empty green bottle.

"I shan't be outdone by a bloody French-born wench, or this ship's capt'n." Mary tossed her head back and laughed her throaty laugh.

Winne dabbed her arm, then joined in. "Oh, Mary, you do shame the best of 'em!"

The inoculations continued methodically as the majority of the pirates complied with the treatment, though mostly due to peer pressure and the threat of being labeled a coward. Particularly difficult would be the fate of anyone who had to bear the shame: two women, the first volunteers, had bested them.

Archer immediately protested and refused to let Kathryn be the one to perform the act. Winne stepped forward and sliced—not so gently—into the quarter-master's arm, then placed the pox inside. He cursed her and was met with the captain's warning look to, once again, mind his intentions.

Kathryn welcomed the break and met Winne's eyes with gratitude as she resumed a place next to Mary and Jacquotte Delahaye.

The rest of the crew soon followed. Backing out now would only seal one's reputation as "faint-hearted." No hearty pirate would stand for that epithet. Curses flowed and grog was consumed as the blood trickled from forearm after leathery forearm. Drinking rum, while under full sail, was generally not tolerated, but Captain Phillips had turned a blind eye to their lawlessness, given their current circumstances.

As the last of the pirates were treated, Captain Rackham stepped forward. "What say ye, Annie? Be this the means for our mateys to stave off th' pox, as well?"

She doused the rag once again, then lifted the bottle to her lips and chugged some of the contents before setting it down again. Without hesitation, she swept the cloth over her own skin with one hand. In her other, she held the pox-laced dagger. She then dug the tip of her own dagger deep into the pale flesh of her forearm. Kathryn watched her cousin's face fix on Calico Jack. The corner of her mouth twitched only once as the blade separated the skin and blood surfaced. "This is how it's done, Jack." When she had finished, she held out her arm for Calico Jack to see and replied in a lively voice, "Aye, there be no other way to be sure of it."

Kathryn moved forward and dressed her cousin's wound. Afterward, she ambled over to Mary and Jacquotte, standing silently amused as they watched the whole proceeding. The now-empty green bottle was cast aside and a new one offered to Winne as she approached. Mary wrapped an arm around Winne's shoulder as she heartily drank from the bottle shared by the women.

"Line up, me hearties," Calico Jack called loudly. An unsuccessful attempt to remain unnoticed had exposed the last few pirates huddled in a far corner. "Ye're just as prime as these scurvy dogs sailin' aboard this 'ere ship! Line up an' get what's comin' to ye, says I."

Once again, flesh was pierced and black pox was placed in the open wounds. Kathryn attended to the entire process herself, as Winne was indisposed with the women. When she had finished the last, she lifted her gaze to the sea skies and wiped her forehead with the back of her sleeve. The afternoon had grown hot and muggy, and the sun was baking the flesh on her back. She dipped her dagger once more into the purulent glass and laid it down, ready for use one last time.

"So be it," said Calico Jack "Nay," she responded sullenly as her eyes met Captain Phillips' gaze. "There's yet one left undone."

Rolling up her sleeve, she studied his face and lifted the waiting dagger by the blade, offering the hilt to the captain. He hesitated, then stepped forward and took it from her outstretched hand. Carefully, he made the incision on the moist surface of her skin. He felt his own skin crawl when the blade penetrated her flesh, and the infection oozed inside. She winced silently and his eyes darted to her face. Nodding, she smiled reassuringly as he finished the deed.

"So, now, it's done. Should death meet us from this, it is by our own hands and not a stranger's," she whispered.

Captain Phillips said nothing but held onto her wrist for a moment. In his eyes, she saw sorrow for the task just done. She smiled at him lovingly, an expression of forgiveness mixed with gratitude for his help in a medicinal undertaking he did not wholeheartedly understand.

"Let's pray we survive."

"Winne foresaw the outcome, John. The crew will be saved, all but perhaps two or three,

who'll face their doom regardless of the remedy just applied."

"And the visions of your cousin…or Anne, as she is known…can they be trusted?"

"Aye, her musings are true, and her prophesy is nearly always accurate. The ship will be saved from the blight of pox." Kathryn glanced at Winne. "Still, rough days lie ahead for most, as we'll all be racked with a form of the disease, though not in its entirety. The remedies given in grog will aide with the fevers and such."

"Aye, then. The men best be about the business of sailin' this ship until that time." He gave the order to Archer to set the men back to work.

All hands returned to their duties, though somewhat rum-soaked. Calico Jack gave similar orders, and the *William* kept pace alongside the *Revenge*.

Kathryn felt relieved at having completed the daunting task of inoculating a full crew from two ships. She watched contentedly as both vessels took to sail. Her arm smarted at the point of incision, and she rubbed at it absentmindedly.

The sun warmed her aching joints, so she allowed herself a moment's pause to raise her face skyward. Warmth radiated over her body and soothed the chilling thoughts of pox. Golden rays danced over her closed eyelids as she slowed her breathing to match the rise and fall of the ship on the swells. Sea spray filled her nostrils with the comforting scents of old wood and saltwater. She felt her muscles relax, and peace once again filled her soul. This was where she found her solace, amongst the sea and sunlight. Unintentionally, a soft smile crossed her lips, and she inhaled contentedly.

Abruptly, her peace was interrupted by the sounds of male voices. She lifted her head and blinked in the direction of the offensive noise, recognizing one in particular. The deep bass voice sounded irritated.

"Ye drink this, man, else face the consequences," Captain Phillips ordered.

Kathryn nearly leapt to her feet and dashed across mid-ship to where a small gathering of men surrounded a young boy. She recognized the young Filamore, abandoned by his own fishing vessel not long ago. Captain Phillips stood before the lad with a pistol aimed at the youth's belly. In one hand, the captain held a goblet.

"Drink it, I say, or ye'll be dead 'fore sunrise," the captain growled.

Kathryn approached them to the protestations of the young boy. She wondered why the boy refusing to drink should cause such concern, even provoking the captain to rage.

"This be none o' yer business, witch," Archer spat as she circled the crowd of men, aiming for a better look.

Captain Phillips glanced in her direction, then cocked the pistol in his outstretched hand. "Nay, Mister Archer. This is very much the lady's affair. It's the remedy she gives us to ward off the pox that young Filamore refuses to drink. Perhaps the chirurgeon will be able to convince this bloody coward to save himself from certain demise and drink it."

"I will not drink it!" Filamore protested once again.

Kathryn brushed past the men and gave Archer a black look, which he returned. She stepped up to the youth, crouched at eye-level, and peered into the young boy's face.

"These men mean no harm, lad. The capt'n is keepin' you well cared for and fed, takin' you aboard when your own capt'n left you for dead, or worse. Remember it, lad, for that's the truth." Her voice soothed him, and the young man nodded. She placed her fingers gently on his trembling hand. "We all bear the sting of the pox, though grave it may be." She pointed to her own open wound. "Yet, a remedy is ours, lad! The drink supplies it, and we all partook of it…see?"

"Nay. I won't do it!"

She reached for the captain, who handed the goblet to her. Turning back to check on the lad again, she lifted the rim to her lips and swallowed some of the bitter amber liquid.

"Let me show you. I'll drink it first. Though it's bitter, it staves off the fevers. All will be well…you'll see." She carefully placed the goblet into the young man's hand. "Drink, Mister Filamore, and ease your mind o're the matter."

The youth lifted the goblet slowly, his attention glued to the azure blue of Kathryn's eyes. She smiled, nodded, and urged him to drink. He placed the mug to his lips and took several swallows as tears ran down his cheeks.

"That's a good one, and hearty, too! Now finish it up and be done with your frettin'." Kathryn stood upright and faced the rest of the gathered men, her eyes locked on Archer. "Anyone who doubts my word on it best speak with me face to face!"

Dropping her hands to her hips, she scanned the pirates, who slowly turned one by one from the circle and returned to their positions on the ship. The captain replaced his pistol at his side, dismissed Filamore to his duties, and turned to face Kathryn.

"Your ways are crafty, lass. You have a gift about you, and I'm beholdin' to you once again." He smiled at her, and she felt her heart leap.

"Woman's words to a frightened boy, that's all I've done here. Young Filamore is still but a youth, scared, and without knowledge. Watch him, John. I sense he is a lad subject to wild thoughts and reckless actions. He could be dangerous to the crew, should his fears overtake him."

"Aye, I've sensed the same about the lad, myself," the captain responded. "Nevertheless, my thanks be to you, Kathryn."

She smiled in return and turned to go.

"Capt'n Rackham plans to part ways at the next sunset. Your time's limited with your kin," he said.

Kathryn stopped in her tracks. Her heart sank. "I was not aware. Time grows short too rapidly at sea," she replied. "I will be spending what's left of our time together with Anne and Mary, then." He cast a sideways glance, and she continued, "And, of course, attending to my duties in the sick bay."

Having said this, she turned back to the open deck and made her way quickly to where She'd last seen her cousin and the other women.

Forty-Seven

SERENITY FLED THE EVENING HOURS much the same way rats flee from a sinking ship.

Before sunset, the merry-making had begun, and spirits were lifted as rich rum and fine wine flowed freely from barrels and bottles no longer held captive within both ships. Sleep, likewise, abandoned both crews as music and laughter rumbled forth from the farewell celebration. Everything was done in honor of parting friends, not an odd practice—even in the company of pirates.

Kathryn huddled around a barrel heaped to over-flowing with fine fruits, greasy mutton, salty fish, and crusted bread. Its staleness was made sufficiently palatable by dipping it into the nearest mug, which turned the pale white center a deep amber or rich cerise, depending on the liquid within.

To one side, Winne sat with her arm around Kathryn's waist. To the other, Mary and Jacquotte hunkered down together. All four women were heavily engaged in deep conversation, with topics that changed almost as rapidly as Jacquotte's lovers. It was obvious this was "women's talk"—the subject matter unwelcomed to men. She was doubtful any man could keep up, or so Winne had said once.

Kathryn's heart ached as she sat near her cousin, knowing the opportunity to meet again would not be for a long time, if ever. Either could run afoul of nature or bad blood, for a pirate's life held risks. Always in the back of her mind was the knowledge that Archer—or worse, Morrigan—sought to destroy her. It kept her wary.

Kathryn pulled Winne in closer and gave her a subtle squeeze. Winne cast a strange look her cousin's way, then leaned over and kissed Kathryn's cheek before lifting her mug overhead.

"A toast!" Winne's raspy voice was joyous. "To colleagues, kin, and newly acquired acquaintances!"

"Here! Here!" All four women raised their mugs.

Kathryn took a long sip as her eyes drifted to the full moon overhead. Abruptly, she froze with the mug against her lower lip. Overhead, a silver mist wove long, glimmering strands around the bright orb. Ghostly apparitions danced menacingly in the black night.

Kathryn elbowed her cousin, who tossed an irritated look. "What is it?"

"The omen," Kathryn said, nodding skyward.

Winne looked up into the night sky. "Holy Saints have mercy on us!" Winne gasped and clambered to her feet.

"Do you see it? What is it, Winne?" Kathryn's voice stayed low so as not to alarm the others, but it was too late. Both Mary and Jacquotte had already fixed their gazes on the omen.

"It's the sign of the Silver Moon," Winne whispered. "The Silver Moon Omen."

Kathryn swallowed hard. Her heart pounded in her chest. She shuddered as she recalled the dead eyes staring up at her from within a detached head. She had seen the very same omen many months ago.

"What's a Silver Moon Omen?" Mary asked casually, gazing up.

Jacquotte, perched upon a barrel, grasped another piece of bread and dunked it heartily into a nearby mug. Its deep plum color dripped wine as she lifted it to her mouth. "It means nothing, says I. The moon plays tricks o' the eyes o' most sailors…drunken scallywags, to be certain." She snorted.

Mary turned from the moon and joined her new friend at the barrel, satisfied with Jacquotte's explanation.

"I hope you're right on that account," Kathryn said to Jacquotte. She stood alongside Winne, whose eyes were fixed ahead as she stared into the night. Kathryn waited patiently as her cousin stared at the moon and hoped Winne would receive some kind of prophetic insight into the omen's meaning.

Instead, Winne was silent.

"So, what is it?" Mary crossed her arms.

"The mist hovers close to the orb. There's foul play ahead, but it won't be this night, methinks. Perhaps it's meant for another ship. These be large waters, Kat, and we're not the only ships under sail." Winne spoke in low tones.

"Aye, 'tis true," Kathryn replied. "The last time the Silver Moon Omen revealed itself,

Morrigan attacked our ship and butchered many of the crew. That was the night the *Mellt Sosye* woke… here, in the palms of my hands." Kathryn glanced down at her palms and wondered if she would soon need to call upon their hidden power again.

"Aye, dubbin' you the Skyfyre Witch, I hear told." Jacquotte sneered and elbowed Mary.

"Aye, t'was the name given me by the Vodoun priest…*Mellt Sosye*, he called it."

Winne glanced at her cousin—the ancient Celtic title had struck a nerve. She swallowed her thoughts and turned back to the moon.

"Well, ye best get the meanin' of those symbols learnt from off of the Straif. I have a feelin' you'll be needin' its power sooner than you presume." Winne stared at Kathryn, who conceded.

"Aye, Winne. Does your *Gifted* vision see Morrigan in this?" Kathryn studied her cousin intently and hoped the vision for prophecy would reveal something.

Winne closed her eyes, and the *Gifted* eye of prophecy opened. Subtly, her blonde curls shook, and Winne gazed at her cousin. "I see nothin' o're it. My vision is dark, but the heart senses there's trouble ahead, and we best be prepared for it." Winne tapped one finger against her chest and nodded to the moon overhead.

Kathryn agreed. Her mind raced, and a shiver ran up her spine, confirming what her cousin had said. She put the mug to her lips, swallowed the rum, and felt it warm her from the inside. Light flickered over the deck, and her eyes focused on the silver mist. Again, she shivered in spite of the drink.

The pirates continued their celebration, oblivious to the omen overhead, while Kathryn and Winne stayed vigilant. For nearly two hours, they kept watch over the ship. The majority of the pirates had fallen into a drunken sleep with bottles still grasped in flaccid hands and snores erupting from gaping mouths.

Mary sat not far off, slumped against Calico Jack's shoulder. He also slept, hunkered down comfortably for the night, nestled on the sheets. Winne smiled at the sight and commented offhandedly. "Blessed they be, so reposed without concern, as you and I seem to be, Kat."

Kathryn smiled. "Walk with me." They crossed the deck, eyes drifting from the sleeping bodies scattered across the deck to the ethereal moon overhead. "Would that we could be as lucky as they, eh Winne?"

"Aye. But, where has Jacquotte disappeared this night? No doubt, she too found her way into a brusque pair of arms to sleep off her indulgence this eve." Winne chuckled.

The women circled the capstan while the moon followed them, casting an eerie light on the ship. As they made their way to the opposite side, Kathryn caught sight of a strange shadow poised just off the starboard quarterdeck. She squinted against the darkness at the shape,

familiar, yet unrecognizable, in the darkness. Four legs, nearly intertwined, propped up a bulky trunk which appeared to have no definition, per se. Kathryn studied the shadow as she walked and wondered what entity had made its way, unnoticed, aboard the *Revenge*.

Suddenly, the shadow moved, and the sound that followed was deep, bold, and chilling. Kathryn froze in place. Her spine ached with the icy chill that accompanied death. Inside, her gut wrenched, and bile rose inside her throat, while fire filled the place where her heart pounded.

"Kat, what is it…?" Winne's voice trailed off as she spotted the shadow.

A sultry female's voice drifted across the deck, words without meaning—paired with the image, ominous and chilling. Winne shifted her weight, and both women stood with their focus glued to the quarterdeck and the shadowy form standing upon it.

"I…they…" Kathryn choked.

The *Revenge* rolled with the current, and moonlight poured onto the shadow. Kathryn gasped and grabbed hold of Winne for support. Jacquotte stood, wrapped in the arms of Kathryn's beloved Captain

Phillips. Drawn together in a passionate kiss—his hands rested on her shoulders, while she clutched the nape of his neck.

"Jacquotte Delahaye?" Winne's voice was incredulous.

Kathryn could not speak. She could not breathe. Tears spilled from her eyes, hot and bitter. Her hands flew to her chest, pressed against the place where her heart struggled to beat.

"John…how could you?" Kathryn whispered.

"Come, Kat. The Omen speaks, and you need not be destroyed by it, as well. Come away from this bloody, repulsive scene, Kat." Winne placed a strong hand over her cousin's shoulder and pulled her in the opposite direction.

Strength fled Kathryn's limbs, and she began to crumple where she stood. Winne's grip tightened as she clutched her cousin closer, supporting Kathryn with her own body. They moved with long strides toward Kathryn's quarters.

When they reached the threshold, Winne spoke again, this time forcefully. "You cannot stay here, Kat. You cannot stay aboard this bloody ship! Come with me, Kathryn. Capt'n Jack will take you in and treat you well, not like that bloody bilge scum who plundered your heart and cast it aside with no mind for the likes of that bawdy Delahaye!"

"Winne, I cannot believe he cares so little. How could he? How could my John run into another's arms?"

Kathryn buried her face in her hands and broke into voiceless sobs.

"There may be more to it than just passion, Kat." Winne glanced up at the moon and Kathryn followed her gaze.

"The Omen?" Kathryn shook her head. "Then the bloody moon has taken me twice. I cannot escape it. Winne, I cannot bear it!"

Winne left her curled up against the doorway arch, and scurried about the cabin to collect Kathryn's personal effects. Moving to a darkened corner, Winne searched a small recess in the wall and gasped.

"Mariel's book. I cannot find it. Kat, do you have the pages from her book? And the Seren…do you still have it with you? I cannot find it here." Winne's voice sounded urgent.

Kathryn reached a trembling hand to her throat and grasped hold of the pale, cool stone about her neck. "Aye," she sputtered. "I have the Seren with me."

Winne rummaged through the trinkets, vials, and charms that lay about the cabin. When she reached the surgeon's satchel, she paused and glanced back at her cousin. "And this…these instruments? Are these some of your most valuable effects, Kat?" She paused, but Kathryn said nothing. "Fine. We'll have to leave the rest—Mariel's book, too. I cannot find it!"

Kathryn shook her head, slowly stood upright, and clutched the wall for support. "There's no reason to take those things." Objects with deep significance – objects that she knew she should carry with her, as chirurgeon of a pirate ship—those she would leave behind.

As Kathryn neared the tiny porthole window, her eyes fell upon the brass hourglass John had given her when she first boarded the *Revenge*. Staring up at her were the initials, *JPB*, scratched in his handwriting. Hot tears appeared once again, and Kathryn fought them back as indignation rose to take their place.

"I won't be needin' this," she said, and swallowed hard.

Winne glanced at the hourglass in Kathryn's hand and smiled compassionately. "Of course, ye won't." She lifted the hourglass, then gently placed it on a shelf hidden behind the door. Winne quickly scanned the cabin once more, turned, and paused to face a dark corner. "What of the staff?"

Kathryn followed her cousin to the corner and the Straif, dormant in the darkness. The women stared at it for a moment before Kathryn suddenly reached out and grasped hold of the blackthorn totem.

"This goes with me. It belongs to the *Mellt Sosye* and not this ship."

"There's my girl!" Winne gathered up the last of the herbs in the tiny cabin. "Now, we must leave."

They bundled a few pieces of clothing and shoved them into a bag, then hastily retreated. The *Mellt Sosye* hesitated only a moment before closing the door behind her.

Kathryn abandoned the *Revenge* without looking back.

Forty-Eight

MIST CURLED IN RIBBONS, FINGERING the dark skies where it crept down from the moon—and in that moment, Kathryn stepped aboard the *William*.

Resolve pushed her forward as she made her way aboard the vessel and took her place alongside Anne and Mary. There was no turning back now that she had been granted aboard. Captain Jack Rackham had been more than cordial, given the circumstances and the elaborate explanation provided by Winne.

"Seems I've plundered the good Capt'n Phillips, after all," Calico Jack said, winking at Kathryn.

Nothing more had been said about Jacquotte and the captain, outside of Mary's abrupt stream of curses, which she let loose the moment Winne spilled the details.

"Th' bloody dog an' his bilge scum tart! May they both rot in th' bowels o' Purgatory, an' th' devil wit''em!" Mary spat and cursed again.

Kathryn said nothing, but leaned against the rails, and scanned the panorama for the *Revenge*. Her gaze stopped near the rear of the ship. She checked the quarterdeck and found it empty. Apparently, Captain Phillips and Jacquotte Delahaye had vacated, a blemished station of passion, in Kathryn's mind, and she felt the tears welling up again in her eyes. She knew it would be days before anyone noticed her absence from the *Revenge*.

"Perhaps Seth will make note," she whispered to no one.

Crewmen from the *William* had begun the arduous process of gathering belongings and loading the vessel. The planks laid between ships were heavy with traffic as goods were transferred between ships. Kathryn looked from the stern of the ship to the horizon. She noticed the glinting gold of dawn had floated over the water's surface.

"Sunrise will be upon us soon, and we'll set sail," Winne announced behind Kathryn.

"Aye," Kathryn replied and glanced skyward to take in the ominous moon still hovering overhead. "The Silver Moon Omen remains." She nodded imperceptibly toward the grey sky.

Winne's attention drifted upward. "It's best we leave this place. I feel evil surrounding your beloved *Revenge*, Kat. I don't know what it means, but you best not be present when evil takes its own."

"This is a hard life, Winne. I know not whether I've strength enough to bear it."

"A pirate's life is always hard, Kat. You've borne it well enough. Assuming you've many fine years ahead, the direction you sail may be different from the one you've planned. Still, all is in God's hands, and it fares best for those who let Him steer course." Winne smiled gently as she spoke.

Kathryn sighed and watched the last of the crew from the *William* carry barrels onboard that she assumed were filled with flour or rum. The planks were pulled, and Calico Jack paced alongside the mid-ship rails, not far from where Kathryn stood with Winne.

"Hail, Capt'n Phillips!" Jack Rackham bellowed and waved a beryl silk scarf in one hand. "Alas, we must bid ye adieu an' set our sails to J'maica."

Captain Phillips stepped up to the *Revenge's* starboard gunwales and hailed in response. Kathryn's heart stopped. She lifted a hand to her mouth, and the tears spilled unchecked down her cheeks as she watched the man who had betrayed her.

"Fair winds in your sails, Capt'n Rackham. Perhaps we shall meet again," Captain Phillips called back. He tapped his brow in salute to Calico Jack and the *William*—then stopped and gripped the rails violently. Their eyes locked, and she couldn't look away. "Kathryn! What are you doin'? Stop this!" Captain Phillips screamed, desperation in his voice. "*Kathryn!*"

The *William* pulled away from the *Revenge*, and turquoise swells divided the ships with an ever-widening expanse. Winne placed an arm about her cousin's shoulders as Kathryn shuddered under heavy sobs. Mary stepped forward to join the other women against the rails, and the three women watched as a frantic Captain Phillips ran the length of his ship and cried out for Kathryn.

Forty-Nine

SEVERAL WEEKS PASSED WHILE THE *William* made
its way south. Kathryn kept vigil during the deep
nights, surveyed the moon, and silently mourned the
loss of her captain. Strangely, the ominous orb had
not moved itself into a waxing phase, but remained as
it was, bright with silvery mist that encircled it with
web-like appendages.

The moon was alive and seemed to be giving birth to
some ghastly form—one that was pure evil, with purpose.
It remained this way until, one night, when Kathryn
stepped onto the deck—as had become her usual practice—and noticed the moon grinning down on her with
an evil crescent smile. She quickly glanced out over the
sparkling water. Snaking its way over the sea caps, the
ominous mist slithered against the ship's wake. In its path,
the *William's* current heading moved directly forward.

The Silver Moon Omen is meant for another ship.
Without warning, death seemed to envelop her as it
bathed her body with a suffocating chill. She could not
breathe. Gasping, she clawed at the space around her

face, her arms flailing against an invisible entity that kept her submerged and devoid of oxygen.

Kathryn was drowning. She began to panic, and, though to the visible eye it appeared as if nothing was wrong, she knew that within moments, she would die. She could feel herself drowning. Her lungs burned. She reached for to the Seren and called upon the power of the stone. Instantly, blue heat welled up in the palms of her hands.

The sorceress lifted them to the sea and chanted an ancient Celtic spell—one used to banish evil and bring new life. Her mind cried out the magic:

Mal se pasou,
Traia o golpe de vida.

Blue light flashed, spilling electricity across the ocean as Kathryn's hands radiated light. Instantly, the sky opened itself to her, and Kathryn gasped large gulps of oxygen into her blistered lungs. She held tight to the rails as she gulped for air.

"Kathryn! Kat!"

Just then, Winne rushed up beside her. Urgency flashed behind her eyes as she took Kathryn by the shoulders. "Kat, what is it? What has happened?" Fear replaced the rasp in her voice.

"Something's happened, Winne. Something… someone is drowning. I felt it…no…I experienced it myself!" Kathryn coughed as she finished her reply.

"Drowning? What do you mean, Kat? You're dry as a bone here."

Kathryn motioned to the water, and Winne followed. The same silvery mist was slowly moving away from the ship. At Kathryn's feet, water began to pool.

"See the Omen, Winne. The sign of the Silver Moon has come alive…it travels north toward the *Revenge* and her crew!" Kathryn pointed to her feet. "It follows me even now."

Winne glanced at the mist and then to the sopping planks beneath Kathryn. She sensed the same foreboding as Kathryn. Glancing up at the moon, Winne finally spoke. "Kat, the Omen has marked your capt'n and his crew. This," she pointed to the water collecting at Kathryn's feet, "is a manifestation of it. You're dry as a bone, yet the water follows you, still—just as the moon omen does. You must protect yourself. Come!"

Winne grasped hold of her cousin's forearm and dragged her into a darkened alcove near piled lines. Away from the visibility of onlookers, Winne pulled a small pouch hanging about her neck from inside her blouse and cautiously untied it. She tipped the tiny leather bag upside down and poured the contents onto the surface of an upright barrel. Small lengths of twig, in various colors, scattered across its surface.

Ilumina…Ilumina…Profetiza.

Winne waved her hands over the spilled twigs as she spoke. The small bits of wood vibrated, and a few of them flipped before falling still. Kathryn watched in awe as her cousin performed the ritual. As she studied the pieces of twig, she noticed small carvings etched randomly on the sides of each piece of wood. The markings looked familiar, and she caught her breath when she recognized that the symbols matched those carved into the Straif.

"These are the markings of the Ogham," Kathryn whispered.

"Aye, that they be…now, hush! I need to concentrate on what they're sayin' to me."

Kathryn watched her cousin study the twigs. Occasionally, she'd stand and circle the barrel, then view them from a different angle. A gentle, "Ahhh" would escape her lips intermittently. The runes held meaning—or so Kathryn hoped. When, finally, Winne returned to her place, sitting opposite Kathryn, she raised her eyes and stared hard at Kathryn.

"There's trouble, indeed, Kat. The Silver Moon sign has already marked your capt'n, to be certain. I fear his life's in peril."

Kathryn swallowed hard. "Continue."

"The Morrigan comes within the mist and aggravates the men against their capt'n." Winne paused to study her cousin.

"What's the outcome, Winne? Have these events already happened, or is this prophecy?"

Winne leaned forward and blew over the twigs. She closed her eyes and chanted silently as she waved her hands once more over the barrel. Kathryn watched as Winne's full lips moved without sound. The twigs vibrated once more as two rolled over to reveal their marks.

"They speak of things from the past…these events have already come to pass." Winne paused only briefly. "There's more, cousin." Her voice took on a somber tone. "The Ogham spells two words that cross betwixt themselves. Mutiny is the first."

"Mutiny!" Kathryn jumped to her feet. "There's mutiny aboard the *Revenge*?"

This couldn't be happening. "And the other? The word betwixt it?"

Winne stared hard at her cousin, then glanced up at the ominous moon. "Murder."

Fifty

"WHO'S MURDER, WINNE?" KATHRYN GRASPED her cousin by the shoulders and spun her around to face her.

"Capt'n Phillips has been murdered, Kat," Winne answered solemnly.

Kathryn's eyes darted to the runes. Losing strength, she collapsed to her knees and cried out in agony. Winne took hold of both of Kathryn's hands. "Look at them, Kat. You cannot change what's happened."

"It has to be wrong. The runes lie!" Kathryn cried out and balled her fists.

"They never lie."

"How? Who? Is the deed done? Winne, tell me all. I'll cut them down myself, I will!" The Seren began to glow as Kathryn's rage grew.

"You'd best calm yourself, cousin. The Seren has awakened." She waited as Kathryn lifted a hand to the stone and took a deep breath. When Kathryn had composed herself again, Winne spoke softly, a warning in her voice. "Kat. There's more."

Kathryn's eyes darted from Winne to the runes. "Tell me."

Winne bent over the barrel and spit onto the twigs. Using one finger, she traced a series of concentric circles that weaved in and out of the runes. Kathryn recognized the pattern as that of an ancient Celtic knot, symbolizing truth and revelation. Next, she clapped her hands three times over the barrel and began to chant. Her lips moved rapidly as she swirled her hands over it. As the runes again vibrated, they increased in speed until they began to swirl in mid-air just above the surface of the barrel's rim. Suddenly, Winne's lips stopped moving, and the objects fell motionless. A fine, pale green smoke rose from them, which dissipated almost as rapidly as it had appeared.

Both women simultaneously leaned forward, almost imperceptibly, until their faces were only inches from the motionless twigs. Kathryn could find no meaning in the symbols that lay there, but Winne's occasional gasps unsettled her.

"What do you see?" Kathryn finally asked.

Winne looked gently into her cousin's eyes as she grasped Kathryn's hands again. Shaking her head, Winne responded, "Kathryn, the truth may only bring pain to you, my darlin'. I've seen your suffering there." She pointed to the runes. "And so, be glad you're here, aboard the *William* with me and Mary."

Kathryn lifted her eyes to the ethereal moon as tears spilled down her cheeks. "I must know the whole of it, Winne. Tell me all," Kathryn whispered.

"Aye, then." Winne held her cousin's hands firmly in her own. "Your capt'n went mad with the loss of you, Kat. His temper rose greatly against the crew. He grew to distrust every last one of those pirates, thinkin' they drove you from him. He still does not understand why you abandoned the *Revenge*, and there's none aboard to tell the man the truth of it."

Kathryn's tears washed her face. "How could he not know the real reason I fled? Jacquotte Delahaye should be reminder enough."

"Aye. Alas, the dirty git is not visible through the Ogham, though I'm certain she'll meet all that's comin' to her!" Winne spat on the deck to make her point and turned back to Kathryn. "Morrigan watches always and has waited for just such a time as this. She boarded the *Revenge* with her magic and used wistful ways to stir the hearts of the crew into mutiny against Capt'n Phillips. The youth aboard was most susceptible, methinks."

"Young Filamore?" Kathryn asked.

"Aye," Winne responded. "The lad, Filamore, and two others, attacked the capt'n and his quartermaster, woundin' them near mortally. Two others were lost, killed in the fight. It was then the brazen youth pushed Capt'n Phillips overboard, into the dark sea."

"No!" Kathryn turned her back to her cousin.

"Aye, Kat…'tis true. Your beloved is lost to the sea," Winne whispered.

Kathryn groaned, tears blinding her. "Oh, Winne, say it's not true! Say he lives! Truly, you are mistaken. These wretched runes are only twigs. Surely they lie!"

Winne shot her a warning look. Her faith in her own prophecy, as strong as the messages of the runes, was never questioned. "I cannot say whether the man lives or has gone to his death. I only know he's fallen prey to his crew, and to Morrigan, and is gone to the depths of the sea."

Kathryn stood and made her way to the rails, searching the water as if to find something within its dark current to prove her cousin wrong. Her mind raced, and she recalled the panic she had felt only a short time ago as she gasped for breath, a witness to a poor soul in peril.

"I know you speak the truth, Winne. I felt his lungs fill with water myself and nearly collapse under the strain only moments ago. Then, through the light, I was freed from it. My poor John…" Kathryn's voice trailed off.

"What's done is done, Kat," Winne said and joined her at the rails. Both stared out at the dark water.

"Oh, that I could join him! I cannot live this life without him now," Kathryn whispered.

"That is not your path, cousin." Winne glanced at the moon.

Both women stayed at the rails, sharing the silence between them. The powerful Celtic witches waited, vigilant under the Silver Moon, as the great ship, the *William*, carried them over their beloved, but deadly, Caribbean Sea.

Fifty-One

LIGHT FROM A CRESCENT MOON swirled, blurring the turquoise and blues into ribbons above his head. In slow motion, he felt the weight of the water against his chest. He remembered it—the splash exploded before suddenly becoming muffled in his ears as he sank below the surface. Suddenly, He was buoyed up by the oxygen he'd sucked into his lungs at the last minute before hitting the water. At least his body had remembered to take its last breath.

He sensed the void to either side of him. Everything appeared dark and closed-in, except for the moonlight, as his body dropped. His muscles ached and would not respond even as he willed his arms to crawl and legs to kick against the heavy water. Twisting his body, he managed to push his limbs against the current, thrusting his face upward, toward the light. But, it wasn't enough, and he watched in dismay as his body sank.

A course laugh sounded through the current, and he recognized Morrigan's cackle mocking him from the depths of the ocean. Tears rose and spilled into the watery grave that embraced him. His lungs burned, and his chest heaved for the first time. He clamped his lips tighter around his teeth and willed himself to hold on a moment longer. Above him, the silver light narrowed into a single, nearly imperceptible, pinpoint. He knew it would be only a moment before he succumbed to the urge to breathe and filled his lungs with salt water. John Phillips would drown, embraced by the deadly Caribbean waters he loved.

Thoughts flooded his mind as his consciousness went dark. All culminated into one name: Kathryn.

PART THREE

Descent

Epilogue 1

FLICKERING ERRATICALLY, A SOFT GLOW settled across the room and tossed amber and resin hues into dancing shadows as the flames burned soundly from the marble fireplace. Wendy shifted on the oversized leather love-seat and pulled a chenille ivory pillow closer to her. She cradled a mug in one hand, filled with her favorite coconut coffee, heaped with a mountain of whipped cream. Her ruby-colored reading glasses sat perched halfway down her nose. The ends disappeared into tangles of flaxen and honey-streaked curls.

Dean Martin sang softly in the background, while Italian melodies wafted from another room in the house. She flipped a page in the magazine perched across her lap and took another sip. This was Wendy's haven—toasty, comforting, and quiet. The blue-eyed blonde relished the warmth of the moment, her world no bigger than the cozy room she sat in.

The fire sputtered.

Wendy seemed not to notice anything, only sipped again from the mug in her hand. Another pop from the flame—a low sizzle that rattled the serenity of the room. Wendy raised her eyes to peer at the fire that burned quietly. The flames licked at the wrought-iron grate but stayed contained.

A sudden flare darted from the back and reached upward into the chimney before dying out. The fire sizzled as it had only seconds earlier. Wendy cocked her head to one side, purposefully lifted her glasses from her nose and placed them on the antique accent table next to her. She sat forward to watch the fire a little more intently and sipped again from her mug.

Pop. Sizzle.

The flame leapt skyward again and, once again, died down to a rolling sizzle. Wendy blinked and set her mug on the same little table, next to the glasses. She leaned in closer to the fire and listened to the flame spit.

It was then she saw it.

The flame lashed out toward the chimney, its tip turning bright red, then black, as it popped. It then dropped down to the base of the fire as it sizzled back to amber.

Her heart pounded. She picked up her cell phone and quickly dialed the one person who could tell her what to do. The hollow ring sounded through her earpiece, and she prayed Mariel would answer this time. It rang again and again as Wendy watched another flame dart skyward. It reached out with a shadowy fingertip, then dropped to a low, menacing sizzle that settled into the flicker of the fire.

"Hello," the familiar voice chimed.

"Mariel!" Wendy sighed in relief. "Oh, Mum! I'm so glad you answered!"

"For heaven's sake child, what is it?"

"The ebony flame, Mariel. Here! In my own fireplace!"

Suddenly, the joy she heard in her grandmother's voice disappeared. "Slow down, Wendy. Now, tell me exactly what is going on. You're not in danger, are you, child?"

"No. At least, I don't think so." She took a deep breath and chose her words carefully, dropping the pitch of her voice.

"I've had a fire in my fireplace tonight, as usual… well, you know how I love fires at night in the fall…"

"Wendy!"

"Oh, yes…well, all was well with it until a few moments ago. It was rather uncanny. I heard it spit and flare. I didn't see it at first, but eventually, spotted it…"

Mariel cut her off. "What manifested itself, Wendy? What did you see in the fire?"

"A crimson and black-tipped flame, Mum. It was the color of midnight onyx." She paused to let the elderly woman digest her words. "There it goes again. It lasts longer each time, Mum."

"Wendy…" Her grandmother's spoke low and deliberate, "…I want you to look at the moon. Tell me what you see."

Wendy threw aside the chenille throw and nearly ran to the window just off to her right. The sky was dark and starless, which gave the appearance that there might be thunderstorms by dawn. Peeking through the clouds, the pale sliver of a waning moon shone with the entire crescent streaming in cloudy beacons of silver light.

With a trembling voice, Wendy told her grandmother what lay before her eyes. "It's the tail-end sign of the Silver Moon," she half-whispered. "It's morphing into some other entity."

"Listen to me carefully, Wendy." Mariel's austere tone left no doubt about the warning to follow. "Find a mirror and look into it. I want you to tell me exactly what you see when you look into the mirror."

Wendy moved quickly to the hall-tree mirror next to the front door. She gazed into the glass and saw herself staring back with a cell phone held to her right ear.

"I see myself, Mum. Why?"

"Do you see the same glow about yourself? Do you see silver light touching you anywhere? The same light as you see from the moon, girl?"

"No."

"Are you sure you see nothing? Make certain, Wendy."

"No, nothing, Mum." Wendy glanced over her shoulder at the fire sizzling and popping menacingly once again.

"Look outside. Are there tendrils? A mist of any kind nearby?"

Wendy darted to the window again and surveyed the darkness outside. "No." Wendy's voice betrayed her fear.

"Then the sign is not for you," Mariel stated solemnly. "…but you are correct, it shifts to some other entity. Let's pray it's not what I think it is."

Both were silent.

"The sign of the moon is, indeed, an omen—a warning that someone has been culled tonight. It's the mark that Morrigan has found her prey…" Mariel's voice trailed off.

"But who? And why the ebony flame here?"

"The onyx flame rises from your sanctuary in response to the omen. This is a sign that belongs to you, yet you do not bear its mark. It's likely a prophetic warning. Pay attention to your *Gift*, child, and be certain to call me if you see anything unusual. In the meantime, we must be vigilant for anything that suggests the omen has attached itself. It could be for anyone. I'll keep watch for the Onyx Rising Moon."

"The what?" Wendy sounded confused.

"Never mind, child. Keep watch over the omen. Are you certain you have no attachment?"

"Yes…I mean, no, the sign has not attached itself to me, as far as I can tell." Wendy's voice faltered. "Yet, if the sign is given here…" She paused as the flame leapt once again. The black light flickered once before dropping. "It must be for me, unless…" Wendy gasped, one hand flew to her mouth, and her eyes darted to the inky light from the fire.

"Unless it's meant for another of our blood," Mariel finished.

"Do you have the sign of the omen about you, Mariel?" Wendy already knew the answer before Mariel answered.

"No, child, I do not!"

"Then, it can only be for Katherine. Oh, no, not again…not Katherine!"

Tension filled the silence between them. Mariel contemplated the possibility of her other granddaughter again being marked by an omen.

Finally, Mariel spoke. "Where is she? Have you seen her lately?"

"Not for a few days. I'm certain she's still at the hospital. I can get in touch with her there. I'll call you right back."

"She was marked so long ago. How could this be for her…again?" Mariel voiced her concern, but Winne's thoughts were elsewhere. "I'm surprised she hasn't called one of us already. Perhaps she hasn't seen…?" Wendy snapped off her phone, cutting Mariel short, anxious to make the next call.

"Sorry, Mum," Wendy muttered aloud, realizing she'd prematurely hung up on her grandmother. She then quickly punched the green "call" button and brought the phone to life again. Wendy dialed Katherine's cell phone, the one only used for work. The mere flash of Wendy's name on the cell phone's caller ID would be an alarm, the signal of an emergency involving the three women who possessed the *Gift*.

Epilogue 2

KATHERINE HAD STAYED LATE, THE constant demands of the ER blocking her from the end of her workday. She could feel her irritation mounting as her cell phone buzzed in her scrub pocket one more time.

"Come on, people," she whispered through clenched teeth as she reached for the tiny black cell phone one more time. "Is it really this important?"

The words caught in her throat when she saw the name that blinked on the cell phone's screen. No personal contacts ever called her work cell unless there was an emergency. Katherine felt her stomach clench. She nudged her glasses along her nose and turned her back on her co-workers, who were standing a little too close for privacy.

"Wen? What's wrong? What's going on?" The words spilled out as she bolted for an an empty spot in the hallway.

The voice on the other end quavered as its soprano tone echoed through the receiver. "Kat, you've got to listen to me, and listen carefully. Get to a mirror quickly. Tell me what you see."

"What's going on, Wen? What do you mean, 'get to a mirror?' You're not making sense."

"Just do it, Kat. Are you in front of one yet? What do you see?"

Katherine could hear the urgency in Wendy's voice, and she knew her cousin would not back down, so she took off down the hallway in search of a mirror. She broke into a slow jog as she neared the closest bathroom.

"Are you there yet? Do you have a mirror?"

"Almost," Katherine said, rounding the corner. She darted into the public bathroom across from the manager's office and locked the door. Taking a deep breath, she spun around, grabbed hold of the sink for support, and leaned forward until her nose was just inches from the mirror anchored to the wall above it.

"What do you see?"

"Nothing! I don't see anything except my reflection. What am I supposed to be looking for?" Katherine's frustration echoed against the tiled walls.

"Do you see a pale light around your face or your head or anywhere?" Wendy's pitch rose with each syllable.

"Wendy, what's going on? What are you not telling me?" Ice rushed down Katherine's spine. Her tone suggested it wasn't a question.

Wendy paused for a moment before answering. "The sign of the Silver Moon shines tonight, Katherine. I've already spoken with Mariel about it." Wendy waited for a response.

"Go on…"

"I saw an onyx flame tonight…*the* Onyx Moon Omen…in my fireplace. I thought it was for me and called Mariel immediately. I didn't know about the omen until Mariel told me to look at the moon. There it was, Kat, radiating from the moon just like…" She stopped short.

"Just like the night in the cottage." Katherine finished her thought. "The night I was marked with the omen."

"No! That was the Midnight Omen and belongs to another lifetime, Kat. Recently, this was the phase of the Silver Moon. But it's evolving into something different. It's changing, marking someone. You said yourself there's nothing cast over you tonight, so it's not for you, nothing to worry about…right?" Wendy's attempts to reassure them both sounded weak.

"Hang on. I'm going to check out the moon." Katherine dashed from the bathroom and ran to the ambulance bay's glass doors.

Red letters, painted boldly over the glass, spelling out EMERGENCY, yawned open, allowing her to rush through and into the night. Her search skyward was futile under the glare of the hospital lights, so she stepped farther away from the building in hopes of a better view. Hidden behind a large palm tree, she spotted light dripping from a deadly moon.

"Wait a minute," she whispered into the phone and stepped to her right.

There it was.

She gasped and clutched the base of her throat instinctively, as if doing so would protect her from what she saw. Deathly pale, a crescent moon hung prominently in the sky. It seemed to smile at Kathryn as she focused her attention on the omen.

"Silver Moon," she breathed, and she trembled at the sight of it. The recollection of a moon's terror—foreboding from another lifetime—filled her veins with ice. "Oh, Wendy…I…who is it for?"

"I don't know."

"It's different this time. Like it's dripping away into…"

"The Onyx Moon is rising, Kat. It's the same sign, still…the Silver Moon omen, but there's the dark one behind it."

Katherine tore her eyes from the ghastly sight and turned, focusing her attention on her cousin, who still waited on the other end of the phone call. "Wendy, who did Mariel say bears the mark of the omen?"

"She did not say, but the onyx flame was with me, which Mariel said could mean it's meant for one of us, one of our blood."

Katherine listened to her cousin's explanation, but nothing made sense. "That can't be. There are only the three of us…you, me, and Mariel. Who else is there?"

"I don't know!" Wendy's response was less than helpful. Katherine knitted her brows together, and began pacing along a small patch of grass. "Wait a minute," Wendy sang through the receiver. "If the omen is marked for one of us, couldn't it also be marked for someone not yet known but destined to be with one of us? Maybe someone in this lifetime?"

"What are you saying, Wen?"

"What if the moon omens can mark someone who's meant to be with us, even if we haven't met them yet?" Wendy sounded almost jubilant.

"Who in the world would that be?" Katherine's voice took an edge.

"Well, I don't know. I certainly don't have all the answers, so don't snap at me. I'm just the messenger."

"Sorry. I'm scared, I guess."

"I know. Me too. But think about it, Kat—why not? The moon is an entity that works on an eternal time clock. Maybe the omen manifests for those we have eternal relationships with. Maybe there is one of our 'blood'…at least, one of us…a person we will be with, but have not yet crossed paths with during this lifetime."

Wendy's logic was dizzying, but it began to make sense when viewed from a psychic's perspective. Katherine's rational side turned inward to seek answers from her spirit. Clarity slowly made its way into her thoughts.

"Maybe the omen crosses lifetimes with those of the past," Katherine stated in response.

"Or those of the future," Wendy added.

"So, the omen could be marking someone we haven't met but are destined to be with during this lifetime?"

"I think so, yes!" Wendy sounded ecstatic.

Katherine grew solemn. "The Silver Moon's sign is a Celtic omen, Wen. It belongs to…" She couldn't bring herself to say the name.

"Who?"

Katherine cleared her throat. "Wendy, you don't mean *she's* marking someone with the sign, do you?"

"Mariel suggested it, but I couldn't bring myself to even say her name." Wendy swallowed the lump that had risen in her throat.

"Then I'll say it…Morrigan. The Silver Moon sign is her omen. If she's marked someone, she's coming for them."

"Possibly…yes."

"Wendy, we have to find out who she is coming for. The onyx flame was yours to view.

I wasn't there, I was at the hospital, but…" Katherine said.

"…I saw it, instead," Wendy finished her thought.

"Mariel's right…and so are you. This is someone tied to us, either in our past or future." Katherine shivered as she spoke.

"I need to run this by Mariel. Let me call you back. How long are you going to be there, in the ER, Kat? Isn't it way past your usual time to be getting home?"

"Yes, unfortunately. I'll try to leave now. I just need to let someone in charge know I've got an…urgent matter to handle at home." She searched for a plausible excuse to leave. "Call me back once you've talked to

Mariel. Promise." Katherine kept her head down as she spoke into the receiver. She couldn't bear to look at the moon omen again.

"Call you back soon." The dial tone went dead as Wendy hung up.

Katherine closed the phone and stuffed it back into her pocket, then reentered the brightly lit Emergency department. Alarms sang out as the staff bustled about, attentive to their patients. Everyone there was apparently unaware of the ominous silver moonlight overhead in the darkened sky—everyone, except Katherine.

Epilogue 3

"ST. LUKE'S, THIS IS ENGINE 21 calling in report... St. Luke's, Engine 21, do you copy?"

No one responded.

"St. Luke's, this is a priority call, do you copy?"

The flustered young woman entered the empty radio room and clicked off the alarm.

Brushing back her dark, wavy hair with one hand, she took up a pencil with the other and pressed the button to respond.

"Go ahead, 21. This is St. Luke's at 2123."

"St. Luke's, we have a two-victim TC. Engine Four is here with us and is bringing in the second victim."

"Copy that. Engine Four with Victim Number Two. Go ahead with report when you're ready."

Victim One is a male, approximately 28 years old, 180 pounds, unresponsive. He has been in and out of consciousness since our arrival on scene, currently not responsive. Airway intact, although we think he may have possibly aspirated. On arrival, he was found face down in water.

"21, to clarify, did you say you have an airway? And, please repeat, where did you find the patient on arrival?"

"*St. Luke's, the patient was a restrained passenger but was found lying halfway out of an Ambulance, face down in standing water. He's breathing six to eight breaths per minute, irregular. Heart rate 120.*

"Engine 21, did you say he was lying halfway out of an ambulance?" She leaned in a little closer to the crackling ham radio in an effort to hear the medic more clearly.

"*Affirmative, St. Luke's.*" There was a slight pause, and the radio crackled. "*He's one of us. The victim and his partner just left your ER.*"

The nurse at the radio stiffened, and her knuckles grew white as she gripped the pencil tighter. "Medics?"

"*Affirmative, St. Luke's. We're assuming he was partially ejected. The seatbelt failed.*"

"Copy, 21." She swallowed hard. "What's your ETA?"

"*ETA three minutes. We have him in full spinal precautions, 15 liters oxygen, and an IV. We're coming lights and sirens.*" Pause. "*He's one of us.*"

Katherine stood up from the radio and rushed out into the ER's main hallway. "Lis, I need you to get the trauma room ready, and we'll need respiratory. We have a couple of medics involved in a pretty bad MVA. I'll stay to help out, where I can." She squeezed Lissa's arm affectionately and swallowed back the gnawing reminder of the promise she'd just made. There was no way she could leave now.

Quickly, Katherine moved down the hallway toward the ambulance bay just as the alarm sounded from the radio room again.

"Got it," Kaycee called out as she slipped in to take the call.

Katherine ran for the ambulance bay, and the glass doors opened wide. Stepping through, she flipped open her cell phone and dialed.

A raspy soprano voice answered. "Kat...I am still trying to get hold of..." Wendy's voice was quickly cut off.

"Wendy, you need to call Mariel." Kathryn paused for a moment, but was met with only deafening silence.

"Why?" Wendy's voice a whisper through the receiver.

A chill tickled Katherine's spine as she gazed up at the deep night sky. Her lips moved in a whisper.

"Silver Moon...I know who bears its mark."

Bibliography

Nautical Know How. (1996/2010). Retrieved
    September 2010, from Boatsafe.com: http://
    www.boatsafe.com/nauticalknowhow/gloss.htm

Bachigraphics. (2007). Voodoo & Hoodoo.
    Retrieved November 13, 2010, from Voodoo &
    Hoodoo: http://www.hauntedamericatours.com/
    VOODOO.html

Draskoy, A. (1993-2009). Shanties and Sea Songs.
    Retrieved November 27, 2010, from Shanties
    and Sea Songs: http://www.shanty.rendance.org

Glossary of Terms. (n.d.). Retrieved February 22,
    2012, from SalingLinks - Promoting Sailing:
    http://www.sailinglinks.com/glossary.htm

Johnson, C. C. (2002). A General History of the
    Robberies & Murders of the Most Notorious
    Pirates (First paperback edition, fourth printing
    ed.). Guilford, Connecticut: The Lyons Press.

Ossian, R. (n.d.). Pirate's Cove. Retrieved August 2009, from Pirate's Cove: www.thepi-rateking.com

Tresidder, J. (2004). 1001 Symbols, An Illustrated Guide to Imagery and Its Meaning. San Francisco: Chronicle Books, LLC.

Glossary Of Terms

Abaft – Toward the back of the ship.

Avast – Pay attention. Stop what you are doing.

Binnacle List – A ship's sick list.

Bosun – Boatswain, officer in charge of sails, lines, and rigging of a ship.

Capstan – A drum-shaped part of the windlass used to wind rope or line connected to cargo or the anchor.

Cast off – To let go, break free.

Chirurgeon – Surgeon.

Colambre – A wine skin whose origin comes from the 16th century, used to hold liquids.

Companionway – The main entrance to a cabin, usually a short stairwell.

Dead Ahead – Directly ahead.

Dead Astern – Directly behind.

Dinghy – A small, open boat, usually used for transport from a larger ship to another location.

Ditty Bag – A small bag for stowing personal items.

Fathom – Six feet.

Fo'c's'le – Forecastle, a partial deck above the upper deck at the head of the vessel, typically the living quarters for the crew.

Foreward – Toward the bow or front of the ship.

Galley – Kitchen or cooking quarters for a ship.

Gangway – The area along the side of a ship where people board and disembark.

Gunwale – The upper edge of the side of a ship.

Heading – The direction ahead of the bow of the ship.

Helm – The wheel.

Helmsman – One who steers the ship.

Hoay – A slang version of "hoy" or "ho." Its purpose is to draw attention to something: "Land ho!"

Hold – The compartment below deck used for carrying cargo.

Hull – The main body of a vessel.

Leeward – The direction away from the wind, opposite of Windward.

Line – Rope used on board a ship.

Monkeys – Guns, cannons used on a ship.

No Quarter Given – Death to all. No lives spared in a capture.

Rails – A narrow length of wood forming the top of a ship's bulwarks.

Rigging – The lines that hold up the masts and move the sails.

Sea Chantey – A maritime work song sung by the crew on board ships while working.

Secure – To make fast, fasten securely.

Sheets – Lines used to control the position of the sails.

Shrouds – Lines running from the top of the mast and attaching to the side of the ship.

Slack – Not fastened, loose.

Starboard – The right side of the boat.

Stow – To put something away, put in its proper place.

Taffrail – The rail at the stern of the boat.

Waist – The deck between the quarter-deck and forecastle.

Enjoy Other Books By

Doce Blant Publishing
www.DoceBlant.com

Alys
by Kiri Callaghan

Hardbound ISBN: 978-0-9978913-8-6
Paperback ISBN: 978-0-9978913-9-3
ePub ISBN: 978-0-9984294-0-3

The Déjà vu Chronicles
by Marti Melville
Midnight Omen (book 1)
Hardbound ISBN: 978-0-9971023-3-8
Paperback ISBN: 978-0-9971023-4-5
ePub ISBN: 978-0-9971023-5-2
Library of Congress Control Number:
2016906558

The Tales of Barnacle Bill: Skeleton Krewe
by Barnacle Bill Bedlam

Hardbound ISBN: 978-0-9967622-3-6
Paperback ISBN: 978-0-9967622-2-9
ePub ISBN: 978-0-9967622-4-3

The Next Victim
by Cutter Slagle

Hardbound ISBN: 978-0-9967622-6-7
Paperback ISBN: 978-0-9967622-5-0
ePub ISBN: 978-0-9967622-7-4

'Til Death
by Cutter Slagle

Hardbound ISBN: 978-0-9978913-0-0
Paperback ISBN: 978-0-9978913-1-7
ePub ISBN: 978-0-9978913-2-4
Library of Congress Control Number:
2016949335

Never Surrender
by Deanna Jewel

Hardbound ISBN: 978-0-9971023-0-7
Paperback ISBN: 978-0-9971023-1-4
ePub ISBN: 978-0-9971023-2-1

CPSIA information can be obtained
at www.ICGtesting.com
Printed in the USA
LVHW080234250619
622262LV00010B/142/P

9 780999 493700